# The Circle of Seven

# The Circle of Seven

# David Marshall

iUniverse, Inc.
Bloomington

# The Circle of Seven

iUniverse books may be ordered through booksellers or by contacting:

iUniverse
1663 Liberty Drive
Bloomington, IN 47403
www.iuniverse.com
1-800-Authors (1-800-288-4677)

ISBN: 978-1-4697-8949-1 (sc)
ISBN: 978-1-4697-8947-7 (hc)
ISBN: 978-1-4697-8948-4 (e)

Printed in the United States of America

iUniverse rev. date: 02/29/2012

For Hannah and William, who have taught me to look for more than what there appears to be on the surface, for through the eyes of our children can we truly see, not only what is, but what wonders there may be.

# Prologue

*"I do not believe in a fate that falls on men*
*however they act; but I do believe in a fate*
*that falls on them unless they act."*
**Buddha**

The dreams were coming more often now, at least once a week. They were vivid in their clarity; the colors and sounds almost too vibrant to be real. But they were more than dreams. Somehow, as he slept, he could tell they were more.

There were different dreams, a series of them in fact. But, lately, there was only one dream in particular.

The scene unfolded the same way every time. A crown of pure gold, encrusted with emeralds, floated past. At the front was a peak stretching upwards from the base, pointing, like an arrow, toward the heavens. Arranged down either side were six more peaks, slightly smaller but no less grand than the central one. A second crown, identical to the first in all respects save that it was of a size to fit a small child floated after the first. A large ring of polished silver hung around both crowns.

The two crowns floated around each other for a time. There was a mounting foreboding. He tried to call out, to warn the crowns of his feelings, but he had no voice. Then, as he reached out with insubstantial hands, his fears came to pass.

The silver ring began to contract around the crowns. The larger crown slipped outside of the constricting ring, but the smaller was too slow. As easily as a fist around an overripe peach, the ring collapsed on the trapped crown. The crown was crushed into a tiny, glittery heap, slowly dimming into nothingness.

With a start, sweat dripping from his face, the dreamer awoke, sitting straight up. Fear radiated through him. Something terrible was in the air, he was sure of it.

# Chapter 1

*"Without courage, wisdom bears no fruit."*
*Baltasar Gracian*

Faith was something Barall held dearly and close to his heart, something strong, undeniable and unshakeable. He had been a servant of Endomar, God of Wisdom for more than a dozen years and never once had he questioned his own calling or his beliefs. Not once had he doubted that he could make a difference. Until tonight.

Glancing furtively down the dim corridor and over his shoulder to check he wasn't being followed, he wiped tears from his eyes. Despite the coolness of the early spring night, he was sweating profusely and wiped a shaking hand over his head. Like all Acolytes, he was required to keep his head shaved, a symbol of innocence in the church. All Initiates and Acolytes kept their head shaved, men and women alike. Barall had been an Acolyte for more years than was normal, but Comfort Vance, his teacher and mentor, felt he wasn't ready to advance yet. Barall stood not quite six feet tall, with bright blue eyes, under sandy brown eyebrows, which gave a hint what color his hair would be, if it were allowed to grow in.

A slender build, common of most priests of his age of twenty four, was accentuated by stark white skin and slender, tapered fingers.

Comfort Vance always joked with him, that if he hadn't joined the church, Barall would have become some sort of musician.

When he'd been elevated to Acolyte, Barall had been assigned to Comfort Vance who was charged with maintaining the cathedral archives. Vance was something of an outcast, though, as well as being the most knowledgeable person about the history of Cherilla and the religion of Endomar.

It wasn't Vance's knowledge that made him a perpetual thorn in the church's side; it was that he was vocal in his denouncement of what he called 'the downfall of the moral guidance and leadership of the church, particularly in Emissary Caven.' The Emissary, of course, didn't care for this talk, but likely would have left it alone, had it stopped there.

But Vance, in his position as the Master of the Archives, was cause for even bigger headaches for the Emissary and his advisory council of Wisdoms. Vance's research had supposedly uncovered evidence of at least six other gods.

These beliefs, which Vance shared with anyone who would listen, were blasphemous in the eyes of the Emissary. The entire country worshipped Endomar: He was the only god, the God of Wisdom, and there were none other like Him. The Emissary denounced Vance and ordered him silent, but the order was ignored. It was just further proof of the lack of leadership in the church and the grab for more power by the Emissary.

Barall had read everything Vance had found, learned and understood and even accepted his findings. But he couldn't see how one as wise and intelligent as Vance could not foresee what would happen. Not until it was almost too late.

The people to whom Vance would talk would listen politely, and then go on their way. "There's no proof," they would say to each other over mugs of spiced wine. "The great Emissary is the Chosen of Endomar, the wisest of the wise. He would not lie to us."

Only yesterday Barall had begged Vance to stop, to try to see that the Emissary, and the church, would not stand for his heretical preaching. The Emissary would not allow his position to be compromised in any way. Of that Barall was certain and even Vance had to concede the point.

Vance had noticed odd things about the Emissary and what occurred around him. Youngest of any preceding Emissary, just thirty-five when he had assumed the mantle of power, Caven was strikingly handsome, with chiselled features, high cheekbones and a cleft chin that only seemed to make him more attractive. He had a deep voice that he was able to use with great ability to put anyone at ease in almost any situation, or that could boom when necessary.

But strange things began to happen once Caven moved from being a Wisdom advisor to being the Emissary. He preached of the declining beliefs of the people and their lack of support for the church. He called for the integration of the neighboring countries of Naer and Conti into the Endomarian religion – not necessarily by peaceable means, either.

But that wasn't the worst of it, not by far. Girls, mostly Acolytes and Initiates, some as young as fifteen, were often called to the Emissary's chambers. Not uncommon, really, since those were the two lowest ranks within the church. They were assigned work as servants, maids, food handlers, message runners and a dozen other tasks in addition to learning the theology of Endomar. They also served as personal attendants to senior officials, such as the Wisdoms and Emissary.

But when the Emissary called girls to personally serve him; they returned different from before. They were subdued and quiet, tentative and often frightened of every sound or touch. Each one would refuse to talk about what had happened to cause such a change, becoming fearful or angry. And that was only if they were seen again as some weren't. Friends who asked after them were told they had been reassigned or transferred. Vance, however, suspected something more sinister.

Which of these Vance was killed over: his preaching of other gods, his denunciation of his own church's highest official, or his suspicions as to the reasons behind the girls' change in behaviour, Barall didn't know. He had gone to Vance's quarters adjacent to the vast library that made up the archives barely an hour ago. He had found Vance there sitting in his padded, patterned chair in front of a cheerily burning fire, a blanket pulled up under his chin. The room was a jumbled mess of books, clothes and furniture, all of it strewn over and around each other so barely a free space was to be found anywhere. The smell of the burning logs helped dispel any mustiness that normally strolled hand in hand with such clutter and disarray.

The student had smiled to find his master in such a state. But the smile quickly faded as Barall saw the splatters of blood on Vance's face and seeping through the thin blanket covering. With a trembling hand he pulled the blanket away. A gasp escaped and a hand flew to Barall's mouth for Vance was quite obviously dead. The proof was evident given the dagger jutting out of his chest, imbedded so far that none of the blade was seen. To add to the horror, Vance's hands had been positioned over his chest in the sign of the circle, fingers of one hand touching the thumb of the other with the handle of the dagger piercing the center of the circle.

It was a message Barall understood immediately. The circle was the symbol of Endomar, the pursuit of wisdom being never-ending. Wisdom, it was taught, came from having knowledge, experience, compassion and honor; the four points of a compass, which formed the circle of life. The dagger through the god's symbol symbolized Vance had broken faith with Endomar. To Barall though, it was more likely meant as a message that Vance had broken trust with the Emissary.

There was no proof of this, however, only the suspicions Vance had had, shared for the most part by Barall. And now a Comfort had been killed in his own chamber. Barall didn't know what to do. His master was dead and he didn't want to learn from any other. Under Vance he had been not only educated in priestly rules and knowledge, but also in all manner of other issues. He had been required to read of history, war, philosophy, geography and more. There had also been a strict exercise regimen, including practice in the use of the hammer, the only weapon Vance considered suitable for a priest to use in times of battle. Not an easy master, Vance had been fair, with expectations of excellence in all areas.

With his master and friend dead before him, Barall selfishly thought of himself. What was he to do? Where could he go? The more he thought about it, the more he felt that he, too, was in danger. While not as outspoken or blatant as Vance, he was well known as Vance's Acolyte, and his own feelings toward Caven were no secret.

If they could kill a Comfort, there would be no problems killing an Acolyte. A cold sweat broke out over his bald head then, as fear gripped his heart. As if dreading the killers, or even the Emissary, were still in the room, Barall's eyes roved about, flitting anxiously from spot to spot.

Finding no one else in the room, cool thinking momentarily controlled the panic threatening to overwhelm him. A few steadying breaths and Barall felt himself in control enough to decide what to do. He had to leave the cathedral, that much was certain. To stay would only be asking to be killed as well. But where would he go? What would he do? All he knew was how to be a priest. All his training and experience were dedicated to Endomar, and through Him, to the people of Cherilla.

He considered travelling to some of the outer reaching towns, Casban or Erskin perhaps, and finding a new life there. Vance had made some cryptic references to some group he was in contact with that shared his beliefs. If Barall could somehow find this group, maybe there was something he could do to help them. Of course, he didn't know anyone in this group or where they were, or really, what they were planning to do.

Glancing around, Barall realized he had been standing debating with himself for quite a long while. There was nothing left for him here, nothing to keep him in the cathedral beyond his dedication to his faith. That was something that could never be taken from him, never soiled the way the Emissary had soiled his, and it was something he could practice anywhere.

Finding an empty pack in a nearby corner, Barall hurried about the room stuffing in all manner of things he thought he might need. Vance had not been a neat or tidy man, so finding things was a bit of a chore. However, he eventually found a round of crusty bread, a wheel of cheese, a warm woollen cloak and several changes of clothes Vance no longer needed.

It was a strange feeling to be rummaging through his master's belongings as his corpse looked on. Even stranger now that he was finished and ready to go, to leave the only life he had ever known.

He paused and gazed again at the man who had been his mentor, master and friend for more than half his life. Impulsively, he reached out and touched Vance's forehead with the tips of his fingers, registering the coolness of the skin against his fingers, and the surprising steadiness of his own hand as it stretched outward. A part of life, death and the rituals associated with it are an integral part of a priest's work. Barall had been instructed in all aspects of a Comfort's job, including the blessings for the dead, to help guide the soul to its next destination. The prayer came quickly and easily to Barall, just as tears once again filled his eyes. As he began, though, he was shocked to see an eerie glow suffuse Vance's body, blurring the scene before him, like he was looking through a curtain of haze or fine mist. Then, through the fog, as if from a great distance, came Vance's voice.

Barall recoiled in fear. As his fingers left Vance's skin the voice and the fogginess disappeared, leaving Barall to wonder if it had ever even happened. His brows narrowed in thought as he considered what had happened.

There were some basic and rudimentary prayers that were said to work miracles if the priest was devout. A priest could ask for blessings from Endomar, the results manifesting through the priest. That was another blasphemous belief the Emissary was striking from the commonly held church tenets, and another mark against Vance who refused to conform. Barall had never heard of anything even close to resembling this. However, now that his fear at the shock of the event was lessening, his curiosity was mounting. Was it really Vance who called out? How had he managed to do this? Would he be able to speak to him again if he repeated the prayer?

With a small shrug since there was no way to know the answer to any of these questions without trying, he again touched his fingers to Vance's forehead and began to pray. Almost as soon as the first words were out of his mouth the foggy glow again filled the room. This time, Barall controlled the fear that swept through him.

"Barall," came a voice from the fog. "You must flee at once."

"V-Vance?" replied Barall, fear still evident in his voice.

"Of course, boy! Who do you think would be talking to you as you say the death prayer over his body?" said the sarcastic, yet still sepulchral voice that was only vaguely recognizable as Vance's.

"H-h-how … ?" started Barall.

"The how doesn't matter at the moment, lad," said Vance, his voice somewhat tempered. "I don't have much time; the spell won't last long, given the condition I was in when I cast it, so you need to listen."

"Yes, Comfort," came the automatic reply, which served to lessen Barall's fear.

Slowly, as Barall listened to the disembodied voice that was his master, rage and determination, mingled with fear fought for control within him. He was told of how Vance had been confronted by the Emissary's personal guards, charged with treason, blasphemy and failing to uphold the office and position of Comfort. The punishment, they said, was death. And with that they had plunged the dagger into his chest and left him for dead.

Barall shivered to hear the cold, dispassionate, telling of murder from the dead man himself, and struggled to keep focussed on what he was being told.

Vance had not died immediately from the dagger wound; he was alive enough to whisper his own prayer to Endomar. A last act of defiance against Caven, to cast a spell the Emissary called blasphemous but which, obviously, the god had granted.

Barall smiled as Vance's voice settled into a moment of quiet. That Endomar had granted Vance's prayer only served to validate what Vance had been proclaiming all along.

"Exactly," hissed Vance, somehow reading Barall's thoughts. "And now you must run, lad," he continued. "Hidden in the seat of this chair is a book. You will know what to do with it, but do not open it, nor even read its title, until you are away from here. Get out of the cathedral and move toward Vanerry to begin your journey for true wisdom. You will be the greatest of us all. You have already made me proud."

❧

Glancing out a window, unshuttered to let some of the cool spring air into the otherwise stuffy cathedral, Barall noticed he was very close to the door he was seeking. Soon he would learn if he was to share in Vance's fate. He had, so far, seen no one about. The hour was late and most of his brethren would be asleep in their beds, unaware of what had transpired while they dreamed.

The corridors were empty so it seemed his footfalls rang louder than normal. Most of the torches had been doused as well, but Barall moved through the well-known halls easily, yet with the fear of one expecting to be caught.

*"You will be the greatest of us all. You have already made me proud."*

Two simple phrases, but they carried so much weight with them, implied so much responsibility. Of course Barall didn't have the slightest idea what Vance had been talking about. The greatest of them all? At what? All of whom?

He had found the book, hidden in the stitching underneath the seat upon which his master had died, and, as warned, had not opened or read anything of it. He barely even glanced at it as he slid it into the pack and slung it over his shoulder before leaving without a backward glance.

Nearing the southern gate now, though, Barall could feel fear creeping back. It insinuated itself into every nook and cranny of every thought. The guards would have been warned to look out for him, kill him on sight. The book Comfort Vance had instructed him to take must have been precious to the Emissary. These and a hundred other thoughts pressed down upon him with such weight that he was finding it hard to breathe. When a guard, unnoticed until now, clapped a hand on his shoulder from behind, Barall nearly leapt out of his skin. It was a very undignified and unpriestly squeak that escaped his lips as his feet left the ground.

He turned around, his heart thudding so loudly he was sure even the guard standing in front of him could hear it. Before him stood one of the Emissary's guards, resplendent in his uniform of rich purple. Bands of immaculate white circled wrists, waist and neck, with the circle of wisdom in the center of the chest. The surcoat covered a shirt of chain mail armor that, even though he couldn't see it, Barall knew was buffed to a near mirror finish. He could even smell the oil the man had used to clean it over his own smell of fear.

Black boots similarly polished to a gleaming shine, into which crisp blue pants were tucked, completed the uniform.

Normally, Barall admired the strict discipline and smart dress of the Emissary's guards, but today it seemed ostentatious and a too-rigid requirement of the Emissary's. It was like he had to control everything. Add to that the fear Barall felt at seeing a guard after being told his master had been killed by them, and he nearly fainted in pure fright.

Barall looked into the face of the guard. There was no glimpse of the leering excitement or haughty expression of one who has caught a man wanted by the Emissary himself. Such a deed would surely move a lowly guard into the Emissary's good graces. None of that puffed up pride was there; only a slightly amused look of someone who has just startled another completely out of their composure.

"Acolyte?" asked the guard deferentially.

Taking a moment to catch his breath, Barall didn't reply at first, which only served to further amuse the guard. They exchanged a small smile at the humor of the situation and Barall realized that this man didn't know it was likely the Emissary was looking for this particular Acolyte.

"My apologies for startling you, Acolyte, I didn't realize I was so stealthy."

"No, no," replied Barall, amazed at how calm his voice sounded. "It was all my fault; too preoccupied in my own thinking. Just another lesson in wisdom granted by the great God as I am about to set out on a task in His name."

It was a calculated gamble, Barall took, hoping to distract the guard from the real reason for stopping him. The guard might demand to know just what task would take a mere Acolyte out of the cathedral in the middle of the night, but Endomar granted Barall a truly pious guard, for he merely nodded his head and made the sign of the circle in front of his chest.

"One should always be aware of one's surroundings," said the guard knowingly. "You never know what, or who, is waiting for you. That is when men, and life, seem to catch you unaware."

Returning the circle in blessing, Barall turned and continued down the corridor, the sound of his boots echoing around him, and exited the cathedral without so much as a raised eyebrow from the guards.

Even as he crossed the lake that surrounded the island upon which the cathedral was built, he couldn't shake the feeling the guard's words were somehow prophetic.

# Chapter 2

*"It is unwise to be too sure of one's own wisdom.
It is healthy to be reminded that the strongest
might weaken and the wisest might err."*
*Mohandas K. Gandhi.*

Caven, Emissary to Endomar, the God of Wisdom, stretched languidly, relishing in the loosening of tight muscles. His private bedroom was located high within the cathedral, and sumptuously decorated with soft carpets, lavish furniture of a dozen different woods and masterful pieces of art placed throughout. Dominating the room, however, was a massive bed, covered in the finest silk and the warmest blankets.

He glanced casually toward the bed and scowled to see the tangle of sheets and smooth, young limbs even as the unmistakable odor of their lovemaking wafted toward him as she moved.

The girl, he hadn't bothered to learn her name when she came to him last night, snored lightly as she slept, further deepening his scowl as the sound intruded on his thoughts. A soft robe, pulled over his nakedness, covered his smooth, rippling muscles and made a soft rustling sound as he moved to pull a small chain beside the bed.

Somewhere, he never cared to learn where, a bell rang summoning guards to his chamber. While he waited, he strode to his desk on the opposite side of the room. It was not the largest room in the cathedral. That distinction was saved for the great Hall of Wisdom where all devotees of Endomar, from the Emissary down to the lowliest servant on the island came to worship every twenty days. The Emissary's bedchamber was biggest after that, though.

For the moment, the Emissary wasn't considering his next sermon, nor even the hundreds of details required to run the only church in the country. He was thinking, instead, of treachery. His desk was covered with pages and scrolls, each one sensitive in nature and not for any other eyes than his. They were all taken from Comfort Vance's office just last night. In them, he was sure, would be the names of his mysterious group of conspirators, threatening to spread chaos throughout Caven's world.

Thinking of Vance brought a still deeper scowl to the Emissary's face, and his brows came together over clear, sharp brown eyes. Vance, the fat fool, was more dangerous than probably even he realized. The Emissary had plans for his church. Plans that went beyond the city of Anklesh, beyond even the country of Cherilla.

The worship of Endomar was to be expanded!

As altruistic as that sounded when the Emissary discussed it with the Council of Wisdoms, it really wasn't.

The council was a group of priests with experience and knowledge who acted as advisors to the Emissary. The rules stated there had to be at least three Wisdoms on the council, but there was no maximum. Caven allowed only the barest minimum.

When he assumed the position of Emissary, there had been almost two dozen Wisdoms on the council. All but three, Lassand, Virez and Destrin, had been dismissed and returned to normal duties of managing the Primates and Comforts, and running the church. Of course the three chosen to remain were fiercely loyal to Caven, but even they were not aware or informed of all the Emissary's plans.

They all saw the benefits of expanding the church. The people needed their guidance and structure, needed the wisdom they preached and fairly demanded the calm and judicious Comforts to minister to the wicked and uncontrollable. But none would have guessed the Emissary saw only to increase his own personal power. With an increased congregation, there would be more money flowing into his coffers, more men willing to carry out his every whim, for after all, he was the manifestation of god.

Fools! All of them fools. What did Endomar care for any of them? If He was even there in the first place.

Caven had entered the church just like many before and after him, because his parents couldn't pay their taxes. The youngest son of a poor farmer, Caven's servitude ensured the family's security for, at least, another year. But Caven hadn't forgotten that lesson learned at such a young age: money controlled everything.

Working with the money-counters as an Initiate, Caven had been able to see the vast amounts of gold and silver that poured into the church, donated by the faithful and the stupid. And he had been appalled at how much was then just given away. When he questioned it, he was told that it was the church's duty to provide for the welfare of others, so the money went out to build houses, buy food and a thousand other things the Emissary decided the people needed.

The more Caven learned, the more he realized the Emissary was in charge of it all, and not only in the cathedral. He had influence with the king, for priests were often used as mediators or judges in disputes. There was even a guard contingent at his command. As Caven moved through the ranks, increasing his power and influence, his sights were always set on being Emissary, with all that power at his fingertips.

Now here he was, and a minor, insignificant Comfort was trying to ruin it all. Vance's notes and books were spread across the desk. He had no idea if Vance's theories of multiple gods were true or not, and he honestly didn't even care. He did care in that it gave him the opening he needed to discredit Vance, and set plans for his removal in motion. The guards had performed their duty without qualm or question, leaving nothing in the Emissary's way.

They had returned with information about a group of six or seven others, scattered throughout Cherilla, who were working with Vance. But there were no names mentioned, nothing that pointed in a direction in which to search.

With Vance now taken care of, the only questions remaining were how much the Comfort knew of the Emissary's plans and whether he had told anyone else. The pages on the desk before him revealed nothing. There were requests for additional books for the archive, accounting of volumes lent out to various Comforts or Primates, and more. Useless drivel.

He was still staring at those pages in disgust when there was a soft knock at the door. Guards materialized silently through the door without waiting for him to bid them to enter. The Emissary didn't move from his seat at the desk, didn't even turn around to watch as the two men clapped rough hands on the still sleeping firl in his bed.

As her naked body was hauled from beneath the sheets, a hand was clapped over her mouth and her hands pinned behind her back. Her eyes had snapped open as soon as the hands touched her, but her struggles were in vain. There was no way she would be able to free her arms.

Oblivious to the turmoil around him, the Emissary made the mistake of looking up as the girl made a soft choking sound. The girl had been watching him the entire time, her eyes pleading, begging for him to help her. With a last wrenching lunge, she managed to jerk her mouth free of its muffling hand.

"My lord …?" she started, before the hand resumed its place, none too gently across her mouth.

A small crinkling of the eyes was the only sign of the Emissary's irritation as he stood and raised one, well manicured, almost delicate hand, to the guards. His very presence commanded authority and he strode through the silence like a conquering general into the city of a defeated enemy. He walked with his back straight and eyes focussed solely on the girl.

Stopping in front of her, he stood looking down at her, not saying a word. A hand reached up and, almost tenderly, ran across her naked shoulder, marvelling that a bald woman could still be attractive. He might have to reconsider the requirement that all Initiates and Acolytes shave their heads.

Making the sign of the circle between them, he finally turned away, missing the look of pain that filled the girl's eyes as he abandoned her. The look of pain changed to horror as his next words, thrown over his shoulder, pronounced her sentence.

"Bless you, child. Thank you for fulfilling your purpose."

# Chapter 3

*"Wisdom consists of the anticipation of consequences."*
*Norman Cousins*

Barall left the cathedral through the southern gate and managed to find a boat large enough to carry himself and his pack, tied at the water's edge. With a whispered prayer that the owner of the boat would be able to find another way home, he untied the single rope that held it in place and pushed off. An alarming amount of water poured into the boat, quickly soaking his worn brown boots and pants.

With no clear idea of what he was doing, he had somehow managed to paddle himself the short distance across the lake without capsizing the boat or dunking himself, though he missed the docks he was aiming for by several hundred feet. Another prayer followed his landing on the shore to the south of the island that had been his home. It was dark now, and barely any light shone from the massive structure; its windows and gracefully beauty hidden by the night.

There was still some activity within the city, though, even at this time of night. Guards in the king's colors of blue on white, looking bored, patrolled the streets; workers loaded or unloaded ships; and others who just seemed to be wandering. With a last backward look at the cathedral, Barall moved deeper into the city, becoming just another anonymous face.

He had travelled into Anklesh on occasion, running errands for Vance or one Comfort or Primate or another, so knew his way well enough.

The city had grown concentrically around the lake with Cathedral Island as its center. The king's palace and many noble estates abutted the lake in the northwest quadrant. To the west were the open air food and goods markets, while the main docks, with their accompanying warehouses were to the south and southeast. The northeast quadrant led to the open sea, under the Bridge of Micarad. Further away from the lake were the merchant houses, traders and other wealthy families followed by the businesses and shops all cities had and needed for commerce. Lastly, furthest from the delicate eyes and sensibilities of the wealthy, were the homes and lives of the poor, living closest to the walls and the dangers that lay beyond them.

His walk through the city, while uneventful, was marred by Barall's fears showing themselves at every corner. Every sound became the Emissary's men closing in on him; every silence was a trap just waiting to be sprung.

The guards at the main gate watched him with unconcealed amusement as he fairly ran up to them. The sky was still dark, but the sun would not be hidden much longer. Above him, Barall could see more guards manning the walls. Silent sentries that watched the landscape surrounding Anklesh.

Nearing the gate with more than a little trepidation, Barall could feel his heart hammering in his chest, and beads of sweat blossomed across his hairless scalp. Crossing the last dozen feet, he swiped one arm across his face, trying to regain some semblance of his dignity. But as he approached the guards, he found he was unable to meet their eyes.

"Aw, forget it. There's no bet. He's crying!" said the guard on the left.

Barall's head snapped up at the words, staring from one man to the other, a mixture of shock and anger on his face.

"Ooh, careful there, Tigell," said the man on the right. "You made him mad."

"Now I'm scared," retorted Tigell. "What is this anyway, the third one kicked out this season?"

"Yeah, must be hard being a priest with all that praying all day and everything."

Cruel guffaws followed, but Barall barely heard them. They obviously didn't know or care who he was, but more importantly, they thought him a disgraced priest. Occasionally one was asked to leave by the Council as being unfit for one reason or another.

Thinking quickly, Barall put what he hoped was a pitiful expression on his face and looked to the two men.

"Please, sirs," he said meekly. "May I pass?"

More laughter met his question and Barall could feel heat flush his face. Even though he wasn't, yet, disgraced, he could well imagine the feelings such men and women would experience coming upon such cruel, insensitive, men as these. They didn't care about what the poor person would be going through. His anger at this treatment was cut short when one of the guards poked him.

"Hey! You listening?"

Barall started in surprise. He hadn't heard a thing they had said.

"Huh?" he blurted.

The two laughed at him again.

"Not much of a talker is he, Tigell?"

"Or a listener either, Sovran. Think that's why he got kicked out?"

Barall listened as they continued to talk about him as if he wasn't there. He felt angry at their words but tried to hide it to maintain the role of outcast. Finally, he simply broke in on their laughter asking again if he could leave.

As if his interruption was all they were waiting for, they stepped aside pointing to the side door, rather than opening the full main gate before daybreak. Their laughter followed him out of the city.

☙

Barall stood still, silently watching the couple who stood watching him. For three days he had moved further and further from Anklesh, heading roughly west, never once seeing another soul. Until now.

The landscape had not changed at all since he had exited the city. The great, tall walls seemed to mock him as he farily ran from the guards within. Once he was well away, he slowed his pace, keeping to the worn, packed dirt road. The area immediately around the city was open farmland and continued that way for as far as Barall could see. The air was crisp and clear, the sounds and smells of farms and animals cloaking the air like a fog. But this was a welcome fog, bringing new wonders and feelings to Barall, who had been living inside the cathedral for most of his life. It was a feeling that he didn't want to end.

Then the man and a woman appeared. Both looked to be young, but both were likely still older than him. The man was slightly taller than Barall, perhaps half a head taller, with black hair that framed his face. He was dressed simply in plain brown woollen pants, a white shirt and black vest that left his arms bare. Barall could only stare at those arms. They were absolutely huge, with muscles bunching one atop another. He would have expected such a man to be extremely confident, for the simple sight of him would have had most people fawning over him or running away. Instead this man's expression gave Barall the feeling of melancholy. He looked sad, like he had never been happy in his life.

The man's companion could not be more unlike him. She was very short but with long, flowing hair of fiery red curls. She did not have the obvious physical strength of the man, but she looked back at Barall with such directness that he couldn't hold her gaze for long. It was the woman who finally broke the silence, her directness coming out in her voice and manner as much as her eyes.

"Who are you?" she demanded.

Barall's brows narrowed and he adjusted the pack on his back.

"Who are you?" he shot back.

"Look whelp …" started the woman, but the man placed a surprisingly gentle hand on her shoulder.

"Peace, Cura. He has as much a right to know us as we do him."

His eyes had never left Barall while he was talking. "My name, young sir, is Dalis, and my friend here is Cura. We are simply travellers."

His speech was very much like his appearance. He spoke methodically and slowly, like he had to pull the words out of his throat to speak them.

"Thank you, Dalis," replied Barall, pointedly ignoring Cura. "My name is Barall. I too am travelling."

At the mention of the name, Dalis gave a start and his eyes opened wide. Before Barall could notice, Cura spoke up, drawing Barall's attention.

"Well, Barall, seems like we're all just wandering around. We were about to take some food. Would you care to join us?"

Her manner had changed completely. No longer brusque or rude, she was being nice and polite. Oddly, this put Barall more on his guard than anything else, and he looked back and forth between the two, trying to glean some idea of whether he could trust them or not.

For the first time he noticed the weapons they carried. Dalis carried a massive hammer. A block of stone, as long as a forearm and half as wide, was mounted atop a thick shaft of wood. A cord of what appeared to be leather was wrapped around that shaft, ending in a stubby pommel at the bottom.

Cura, too, was armed. Strapped across her back was the shaft of a bow, which meant there was probably a pile of arrows on her somewhere too. He didn't know how he had missed seeing the weapons before, but suddenly Cura and Dalis took on a lot more sinister appearance. Now they were warriors and dangerous. He didn't really want to spend any more time with them than absolutely necessary, but didn't know how to get out of it.

Dalis took the question away from him though, by picking up a bag from behind him and tossing it to the ground between them. Then he reached back again and picked up another bag and, reaching inside it, pulled out a blanket. Spreading it on the ground, he promptly sat down and began unpacking food.

Looking at him, Barall and Cura shared an amused look before shrugging and joining him on the blanket.

"I have a little food I can share," said Barall opening his own pack and starting to pull items out. Clothes and a book came out as well as the food he had taken from Vance's chamber. All made its way onto the blanket as he searched through the pack.

Watching him, Cura was at first amused, but at the sight of the book, she snatched it up and quickly opened the cover to read the first page. Her face quickly suffused with anger as she read.

"Where did you get this, boy?!?" she demanded waving the book in the air.

Both Barall and Dalis looked at her in surprise, also noting the edge to her voice.

"My … friend … gave it to me," Barall said hesitantly. He didn't want to say 'master' in case he had to maintain the ruse of being asked to leave the church.

"Is that what I think it is, but hope that it is not?" asked Dalis quietly, eyes shifting between Cura and Barall.

"Yes!" The word fairly spat from Cura's mouth. "And he's just casually tossing it around."

Then to Barall she hissed, "Your 'friend' gave it to you, eh? You sure you didn't steal it?"

His own anger rising to meet hers, Barall could feel the loss of Vance even more deeply now. "I did not steal it!" he said hotly, trying in vain to grab it out of Cura's hand. "I told you. It was given to me."

A shared look between the two companions told Barall their disbelief more than any words could. They didn't believe him and he didn't know why. In truth, he hadn't even looked at the book yet, hadn't even pulled it out of his pack. They seemed to think there was something special about this book. They had recognized it at once and must know who its owner was. The question that floated through Barall's mind was: where did Vance get the book?

"Barall," said Dalis slowly, his gaze intently focussed on the confused Acolyte. "This is very important, my friend. Where did you get this book?"

Perhaps it was Dalis' penetrating gaze, or the quiet, sure tone of his words, but Barall found he was unable to look away from the mud brown of his eyes. Suddenly intensely aware of his surroundings, Barall could smell the scent of the grass crushed by their bodies when they sat down and he could hear the trill of the birds flying overhead. Looking into those eyes, Barall was mesmerized. He felt no desire to lie or to not tell Dalis anything but the entire truth. Without another pause, he related the entire story of three nights earlier.

When at last he finished, the other two sat in silence, contemplating what he had said. Finally, it was Dalis again, who broke the silence.

"Vance is dead." It was a statement, not a question. "This changes everything."

"No!" exclaimed Cura. "It changes nothing."

"Cura …"

'No Dalis. What has changed? The others are ready. We just have a new member, that's all. Nothing else."

"Who's the new … ?" Then he glanced at Barall. "No, Cura. You can't possibly be thinking …"

Only a raised eyebrow met this revelation, to which Dalis could only groan and hold his head in his hands, as if the mere thought of what Cura was suggesting was making it ache. Barall sat silently throughout this short exchange, not really knowing what they were talking about, just that it somehow involved him. He took the opportunity to snatch the book back from where it sat in front of Cura.

It was a nondescript book, approximately three fingers thick, bound plainly with what looked to be cured animal hide. The simple title, *A Priest's Life*, was etched into the cover in a bright blue color, and though the book seemed brand new, he could sense an air of age about it.

Almost reverently he opened the cover and read the first page: *The life and thoughts of Gibson, priest of Endomar.*

A diary? All of this was because of some old diary? Barall didn't understand. He flipped through the pages of the book and found them filled with the same neat, flowing script. Each page seemed complete with this Gibson's days and weeks as he lived his life in service to his god.

Then, as he neared the end of the book, Barall noticed a change in the text. No longer did it flow from one page to the next, but seemed to be more like a list. He paused at one such page and gasped at what he found there. He quickly flipped to another page and then another.

*Bless* was written at the top of one, *Light* on another, *Cure Disease* on the next, *Heal*, on yet another.

"This is a spellbook!" he said excitedly to no one in particular, quickly flipping through page after page of spells he hadn't even known existed. Most of which, he was sure, the Emissary would have declared blasphemous, but here they were written in the diary of an ancient priest.

"It is more than that, Barall," said Cura, her tone and manner again respectful. "Gibson was a true priest of your God Endomar. He was also an Emissary, albeit for only a short period. Vance found this diary and slowly found the rest of us."

A dozen questions came immediately to Barall as he listened. There were so many, he didn't know which to ask first, so he stayed silent. He watched as Dalis combined their foods together and served everyone a small meal. As they ate, Cura and Dalis took turns telling their story.

They, and four others, all knew Vance. Until recently, none of the others had known each other, except for Cura and Dalis. Vance was very discrete and circumspect in his dealings with his six companions, but then, as he became surer of them, brought them all in on his plans. The Emissary of Endomar was a cruel, corrupt man, using his position not for the betterment of the people, but for his own greed. Even more than that, however, there was proof of the existence of other gods; a pantheon of sorts.

Six other gods and goddesses, also existed, three of good and three of evil. Neutral Endomar ruled with them. The seven priests of the gods, Vance, Cura, Dalis and the others were to band together and spread the word throughout Cherilla. Their goal was not to destroy belief in Endomar, but rather to return truth to the people.

"Do you know why, Barall?" asked Cura at the end of their story.

"Balance," he replied immediately. "The entire world is governed by the balance of opposites: men and women, strength and weakness, good and evil. In this the world is maintained. If it tips too far in either direction, there is stagnation, chaos and death."

"Vance taught you well, Acolyte Barall," said Cura with a smile.

"What? No! I'm not …"

"Yes you are, Barall," cut in Dalis. "We recognized the name immediately from Vance's letters. He always spoke very highly of you. We are very sorry to hear of his death."

Barall could say nothing for a moment. The feeling of loss clamped so tightly around his heart that he found breathing difficult. When he finally looked up, he wiped tears from his eyes and tried to give them a smile, but failed. Then, with a gusty sigh, he asked what was to happen next.

"Well, you'll come with us to Guilder, of course, to complete the circle."

# Chapter 4

*"By three methods we may learn wisdom:
First, by reflection, which is noblest; Second,
by imitation, which is easiest; and third
by experience, which is the bitterest."*
**Confucius**

The journey to Guilder passed uneventfully for Cura and Dalis. They led Barall overland, stopping frequently, as the young Acolyte was not yet accustomed to walking from sunup to sundown. At every opportunity, Barall had Vance's book out and was voraciously reading of the life and thoughts of the long-dead Gibson. Given that they were walking all day, he didn't get a lot of opportunity before he fell into his bedroll, exhausted each night. By the time they reached Guilder, nearly two weeks later, he had not even finished reading the first dozen or so pages.

Guilder was a town of large enough size to warrant its own Comfort to speak to the people. The church built here was old, and showed its age, but it was beautifully constructed. Huge blocks of brown stone, used to form the walls, were left in their natural state rather than being filed smooth. The roof was wooden and covered with overlapping slate tiles to protect it from the elements. Despite the incredible architecture and grandeur the church evinced, it was the doors that drew Barall's eyes.

Made of solid walnut, the size of the two doors dominated the front of the building. Cleverly crafted, each door appeared to be made out of a single board. Carved into each door was half of the circle of Endomar, the two halves joining to form the whole where the doors met.

As immense and almost overpowering as was the cathedral in Anklesh, this small church was just as memorable for its simple beauty. Barall had never been one to be struck or inspired by a building. They were only man-made after all, and how could something created by man ever compare to the wonders of Endomar? But this gave him pause.

He stopped in the street in front of the church and simply gazed up at it. Though small, it seemed to dominate the town, like it was there first and the town grew up to support it, rather than the other way around.

They didn't linger long, not wanting to draw attention to themselves. Cura led them to a small house, a stone's throw from the church. Though close to what was obviously the central building in town, the house was worse than anything Barall had ever seen before. It leaned more than a little to one side and seemed to be in great danger of falling over. Shingles of some indistinguishable grayish wood covered the frame in most places. Several were missing and the interior of the house could be seen through the gaps.

As they neared Barall detected the unmistakeable odor of mould and rot.

"Looks like they've made some improvements since we've left," said Cura.

A non-committal grunt was Dalis' only reply. Barall stayed silent, though he was sure his disgust at the house and surprise at Cura's remark were plain enough on his face.

The trio marched along the hard-packed path that ran down the side of the house. The way was so narrow Dalis had to walk sideways to avoid scraping his shoulders against the walls on both sides. Near the back of the house was a door, cleverly hidden and invisible from the road.

Without bothering to knock or announce themselves in any way, they pushed through the door which opened on surprisingly silent hinges.

Barall could only gape at the condition of the interior. Where the outside of the building was falling down and dilapidated, the inside was the opposite. There was only a single room, with no windows or other doors. It was fairly clean, with a single stove, unlit at the moment, tucked into a corner. The only furniture was a long table in the center of the room, with three chairs down each side and a seventh placed at one end, nearest the door where he stood.

Dalis noticed Barall looking curiously at the room and edged closer to whisper in his ear.

"The inside is smaller than the outside. These walls are several feet within the house, and cleverly painted so anyone looking in a window, or even opening the front door, sees only a run down, old house."

Having said his piece, Dalis gave Barall a clap on the shoulder that nearly sent the young priest sprawling, and moved into the room to greet others already there.

Four people, two men and two women, had stopped what they were doing and now stared at the newly arrived trio. Each of them showed some sign of surprise at the arrival, but all stared mainly at Barall; Dalis and Cura obviously known to them.

Groaning, Cura stretched her shoulders and rolled her head and stepped deeper into the room. She walked purposefully toward the table standing the center of the room upon which a pitcher stood and trays of different foods. A sweet scent came to Barall as she poured a glass of rich amber wine into a glass and drank deeply.

"Damn travelling upsets my stomach," she muttered, draining her glass.

"Who's this?" demanded an older man standing off to one side with another man and a woman.

"This is Vance?" asked the woman with the first man incredulously.

"What have you done, Dalis?" accused the last of the trio, pointedly ignoring both Cura and Barall.

Barall's head swivelled from one person to the next as each spoke. None seemed overly pleased to see him. The woman in particular stood tapping one foot, her icy gaze sweeping from Barall to Dalis and back again.

"Cerrok, Seskia, Venick," said Dalis, nodding to each in turn. "Tella," he added to the other woman standing off by herself at the other side of the room. "We need to talk. Things have changed."

"No they haven't," said Cura still standing by the table.

"Despite your feelings, Cura, they have. We need to discuss this."

The sure way Dalis spoke as well as his penetrating look quieted even the fiery Cura. She stood, her fingers gently drumming on the table. Finally she lowered her eyes and nodded.

As if that simple gesture was enough to break the tension, everyone seemed to move at once. Six people converged on the table centered in the room, removing wine and food and replacing everything with a seven candle candelabra and a glass of clean water at each place.

Each of the six people took a position behind a chair. From where Barall stood, he could see an image carved into each one. Down his left, there was a heart, a tree and what looked to be a large rock or boulder. Opposite those were a skull with its eyes covered, two clasping hands and a cross made of two arms, one over top of the other. Given his position, he couldn't see the symbol on the seventh chair, positioned at the end of the table nearest to him.

When the six were arranged, each head turned to Barall, watching him as if expecting something. It was uncomfortable to have such intense looks focussed solely on him, not talking, like they knew something he didn't.

"Well, Vance?" barked one of the men. "Are you going sit down or just stand around all day?"

Shock rippled through Barall. Vance? How could they think he was Vance? He lowered his head as the feelings of loss came over him again. No one spoke, the silence absolute until finally Dalis spoke, his words startling everyone, first with the shock of the sound, then with what was said.

"Please, Barall, come and sit down. We will start with introductions, and then you can tell us your story."

Slowly, Barall made his way to the table, struggling to make his legs obey his commands. Reaching the chair, he looked at the back and noticed a perfect circle carved into the dark wood.

"A circle," he said softly, his fingers tracing the symbol of his god.

"Yes, Barall," said Dalis. "Just as the symbol of Endomar graces your chair, our gods' symbols adorn ours."

Vance had taught Barall about the possibility of gods other than Endomar, a fact they had hotly debated. But now he was confronted with, if not their existence, at least the belief in their existence. Never had Vance ever let on that he knew anything about these other gods, other than a general feeling of their existence.

"Friends," started Dalis, "this is Barall, Acolyte of Endomar, apprentice and friend to Comfort Vance. Before we explain why Barall is here, let us introduce ourselves to him. My name is Dalis, priest of Sleonde, Goddess of Love and Loyalty."

Dalis pulled out the chair with the heart symbol and sat down. Beside him, in the middle of the table, stood Cura.

"My name is Cura, priestess of Aronya, Goddess of Health and Healing."

The chair that she sat down in was carved with the symbol of a tree. As she sat down, a tall woman who stood next to her, to Barall's immediate left looked to him. She was taller than Barall, and looked to be slightly older as well. Her frame was thin and wiry without appearing to be macerated. What shocked Barall though was her head.

Her eyes were a vibrant, striking blue, the color of a cloudless summer sky. It felt to him like he could stare into those eyes forever. The effect of her eyes was marred however, by her shaved head. Its baldness mirrored his, and it was with great effort that he resisted the urge to run a hand over his scalp in recognition.

"Tella," she stated gruffly, her voice nearly as deep as a man's. "Follower of the God of Strength, Gefrin."

Her introduction made, she abruptly sat down in the chair with the rock carved into it, and sat stiffly, staring straight ahead.

With a small grin to himself, Barall turned to his right and looked down that side of the table. The first person, standing at the far end, was an expressionless woman of average height. She was reed thin with a small nose and green eyes, framed by short dark hair.

"I am called Seskia and I am a priestess of Rettela, the great Goddess of Disease."

Her chair was carved with the image of the skull and she sat in it with a calm air of certainty and a smug look toward Cura. Though she only gave a dismissive sniff in reply, Cura's eyes had narrowed and her hands were clenched into fists.

The man next to Seskia cleared his throat in an obvious attempt to draw attention to himself. Because Barall happened to be watching Cura at the time, he noticed the softening of her gaze. It was there only for an instant before being replaced with something that looked like disgust.

Following Cura's gaze, Barall found an extremely handsome man gazing down his sculpted nose at him. He stood at Barall's height, perhaps a shade taller with hair the color of wheat that hung to below his shoulders. His clothes were well tailored and appeared to be of the finest fabric. Just from those few seconds, Barall could tell he was a proud, well-to-do man. He was much older; perhaps twice Barall's age, and kept tossing his hair and picking at miniscule particles of dirt on his clothes. When he spoke, the same haughtiness that was presented through his clothes and mannerisms came through.

"I am Cerrok, boy, high priest to Xelteran, the God of Greed. Every man's true desire is to own or control others and what they have, and Xelteran is there for them."

He drew breath to speak again, but was cut off by the last man, nearest to Barall's right. This man, too, was much older than Barall, though slightly shorter. He had rich brown hair, just starting to gray around the temples, with long sideburns running down his cheeks to connect to a short, scruff beard.

A scowl seemed permanently carved onto his face as he looked over Barall. His eyes roved up and down, taking in Barall's youth and unkempt, travel-worn appearance. A glance at Cerrok spoke volumes of his opinion of Barall.

"Call me Venick, first priest of Melnock, God of Strife."

The chair with the crossed arms was Venick's, and he sat in it like it was the grandest throne of any king.

The only person left standing now was Barall. Not knowing what else to do he followed what the others had done.

"My name is Barall. I am an Acolyte of Endomar, God of Wisdom."

"An Acolyte?" sneered Cerrok. "Not even a full-fledged priest, yet." When Venick had started talking, Cerrok had sat down grumpily in the chair with the grasping hands.

"What are you playing at Cura?" sniffed Seskia, sounding smug and angry at the same time. "You were to bring Vance, not some undisciplined, unproven boy."

Seskia leaned forward to stare intently at Cura. "Could you not even follow those simple instructions?"

Heat rushed into Cura's face as anger flooded her. Before she could find any words to retort however, Tella interjected, her deep voice stopping the impending fight before it could begin. "Perhaps we should let them tell their story before we come to any conclusions?"

The simple suggestion was met with nods all around, even Seskia, begrudgingly accepting. Soon six sets of eyes were again focussed on Barall, and, for a second time, he found himself relating the tale of finding Vance, killed by the Emissary's guards, his flight from Anklesh and meeting Dalis and Cura.

When his story came to an end, there was silence in the small room. Barall gratefully accepted a glass of water from Tella and, giving her a weak smile of thanks, tried to sort through what he had just heard. Not only were there apparently other gods, just as Vance had argued, but there were religions and followers devoted to them as well.

Strangely, Barall did not feel threatened or offended by this. He thought he should be; after all, the worship of Endomar was all he knew and wanted in his life. He had no need or desire for any other god. He was wise enough, though, if he could be so bold as to believe himself wise, to recognize a possible need for others. A whole people dedicated to one god, with a single set of beliefs and thinking would eventually lead to imbalance.

That particular thought led Barall to thinking of Caven and what he was doing to, and within, the church. If there was only one religion, and Caven was at its head, and his policies of subjugating the other religions, then the spirit of the people was in serious jeopardy of losing itself.

That was what the theory of balance, and Vance, really spoke about. It was not only about good versus evil, right versus wrong and the equality of opposites. It was also about different views and opinions being allowed to flourish and grow without fear of automatic reprisals.

Into the silence, Barall's voice sounded like a gong. Six heads swivelled to look at him, some in shock, and others in welcome. By the time he had finished, all looked on him as a member of their group.

"The current order of things is wrong. Your religions are floundering due to lack of knowledge and support, mine due to mismanagement, and too much support. That has led to corruption and the pursuit of personal goals over the needs of the faith and the people. While it may be inevitable for a man," he continued with a nod to Cerrok, "it is not at all permissible in a religion. My master, Vance, has been preaching of this imbalance for years, and instructing me in its causes and the likely results if not stopped. It cost him his life. He has charged me with finding you and helping to restore the balance. To do that we must educate the people of the existence of a pantheon of gods, and push the corrupt Caven from his position of power."

# Chapter 5

*"The beginning of wisdom is found in doubting;*
*by doubting we come to the question, and by*
*seeking we may come upon the truth."*
*Pierre Abelard*

The discussion following Barall's speech was short but energetic, as the seven debated the best way to achieve their goals. As the newest member, and in his mind, the least educated in the manipulation of politics, Barall listened for the most part. He found by doing this that there were definite sides to the sideless circle, and very specific animosities between individuals. Tella and Cerrok in particular fought for control of the circle through very different means.

The priestess of Gefrin bullied and tried to force her views on the others while Cerrok of Xelteran chose a subtler means. He would bide his time and then pick opportune moments to discredit or devalue Tella; showing her as a poor candidate for leader.

Some were more personal in their feelings toward each other such as Dalis and Venick. They seemed to have a mutual respect for the other's ability, but an equal dislike for the other personally. It took a lot of effort to get them to acknowledge a valid point made by the other.

Lastly there was Cura. In the short time they had travelled together, Barall had found she could be abrupt, mean, cold-hearted and quick to judge. But she had also proven to have a sense of humor, fierce loyalty and a devotion to her friends, faith and purpose. In her, he could see someone in whom he could entrust his life and become honest friends, for she would always speak her mind and the truth.

Except when faced with Seskia.

The priestess of Retella seemed more interested in throwing cutting remarks and insults at Cura than anything else. It was obvious to everyone that Cura wished to lash out, to respond in kind, but always held her tongue, keeping to the issue at hand.

With all of the inner conflicts and in-fighting within the group itself, Barall found he was the one who was forced to guide the discussion. Surprising himself, he fell into the role easily; using his own thoughts and feelings to flesh out the plan. It was a complex situation in which they found themselves; seven people striving to change a country of one faith into numerous religions. The method for doing this turned out to be surprisingly simple.

The country of Cherilla was made up of relatively few large cities, Anklesh being the largest, and therefore the capital and home to the cathedral of Endomar. There were also Erskin and Wilrien, one to the west and the other far to the south and east. Both of these were roughly the same size, just slightly smaller than Anklesh. Other, somewhat smaller towns, including Bajanor, Casban, Laufrid and Mordrum, were scattered across the country.

All of these places were large enough to support not only a Primate, a senior priest of Endomar to whom any number of Comforts reported, but also a large contingent of church guards. The guards protected the churches from robbers and vandals and escorted Comforts as they travelled to outlying towns and villages.

Needless to say, such forces were beyond the abilities of seven people to defeat. So they would first travel to the small villages and outlying towns, too small for a Primate's residence. They would visit only those towns with either no Endomarian priests, or at the most, limited to a Comfort. A town such as Guilder.

❦

The job of a Comfort stationed in a small town or village was very different from those working in larger locales. The large centers usually had more than one Comfort, sometimes even a Primate, and that, Rischa thought, made all the difference.

A small town Comfort not only preached to their people every twenty days about the four pillars of faith, but also served as confidant, counsellor and advisor. Most of them also worked as independent arbitrators to disputes in all manner of issues, and even as teachers to children.

As the Comfort of Guilder, Rischa would not change positions with a large city Comfort for anything. She thoroughly enjoyed the challenges and variety her role in Guilder provided. It was not that she craved power or influence over the townspeople; in fact it was the exact opposite. She served to guide the people to attain their own wisdom and ability, to teach them to work toward the four pillars in all aspects of their life. It was not an easy task she asked of them; the pillars were extremely difficult.

The pillars represented the characteristics Endomarian religion declared necessary in order to reach wisdom. The first two, knowledge and experience, were not that difficult for they asked for very little of an individual. Experience was gathered every day just by living, and knowledge followed with every success, failure and trial. Compassion and honor were much harder for they required effort. Compassion guides that logic may not always lead to the right decision and that the heart, as well as the mind, should lead a person. Harder still was honor. That pillar required that a person do what is right, guided by the other three pillars, even at the peril of one's own self, to put the good and well-being of the whole first.

It was a thrilling and exciting life for Rischa and she savored every success she saw with her town. While she may not necessarily have agreed with all of the edicts coming from the cathedral, she still worked to implement them and explain the reasons behind them.

Of course there were always questions, and she welcomed all of them, for was questioning not the root of the pillar of knowledge? It was rare that she could not provide an answer or guide the questioner on the path toward finding one on his or her own. Lately, however, more and more people were arriving at her door with questions for which she did not have answers. Never before had she been asked about the existence of gods other than Endomar.

"There are no other gods," she stated to Hockne, a well respected cobbler in town.

He had come to Rischa, meekly asking the question she had now been hearing for over two weeks. She answered him patiently, but her mind was reeling. Where had all these questions come from, and how was she to properly answer them? Endomar was the one and only god.

He required balance in life. Other gods could only disrupt that balance by creating uncertainty and confusion. The four pillars all worked toward maintaining that balance, all flowing together, reinforced and encouraged with each mass.

Every twenty days mass was held because, in that length of time, a person would have gained enough experience that it was necessary to temper it with compassion from their own and the Comfort's knowledge to maintain an honorable life.

Now, even long-standing members like Hockne were questioning a belief Rischa had thought unshakeable. It was only with someone like Hockne that Rischa would pursue this issue further. He was a friend and would give and expect honesty.

"Why do you ask, my friend?" she posed, leaning forward toward him, both anticipating and dreading his answer.

They were sitting in her simple, yet comfortable office, another indicator of her trust in the man before her now. Everything about her indicated relaxation and casualness. She sat in a plain, high-backed wooden chair, her shoulder length brown hair, neatly tied back, was framed by the circle of Endomar that made up the very top of her chair. Her hands were kept loosely clasped in her lap, and one leg crossed over the other. A robe of the Comfort's pale green, belted at the waist with a sash of deeper green, hung easily from her shoulders and revealed an average build for a woman of her forty years. The only adornment she wore was a silver chain with a three finger wide silver circle. The room was quiet and still, as no sounds from outside could intrude on them here. Even the smell of a root tea, brewing off to one side, helped to make the room more pleasant and comfortable.

Surprisingly, Hockne would not meet her eyes. He looked almost ashamed as he smoothed out invisible wrinkles in his woollen pants. Eventually, when it became obvious that Rischa was not going to let him go without an answer, he glanced up, and with an abashed look, finally answered.

"I'm sorry for my question, Comfort," he started. "It's just that there has been a lot of talk lately, and they are very convincing with their words."

"'They,' Hockne? Who are 'they'?" Rischa asked softly, struggling to keep the concern from creeping into her voice.

Hockne looked up at her now. "Comfort," he said mildly reproachful, "you need to get out of this church once in a while. There is a group of people in town who are talking to people about other gods. They claim that Endomar is but one of seven gods who watch over us."

Rischa sat back heavily in her chair, shock evident on her face.

For a moment she said nothing and merely sat staring as if seeing nothing. How could she have been so blind, so oblivious to what was happening around her?

It had been so busy lately, with all the audiences she had been giving, instructing the Initiates and Acolytes assigned to her care, and all the other day-to-day chores that came with running and managing her own church. It had gotten to the point where she hadn't been able to even read the letters sent to her over the past several days. The pile, organized by an Initiate, sat at the other side of the desk as a glaring reminder even now.

"What are these people saying?" she finally asked, no longer holding her emotions in check. Even to her own ears, she heard anger and frustration, so she tempered her question, hoping to allay any fears she may have raised in Hockne.

"Please, Hockne. Your knowledge will help me to learn about who these people are and what they are about."

"I took no offence, Comfort," replied Hockne, though a moment ago his eyebrows had been lost in the hair falling over his forehead.

They talked for another hour, Rischa calling for tea and food for them both. When Hockne finally left, Rischa felt she had at least some understanding of what was going on in Guilder. The situation was definitely something she needed to report to the cathedral. First, though, she might as well see if there was anything in her unread correspondence from Anklesh that required an answer as well.

෧෨

The Emissary was in a foul mood by the time he reached his office. The day had been full of dull meetings and reports he had been forced to sit through. His position seemed to mean that he was required to make every decision. The Wisdoms were going to be taking a lot of these mundane tasks from him, and let them just try to complain about it! There were more where they came from, so they could quickly be replaced.

As if thinking about the council summoned them, when the Emissary opened the door to his study, he found Virez standing by his desk. A glance he didn't bother to hide from her showed that nothing appeared to have been disturbed. His office was a large room, with a massive desk sitting near the fall wall. The floor displayed a simple carpet, dyed a deep purple to correspond with the Emissary's colors. There were no other adornments or embellishments in the office. In fact, beyond the desk and chair for the Emissary, there was no other furniture. Any visitors were expected to stand, conduct their business and leave.

"What?" he demanded moving past her without a look, pulling off the heavy chain with Endomar's circle and placing it on a hook embedded in the wall. He rubbed his neck and rolled his head to try to ease the tension causing them to ache miserably.

A rustle of paper and a soft step warned him of Virez's approach. He turned to watch as she moved around his desk, flexing her fingers, a slight smile on her face.

"Your purpose here, Virez?" he growled at her.

The Wisdom was young, approaching her late thirties, and was a handsome woman who would never be considered beautiful. She stood about half a head shorter than the Emissary with short, wavy blond hair. Her robe of earthy brown was belted across hips just starting to lose some of their curve. A small purse was looped on a long strap over one shoulder and across her chest in what the Emissary took to be an obvious attempt to draw attention to the bosom hidden behind the robe.

"Your Eminence is obviously overworked. If you will permit me …?"

After a thoughtful look at Virez, the Emissary finally sighed.

Rather than turning around and facing toward the wall, he pushed past her and sank into the padded wooden chair behind the desk. Doggedly following, Virez squeezed in behind him and began massaging his neck and shoulders.

Despite himself, the Emissary could feel himself responding to her ministrations. As Virez's fingers pressed and rubbed against the knots created by the strain of the day, a low moan of satisfaction escaped from between his lips.

"I'm glad that I'm able to ease some of my lord's tensions," purred Virez. "I am available for any such relief that you wish," she added after another long moment.

The suggestion of what she was offering hung in the air. The Emissary said nothing at first, considering how best to respond. Virez was not someone he would normally even glance at twice, but he had to consider his future plans for the church and what type of allies he would need. She was a high ranking, and fairly well-respected, priestess. He had chosen the three Wisdoms for their tractability, their willingness to obey his commands when required and look the other way when not. They were not in their positions because of thinking freely or creatively.

Still, her suggestion intrigued him, not so much for what she offered, but that she had even thought to offer it all. A grin creased his face as he decided what to do.

"Your offer is very much appreciated, Wisdom Virez. I can think of nothing I would enjoy more than your helping with my tensions." He started laying his hand on hers as it moved across his shoulder. "But first, you still have not explained your presence."

"My apologies, Emissary," said Virez. "I received this letter from a Comfort stationed in a village two weeks journey from here. If what she says is true, then this is something that you will want to deal with immediately."

A neatly folded letter was placed on the desk before Caven.

Virez used the opportunity to press herself firmly against his back, allowing him to feel what she was offering. She stayed that way as the Emissary opened the letter.

Almost immediately the knots of tension returned to his shoulders, bringing with them all their aches and pains. He batted away Virez's useless attempts to seduce him and rounded violently on her.

"How long have you had this?" he roared at her.

"I came to you as soon as I had seen it," she replied, stunned by his outburst. "Why?"

"Why? Why? You useless cow, Virez! This Comfort in Guilder is sitting on the biggest threat the church has ever seen, and you don't even see it."

"I want a contingent of guards sent to Guilder immediately. They are not to simply arrest these people, I want them killed outright. The charges are blasphemy, hereticism and treason."

"But Emissary, only King Zithius may lay a charge of treason," started Virez. She stopped when she saw the rage boiling up in the Emissary, his face purpling and his hands clenching into white-knuckled fists.

"Yes, Emissary," she amended hastily. "It will be done immediately."

The Wisdom moved with remarkable speed toward the door, when a call from behind stopped her.

"You forgot about your offer to help me with my sore muscles," he said.

Virez froze with her hand on the handle of the door. She was trapped, and she knew it, and so turned back toward the room slowly. Still seated behind his desk, Caven was busily writing. The scratch of the quill across the parchment was the only sound.

"Yes, Emissary."

"You will now attend all First Primate meetings in my stead. I will expect a written report, of no more than two pages, an hour after each meeting advising me of its outcome. Thank you for relieving me of that stressful burden," he said, never once looking up.

"Of course, Emissary, it will be my pleasure," was Virez's only reply. The tone of her voice said that it would be anything but a pleasure to sit through the ordeal.

"And Virez …?"

"Yes, Emissary?"

"Never question my orders again. I am the Emissary of Endomar and despite the title Zithius may currently hold, I rule this country, and I will decide its future and that of its citizens."

# Chapter 6

*"Kindness is more important than wisdom, and the recognition of this is the beginning of wisdom."*
Theodore Rubin

The air was heavy with the smell of impending rain and lightning lit the night sky almost continuously. So far, not a single drop had fallen, but it was only a matter of time. The wind blew fiercely, whipping dirt and leaves around Barall's ankles. Despite the threatening storm, Barall's mood was light. The knowledge and insight he had gained from reading of Gibson's life was buoying him up, even in the face of the group's disappointing lack of success.

While the people of Guilder seemed interested, almost eager, to learn of the other gods, there had been no change to their lives. Barall didn't really know what he had expected to happen, but upon his first reading of *A Priest's Life*, he had felt a sense of rightness about it, as if something had been missing, or wrong, in his life and he hadn't known about it until now.

After that first reading, he had re-read it, much more carefully this time, thinking more about what he was learning. Gibson had been an unremarkable and ordinary priest of Endomar, reminding Barall of himself actually. He was devout and faithful, enjoying the challenges that being an Acolyte, then a Comfort, entailed. Cura had been mistaken in saying that Gibson had been an Emissary. He had not. Though he had been very close, perhaps even likely to attain that illustrious post, he had apparently died as a Wisdom, counsellor to Emissary Aiximor.

Perhaps Gibson had been unremarkable as a priest, but he was diligent in recording his thoughts and ideas as he progressed through life. Within his diary, written in the same compact, neat handwriting throughout, he talked about meeting priests and priestesses of the other gods. He spoke of the friendly debates with them over religious differences and gossiped over what the heads of the seven orders discussed when they met. Most shocking of all, Gibson described his participation in a joint effort of priests of all seven gods and goddesses to work with the dwarves and people of the Tekil Mountains to overcome a large and brutal tribe of mountain trolls. The Tekil Mountains were found in south central Cherilla and extended into neighboring Naer.

Barall had never heard of trolls marauding through the countryside, much less banding together in tribes to do so. As shocking as that was, though, what he took from the tale was that the different priests fought together against a common enemy, to defend friends. Non-human friends at that.

The impending storm intruded on his thoughts with a resounding clap of thunder. Barall stopped in shock as the sound echoed eerily through his head.

The village of Guilder was bracing for the onslaught of the storm with people barricading themselves inside their homes. Shops had closed early, their doors barred as much against the rain as against those who would wish to profit from it. Even Barall's small group had ended their talks early, sending remaining villagers home. While none had come out and pronounced themselves a devotee to any of the 'new' religions, there were a lot who continued to attend meetings and ask questions. Tella had even boldly proclaimed that villagers were starting to question Rischa, the Comfort stationed within the church in Guilder.

Tomorrow was the day of worship, the end of the twenty-day period when Comforts all over the country opened their church doors to any and all comers to hear of the four pillars of faith. It was also a time when anyone could question the priest. This was normally used as a time to expound on one's problems that the Comfort could resolve, but there was nothing written about what could, or more importantly, could not, be asked about.

Barall had tried numerous times to get into the church to see Comfort Rischa. Each time he had been denied, turned away at the door by an Acolyte expressing dismay at the Comfort's busy schedule. No one, of course, was fooled by this. Rischa was simply refusing to meet with him. It was the why that Barall did not understand. He simply wanted to talk to her. But the Acolytes had been adamant in their refusals.

Until today. Today, Barall had been greeted at the door by the same, fresh-faced Acolyte as every other time. Not deterred, Barall kept his face serene as he, again, politely asked permission to see Comfort Rischa.

"She is not available at the moment, good sir," responded the Acolyte, equally politely, though with a mixed expression of awe and fear.

"Thank you for your time, my friend," said Barall, already turning to go and join the others at the meeting place.

"But she is available this evening," the Acolyte called after him. As Barall turned back, the surprise evident on his face, the young priest spoke again. "She asks that you return here, alone, two hours after sundown and she will see you then."

The sound of the door closing nearly caused Barall to miss the last of the words. It was an odd time for meeting, but he was happy nonetheless. Finally he would be able to present his issues to someone within the church and be able to show what he had learned about Endomar and His religion. Gibson's diary had revealed so much more than the friendly existence of six other gods. There was more to the religion of Endomar than any of them had believed.

The others were somewhat less enthusiastic about the news.

"It's a trap for sure," said Cerrok.

"Aye!" agreed several of the others.

Barall pushed their fears aside; this was a Comfort of Endomar, not an enemy general he was going to meet. But Cerrok would not be deterred so easily. "They're the same thing lad," he said, his normal testiness replaced with concern. "Everyone has their own goals, their own personal desires. Sometimes they're right there in the open, laid bare for anyone to see. In others, they're buried deep, hidden to all but themselves."

"You don't know but that this Rischa doesn't need to curry favor with the Emissary. What kind of honors could she expect for lopping the head off our little movement here before it even gets going?"

It had taken the weeks they had been together for Barall to prove, not only to the others, but to himself as well, that he was an equal member of this group. He had argued with the group, and had won and lost points in those discussions. But he had not been bullied by Tella, or connived by Cerrok, and had kept to his own opinions. That, more than anything else, granted him the acceptance of the others, but never had he considered himself the head of the group. Noticing his shocked expression, Venick clapped him on the shoulder.

"Don't even know your own place, do you boy?" he said, his tone gruff, but his manner not unkind. "Despite how much we might wish otherwise, you're it."

"It is actually the way it always has been," added Seskia, coming up to the three men from the other side of the square where they had gathered to meet with any interested townspeople.

"What?" said all three men at once.

"Endomar has always been the leader, the guide. He draws the others like the flame draws the moth. He is, after all, the God of Wisdom."

Having said her piece, Seskia wandered over to greet some people arriving in the square, her slender figure easy to pick out among the more robust townsfolk.

In the end, Barall listened to his friends' arguments and decided to attend the meeting anyway. The storm was not something that would deter him from going; he just hoped that it would hold off long enough for him to get inside. As if in defiance of his wish, small, stinging rain drops began spattering him. The sound of the rain soon mingled with that of the wind to drown out just about everything else. The darkness seemed to deepen with the rain, and what little light leaked from the passing windows shrunk even further in upon itself.

Quickening his steps, Barall didn't notice several shadows detach themselves from the front of the church and make their way toward him. With only the fiercely blowing wind sounding in his ears, it was without warning that Barall found himself lying face down in the rapidly soaking ground, the smell and taste of the mud in his face as a heavy weight pressed into him. In front of his face was a pair of muddy boots, several pairs in fact.

As he tried to push himself over, the weight pushed him deeper into the mud.

"Hold still," a gruff voice commanded. The sharp point of a knife pressed to the back of Barall's neck emphasized the point.

"Who … who are you?" stammered Barall not daring to move. "What do you want?"

"Quiet!" growled a voice from above.

There was an interminable silence while Barall struggled to understand what was happening to him and who these men were.

Eventually, rough hands grabbed him and hauled him bodily to his feet. Without a chance to see the faces of the men, he was shoved from behind in the direction of the church.

Lightning flashed suddenly, illuminating the area all around. Arranged around Barall were several soldiers. All wore the uniforms of soldiers of Cherilla, a blue uniform with bands of white. The men were soaked through and appeared exhausted but determined.

He slugged through the mud, slipping every other step toward the dark church, dim lines of light gleaming around the door. Slipping again, he nearly lost his balance, but caught himself against the soldier next to him. The soldier jerked his arm away, pushing Barall back to the center of their circle with a laugh.

The man's coarse laugh, however, was cut short with a gurgle. Another flash of lightning quickly followed by another and another lit the area as brightly as any day. The man fell forward, an arrow piercing his neck.

Everyone stood, shocked to stillness by the scene before them. Only when another arrow sailed past everyone, narrowly missing another soldier, did they recover.

The arrow sent a whirlwind into motion. Five soldiers who had been surrounding Barall at a distance of several paces, moved closer, completely blocking him from escape. All drew their swords, the sound coming to Barall even over the wind and rain. For his part, he stayed huddled in the center, too scared to move and not really knowing who was on his side, if anyone.

Lightning continued to flash so he was able to get intermittent flashes of movement from all around him. Through the curtain of rain he could see shapes moving about, metal glinting in the dim light. The men surrounding Barall tensed as they too caught sight of the indistinct shapes. Hands tightened unconsciously around their weapons and they shifted slightly to adjust their balance.

Through the darkness five new figures approached, cautious of their footing, and another arrow soared through their midst. This one, too, didn't do any damage even though it managed to strike a glancing blow off the man to Barall's right. The sound of the hit against the man's breastplate caused Barall to jump in surprise. The soldier, clearly uncaring of his own mortality, merely shrugged as if it were only a fly that had hit him and not a steel-tipped arrow.

"Too much wind," someone muttered.

"Aye, but good enough to get Pillo on the first shot," remarked another.

After that there were no more words between them as the five forms materialized into men and women, each with weapons drawn. Each had selected a target and they moved forward with obvious intent.

"Hold!" shouted the apparent leader of the quintet surrounding Barall. "You are interfering in the work of the Emissary of Endomar. Lay down your weapons and no harm shall come to you."

"Any Emissary that sends soldiers to attack one of their own holds no authority with us," came the shouted reply.

On the heels of this declaration a long, thin dagger came slicing through the rain and darkness. The blade flew straight and true, directly into the shoulder of the leader. The impact spun him about until he lay flat on his back in the mud, groaning and clutching at the dagger.

Momentarily stunned, the remaining soldiers quickly recovered and three moved to intercept the five attackers. The last stayed with Barall, his sword resting none too casually against Barall's shoulder. Turning to look up the blade, Barall noticed the tight, two handed grip his guard had on his weapon, and the steely eyes focussed on him.

With a shudder, Barall turned back to the battle unfolding before him. Although outnumbered, the remaining guards did not hesitate in spreading out to protect the rest of their unit, and their prisoner. Grim, rain soaked visages approached, also spread out in a line. For the moment, all animosity and disagreements among the seven priests were forgotten as Tella, Dalis, Cerrok, Venick and Seskia joined in battle with the Emissary's soldiers. Each carried a different weapon, but they wielded them with the comfort and confidence of long use.

Tella launched herself at the nearest soldier with a knife in each hand. The soldier sneered to see a woman, armed only with knives come at him. He slashed at her, almost casually, already intent on helping his partner fend off his attacker.

But Tella was obviously very used to fighting men armed with weapons with a longer reach. Using the momentum of her run, she fell to her side and slid right under the soldier's wild swing. Coming to a stop butted up against his legs, she didn't hesitate, but lashed out viciously with both knives. Spurts of blood gushed from the inside thigh of both legs. With a cry he dropped his sword and clutched at his legs in a feeble attempt to staunch the flow of blood. Tella stood and kicked his sword away. Coming up behind the man she grabbed a fistful of hair and pulled, baring his throat. In one swift motion she ended his life with a pull of her knife.

Looking around, Barall could see the others were having similar success. Dalis was trading blows with another soldier, his hammer weaving a web that the other's sword could not penetrate. The huge priest of Sleonde had his opponent continually retreating, so it was only a matter of time.

To Barall's left, Cerrok and Venick, armed with a mace and a sword, respectively, had ganged up on the third soldier. By the time Barall looked over to where they were, the soldier was already dead, lying on the ground at the feet to the two priests.

With the three soldiers dead that left only …

The thought in Barall's head was shaken as he felt the sword at his neck suddenly jerk. The well-honed blade bit into his neck as the man holding it toppled backward, two arrows sprouting from his chest.

Rolling forward, Barall came to rest against a dropped sword. As his fingers closed around the hilt, his eyes met those of the fallen unit leader. He was an average looking man, with short blond hair and blue eyes. Travelling to Guilder had obviously been hard, for he had not even taken the time to shave. Fatigue, now mixed with the pain of his wound, showed in his eyes.

With a grimace, the guard pushed himself to his feet, and slowly drew his sword. Intent on his duty, he shuffled toward Barall, his left arm kept cradled against his chest to avoid moving the dagger that jutted sickeningly from his shoulder. His right arm seemed barely able to hold his sword, but he still managed to keep it raised.

Barall looked wildly around, hoping for some sort of support, but the others were all too far away or not aware of his predicament. He stood, clumsily holding the dead soldier's sword before him.

The weight of the weapon surprised him and he wondered how men could so easily use them. He tried to back away, but even wounded, the leader was quicker.

"Lay down your weapon," said the man. "and tell these others to do the same."

"You attacked us!" exclaimed Barall, continuing his retreat.

"No. You are under arrest for blasphemy, hereticism and treason, by the order of the Emissary himself. Now yield!"

Though his eyes opened wide in shock at the charges against him, it was really no less than Barall had expected. He would not quit this course so soon simply because he was now a wanted man. Vance's memory demanded more.

"I will not," he called back, stopping where he was and lifting the sword to what he felt was a proper position to defend himself.

The soldier shook his head sadly as if regretting what he must do. With a determined look, he advanced on Barall, his sword held low. As he neared, he swept the blade upward, intending to catch Barall unaware.

Not at all expecting the move, Barall jerked his head backward to avoid the blade aimed for him. Moving too fast, he could feel his feet slipping out from under him. He fell to his back with a whump and a splash of mud.

Above him, he heard a shout of triumph from the guard who raised the sword to stab Barall through the heart. Closing his eyes to the inevitable, Barall whispered a final prayer.

# Chapter 7

*"Nine-tenths of wisdom consists in being wise in time."*
*Theodore Roosevelt*

The sword was carefully pried from his fingers and gentle hands began to probe at the wound on his neck. Opening his eyes, Barall was shocked to see Cura kneeling over him.

"Hold still," she said gently. She was covered in mud and appeared slightly out of breath. As she leaned over him, Barall inhaled the smell of rain and earth coming from her hair.

"That's not bad," she declared at last. "Not even bleeding anymore." Then, as she turned away, giving his shoulder a pat, "Now let's see about your friend."

Confused, and more than a little shocked at being alive, Barall pushed himself up to watch as Cura moved to tend to another wounded man.

"Oh no," breathed Barall. He heaved himself the rest of the way up, helped unexpectedly from behind by Dalis. The large man grabbed Barall under the arms and lifted him easily to his feet.

"Thanks," gasped Barall, immediately asking what had happened.

Sensing Barall's urgency, Cerrok answered, thinking that Dalis' deliberate way of talking would grate on Barall.

"We didn't trust this Comfort as you did, so we followed you to make sure you actually made it to your meeting," said the priest simply, as if attacking and killing six soldiers was an everyday event.

"If there ever even was a meeting," added Tella, the rain fairly flowing off her bald head as she cleaned her knives.

Barall shivered at the sight of the woman calmly cleaning the blood of the man she had just killed from her knives as if it were nothing more than a common chore.

"What do you mean?" demanded Barall. "All of you. Do any of you understand what you've done?"

"Other than save your life?" shot back Cerrok.

"And the movement itself," added Tella.

Cerrok glanced at her, surprised at finding support coming from one he was usually at odds with. Barall noticed it too, but chose to ignore it.

"Have you?" demanded Barall. "You have killed six of the king's soldiers on duty for the Emissary. Will that save the movement or speed its destruction?"

"Five," broke in Cura, cutting off Cerrok before he could retort.

"What?" exclaimed Barall.

"That's easily fixed," stated Venick moving toward the wounded man and pulling his sword from the sheath belted at his waist.

"No," Cura stated flatly, placing her body between Venick and the soldier. "We are not killing a helpless man for no reason."

"Oh no? They attacked us. They wanted to drag Barall back to Anklesh in chains. That is reason enough."

"No, it's not," said Dalis. "There's a big difference between killing in defence and murder. Had Barall struck deeper, there would be no question, but he did not. So now we should work to minimize the harm we have caused."

"Exactly," started Barall. "Wait. What? Struck deeper? What are you saying?"

His eyes swivelled from one to another in confusion, clearly not understanding what Dalis has said.

"Dalis, help me here," commanded Cura in exasperation. "Barall, your sword hit the captain here when he rushed in as you were falling. He impaled himself."

As Dalis bent and easily lifted the man into his arms, Cura continued telling the others how she might be able to save his life, despite the loss of blood and damage to his body. She needed a quiet and preferably warm, peaceful place to work.

Looking up, Barall found the church directly in his line of sight. Anger and cold purpose filled him. He reached down and picked up a sword at random from the pile amassed by the others and strode off toward the church. No longer worried about appearances or being polite, he was not about to be rebuffed again. Tonight, Comfort Rischa would meet with him.

Holding his borrowed sword in both hands at about chest height, Barall leaned forward until the sword touched the ornate doors he had so admired earlier. Closing his eyes, he began his prayer. Gibson had described this spell as being used to gain access to cursed buildings in order to cleanse them of evil. However, Barall saw no reason why it wouldn't work here as well. The other six members of his group were arranged in a semi-circle behind him, Dalis still effortlessly carrying the wounded soldier when Barall opened his eyes.

"Knock," said Barall quietly, using the sword to push against the door.

Instantly, the beautiful doors flew inward. They smashed against the wall just inside the opening, tearing the hinges from their sockets and careening further into the church.

Barall stood blinking at the effects of the spell; he had not expected so powerful a reaction. A slight cough from behind brought him back to the present, so without looking back, he marched into the church. The inside was dimly lit with torches spaced intermittently along the walls. They sputtered and waved as gusts of wind from the storm blew in the now doorless opening. Row after row of benches lined a central corridor, at the end of which stood a lectern with Endomar's circle embossed on its forward side. Two doors led off this central room to both the left and right.

"Rischa!" yelled Barall striding down the corridor, his boots echoing in the vaulted room, gobbets of mud dropping off with each step. Inside, the church was as resplendent as it was outside. But Barall ignored it all as he continued calling for the Comfort. He stopped at the lectern not only because he was unsure of where to go, but also because he felt that here, at the spot where the faith of Endomar was preached, was where the soldier should be tended. The soldier that he had caused to be injured.

Acolytes arrived in the central chamber from the different doorways, distinguished by their shaved heads and white robes. Their shocked expressions at his shouting, and the presence of armed men and women in their church, were only diminished when they saw the wounded soldier being laid at the base of the Comfort's lectern. A low moan escaped the man as Dalis placed him gently on the ground.

Two Acolytes rushed immediately to the lectern and started examining the man. Barall turned his attention to the third, who remained in the doorway from which she had appeared.

"Comfort Rischa," stated Barall walking up to her with a perfunctory bow.

"I take it you are Barall?" said Rischa, nonplussed by his awareness of who she was. Then, at his nod, "How did you know it was me?"

"You didn't move to help the soldier you sent," he replied angrily.

Rischa, too, was in no mood to brook the tone she heard in Barall's voice. She strode out of the doorway right up to Barall, uncaring of the sword still in his hand and the mud and blood caking his clothes and hair.

"I sent no soldiers. I only sent the invitation as you have repeatedly asked for. And you come to this meeting armed, dirty and bellowing like an animal. Is this how you show your respect?"

"Respect is earned, not granted," he shot back.

"Perhaps, but do you normally start a relationship in this way?"

"Of course not, I get this way after being attacked in the street."

"I repeat, I sent no one."

"Well someone did."

"My apologies, Comfort," broke in one of the Acolytes. The two white-robed Acolytes had fairly bullied their way to the man and had, as gently as possible, removed his tabard and mail shirt to examine the two wounds marring his, otherwise muscular, body. From where Barall stood, they looked ugly and ragged.

"Yes, Vitas?" Rischa answered, her voice again calm.

"I do not believe there is anything we can do for this man. His wounds are just too grievous."

The woman spoke deferentially to Rischa, but her eyes constantly roved among the seven strangers. They seemed to linger longest on the handsome Cerrok. The priest was likely more than twice her age, but still he gave every indication of being interested in the girl.

By now, a small group of villagers had gathered at the door, drawn by the commotion in the square and Barall's spell at the door. They stood in a group just inside the doorway; unsure what to do now that they realized the church was not under attack.

"With a sigh, Rischa thanked her subordinate. "I know you did your best, Vitas. Just try to make him comfortable. I will see to our guests."

She moved past Barall to talk to the villagers clustered together and dripping from the rain. Knowing that more could be done for the man, Barall made his way to where Cura and the others waited after being pushed aside by the Acolytes.

"You've got to do something, Barall," said Cura as Barall approached.

"Me? You're the priestess of health and healing."

"Yes, but we are within your church, surrounded by the faithful. Your casting of the spell will do more to advance our cause, than if I did it myself."

As Barall hesitated, Cura pushed him toward the moaning soldier. "Seeing how we got in here in the first place, I know you've studied the diary. I also know that you wouldn't be foolish enough to not have learned the healing spell."

"Yes, but …"

"No. There are no 'buts'. You can do this."

He looked down into Cura's green eyes and saw only trust and faith. Faith in him and his ability to heal another.

"What do I do?" he asked.

Smiling, Cura explained that he simply needed to be in contact with the wounded or sick, and then to pray. "The prayer is the spell and its power is drawn from the strength of the priest's faith."

The soldier was still moaning softly, but they were coming more pitifully each time. Barall knelt at his side, sickened at the sight of the wound he, himself, had inflicted. It still oozed blood, but sluggishly, as if the body was running out of blood. The wounds seemed almost too small and precise for the amount of damage they had caused.

Ignoring the protests of the two Acolytes, Barall placed his hands directly on the wounds, one on the shoulder and one over the jagged gash in the stomach. Closing his eyes, he prayed to Endomar. He prayed for the soldier's life. He prayed for the strength to help not only this man, but the entire country as well. He prayed for the wisdom to do the right thing.

How long he prayed, he didn't know; time lost all meaning to him. But then, beneath his hands, the body twitched. The twitch turned into a sigh and the man suddenly sat up.

# Chapter 8

*"He that never changes his opinions, never
corrects his mistakes, and will never be
wiser on the morrow than he is today."*
*Tyron Edwards*

It was a very different and distracted Rischa who held mass the next
morning. She had spent the night in discussion with Barall, their
words, at times, heated, as Barall explained their purpose and the
reasons for what they were doing.

More than his healing of the soldier and the production of
Gibson's diary, a priest that Rischa had actually heard of, it was the
revelation from Captain Kayir that proved most convincing to the
Comfort. The formally wounded soldier had fairly demanded to be
a part of their discussion. When he revealed that he had been sent
by the Emissary, with orders to kill the seven members of Barall's
group, Rischa grew introspective. While she thought through all she
had learned, Kayir turned to Barall.

"What of me now, my lord?"

"I am no 'lord,' Kayir. I am the son of a glass blower who heard
the call to serve. You are not beholden to me in any way, so you may
do as you wish."

Kayir chuckled mirthlessly. "I am a soldier, my lord. It is rare that I can ever 'do as I wish.' You say you are not a lord, yet you hold the power of a god in your hands."

Barall thought for a moment, wanting to pick his works carefully. He knew Rischa was listening as well, and how he answered may weigh on her own thoughts. "I am merely the vessel through which He worked," he answered at last. "It was Endomar's decision whether to heal you or not, I merely offered the request. Please, just do what you think is right."

They sat around a fire in Rischa's personal rooms, these being deeper within the church and therefore away from the battering wind and rain. Fatigue was quickly claiming Barall after the battle and then being up more than half the night talking. Despite his best efforts, he could feel his eyes sliding shut and by the time he woke, it was already morning and he was alone in Rischa's chambers. After a quick breakfast of bread and fruit, left behind presumably by a thoughtful Rischa, he opened the door to go and listen to Rischa address her people.

"My friends," she began just as Barall reached the main chamber, "it is said that the path to wisdom begins with a question. It could be 'why' or 'how'. The question leads to a search for answers, which in turn leads to the first two pillars of wisdom. The experience gained in the search and the knowledge obtained by it."

Barall edged around one side of the room, but he couldn't get far. The church was bursting with what looked like the entire village, the air heavy and cloying with so many people. He noticed Dalis and Tella first, then the rest standing near the gap where the doors had been. Workers had obviously been busy through the night while he had talked and slept. The doors themselves were nowhere to be seen, and Kayir's blood had been washed away.

While he was looking around, Rischa continued. "The other pillars are, at the same time, very simple and extremely difficult to achieve. It is easy to show compassion to those who are sick or poor or injured, and honor is such a vague and esoteric principle that one could easily explain away murder as an honorable act."

Barall's head snapped up and his eyes quickly sought those of Rischa, but the Comfort kept her head down as if ashamed of her chosen course. Unable to glean her intentions, Barall then looked to the others. They, too, apparently took Rischa's words the way he had. Rischa was about to denounce them all in front of the village. While the others, standing right by the door would be able to escape, there was no way Barall could make it out. As Rischa continued, however, it became obvious she not going to denounce the movement, she was fully endorsing and supporting it.

"While the four pillars are preached to you and we all try to live up to them, we have become complacent. The church has let you down, and I have let you down, for it is the church, and I, that instructs and leads, and so it is the church, and I, that have lost focus and purpose."

"You have heard the group of people who have been speaking in the village. These seven people, priests of different gods and goddesses, are here to educate us all. As I said earlier, the path to wisdom starts with a single question. Well, I will be the first to admit that I don't know where to start. Where did these supposed other gods come from? Where have they been? Why are they here now?"

There were nods and shouts of agreement with each question posed. At the back, heads started to turn to look at the group of priests, making more than one slightly uncomfortable, as they wondered what was meant or intended by those looks.

"I have spoken directly with Barall, the leader of this circle of priests. I find him to be eloquent, passionate and entirely honest. What you don't know, and in fact what I myself learned only last night, is that Barall is a full Comfort of Endomar."

Gasps of astonishment met Rischa's declaration as apparently no one had thought to guess at Barall's religious allegiances. Only Barall and his friends knew this was not true, but they stayed silent wondering what Rischa was doing by elevating him now, and in so public a forum. Clearly Barall wanted to ask Rischa that very question.

"But there's more," continued Rischa. "That alone would not be enough to convince me of anything for how do we know there are gods other than Endomar? Before I even try to reply, let me ask another question: How do you know there is an Endomar?"

Silence met her last question, said with quiet insistence. No one had ever asked that question before, let alone their own trusted and respected Comfort, and it made everyone who heard it pause.

"Faith," said Barall into the silence.

"Exactly," replied Rischa nodding in Barall's direction. "Faith is all we have, and all we really need. If you require proof, you are not, truly, a believer. However, knowledge or belief in Endomar is all we have had for generations. How can we suddenly, now, be expected to believe in these others?"

"Faith!" shouted Tella from the back of the room. "We are not asking you for anything: no coins need be spent, no oaths given. All we ask is that you listen and learn and keep an open mind. If what we say appeals to you then we can talk more."

"It's not enough," came a shout from the far side of the church. When shouts of agreement met this declaration, a woman of middle age, plump with stringy brown hair stood up.

"I'm sorry, Comforts," she started, nodding to Barall and Rischa. "I don't know nothing about no learning. I believe in Endomar because that's what I was brought up to do. Nobody's never heard of no others."

Having said her piece, the woman sat down, to the delight of the man beside her who had been grasping at her arm trying in vain to pull her back into her seat. Barall happened to glance over to the door, and noticed Tella glaring at him. He lifted his shoulders in question, and Tella responded with a lowering of her eyebrows and an angry jerk of her head toward the outspoken woman.

He thought for a moment but shook his head. While he could formulate a response, he decided to take a page from Cura's book and turned to listen to how Rischa would respond.

Before she could say anything, however, another accusation rang out into the hall. "What about them weapons? I ain't heard of no priest who used weapons," called out a man glaring accusingly at the back of the room.

This time it was Venick who answered, slowly drawing his sword so the sound of the steel scraping along the side of its sheath drew all attention to him. "The use of a weapon," started Venick, "requires a certain amount of training and discipline, just like being a priest. Both also require the time to practice in order to be proficient. Your priests do not have that time as they have a congregation to tend to. As you have all said, no one has heard of us, so we don't have many people to preach to."

Venick grinned as the sword returned to its sheath. "We used our free time to learn to protect ourselves from those who would persecute us."

Looks of fear and disbelief spread across every face, except those of Venick's friends; they looked on him with lowered brows and frowns. His comments, while true, would certainly not endear them to the locals.

Rischa chose to ignore the last comments and instead returned to the original question asked of her.

"Why do we require any proof? There is no way to prove the true existence of Endomar, or any other god, yet we still believe, or can believe."

She paused a moment and gathered herself. As if coming to a hard decision, she sighed deeply, stepped away from the lectern and walked forward several steps. "I hesitated to tell you this," she said, "but I think that you need to know what has happened. I will start with a personal revelation. Most of you know that I have been against the acknowledgement of other gods. I was confident in my opinion that Endomar was the only god there was, and the only one we need. But, I too, have become complacent. There is a balance that must be maintained. Balance between opposites keeps everything aligned. In nature, there are predators and prey. There is a balance between them. There cannot be too many predators or they will eat all the prey, and then the predators, too, will die. The same is true in life. There must be a balance between good and evil, men and women, religion and secularism. Without this balance, chaos will erupt or stagnation will occur."

"For the reason of balance alone, I will, at least, maintain an open mind and a willingness to believe in other gods. However, while I have no hard proof of their existence, the incident of last night certainly does, in my mind, lend credence to Comfort Barall's position. Last night, soldiers attacked and tried to kill Comfort Barall and his friends, and in their defence, several of those soldiers were killed and another severely wounded. That wounded soldier was brought here for our healing, but his wounds were too serious for us to help him. However, before the eyes of several witnesses, myself included, Comfort Barall, through prayer alone, healed him. As we watched, blood stopped flowing, wounds closed and mended themselves, and color returned to the skin that was as pale as snow. The man, this soldier who was trying to kill Comfort Barall, stood up, as hale and healthy as I am, thanks to Comfort Barall. For these reasons, I choose to believe in Barall's circle and will support him in any way I can."

༄

"What are you doing?" demanded Barall of Rischa following the tumult of her service. "I am glad and honored that you, at least, accept what we say, but do you realize what you've done? The Emissary will not sit idly by while you support us, and certainly not for elevating me to Comfort. He will come after you now."

The senior Comfort sat calmly on the edge of her desk still dressed in her formal robes of pale green. Crammed into the room with them was the rest of the 'circle' as Rischa termed them, as well as several of Rischa's more senior Acolytes. As much as space allowed, Barall paced back and forth in front of the desk, arms punching the air for emphasis. He was obviously upset, judging by how heavily he was breathing and how concerned he appeared for Rischa and her underlings.

"I did what I thought was right; what the seven pillars require of me," Rischa replied softly.

Almost immediately, Barall stopped pacing and looked around to see if the others had heard as he had, which, judging by the looks on every face in the small room, they had.

The Acolytes shared the looks, as if Rischa had either just betrayed them or released them. The dichotomy was not lost on either Barall or Rischa.

"Friends," started Rischa, feeling it was her place to explain what she had just set in motion and why. "I did not make this decision lightly or without due thought. I recognize I have crossed the Emissary and his chosen course for the church. Given what he was willing to do to Barall to protect his position, my decision may place us all in danger. Knowing that, I still chose to support Comfort Barall and his circle as they fight to restore the balance. This was my choice, and mine alone, and you are all free to make your own choice, as Endomar has always allowed. Please, think about what you have learned, talk among yourselves and do what you feel is right. We will all talk together later if you wish."

Knowing a dismissal when they heard one, the half dozen or so Acolytes filed out of the room, already whispering together with sidelong looks at Barall. Once the last had left, closing the door behind her, Rischa let out a long sigh.

"They're all good priests," she said with a smile, "but this may be a bit too much for them."

Barall moved to help her remove the robes of office, for which he received a nod of thanks.

"The Emissary will not accept anyone undermining him," stated Tella frankly. "He cannot allow his position to weaken."

"Agreed," said Cerrok nodding to Tella and approaching Rischa. "But then you knew that, didn't you? What are you planning?"

Rischa smiled and laid a hand on Barall's arm, stalling his defence of her. "I suspect the Emissary will not be pleased, but then I also suspect that you seven are not long for Guilder and will soon move on. And, as I said, I believe what you are saying, priest of Xelteran."

Cerrok bowed his head in acknowledgement of her deduction. "Still …" he started.

"No, there is no underlying motive. Some people act simply because it is right to do so." Then turning to Barall, she added, "If you could stay long enough for us to copy that wonderful book …"

"We cannot," said Barall, "But I have already copied some of it. You can have that and I will have to send you the rest."

"Barall …" started Cura, hesitantly. The copying of Gibson's diary was not something any of them had discussed. While there were definite advantages, there were also great risks, not the least of which was the Emissary obtaining it. At the moment, they had the upper hand for they had the diary and, therefore, the knowledge. If the Emissary had it too, he could find some way to discredit it, and them.

"No, Cura. While Vance was right in concealing the diary, he was alone in Anklesh where, if the Emissary had found it, it would have been disastrous. Now, though, we need to spread the word, and as quickly as possible. Gibson was a priest of Endomar, and remembered by at least some of the current clergy. They deserve to see his works first hand."

"I agree with Barall," said Dalis, his deep voice and huge frame seeming to fill the room. "The decision is sound and shows the faith he has for his god and the priests that follow Him. But there is still the matter of his elevation."

At this, Rischa's eyes twinkled in suppressed mirth. From a drawer in her desk she pulled out a set of pale green Comfort's robes. The neatly folded robes were held between her hands and smelled faintly of soap, like they had been freshly washed.

"An Acolyte can be raised by any Comfort of sufficient experience. Normally it is considered bad manners for one Comfort to elevate another's Acolyte. But in this case, I don't think Vance will mind."

# Chapter 9

*"There has to be evil so that good can*
*prove its purity above it."*
**Buddha**

The storm that hit Guilder through the night lingered longer over Anklesh, though not as powerfully. The rain was still falling as the Emissary concluded his own services in a conspicuously under-filled cathedral. Few citizens braved the wind and rain to attend the service, but the Emissary knew it was more than weather that kept the people away. The people were turning away from him. And if they were turning away from him, then they were turning away from Endomar.

In the days that followed, the Emissary's feelings at the sleight afforded him were felt by all. He harangued prominent individuals and business owners for their lack of faith; Comforts ranged through the city proclaiming an overall lack of faith in the realm and deploring the evil that must be in the hearts of the faithless. The Emissary proposed policies of minimum donations to the church for all citizens, and mandatory service in the church guard for all youths.

The second service following the storm it was another gray and rainy day. On a day such as this, it would not have been odd to see more than a few empty seats in the grand hall. But by then, most people had heard of the Emissary's volatile temper and so the lords and ladies came across Cathedral Lake in their covered boats and mingled with the commoners on the docks in front of the great doors. The Emissary, in another gesture to prove his power, made them wait outside, soaking them through to the skin.

"It never used to be this way," more than a few could be heard to mutter, and it was true. Most there could remember when it was customary for the Emissary to come to them, rather than the other way around. Past Emissaries would venture out into the city and across the country to talk to the people and hear of their lives and troubles. Masses had been held in parks and on street corners, even in the kitchens of the homes he had been invited into. Most, too, knew that that was before Caven. This Emissary hadn't been seen outside of the cathedral since he had been elected Emissary.

When they were finally let into the hall, everyone rushing in like cattle into the barn, the service was dull, almost perfunctory. It was like the Emissary was merely going through the motions of the service, saying what they all knew already, just to get it over with and on to business more worthy of his attention. There was no mention of the rumors of new gods that were being heard from the west. Nothing was said about the strange growth in the number of soldiers wearing the Emissary's colors. It even seemed as though he was going to end his sermon without the customary question period.

"My lord," one brave man called out from the back of the room, "wait!"

Most in the crowd gasped at the tone used by the man, and waited for the Emissary's wrath to descend. No one dared to call to the Emissary in such a common way. From the dais where he stood, the Emissary turned slowly back to the people. The look on his face was unreadable, and so the people waited with breath held, to see how he would react. The Emissary's sharp eyes sought the man who spoke but there were too many to choose from, until the man called out again, just as the Emissary was turning to leave.

"I have a question, my lord."

A flicker of annoyance flashed across the Emissary's face, but even he recognized he was caught. Not even the Emissary could avoid hearing a question asked during a formal service, as much as he might want to.

"Ask my son," he said grandly, "but, please, approach that we might all see he who asks."

From the back of the room, an average looking man started moving. He was dressed plainly, though probably in his best clothes, of plain linen, marred at the cuffs and elbows and showing the wear and tear of a labourer. His pants of non-descript brown were torn in some places and threadbare in others. As he walked to the front of the church, his boots made wet, slapping sounds and bits of mud trailed behind him across the smooth marble tiles.

The Emissary watched him come. He knew what the people thought of him behind his back; they feared him and thought him harsh and unreasonable compared him to other, gentler, kinder Emissaries from before.

*Well, let them,* he thought. None of the prior Emissaries had the foresight or ambition to expand their domain. None of them had to deal with new religions, blossoming from within their own and threatening the very essence of who they were. None of them had the strength to stand up to those who considered themselves in power, whether political or mercantile. The entire country was dedicated to Endomar, and he held onto them with an iron grip. Any wavering of faith could lead to the downfall of the entire church. The people would abandon him and leave him begging for scraps from those who used to worship at his feet. The people did not need other gods. They needed only direction and leadership to tell them what to do and believe. The pursuit of wisdom was a lifelong goal, never truly attainable. That was the eternal secret of the church, one that could never be shared or spoken of. The church would vehemently denounce any who would dare say otherwise, but anyone who questioned hard enough could see that. New religions would do nothing to enhance the lives of the people; they would only cause confusion, doubt and discord.

The leaders were obviously charlatans, seeking the precious few coins that could be squeezed out of the people to line their own pockets. And then what? They would disappear as quickly as they had come. But not soon enough by Caven's reckoning. The common people were fools and would listen to anyone who knew how to talk to their baser needs. Find what scares them, find someone to blame, and direct the people to the church as the only one willing to say it.

But he was no fool. He could see what was happening and could take steps to thwart it. He had already sent a unit of guards to deal with the matter after all, and that should end things before they got going. He needed those coins for his own plans.

"My lord?" said the man, breaking into Caven's thoughts, giving the impression the man had been standing there waiting for awhile. He covered his lack of attention by simply ignoring it. Putting a false smile to his lips, he looked down at the man standing below him.

"You have a question." It was a statement not a question.

"My lord," the man began, falling to one knee before the Emissary. "Why are you taking my son, my lord?"

"Your son?" He looked to the side of the dais where the Wisdoms sat. "What is he talking about?" he demanded.

Destrin stood and made the sign of the circle toward the Emissary.

"Emissary, if I may? I don't know this man specifically, but I believe his son has likely just joined the ranks of your guard."

"Ah," said Caven dumbly. Thinking quickly and gripping his tall staff topped with Endomar's circle, he turned back to the man before him.

"My son," he began in a tone normally used for speaking to a child, "the issue is simple. Men of faith are needed by Endomar to support the efforts of His church. Your son obviously felt worthy enough to join others of similar feelings. His, and your, sacrifice is appreciated and we will pray for you both."

"Thank you, Emissary," gushed the man, obviously taken in by Caven's flattery. He bent to kiss the Emissary's outstretched hand and dropped a coin in the box beside the first pew as he made his way back down the aisle.

"Thank you, my son, for your donation to Endomar," called the Emissary. "If only more were like …"

"What efforts, my lord?" interrupted another shout from the back.

The Emissary's brows curled downward at being interrupted by another shouted question. Didn't these people realize he was to be treated with greater respect than with shouts from a mob? Still, he supposed, could any better be expected from such common stock? He decided he could be magnanimous and answer some questions. There was nothing extremely pressing at the moment.

"Friends, you should all realize that the church is here to support you, and work for the betterment of all. There is more of the world than Anklesh, more even than the entire country of Cherilla. There are peoples beyond our borders who would benefit from my wisdom and teachings. Who are we to deny them such? We need to look beyond our borders, to expand the benefit of our Lord Endomar."

The hall erupted in spontaneous shouts and cheers for the Emissary, who stood, soaking it all in with his arms stretched out to either side. He wore a rapturous expression and a beatific smile as the people responded to his declaration. To the side of the dais, however, the three Wisdoms exchanged looks. This was the first they had heard of any plans for the church. They were not as attuned to the political climate as their more secular brethren, but common sense would say that armed soldiers, even those under the guise of the church, would not be looked upon favorably by their neighbors.

Both Naer and Ponti, their neighbors to the east, while not enemies, were not allies either. There were little relations between them as far as the Wisdoms could tell. The Emissary was aware of this, and yet he was proclaiming his intention to send men into those countries to advance Endomar's teachings. This would be tantamount to an invasion.

Lassand, sitting the middle, with Destrin on his left and Virez on the right, whispered to his fellow Wisdoms, "We must proceed carefully if we are to survive."

"Agreed," said Virez, her eyes focussed solely on the Emissary.

"Why?" asked Destrin. "Our lord is brilliant, and his plan ingenious. What is there to fear?"

Lassand shot him a quick glance, his face filled with disgust. Wisdom Lassand was older, by far, than his two companions, having spent nearly fifty years in service to Endomar. He was not a handsome man, nor had he ever been. His head appeared overly large, covered in wrinkles, and sat atop a body seemingly too small to support it. Unlike most Comforts, when raised from Acolyte status, Lassand kept his head shaved. While the others suspected this was due to his increasing lack of real hair, it did serve to highlight his deep brown eyes, and gave him the look of one truly wise. Of the three Wisdoms, he, and he alone, had the support of individuals who actually felt he deserved the position.

"You are as foolish as you are naïve, Destrin," he whispered hotly. "Do you think Naer and Ponti will calmly accept armed men and women into their countries? Do you think whatever gods they worship will welcome the conversion of their people? Do you think the people of Cherilla will thank us for killing their sons and daughters? Do you even think at all?"

"Lassand ..." began Virez.

"Tell me, Lassand," began Destrin with equal heat in his voice, "do you always question your Lord Emissary? Are you truly as faithful as you claim?"

Surges of emotion raced through Lassand at the accusations. Shock and rage paramount among them, but reason and wisdom won out. Perhaps Destrin truly didn't see the dangers and foolishness the Emissary's plans evinced, so rather than reply hotly, he spoke with cool detachment.

"Of course I question, my brother, for that is truly our purpose. It is this council's duty to question the Emissary, to ensure he works for the good, not only of Endomar, but for the people as well. But this is neither the time, nor the place, to debate it. For now, let us agree to meet again, an hour hence, to discuss options."

℘

The purple robes of his office followed the solid gold circle with matching chain onto the hook behind the desk. A sigh of relief hissed from between Caven's lips and he stretched contentedly, relieving taut muscles. From behind him a pair of slender hands slid a more comfortable robe over his shoulders, this one, made of soft silk and feeling deliciously cool, and light, against his skin. The Acolyte who attended him this morning made herself busy brushing out the folds of his formal robe and eyeing it critically for any imperfection that would cause these robes to be discarded as unfit for his august person.

"You seem so tense, Emissary," she stated. "I can draw you a hot bath if you'd like?"

Caven looked at the girl for a moment. Typical of Acolytes her head was clean shaven, made all the more obvious as she demurely looked down, probably intimidated and awed by his position. He reached out one hand, his long fingers gently tipping her head up to look at him. A pair of brilliant emerald eyes topped by wonderfully long lashes gazed back at him. Her white robe, in pristine condition, was cinched about her trim waist with a loop of white cord. The robe must have been just a little too small, for it hugged her figure, nicely accentuating the curves of her hips and breasts.

Feeling the now familiar urges within him, Caven placed a gentle hand on her shoulder, pleased to feel her tremble at his touch. "I would like that, but the day is still young. Perhaps you could return tonight?"

"Of course, Emissary. It would be my pleasure," the girly gushed.

"Excellent. I look forward to it," he finished, turning away, his thoughts already turning to the day's schedule.

The girl, however, remained, standing by his desk, shuffling uneasily from foot to foot. They remained so for several heartbeats, the Acolyte obviously not recognizing she had been dismissed. Eventually, it was the Emissary who conceded and broke the silence.

"Yes," he demanded impatiently, looking up from his desk.

"I'm sorry, Emissary, but your service this morning ..."

"Yes? What about it?"

As if his question opened a floodgate, the words poured out of the girl, almost too fast for Caven to follow, but obviously this girl found his service to be much more than everyone else.

"Oh, Emissary, it was just wonderful," she gushed. "It was stirring and romantic and inspiring, and yet, scary at the same time. Not scary like terrifying, but scary as in being a part of history itself. I don't know if that makes sense to you, since you are the Emissary after all, but I just wanted to thank you, Emissary."

It took a moment for Caven to realize she had stopped talking, and another to realize he was confused.

"Thank me? For what, child?"

"For being so wonderful and … and, inspiring and handsome and courageous and brave."

With that she leapt into his surprised arms and hugged him tightly. Then, before he knew it, she had released him and was already heading toward the door, her face hot with embarrassment.

"I will be here to serve your dinner and ready your bath Emissary. May Endomar continue to bless you, my lord."

The scarlet blush of embarrassment was the last the Emissary saw as she fairly fled the room, but he puffed himself up in self-congratulation. He was loved and admired, and desired, by the people. Truly, there was no way his plans could fail.

❧

The feeling of euphoric invulnerability the Emissary had felt following the morning's service was, slowly but inevitably, quashed throughout the remainder of the day. Despite the endless parade of useless meetings and pedantic reports he was forced to endure, he could feel his spirits return as he walked to his last meeting. This last minute meeting was the one he had been waiting for and it would not be plodding or irrelevant, with mind-numbing droning. Finally his plans would be set, fully, in motion.

He strode down the hallway like one in charge of his own destiny. *That's what I am,* he thought to himself, his circle topped staff striking a cadence with his steps. *I have such forces and power at my command that I shape my own destiny.*

So with arms swinging confidently, the Emissary burst through the wide, double doors held open for him by two church guards, and into the meeting chamber. This particular room was situated between the grand hall where services were held, and the Emissary's office. Usually, advisors and researchers used the room, waiting to be called by the Emissary to provide assistance on whatever matter he was currently dealing with. Tonight, however, only a single individual, standing smartly at attention, occupied the room. With evening approaching, Acolytes had already been in to light the candles that illuminated the room. Hundreds of flickering flames danced and swirled as the Emissary swept by, ignoring the man to lean his staff against the arm of a comfortable-looking but utilitarian chair.

He turned suddenly to face his guest. The quick movement caused his robes to float upward and then settle perfectly in place, every pleat and fold exactly where it was supposed to be. If Kayir was impressed by this display, he didn't show it, but remained in place as if rooted to the spot.

"Well, Captain? I see you have returned, and still covered in the dust and dirt of the road as well," sniffed the Emissary.

"I assumed your Eminence would wish to hear my report straight away," replied Kayir.

"So you made no stops before coming to me," the Emissary presumed, "excellent. What news from Guilder?"

The Emissary could barely contain his excitement. Captain Kayir's unit had not been expected back for another few days, or even a week had they been forced to transport prisoners, so that he was back so quickly was a sign of good fortune.

"I fear you will not like the news, my Lord Emissary," Kayir started.

"Pray that I do," replied the Emissary, his voice quiet.

Kayir, to his credit, did not react to the veiled threat. Most assuredly, he heard and recognized the comment for what it was. This was the Emissary of Endomar, the highest religious authority after the God Himself and some would argue he had more power than even the king.

"I'm afraid I can only report the facts, my lord. The mission with which we were charged was not completed successfully. Lord Barall and his circle all still live, my lord."

For a moment the Emissary said nothing, appearing to not even breathe. "Circle?" he asked quietly, masking his growing anger.

"Yes, my lord. That is what the people are calling them."

"I see. So you spoke with them, the members of this 'circle' did you, Captain?"

"Briefly, my lord. It was after …"

The back of the Emissary's hand struck Kayir's cheek, followed quickly by another to the other side of his face. The blows stung but did little else to affect the hardened soldier. Likely, they caused the Emissary more hurt than Kayir.

"Are you proud of your failure, Captain, for you seem to be?" the Emissary demanded, his voice no longer quiet, but filled with outrage.

"Proud? No, I'm not proud. Losing five men in battle is not something to be proud of."

"And yet here you stand, unscathed, when you should have stayed and continued to work to fulfill your mission."

"I was not unharmed, Emissary," Kayir began, his own temper starting to rise, but being held in check by his training and discipline.

"Explain," demanded the Emissary, leaving Kayir standing where he was and starting to pace around him, snatching up his staff as he went by.

As Kayir told his story, starting with his unit's arrival in Guilder and their plan for arresting Barall, the only other sound was the rhythmic clack, clack of the Emissary's staff striking the tiled floor.   By the time the tale reached the battle and the subsequent wounding of the captain, the Emissary was breathing heavily and his knuckles were white around the smooth, polished wood of the staff. He could sense what was coming deep within him; he knew it, but fought against it. It just wasn't possible. Wisdom was knowledge through experience, tempered with honor and compassion. What Kayir was about to describe was the blackest evil. To believe that a priest could call upon the power of their god, to wield as He would, was blasphemy. Believing oneself equal to a god was the epitome of arrogance.

As Emissary, he saw it as his responsibility to eliminate such problems. This Barall was proving to be more of an issue than he had thought. He listened as Kayir spoke of Barall breaking down the door to the church as though it were nothing more than parchment. Then he picked out the Comfort, never having met her before. The details were somewhat fuzzy in Kayir's head for he was only barely conscious at the time.

Finally, what the Emissary suspected was coming, was said. "He healed me, my lord. The wounds I had were suddenly gone. My flesh mended, and blood …"

Whatever else Kayir had been about to say, was cut cruelly short by the sickening thunk of the Emissary's staff caving in the back of his head. The lifeless body pitched forward, bouncing once off the side of a chair before settling on the floor at the Emissary's feet.

Caven stood over the body, bits of blood and gore dripping from the circle topping his staff, "A pity your Lord Barall is not here now, Captain."

# Chapter 10

*"In a controversy the instant we feel anger*
*we have already ceased striving for the truth,*
*and have begun striving for ourselves."*
**Buddha**

The meeting had gone on longer than any of the Wisdoms had thought or wanted. They had gathered immediately after the Emissary's service to debate his pronouncement. Destrin hotly contested their right to even question the path the church should take, arguing it was the job of a Wisdom to support the Emissary's decision. "He is the voice of the god, after all," he said.

Oddly, it was the normally contrite Virez who spoke out against Destrin. She argued, just as vocally, that it was exactly their role to question the Emissary, to ensure he was doing what was best. Lassand stayed silent. Listening to his companions he could see valid points for both sides, but determined the actual point of the discussion was off the mark.

"The issue," he pointed out quietly when a moment presented itself, "is not whether we should be expanding the church …"

"What is it then?" demanded Destrin, not bothering to hide his irritation.

"The Emissary has already made the decision, and announced it in front of the city. At this point, it is irrelevant what we think about it, it's already done."

He let that thought sink in for a moment, watching their expressions as the realization hit them, practically at the same time. "We should be discussing *how* to implement what was proclaimed."

❦

Behind him, the door opened on silent hinges and three figures stared at the scene before them. The Emissary stood with his staff of office, covered in blood, and a body at his feet.

"A pity your 'Lord Barall' is not here now, Captain," said the Emissary dispassionately.

A small gasp escaped from Destrin, alerting the Emissary to the trio's presence. He whirled around, his face contorted in rage.

"What are you doing here?" he spat at them, none of the anger leaving his eyes.

The trio of Wisdoms stood gaping at the Emissary and the dead body behind him. Looking at his face, the three were equally stunned at what they saw there. The Emissary's eyes were wide and staring, the pupils appearing as mere pinpricks in an ocean of surrounding white. Making his eyes even more pronounced, his cheeks were flushed a bright red, though whether from exertion, guilt or excitement, was unknown. But none of this was what caused the Wisdoms to stop short in appalled fascination. It was the wide, almost euphoric, grin that spread across the Emissary's face.

Virez shuddered in seeing that look. One very similar to it was on the Emissary's face when he rebuffed her advances and threatened her. The look he wore now was frightening to her, for it seemed like he enjoyed hurting people in any way he could. Was this the man who they had elected to run the church?

It was Lassand who recovered first. His normally calm face was frozen in horror. "M-my lord?" he stammered. "What has happened here?"

"Fools! All of you are fools. You dare to barge in here unannounced, and unwelcome? Do you wish to share this fate?" In some macabre vision, they watched the blood covered Circle of Endomar flash by them in an arc to end pointing at the dead body on the floor.

All the Wisdoms could do was stare back at their leader. Virez shuddered in thinly-veiled fear. More and more, the Emissary frightened her with his quick and violent temper. Once, she had thought him to be charismatic and handsome, but seeing him now, she wondered where that man had gone, for there was nothing even remotely appealing about him. The others knew nothing about her failed attempt to seduce their leader. Without a doubt, they would scorn her for even attempting such a thing. Had she succeeded, it would undermine their own positions within the council and with the Emissary.

Caven must have seen her reaction, for his grin widened.

"Do I frighten you, dear Virez? I should, you know. I should frighten all of you. Next to me, you are nothing."

For a moment, no one spoke. Only the hissing of the wicks in the candles could be heard. Then, in a voice barely above a whisper, Destrin broke the silence.

"What have you done?" he asked, his head shaking slowly back and forth causing his long, black hair to sway with the motion.

The normal ingratiating look he wore in front of the Emissary was replaced by one of horror. His eyes kept flicking back to the body, slowly cooling on the floor, as if they desperately wanted, but just couldn't, stay away. Mistaking Destrin's look to be the same as Virez's, Caven ignored him, and turned instead to Lassand.

"What say you, Lassand?" he asked in a voice that made it clear he didn't care in the slightest what Lassand thought.

The older Wisdom did not respond at first. He was clearly able to better master his emotions than the others, but he, too, was deeply shocked at what he saw. Running a hand over his bald scalp, he refused to acknowledge the sweat he felt there, and instead took a steadying breath.

"I do not presume to know what happened here, my lord," he began. "I would hazard to guess that this man deserved the fate before him."

"Ha!" barked the Emissary, seeming to relax a little. "Ever logical, Lassand."

"No," broke in Destrin. "No. No. No. No." His shaking head had increased so his hair was now flying across his back, spreading out like a fan behind him. "Do you even know what you've done?" he fairly spat at the Emissary. Then, "Oh Good Lord Endomar preserve us," he prayed.

"What are you whining about now?" said Caven tiredly.

Without waiting for an answer, he stepped over the body at his feet and poured himself a drink from a waiting pitcher. Drinking slowly, he seemed to notice the blood coating the circle mounted to the top of his staff and scowled at its sight. Nonchalantly, he flipped his staff end for end and wiped it off on the plush carpet not caring that it had been donated to the church by its makers generations ago.

Looking up, the Emissary raised a casual eyebrow at his Wisdoms, as if daring them to comment. None did, though their reactions to this mirrored those at the sight of the dead soldier.

"Well, Destrin?" he asked, sinking his lanky frame into a chair.

"This is Kayir," said Destrin pointing at the body.

"Yes, I believe he said that was his name."

"Kayir," continued Destrin, "As in Kayir, son of Zithius, King of Cherilla, and himself the Crown Prince to the throne. And you've just killed him in cold blood."

"What?!?" Caven roared in fury, launching himself to his feet. "You did not think this information important?"

"That you do not know the name of the next king, or his face, is no fault of mine. Nor that you so casually take his life," Destrin yelled back with equal heat.

"You would do well to watch your tongue, Destrin," said the Emissary quietly, his brows narrowing over his eyes.

"And you would do well to watch your actions," spat back Destrin vehemently.

Without a sound, Caven swung his staff toward Destrin's head. The speed and force of the attack froze both Destrin and Virez, but Lassand stepped neatly into the attack, stopping the blow with one hand to the shaft of the staff.

"Hold, my lord," said Lassand, keeping himself between the other two men. "One body will be hard enough to explain, two will be impossible."

"Bah!" breathed the Emissary, wrenching his staff out of Lassand's hand and turning away.

"We can explain this, my lord, so the truth is not known. Did Kayir meet with anyone, see anyone, before you tonight?"

"No," came the reply after a moment. "He said he came right here to deliver his blasphemous news that this Barall had 'healed' him."

"Good, good," murmured Lassand, for the moment ignoring the information of what Barall had somehow done. "We can work with this, lord. You should return to your chambers, rest and refresh yourself. We will handle this."

At first, it seemed as if the Emissary was going to let himself he handled. He walked to the door, not even sparing a glance for the king's son as he passed. But then, standing on the threshold of the door, he stopped. "Destrin," he started, slowly turning to face them with the same, wide-eyed look and evil smile. "You are relieved of your rank and position. You are hereby relegated to the rank of Acolyte. When next I see you, should you ever be in my presence again, I expect to see you dressed in white and your head shaved as befits your worth."

Listening, Destrin blanched at the first pronouncement, and nearly collapsed at the second. His hands flew to his hair before he could control them.

"You ..." started Destrin.

"... can't?" finished the Emissary. "Actually, I can, and I have."

"Actually," broke in Virez, surprising more than herself by speaking, "you can't. You need the approval of the council to remove a sitting Wisdom."

It looked as if Caven would strike out at her now too, for the Emissary's fingers clenched the staff so tightly, Virez thought she could here the wood groan in protest. "Fine," he said instead. "Then the council is hereby disbanded. None of your worthless services are required."

# Chapter 11

*"Learn wisdom from the ways of a seedling. A seedling which is never hardened off through stressful situations will never become a strong productive plant."*
**Stephen Sigmund**

The Emissary left, letting the door slam shut behind him. The three former Wisdoms didn't move, barely daring to breath, in shock at what had just happened. Softly, Lassand crept to the door and listened for a moment. Daring to crack it open, he saw the empty hallway stretch out before him, the guards leaving with the Emissary. Closing it again, he turned to face the others.

"He can't do that, either," he said.

"Really?" said Destrin, his voice raising an octave as he spoke rapidly. "Really? It seems he just has. And who do you think people will believe, Lassand, us or him?"

"How could you?" asked Virez. She looked calm to Lassand but her voice, too, betrayed how shaken she was.

"How could I what?"

"Offer to cover for him? To cover up this … murder," she concluded in a whisper.

Lassand sighed heavily and looked down at Kayir's body. "Kayir," he seemed to whisper, "Of course it had to be you."

With a slight shake of his head, Lassand composed himself, and apparently coming to a decision, faced the others again.

"It wasn't for him, despite what it looked like," he started. "I needed him back in his own rooms."

Virez looked at Destrin, and it was clear neither of them understood.

"Let me explain."

❧

Caven entered his rooms and knew immediately, though there was no one visible, he wasn't alone. Holding his staff before him, he advanced slowly into the room, cursing himself silently for dismissing the guards at the door before he entered. He could call them back, and hesitated a moment as he thought to do so. *No,* he decided. *I'll appear the fool if there's no one here.*

The decision made, he ventured deeper into the spacious rooms. Only when the sound of water came to him, and he noticed the vials of oils and balms on the table by his bed, did he remember. The girl, that beautiful, young Acolyte who had attended him after the service this morning. She had promised to return tonight to help him relieve his stress.

*Ah, yes,* he thought. *And it needs relieving. I can feel it tightening even now.*

With his most charming smile on his face, the Emissary entered his bathing chamber to find the girl there, adding rose petals and lavender to the steaming water, the scent of the oils and balms enveloping him.

"That looks absolutely delicious," he said, his brown eyes never straying from the curves of the girl's body.

She looked up at his words and smiled, revealing clean, straight white teeth.

"The heat should be just about right," she answered.

Then she surprised him. Instead of leaving, as most of the girls who attended him did, she advanced and began loosening the ties of his robes. He leaned his staff against a corner and enjoyed the feeling of being undressed by this beautiful vision of a girl. She was not some shy, naïve waif, he realized. She has been with a man before. Surprisingly, this did not bother him as much as he thought it would have. Her hands gently but confidently removed his clothing. Was it a mistake when those hands brushed against his skin? Was her breathing quickening too?

These thoughts and more ran through Caven's head as he stood before her, naked. She watched him, not looking away, as he climbed into the bath, sucking in his breath as the hot water enveloped his body.

"I will ready your massage, my lord," she said heading out of the room. "And don't worry; I know all the places you need taken care of to make you feel just right."

Sighing luxuriously, he sank deeper into the bath. *This night is turning out just perfectly,* he thought.

❦

Their reactions were as varied as the individuals themselves. The three, not quite friends, but colleagues, had worked over the body of Prince Kayir as Lassand talked, telling them of what he was doing, and why. The body had all personal items removed and the lie to be told agreed upon. But then his story turned from the practical to planning for the future. As that discussion concluded, Virez sat down heavily, a mixture of disbelief and awe on her face. If Lassand had actually done what he'd described … it was unthinkable. But had she not tried, essentially, the same thing? The story only seemed to fuel Destrin's anger, only the rage he had felt at the Emissary was now directed toward Lassand.

"A spy?" he fumed. "You've got a spy on the Emissary? He is our guide, our leader."

"A leader who has murdered how many? There is more than Prince Kayir, you know. How many girls have gone to his chambers, never to be seen again? How many, like Kayir, who have simply displeased him and paid a terrible price?" replied Lassand, speaking in the same calm voice he had used throughout his telling.

"Who did you find, Lassand? What fool did you send to their death, then?" hissed Destrin.

"Nokya is no fool," came the answer. "She is wise in living on the streets; in taking care of herself. Do not think to judge me, Destrin. Or you, Virez. Both of you have tried something similar, I know, so keep your false recriminations to yourselves."

His statement stunned his companions to silence, but he kept the smile from his face. This was no time for self-congratulation. Too much had happened, and there was too little time to plan for what to do next.

"The council has been disbanded," he said then, switching to the more pressing topic. "What should we do?"

"There's nothing we can do," said Virez.

"We do as we're told," said Destrin.

"But we weren't told to do anything," commented Virez.

"I was," said Destrin.

"Oh, yes," broke in Lassand, "your hair."

That Lassand said it without a hint of a smile or mockery in his voice was probably all that kept Destrin from lashing out at him. His face, though, tightened noticeably and his fists clenched at his sides.

"If you will listen," continued Lassand, "I have an idea."

୧୨

They listened, not interrupting or questioning, but becoming more and more stunned as Lassand outlined his thoughts. Once the basic idea was on the table, they spoke openly and, perhaps for the first time, in cooperation. At the end they grew quiet, regarding each other, eye to eye as compatriots. When it was clear that no one had anything new to add, the others looked to Lassand, the unspoken but agreed upon, leader of the group.

"We are agreed, then?" he asked them quietly.

There was no answer at first, and Lassand waited patiently. This was no small thing they were proposing. Casually, he let his eyes wander to the body of Prince Kayir, still laying in the room with them, but changed from what it had been. In the short hour or so since the Emissary had left, the Wisdoms had stripped the body of its clothes and replaced them with Acolyte robes. All jewellery and other possible identifying items had also been removed. Lastly, to keep the disguise as honest as possible, they had shaved his head. Destrin, to his credit, remained stoic and resolute throughout.

But now, the time for a decision was at hand. There were no more delays or hesitations as Lassand returned his gaze to his friends. They were in it now, no turning back, as both Virez and Destrin nodded their agreement.

"Then, truly, our faith is to be tested," said Lassand. For what we are about to do, we shall be either hailed or scorned. Never before has anyone sought to unseat a reigning Emissary."

୧୨

The Emissary stood before the entire priesthood in the cathedral. Every member of the church of Endomar was present, from the highest Primate down to the lowliest Initiate. Rarely was such a special session called, but it was within the purview of the Emissary to call such meetings, should the occasion warrant it.

No one knew what was going on, though rumors ran rampant throughout the great hall. It had not gone unnoticed that the Wisdoms were not in their usual spots. In fact, of the three, only Lassand was present. He sat not in his customary place near the head of the cathedral, but in the front row with the rest of the Primates. He was not even dressed in the brown robes of the Wisdom, but in the blue of a Primate.

Of course, Lassand had also heard the rumors, difficult as it was when people tended to stop speaking as soon as he came in sight. The rumors were circulating just as fast and furious about him and the council as they were about this meeting. He knew, naturally, what it was all about. Even without Nokya to tell him, he could have figured this out. The Emissary was nothing, if not predictable. The girl he had recruited to spy on him had done her job well and already ingratiated herself into Caven's good graces. How she had done that, was not Lassand's concern, although he did hope she kept herself safe and well.

The Emissary had never before kept the same Acolyte as an attendant for more than a few days. That he seemed to have done so now was a favorable sign. The girl, living on the street, without a home or even knowing where her next meal would come from, had been brought to the church by Lassand a year or so before. She had taken to Lassand immediately, like a child to its father and looked up to him and trusted him. He was a mentor of sorts to her, and often spoke of his fears and thoughts to her when they could get a chance together.

It was Nokya herself who had first suggested the possibility of being a spy, openly discussing how she would earn Caven's trust, much to the shock of Lassand's priestly sensibilities. Then when Nokya was actually selected to be the Emissary's next attendant, she took the assignment immediately without even mentioning it to Lassand. It was only after the morning's service that Nokya managed to inform Lassand, and by that time, she had already met with the Emissary and promised to return in the evening. That had been several days ago. There was nothing he could do now to find out what, if anything, had happened between them, or if she had anything to report. They had decided that it would be up to Nokya to decide what was safe for her to do and when.

Just then, the Emissary strode up to the dais amidst a fanfare of trumpet blasts. With a swish of his purple robes, Caven stood at the front of the hall, a somber look on his face. For the first time, Lassand watched one of the Emissary's performances, with the full knowledge of what kind of man he truly was. Knowing the truth about the man, he saw the falseness of him, how much of an actor he really was. The role he played now was that of a grieving father. He spoke of an Acolyte who had been found dead outside the walls of the city, the probable victim of a robbery. He spoke highly of the duties performed by the deceased Acolyte, how devoted he was to the church and how pious and faithful he had been.

Of course no one in the hall actually remembered any such Acolyte but none would ever admit it. No one wanted to be the one to declare that such a wonderful person was not known to them. If asked, people would speak highly of the man as if they had been the closest of friends. Even Lassand perpetuated the lie. He maintained his position as a Primate only at the whim of the Emissary. He could just as easily be demoted further, or even sent away from the cathedral and Anklesh. That was the lie he had created for Virez and Destrin: they had been sent away to do special work for the Emissary. Should Caven ever ask him of it, he would, truthfully admit he didn't know where they had gone, or where they were at the moment. There would only be communication between them in the most extreme circumstances, and then, Lassand could only receive such information, unless, or until, the others revealed where they were.

As the meeting broke up, the lie of Kayir's death told to them all, Lassand moved out of the hall, a cocoon of space around him. No one wanted to be seen as walking with the out-of-favor Lassand. Ironically, that isolation worked against him in terms of being able to speak to Nokya, but he was still a Primate within the hierarchy. He had duties to perform and those would, from time to time, require him to make use of particular Acolytes and Initiates. He only hoped that the others would be able to do their parts as well.

# Chapter 12

*"Thousands of candles can be lit from a single candle,
and the life of the candle will not be shortened.
Happiness never decreases by being shared."*
**Buddha**

The 'circle,' as the group was rapidly becoming known, was camped a half day's walk outside the town of Laufrid, located on the south side of the inlet off Myer Lake. They had all enjoyed the beauty of the sights and sounds of the water. It was one of those inexplicable things that being near to water seemed to make everything more peaceful.

Laufrid was a good sized town, much bigger than Guilder, but smaller than Anklesh. It survived on fishing and farming, but also supported several different business types within its walls. It was one of the few walled towns in Cherilla. A solid looking stone wall surrounded the town on the land side abutting right up to the shores, but leaving the water side open. From where the group sat, enjoying an early supper as the sun was beginning to fall, they could see small boats making their way back to the docks and the supposed comfort of home.

"Stop fussing with it, boy," barked Cerrok.

Caught, Barall meekly lowered his hand from the crop of short, sandy blond hair sprouting all over his head. Since he had been ordained as a Comfort, he had agonized over whether to let it grow or not, trying to come to a decision on whether it was right to do so. Finally, it was Cerrok who made the most convincing argument. "If nothing else," he had said, "you won't have to go through the ordeal of shaving your head any longer."

Barall stood blinking at the older man for a moment, then laughed and clapped him on the shoulder. "If neither answer is right nor wrong, choose what is best for me, is that it?" he chuckled.

"Exactly," smiled Cerrok.

Now, seeing the glint in the old priest's eyes, Barall smiled sheepishly at his friends. "It itches," he said lamely, to the amusement of the others.

"I can't tell if it makes you look younger or older," Tella said in her husky voice.

"Trying to decide if you should let yours grow, too?" purred Venick across from her.

"Hardly," she replied, not even bothering to look at their scruffy companion. "People often see strength, or wisdom," she added with a nod to Barall, "in age. I was trying to determine if Barall would be seen as too young to have either."

The others looked at Barall, who, having now spent numerous days talking to all sized groups of people, sat calmly under their scrutiny. It didn't matter, really, which way they assumed he looked, he would continue to let his hair grow and speak to the people.

They left Guilder immediately after Comfort Rischa's service. There was no fanfare or announcement. They simply gathered their belongings and horses and continued their journey. Behind them, Rischa had watched them leave, smiling as she did so. More than ever, she believed her decision to support Barall was a good one. Good for the people of Cherilla, but also, in the long view, for the

Church of Endomar. Competition was a good thing, and healthy. The people of Guilder were talking about their faith – looking at it in new ways and so they were strengthening it. She, too, felt reenergized, the knowledge of three lost pillars of faith invigorating her. She had learned enough that the pillars of sacrifice, patience and humility simply made sense. They filled in gaps for her.

None of this was what made her smile however. It was the symbol leaving her village. Already, Barall and his circle were causing waves, but they were only the tip of the arrow that would pierce the bubble of complacency that had enveloped her faith. And that was how they rode away, with Barall as the tip and three priests of strange gods flowing outward to either side behind him. The arrow had been loosed, and only the gods knew where it would fly.

The circle, of course, knew none of this. They rode out of Guilder and made their way to the next village. Each new village was approached in the same way as Guilder had been and, for the most part, the results were the same. The villagers were generally sceptical at first, and occasionally hostile, but always the circle was heard. There had been no further contact with Anklesh or the Cathedral, which was taken to be a good thing but with a healthy dose of caution to recognize they had not heard the last from the Emissary.

Barall was the center of the villagers' discussions as the representative of Endomar. Tentative, at first, to accept the attention, he quickly came to realize the importance of his voice to the people. Though barely raised to Comfort, the smaller villages rarely saw church authorities, so any that came through were immediately treated as if they were the Emissary himself. What they found was that people's faith was fairly fluid. They listened to the circle and nodded or shook their heads. Just as in Guilder, each circle member seemed to attract at least one or two villagers after the general meetings had broken up.

Though Barall was intensely curious as to what they discussed in these private sessions, he knew he could not ask or intrude. There had to be trust and acceptance, particularly among themselves, if they were to succeed. As that thought rolled through Barall's head, there was a commotion in the distance. Shouts carried on the wind to the circle, sounding angry from where they sat, though no words could be made out.

Tella caught Barall's look, and in a smooth motion, she rose and moved from the group. Catching the eye of each other member, each indicated they were ready. As Barall's eyes slid away from Cerrok's, he scowled. Barall seemed to favor the priestess of strength. While Cerrok respected Tella's abilities, particularly her proficiency with the knife, he was not impressed with her leadership. As a priest of Xelteran, his own natural tendency was to control and direct, so obviously he was the best choice for leading this group. He had talent and intelligence that were vastly underutilized by the circle, while Barall was young and in need of guidance, which Cerrok was best able to provide.

Then he shook his head. Barall was a better leader than he was giving him credit for. Barall was honest with himself in recognizing what he didn't know and didn't hesitate to ask questions. The boy had an incredible insight and ability to get to the heart of a matter, while not creating enemies of anyone. He had found Barall to be insightful and intelligent, and at the same time sympathetic to the frustration Cerrok was feeling. Unfortunately, that didn't stop the feeling of being slighted just now. As if his thoughts summoned her, Tella reappeared, her face set in a stoic mask. To her credit, she did not report only to Barall, but spoke to the circle as a whole.

"Two men have arrived and are asking to speak to us," she said. "Their insistence is causing our 'guards' to dig in their heels."

The last was said with a smile, a thing that seemed to lighten her whole face and show off just how pretty she truly was.

Each village they talked to seemed to add to the crowd of people following the circle. After visiting a dozen or so small villages since Guilder, they now had a group of twenty or so men and women trailing after them as self-appointed guards. It served well in situations such as this, but Barall still worried over them. He felt responsible for them, for their health and safety while on the road and particularly if the Emissary decided to attack them again.

"Who are they?" asked Dalis.

"Both, apparently, are from Anklesh, though they arrived separately. The first is called simply Stein. He is dressed well, but not elaborately so. The other is Lebair. He is dressed as a Primate of Endomar."

Tella let her announcement hang in the air a moment before continuing. "Neither is armed, and they are being kept apart. Shall I bring them now?" she asked.

Tella was direct and came across as impatient. Usually it was expedience, she knew the circle would want to see these two men, so why not do it now and know what they wanted? The others, of course, wanted to debate and discuss things.

"Why would a Primate be here?" questioned Venick.

"Two men arrive from Anklesh at the same time?" put in Cura.

"An attack is coming!" broke in Cerrok, stopping all conversation.

"Why do you say that?" asked Barall, his voice and manner calm as he regarded the Xelteran priest with interest.

Cerrok looked almost embarrassed as all eyes turned to him. If he thought he spoke too quickly, he covered his feelings well.

"We have already been attacked once when a Comfort informed the citadel of our presence," he started, ticking off each point on long, tapered fingers. "We have been spreading word of the gods across north, central Cherilla for a month and our circle grows in influence, if not also in power. Suddenly, as we are about to enter the largest town yet, not one, but two men arrive from Anklesh, one of them a Primate. A man likely of intelligence and no small power of his own, probably sent by the Emissary himself."

He finished with a large gulp of the bitter tea they were all drinking, a scowl crossing his face as the harsh liquid rushed down his throat. They sat in silence for a moment, considering his words. The fire in the middle popped and crackled merrily in opposition to their darkening mood.

"There may be some truth to his words," said Tella softly, as if agreeing with anything Cerrok said was the hardest thing she's ever had to do. "However," she continued, seeing the look of triumph on Cerrok's face, "there is truly no way to know. It may be that a quiet attack, by one man may succeed where the direct assault failed, it may also be true that this man has come simply to talk."

All eyes turned now to Barall. As the leader, as well as the most likely target for an attack, the decision lay with him. Already, in a few short weeks, he had learned much from his friends and companions. Where Gibson's diary and spell book taught him magic and provided insight to the past, his fellow priests worked on the present, molding Barall and teaching him things he would need to know as the leader of an entire faith, as well as a usurper.

Begrudgingly, he learned of weapons and strategy from Tella, economics and trade from Cerrok. Venick talked of Cherillan history, while Seskia was wise in philosophy and ethics. His first two friends, Cura and Dalis imparted their wisdom as well: Cura spoke of agriculture and the health, not of the body, but of the land and its importance to all, while Dalis spoke simply of respect for everyone.

It was like Barall was a child, growing up with six parents sharing the insights of their lives. He enjoyed the discussions with them, and took each to heart, knowing that the education was necessary. It

also afforded him the opportunity to learn more about the hearts
and minds of his friends for their chosen topics were obviously near
and dear to them and to their own faiths as well. Barall loved and
honored Vance, his first and only teacher to this point, but Vance
knew only of Endomar and His way. That, and how that way had
been corrupted by too much power for too long a time.

Finally, Barall met the eyes of every other priest, looking within
to determine a course of action, like their eyes were a window into
their true feelings. As if gleaning what he needed from them, he
nodded once. "Bring Stein," he said to Tella, and then reached out
his hands to the flickering fire, warming them as they waited.

# Chapter 13

*"The whole problem with the world is that fools and fanatics are always so certain of themselves, and wiser people so full of doubts."*
*Bertrand Russell*

The group appeared out of the growing dark, materializing as if by magic. Only Tella seemed aware of their presence, for everyone else jumped at the trio suddenly in their midst. Before them stood Rillem and Valeria, a husband and wife who had, oddly, followed Cura and Seskia, respectively, out of a tiny village southeast of Guilder. Though the two priestesses seemed indifferent, Barall was mildly concerned over a married couple pursuing such dichotomous faiths.

The pair was politely acknowledged, but the main focus was on the man they were escorting. Sandwiched between the pair, was a tall man standing a head over six feet, with well groomed, silky brown hair. A beard and moustache were trimmed close to his face, each containing the first traces of gray. On his spare and average frame, he wore a simple wool coat, dyed a bright blue, that was held together with large silver buttons. On his feet he wore functional calf-high black boots into which he had tucked the legs of his black pants.

Stein stood in the flickering firelight, withstanding the scrutiny of the assembled priests without flinching. He regarded each of them in turn; trying to put faces to the names he had been given. Allowing them the opportunity to assess him gave Stein the chance to reflect on his mission. On its face it was not the most difficult assignment he had ever been given, but it certainly offered to be one of the most interesting. Long used to gathering information for those of influence, he had privately wondered about the existence of other gods. Now, he would be able to learn first-hand whether his suspicions were true.

"Sit, please," said one of the priests. The youngster, dressed as a common man, could only be Barall.

"My lord," replied Stein with a bow to Barall. He sank gracefully to the ground, seemingly uncaring of the dust and dirt his fine coat would attract.

"My name is …" started the youngster as soon as Stein was settled.

"… Barall," broke in Stein. "Former Acolyte of Endomar newly raised to Comfort. My congratulations, my lord."

His voice and manner were polite, yet several of the priests bristled in apparent suspicion. Stein noticed all this, his eyes flicking around the group, before settling again on Barall.

"You seem well informed for one newly arrived from Anklesh," said a man to Stein's right.

Looking toward the speaker, Stein took in the long blond hair and handsome face, as well as the way he tried to take control of the meeting, and knew instantly who it was.

"Actually, friend Cerrok, I have been thoroughly briefed about this group," came the friendly reply. "Well, as thoroughly as possible, that is. Truly, very little is known about any of you, even Lord Barall."

A dagger found its way to Stein's throat, as Cerrok lunged at their visitor. Barely daring to breathe, Stein looked into Cerrok's eyes, and saw no hatred or malice there, only calculating intellect. Despite his years, the priest could move as fast as a man half his age.

"How does anyone know anything about us?" growled Cerrok.

"Peace, my lord," said Stein. "I mean you no harm."

"Perhaps you don't, but perhaps your lord does."

"Enough, Cerrok," said a huge man sitting to Stein's right.

"No, Dalis. We know nothing of him or whoever pulls his strings."

"Nor will we," started Dalis raising his hand, "if you kill him."

Suddenly the hilt of the dagger in Cerrok's hand started to glow. Crying out, Cerrok dropped the dagger, wringing his hand in obviously pain. Looking down, Stein thought he noticed a hint of red, like embers in a cooling fire, around the dagger. On closer inspections, though, he saw nothing out of the ordinary. Cerrok, however, continued to shake his hand as if burned.

*Odd*, thought Stein, letting his gaze take in the entire group. *Obviously the circle was not as enamored with each other as reports indicated. They suffer one another for what they see as the greater cause.* Stein let the thoughts drop as Barall spoke, bringing the whole group back to the matter at hand. The group might be somewhat disjointed, but they listened to the young man as their leader.

"You, obviously, are well informed of us, friend Stein. Who is it that wants to know so much about us?"

He spoke directly to Stein, looking deeply into his eyes. At first Stein smiled. He was well used to attempts at intimidation and charm, by far better talents than a mere boy on a crusade. But, then, this wasn't intimidation or charm, and Stein found he was unable to look away from the direct, penetrating gaze. While a witty remark came to mind, he was unwilling to disappoint Barall, and certainly not to lie to him.

"My lord is Zithius, King of Cherilla," he said simply. "He is curious about you and your goals. So, I was bidden to find you and to learn."

The way he stopped talking, it was obvious there was more to Stein's orders than "to learn".

"And …" prompted Barall.

"My lord …" hedged Stein.

"I am not a lord, Stein," said Barall kindly. "I am merely a priest trying to follow the seven pillars to the best of my being. Simple enough individually, but what about when they are in conflict? Honor and compassion lead me to trust you until experience teaches me otherwise, but humility and knowledge lead me to think that would be foolish, and perhaps dangerous. So, please my friend, do me the honor of telling us the truth of why you are really here."

The king had warned Stein that his true purpose might have to be told. It was to be withheld as long as possible, but it could be revealed if necessary. Not above lying to further his course, Stein still found himself unwilling to lie to Barall. Was it a fear of seeing disappointment in the eyes he was looking into? He didn't know, only that he wanted, needed, to see approval reflected back instead.

Still, truth withheld was not lying. He found that, on first impressions, he liked this Barall, and his first impressions were generally very good.

"Personally I have found that trust is something that is earned, not granted; easily lost and hard to regain. The king is deeply concerned over the increasing power of the Emissary. In his opinion, the church and state should work together to govern the land, but the Emissary appears, more and more, to act independently, without even advising his secular brother. There are rumors and events that have struck to the king's very heart and no longer can he sit idly by."

The visitor lapsed into silence. The circle contemplated what they had heard, and sifted this new information with things they already knew.

"What does he intend to do, then?" asked Venick quietly.

The priest of the god of strife was staring intently at Stein, his perpetually scruffy hair giving Venick the look of a madman, but there was nothing wrong with his mind.

"Do, my lord?" queried Stein.

Not one to suffer fools lightly, Venick grew obviously angry as Stein feigned ignorance. His response came quick and harsh.

"Barall's reply was couched in polite words and diplomacy," he fairly shouted. "Mine is not! Do not treat us as fools, sir. You stated the king will not sit by as Caven takes power. So, what does Zithius mean to do about it?"

"And us?" added Cura with a nod to Venick.

"And what has happened to cause this change in him?" added Cerrok.

Stein flinched as if stung, and an incredibly sad look crossed his face.

"My lord," he began, looking at Barall, "may we talk apart?"

"What you have to say concerns us all," replied Barall simply with a shake of his head.

At first, Stein looked as if he might protest, but seeing the determined, angry look on the seven faces, he sighed deeply. Before he could respond, however, Barall interrupted, his words proving, to Stein at least, that while the Comfort was young in appearance, he was wise in the hearts of people.

"There must be trust, Stein," Barall said. "Not only between you and I, not only within this circle, but among all men. I will not undermine the efforts of the priests here, nor will they undermine me. For that is how we arrived at our current situation, is it not?"

Stein blinked at the circle before him, humbled as he had never been before, and finding himself, suddenly, in unfamiliar territory. Never before had he been in such a position as to truly like and respect those he was sent to watch or gather information. He wouldn't go so far as to say he believed in everything they professed, there was only so far his spirit would bend, but the kernels were there, seeded by a masterful farmer, deftly woven into the fertile ground of Stein's unconscious. He recognized it for what it was, and strangely, felt no different for it.

"The king's mind is truly not known to me," said Stein at last, including the entire circle for the first time. "But, I believe his intent is to help you, as much as he is able, without drawing the attention of the cathedral."

⌘

The man who next approached the crackling fire was of average height. He came forward, and though flanked by Rillem and Valeria, walked as if he were leading them rather than the reverse. His long black hair had been brushed until it shone and he walked with an erect posture, striding confidently, his frame stern and rigid. He was dressed in simple robes, still covered in dust and rumpled from travel, cinched about his waist with a belt of soft brown leather.

Arriving at the fire, he sat himself in the circle without being invited, sitting cross legged surprisingly easily for a man of his apparent age of early forties. He looked straight at the man directly across from him, in the middle of the seven members.

"My Lord Barall," he started, addressing the man directly, "my name is Lebair. I come from the cathedral in Anklesh." He paused, seeming to be waiting for some form of amazement or recognition. When none was forthcoming, he frowned slightly but continued. "I have travelled to join your worthy band and to offer what guidance I can."

Again he paused, looking from face to face expectantly.

"Are you a man of faith?" asked a short woman to Lebair's left. She stared at him with a directness that surprised him.

"Most certainly, my Lady," came the reply, though his gaze never left that of the man across from him.

"And your purpose here?" asked a scruffy looking man to Lebair's right. He, too, glared at the visitor, his face a mixture of suspicion and anger.

"As I said, good sir," started Lebair, "to offer my guidance."

"Are we in need of guidance, then?" continued the scruffy man.

For the first time, Lebair seemed to notice the animosity directed at him. Every face around the fire was closed and hard. "Have I done something to offend?" he asked slowly, spreading his hands out before him.

"You have lied, 'Lebair'," spat the woman again. "Since you sat down, uninvited I might add, you have pompously and arrogantly uttered not one word of truth. I, for one, do not put much stock in the words of a liar posing as a friend."

As if attuned to her anger, the fire suddenly popped loudly, sending a shower of sparks into the air. Into the awkward silence, a huge man sitting next to the seething woman spoke in a slow, almost wistful voice.

"Now, Cura, that's not entirely true."

"What?" she barked.

"He's not a complete liar. After all, he did come from the cathedral."

Barks of laughter echoed around the circle, as the tension was momentarily broken.

"Perhaps, Dalis, but even without his pretty robes, that is still Destrin, member of the council of Wisdoms and advisor to Emissary Caven.

∽

Cura's accusatory finger, pointed directly at Destrin, was as unwavering as her glare. The eyes of the others, while perhaps not as penetrating, were equally direct.

Destrin didn't know what to do. He had intended to lay low within this 'circle,' try to gather as much information as he could about the members and their goals to report back to Lassand and Virez. Somehow, the three former Wisdoms would use this information to depose Caven for a more suitable Emissary.

So little was known about this group in the cathedral. The Wisdoms knew, vaguely, that one of their own, an Acolyte, was preaching of new gods. Why this Barall would want to subvert the work of the church he would have grown up with, Destrin couldn't fathom, but the Emissary had been concerned enough to send Kayir to arrest them, and the prince must have been suitably impressed that he had risked the Emissary's wrath by reporting his disobedience and failure to the Emissary alone.

With so little information to go on, Destrin had assumed that a position of authority, and an offer to be a mentor, a guide, would have been eagerly accepted. That this was not the case was not nearly as troubling as the fact they knew immediately who he was. Anonymity was a wall of security that had been quickly and easily breached. Caught as easily as a fish in a net, he scrambled to recover his wits and dignity.

"My Lady speaks truly," he said. "My name truly is Destrin, though no longer a Wisdom, and no longer advisor to the Emissary. The Emissary has disbanded the council and no longer requires my services.

"Services which you now wish to impose on us?" asked Seskia snidely.

"I would not say 'impose,' …" Destrin started.

"You still have not answered my question," broke in Venick. "What makes you think we need or want your council?"

"Why did Caven discharge you?" asked Tella.

Suddenly, everyone was speaking at once, badgering Destrin, who was looking around in shock and confusion. The more the group talked the more frustrated they became with each other, and talk turned to shouts. As the shouting reached a crescendo, and it seemed as if blows were soon to follow, the fire suddenly leapt high into the air. Long tongues of flame flared outward and upward, reaching out to the sky and those assembled. Initial cries of fear and surprise were replaced with silence as the flames returned to their former, docile flickering. Now sheepish eyes turned to one, who alone among them had remained silent, pondering what he had heard.

Destrin followed their gazes to a young man, sitting immediately beside him. There was a non-descript youth, with hair cut extremely short and dressed plainly in pants and shirt. Immediately, Destrin knew this was Barall, not the older man across the fire from him. Before he could open his mouth, Barall addressed him.

"How do you define faith, my Lord Destrin?" he asked.

"My lord?" queried Destrin, his confusion evident.

"Faith. What is it to you? You are a man of faith, a high-ranking member of the church, surely you have considered the question of what, exactly, is faith?"

Destrin thought for a moment, considering how to respond. With a nod to himself and a small shrug, he related his opinion.

"Faith is belief. Belief in something larger, stronger and greater than you," he said simply.

"Bah," barked Cerrok. "Too simplistic. I'm bigger, stronger and greater than you. Does that mean you have faith in me, or me in you? No, of course not."

"How would you define it, then?" interjected Seskia curiously to Cerrok.

Unlike Destrin, the priest of Xelteran responded immediately. "It is more than just belief, but a belief in something. I believe in Xelteran as a higher entity who espouses a set of values that I believe in and support."

The debate washed over and around them, but Barall, after his initial question, remained silent. He listened to his companion's theories and opinions but watched Destrin as well, and his reactions. Since he watched continuously, Barall could detect noticeable changes in the Wisdom as different points were made, or countered. He was under no illusions that one simple discussion could change a man's entire outlook, but, this one, at least, seemed to be a start.

Barall was brought abruptly back to the discussion by Destrin himself who had finally noticed Barall's surreptitious attention and turned the tables on him by asking what Barall's definition of faith would be.

Like Cerrok, Barall didn't hesitate before responding. "To me, faith includes much of what has already been said: it's a belief in something, in a greater being than mere man. But it is also trust. Trust in that belief system and the higher entity and the eternalness of both. But, while trust in man can be blind and misplaced, being given because of a title or position rather than because of the person, it *should* be blind in one's god. It is not only trust of your god, but that the beliefs and values set down by the god are as eternal as god himself. I'm not entirely sure that faith can be defined, though. Faith is ephemeral and ethereal and what the mind says *can't* be, the heart and soul insist *must* be."

He shrugged, mocking himself with a lopsided grin. The grin soon faded however. She gazed toward Destrin.

"So, Wisdom, are you curious about how we know about you before your even getting here? I was an Acolyte to Comfort Vance for many years. Vance also found every priest here and committed them to this endeavor."

A snort escaped Destrin at the mention of Vance's name and his work, betraying his opinion of Barall's mentor and friend.

"Do not think for a moment, Wisdom, that you know anything of Vance," snarled Barall, anger creeping into his voice. "You have underestimated us, and you have underestimated him."

"He was a better man than you," added Cura.

Destrin's face flushed with his own anger. "I will not argue the worth of a man, tragically killed, resisting arrest for blasphemy and heresy. Such has always been within the purview of the Emissary's office. Nor should you assume to think you know me, simply because you know my name."

Several members of the circle bristled at the tone Destrin used. All of them knew and respected Vance, and had equally little respect for the Emissary and his lackeys.

A deep sigh escaped from Barall's lips, like the burden of the circle was becoming too much for him to bear.

"You are right, Wisdom, this is not the time, nor the place, to discuss such things," he said.

"Thank you, lad. You are indeed wise. But you seem to keep forgetting that the council has been disbanded, I am but a Primate now."

A small twig Barall had been twisting in his hands was thrown violently into the fire. The anger he felt now was almost palpable. His hands were curled into fists and when he spoke, it was through clenched teeth, each word fairly forced out from between them.

"Enough! You and I both know that the Emissary alone does not have the authority to disband the council. You continue to condescend to us, apparently believing we are all fools," growled Barall. "More and more, *Wisdom*, you give me the impression of a man whose faith and trust is not in Endomar, but in the Emissary. Not necessarily in Caven," he conceded, seeing Destrin start to object, "but in the position. Regardless, let us return to the matter at hand. What has changed in the cathedral that the Emissary disbanded the council and had you seek us out?"

The discussion had now come full circle, and Destrin paused to consider the man before him. Barall's youth was deceiving and hid how highly intelligent and intuitive he was. To be honest with himself, Destrin found Barall's statement about being more faithful to the Emissary than to Endomar, disturbing, especially since Lassand had made a similar accusation. Much prayer and introspection was required before he would be able to understand himself better.

For now, he realized how much his life had changed, and in so little time. It was truly going to test his faith to work with this group, whether he agreed with them or not. Caven, regardless of his rank, was certainly unfit for his position and needed to be removed. Reaching a decision he began to tell the story of his last day in the cathedral. He began with the announcement of the expansion of the faith into Ponti and Naer, to the decision of the Wisdoms to hide the manner of the death of the soldier, and for the Wisdoms to separate.

He left out the reason each Wisdom had to separate and their destinations, figuring that he truly only knew his own reasons for leaving. Accordingly, he ended his explanation with that.

"My decision to leave was based, partly, on the fact that the Emissary removed me from my position. That is, admittedly, a matter of vanity and pride on my part. But, perhaps more so was the callous and cavalier attitude of the Emissary to killing Percinal. That was the deciding factor."

"Percinal?" gasped Dalis. "The Crown Prince? I thought you said he killed one of the soldiers sent after us in Guilder."

"Yes," said Destrin sadly. "The prince uses a different name when on duty."

"What name is that?" asked Barall. He glanced at Venick to see his friend's face was a sickly gray shade. Venick had, some time ago, confided in Barall about the foreboding dream he had had about the circling crown being crushed by the constricting circle. Both men awaited Destrin's response, fearing Venick's dream was about to be proven, painfully, prophetic.

"Kayir," said Destrin.

Lassand sighed quietly to himself and swivelled in his chair to look back at the Emissary. They sat in the Emissary's study, normally a cool, quiet place, but today it felt stuffy and hot to Lassand. In the intervening weeks since the members of the Wisdom's Council went their separate ways, the Emissary had grown increasingly agitated. The growing popularity of the circle of seven movement, as it was becoming known, was taking up more and more of the Emissary's time. He had taken to travelling with armed guards wherever he went, even within the cathedral. Someone tested his food for him before it touched his lips, and he regarded even his most trusted advisors with either fear or scorn.

After the break up of the council, Lassand had worked hard to ingratiate himself back into the Emissary's good graces. He had belittled Virez and Destrin and took to wearing the blue Primate robes instead of the Wisdom brown. Then, in a moment of inspiration, he offered to be the Emissary's personal secretary. That, he argued, would save the Emissary the trouble of having to write his own orders himself.

The Emissary took to the idea too willingly, however. He didn't trust anyone enough to allow them to be the sole drafter of his decrees, so he brought in a whole cadre of them. Lassand seemed to be the favorite, perhaps because he could discuss issues with the Emissary from his role as Wisdom that none of the others could, but he worked hard to keep himself in place.

"My lord," started Lassand patiently. "You sent Destrin away when you disbanded the council."

"I can't do that, and you know it!" spat Caven with a dismissive wave of his hand. He spun suddenly to face Lassand again, his eyes wide in fear, but narrowing to a cold, calculating look as he spoke. "He's left to join *him*, hasn't he?" he hissed.

There was no need to ask who 'he' was for there was only one person on the Emissary's mind these days.

"They've joined forces against me, and are plotting to kill me, aren't they, Lassand?"

"No, my lord," replied Lassand, working shocked disbelief into his voice. "How could you think such a thing?"

The Emissary continued as if Lassand hadn't even spoken. "I want him dealt with. See the proper orders are issued, Lassand."

"Immediately, Emissary," responded Lassand automatically. Putting pen to parchment, he drafted a missive thanking former Wisdom Destrin for his hard work and dedication, and wishing him wisdom as he pursued endeavors outside the cathedral. With the Emissary watching while he paced across the far side of the room, Lassand dripped purple wax at the bottom of the declaration and firmly pressed the Emissary's seal into it. Quickly, before the Emissary decided he wanted to read it first, Lassand handed it to a page waiting in the hallway.

He was playing a dangerous game, particularly with the Emissary's state of mind, but here was where he felt he could do the most good, and keep an ear on the Emissary's plans. Even with Nokya still serving as Caven's personal attendant, precious little information was available. As far as Lassand could tell, conscription was still ongoing and not only in Anklesh, but in most of the major cities of Cherilla. He had seen reports from Erskin, Wilrien and Vanerry. But with the number of men forced to join his army, and the Emissary's feelings of persecution, was he planning on asking, or forcing, the peoples of Naer and Ponti to join the faith?

The Emissary suddenly stopped his whirlwind pacing, a gleam of wicked inspiration in his eye. He ordered Lassand to sit and record a proclamation that would be sent to all corners of Cherilla. Finally, Barall would be brought to heel along with any who follow him.

The message was plain and efficient in its purpose, even as it shook the reader to his very soul:

*To:*     *All true and faithful followers of Endomar, God of*
          *Ultimate Wisdom*
*From:*   *Caven, Emissary and Defender of the Faith, Chosen*
          *of Endomar*

*It has become increasingly obvious, despite my repeated and continuous statements to the contrary, that more people are flocking to the banner of the blasphemer, Barall. Words of comfort and solace, when spoken from the lips of a deceiver, are nothing but air.*

*Still, those of weak minds and weaker will heed his words over those of the duly chosen representative of Endomar. I am the sole voice of the God here on the corporeal plane, and no other can speak for me or for Endomar.*

*Henceforth, Barall, and any who follow him, are not welcome in any temple, church or cathedral. He has forsaken me, and as such, Endomar. His rank of Acolyte is withdrawn, as his purported ascension to Comfort was not authorized, and is illegal.*

*It is proclaimed that the common-born Barall be declared heretic and a disciple of evil and anarchy. His words are poison and designed to inflame passion and strife. The people of Cherilla are content with the one God, Endomar, and have thrived under my leadership. Yea do I proclaim that new temples, dedicated through me to the glory of Endomar, are to be commissioned in the cities of Laufrid, Vanerry, Wilrien and Morgrun. These temples shall prove the glory and love all Cherillans have for their god and His greatest servant.*

*Barall, and those who travel with him, are declared enemies of the church. They are to be found and returned to the cathedral in Anklesh to be laid at my feet, in whatever condition required. Any person found to have granted safe haven, succor, aid or information to the heretic are deemed his allies, and will suffer the same fate.*

*No longer shall this church sit idle while people are free to worship false idols. There is no god other than Endomar, and the cathedral shall immediately begin enforcing that law.*

*Soldiers of the Emissary's army, the sword wielded by the arm of Endomar, are marching to all villages, towns and cities of Cherilla. These men are tasked with maintaining order and in finding those sympathetic to this Circle of Seven. All citizens are to submit to questioning if so ordered by any member of the Emissary's army, with anyone found guilty of any crime against the church, to be immediately imprisoned.*

*For too long have the faithful of Endomar been complacent; willing to sit back while heretics and fools have slandered Him. Know that this shall be the end.*

# Chapter 14

*"I do not feel obliged to believe that the same
God who has endowed us with sense, reason, and
intellect has intended us to forgo their use."*
**Galileo Galilei**

Nokya, watched quietly as Emissary Caven stalked across the room, whirled, and stalked back. Dawn had just arrived, so the air in the bedroom had yet to warm. Despite that, the Emissary was sweating, beads of perspiration glistenen off his brow and down his next. Nokya stood demurely to one side, neither announcing nor hiding her presence. On occasion, when the Emissary was in such a mood, he ranted to himself about his enemies and his plans, which she faithfully reported to Lassand. Caven was in a gloriously foul mood at the moment, she could see, and his normally fastidious appearance was bedraggled and messy. She had arrived this morning, to attend to him as always, and found him thus, agitated but silent.

She watched for a few more moments, chewing on whether to interrupt him or not. Several times before she had been witness and recipient to his temper when she had interrupted his thinking. His temper could flare, white hot without apparent provocation, only to cool just as quickly.

To her mind, the Emissary was rapidly losing his grip on reality. He saw enemies everywhere, and plots against him numbered in the thousands. He thought of little else, but chief among both the list of enemies and plotters was this Barall. She didn't know him, but he was obviously the primary problem the Emissary faced, and therefore someone of interest to Wisdom Lassand.

Making a decision as the Emissary completed yet another circuit in his pacing, Nokya strode across the room, her slippered feet making only a whisper of sound on the soft carpet. Beneath the shuttered window a small table stood upon which servants had placed a tray of fruit, bread and cheese, as well as a pitcher of cool water. Reaching it, she threw open the shutters to admit the warming light of late morning and prepared a plate of food for the Emissary.

Though expecting his reaction, she nevertheless gasped in shock as the plate was suddenly knocked aside. With a growl of anger, the shutters were slammed back into place, even before the sound of the shattering plate reached their ears. Nokya had been thrown to the ground as Caven pushed past her, and he whirled on her now as she was picking herself up. Cruel fingers pressed deeply into her arms, causing her to cry out in pain.

"You're with him aren't you?" hissed Caven, his nose almost touching hers. "You're working to kill me aren't you?"

"W-what? N-no, my lord. Of course not," she stammered. "I thought only that you would want some food. You appeared to be distraught."

Caven said nothing, but neither did he loosen his grip. For several heartbeats he stared into her eyes, unblinking. "Mad eyes," Nokya's Nana used to call them. "Wide, staring and too much white then was normal," she had explained. Seeing them before her, Nokya could well believe the truth in those words.

"Bah!" he hissed shoving her aside. "It won't matter soon

anyway," he said softly to himself as he resumed his frenetic pacing. His walking was punctuated now with a desperate clawing of his hands. They moved from shaking fists to talon-like claws, and back again.

Keeping one eye on her chosen master, Nokya moved slowly to pick up the broken pieces of the plate and strewn food. No stranger to pain, the Emissary's grip had been nothing compared to some she had received. Trying to reason out the meaning of his words, while stealing mouthfuls of bread and cheese, was useless, she knew, without more information. It could be that the Emissary had a plan for dealing with 'him,' or that one was already in place or, more likely, that it was something in the Emissary's mind alone. But then the Emissary continued his whispering, seeming to argue with himself, only the bits were disjointed, unconnected.

"No, no, the ambush will work …"

"Laufrid."

"Ponti and Naer need to be brought to heel."

"The great Endomar will reward me as I deserve."

"Traitorous Destrin. Unfaithful Virez."

"Kayir had to die, he failed."

"Soon, I say. It will happen soon."

They seemed like mad ravings to Nokya, Nana's 'mad eyes' notwithstanding. She couldn't make head nor tail of them, but Lassand would doubtless be interested.

❧

Several days after Destrin and Stein had arrived; the circle members entered the town of Laufrid in pairs. The newcomers had both shown themselves willing and competent suppliers of information, although they were still regarded with suspicion. Destrin in particular was just a small step above being shunned.

Given the increased awareness of the circle and their goals, it was a good bet the cathedral was making their own plans against them. Without any idea as to when, where, how or even if an attack would come, it was only prudent to act cautiously and not move around alone. The combination of pairs, however, didn't please anyone. With the increased likelihood of detection and reprisal, the circle would now present their messages separately in different locations throughout the town, simultaneously. This way it would be harder for anyone tracking them to find the entire group. Each pairing would also be responsible for finding their own locations within the town. If any one group were caught, they couldn't betray the others.

First to enter the town were Cura and Seskia. Easily the two least happy with the pairing, the priestesses of Healing and Disease walked as far from each other as possible while still appearing to be together. Both carried their weapons easily and avoided looking and talking to each other. With cold silence between them, they picked their way through the townsfolk cluttering the streets and moved, generally, in the direction of the waterfront. Here, they had agreed was where they would speak.

Cura, short and plumper, was nearly trotting to keep up with her companion. The scowl and determined look on her face made it difficult to imagine her as the first priestess of the Goddess of Health and Healing, but her stubbornness refused to allow her to ask Seskia to slow down.

Of course, the priestess of Rettela knew that her pace was uncomfortable to Cura, which was why she set it as she did. *Let the haughty shrimp keep up*, she thought. Her cold expression made most of those who met them, turn away, which in one sense, pleased Seskia, for she was not really a 'people-person.' She took a long time to open up to people, needing to know them well before sharing anything of herself. Looking deeply within herself, Seskia would have to admit that was part of the reason she didn't like Cura. A sidelong glance out of the corner of her eye showed the determined, focussed expression on the smaller woman's face. Cura was a priestess whose theology was completely opposite to her own, but more than that, Cura could make friends with just about anyone. Everyone liked her and got along with her.

The two women slowed, unconsciously drawing nearer to each other and matching their paces, as they neared the dock area. Laufrid was one of several towns with access to the sea, so its dock area was large and bustling with sailors and workers moving about importantly. The two women did not garner that much interest despite being dressed as priestesses and carrying bows. The signs of their respective faiths, the tree for Aronya and death for Rettela, hung about each woman's neck, to rest comfortably against their chests. Both reached to grasp their medallions in silent prayer before turning to each other. With a nod, not of friendship, but an acknowledgement of respect and loyalty to a cause bigger then either of them, each conveyed the promise of support and protection as they moved together into the crowd.

They found a good spot, an intersection of sorts between two well-moving ways, with some conveniently overturned crates which they used to stand upon. With quick glances around, the two women hoisted themselves up and turned to face the crowds.

They were now getting some odd looks which they ignored. Now that they were here, they looked at each other, both realizing they hadn't discussed how they were going to conduct their sermon. Neither had ever spoken to groups with a 'partner' before.

Though unrehearsed, they quickly fell into a pattern that surprised them with how well it worked.

"Good people," began Cura loudly, catching the attention of those passing, "have you ever wondered why some people live …"

"While others die?" interjected Seskia. "Why some people get sick …"

"While others seem blessed with eternal good health?" added Cura.

As they spoke, more people stopped to listen as something said caught their interest, or sparked something inside them they didn't even know was waiting to be ignited. Those that stopped caused others and stop to see what was happening, which of course led to even more. The priestesses couldn't help but notice their increasing audience and smiled to themselves to see it happening. On the periphery, however, staying hidden within the growing crowd, several hard-faced men stood staring fixedly at the speakers. These men were not there to listen to anything the women had to say. They were on a mission from their lord and no blasphemous rantings would stay their hands.

⚮

Just as Cura and Seskia were reaching the waterfront area, the next pair entered Laufrid. Cerrok and Dalis entered from the western gate, where the women had entered from the south.

"This is a wonderful town," started Dalis, trying to draw out his more morose companion. The high priest of Xelteran sneered at his larger companion.

"Is it now? And why is that, friend Dalis?" he asked. "Is it because the people have yet to attack us for our beliefs? Or perhaps because the market we just passed carries your favorite wine? Or maybe because your goddess demands you think so?" Cerrok finished with a cruel bark of laughter.

For a long while Dalis didn't respond, appearing content to wend his way through the morning crowds of shoppers. He offered no reply for such a long while that Cerrok snorted in satisfaction and assumed a gloating air. His manner and appearance in robes of fine blue silk and many jewelled fingers had many marking him for a lord of some high station. That didn't stop Dalis from voicing his opinion, however.

"For a man of such obvious intellect," he started, pausing to look around a small square they had just entered, "I would think you would realize that building relationships, maintaining friendships, and simply being nice, would garner you greater support and acceptance for yourself and your god."

Cerrok only had time to gape in astonishment at Dalis, when the younger man suddenly stopped and planted his hands on his hips.

"This will do," he announced staring out at the square before them. Not overly large, it was still the point where four streets emptied. Some enterprising vendors had set up small stalls and were valiantly trying to hawk their wares to anyone who would listen.

Cerrok first narrowed his eyebrows at the sudden change in topic, but then looked around in interest. With a quick nod, he pointed off to the eastern side of the square.

"Over there, I think," he said, then started off without waiting to see if Dalis disagreed or not. Upon reaching their chosen spot, the priests of love and greed set up their own platform from some unused stone blocks and wooden planking. With this crude dais set up, they declared themselves ready.

Before they could step up, however, Cerrok caught Dalis' arm. "When you're rich, friend Dalis, you don't need relationships or love," he said, the last with a sneer. "You have servants to cater to your whims, and as for followers, I don't foresee any problem finding people who believe the same."

"Perhaps, Cerrok, but the same could be said of love, could it not?"

❧

Minutes after Cerrok and Dalis entered through the western gate, the third pairing of Venick and Tella entered the southern gate. The two walked close together, seeming almost to be lovers or a father and his daughter so closely were their heads. Where Cerrok and Dalis did not like each other on a personal level, and Cura and Seskia disagreed theologically, the proponents of the gods of strength and strife disliked each other in both these ways. Each hid it well, out of necessity, for theirs were the most belligerent gods, and the quickest to anger. Both thought the other to be arrogant and demeaning, particularly to the other, and unyielding in acknowledging a different point of view.

They spoke now, in hushed, clipped tones, not looking at each other, but for a good spot to talk to the townspeople.

"How can you be so narrow minded?" hissed Tella.

"Me? Isn't that the pot calling the kettle black?" laughed Venick. "You are the one who can't open her mind. How about over there?"

Tella looked at the spot where Venick pointed. They had entered a small square in a residential district, and the priest of Malnoch had found a likely spot. The priestess of Gefrin disagreed however.

"Not enough people around and no easy way out should things turn bad," she said continuing to walk, turning a corner to find themselves in a much larger and busier area. Everywhere they looked were artisans of every sort: artists, musicians, writers and poets and even jugglers, fire breathers and stilt walkers.

"See?" said Venick, his long scruffy sideburns quivering with unvoiced laughter. "You agree with me more than you let on. You expect an attack to come. You, too, see strife crossing this land in our wake."

As he talked, Tella stopped where she was, her whole body stiffened in response to his words. With obvious effort, she controlled her ragged breathing though her fists continued to clench and unclench at her sides.

"I am nothing like you," she breathed. "It is an insult to the great Gefrin to even think so."

"Tella …" started Venick, surprised at the vehemence of her response and trying to make some amends.

"Your god is powerful," cut in Tella, "very powerful, particularly in such times as these. But He craves war and chaos, for in them lurks the greatest chance for power. People are scared or unhappy or overburdened and they look around for someone to blame."

Tella's voice had risen above the whisper she had used when she started speaking until she had been fairly shouting. Now, though, she seemed to have spent her anger for when she continued she was calm, but passionate.

"You say we are alike, Venick, but in truth we are very different. I worship the God of Strength, which you, like most people, take to mean only the strength of body or arms. There is strength everywhere, however. Strength of mind, of conviction, of purpose. Strength of character, of resolve, and of faith."

When she stopped talking, staring hard at Venick like she could impress her words directly into his head, she noticed several things at once. The first was that it had grown extremely quiet around them. This was odd in that, when they entered the square it had been bustling with noise and activity. The other thing she noticed was that Venick wasn't looking at her, but at something behind her. Turning, Tella noticed a good portion of the people in the crowd had stopped what they were doing and now stood staring at the two priests.

"Well, Tella," started Venick with a chuckle, "it appears we just started our first joint sermon."

❦

Barall strolled the streets of Laufrid casually, not seeking anything in particular, other than to avoid the others. Dalis had made an off-hand remark after leaving one of the small villages that while the people would listen to the 'newcomers,' it wasn't until Barall confirmed what they were saying that anyone took them seriously. It was time that each of the deities began to represent themselves without Endomar overshadowing everything. The pendulum of balance was swinging too far and it was time to set things right again. So, Barall distanced himself from the rest of the circle today to see if the people would hear them of their own accord.

He walked with Destrin, as he, too, had never been to the town. Barall had wanted to talk to the Wisdom and the reasons were swirling in his head like dry leaves in a wind storm. Each time he grasped one, it was whipped away by another, which was almost immediately replaced by yet another.

They walked in silence, strolling aimlessly, leaving their destination to fate. Destrin had chosen to walk without his priestly robes, but Barall had nothing but his robes to wear. As it was, he felt like he stuck out.

The older priest must have noticed his companion's discomfort, for he suggested looking for the clothiers. It was the first time either of them had spoken since entering Laufrid, but with those few words, the tension was broken. Coming to a decision, the younger man motioned for Destrin to lead the way, and then offered the question that had been burning inside him for the past weeks, ever since he had left Anklesh.

"Why?" he asked, nodding his thanks to a resident, dressed in a dark, hooded cloak, who had moved out of his way.

"Why?" repeated Destrin. "Why what?"

"Why was Comfort Vance killed? You all obviously disagreed with Vance's beliefs, but didn't think there were any gods other than Endomar, so why was he murdered?"

With each word, Destrin seemed to shrink further into himself. He appeared both ashamed and angry, though at what or whom, it was impossible to tell. Barall's breathing was coming hard now, as if the mere effort of voicing his questions was the greatest effort of all. Vance had been more than his teacher, he was mentor, father-figure and friend all rolled into one and his death had hit Barall like a physical blow that only the appearance of Cura and Dalis had managed to overcome. Until then, he had been living by instinct and luck.

"V-Vance was not murdered," stammered Destrin. "I know. I saw his body before it was laid to rest. He killed himself, so distraught over his doubts of Endomar, and feelings of inadequacy."

Barall stopped, dumbfounded, in the middle of the sparsely crowded street. There were few people around and those that were kept looking around as if afraid of something. The two priests stood staring at each other, each in their own form of shocked silence, ignorant of the townspeople's fear.

"Are you saying …" started Destrin.

"How can you think …" began Barall.

"Vance did not commit suicide?" asked the Wisdom, a tone of pleading hope reaching from his very soul to suck all the anger out of Barall. The Wisdoms didn't know what was going on in their very midst, Destrin realized. The Emissary had only recently disbanded the council, but it was obvious he had long before deemed them unworthy of certain information or unnecessary for helping him with the running and organization of the church. The realization of the depths of the Emissary's corruption hit both men at the same time.

"Oh dear sweet Endomar," breathed Destrin. Barall hung his head in renewed sorrow and frustration at the continued lack of answers. Destrin's prayer, he believed, was over his new revelation about the Emissary, so he was shocked when Destrin suddenly reached out and grabbed a fistful of Barall's robes and pulled him roughly forward.

Barall stumbled and fell to the ground, landing heavily on one knee before sprawling prostrate on the roadway. He lay stunned until a groan from Destrin forced him to roll over and look around. The once empty roadway was now filled with armed, cloaked men. There were a dozen of them; all dressed identically in hard black boots and simple brown cloaks and pants. Each was armed with a sword, carried with the ease of a seasoned fighter, and daggers tucked into the tops of their boots.

The men blocked both ends of the road and were moving to tighten their noose. Destrin lay with a large dagger protruding from his shoulder, a growing red stain spreading across his body, emanating from his shoulder. Another low groan confirmed the Wisdom was still living, at least for the moment. Barall rolled to his feet, but weaponless there would be little he could do against so many. With his heart pounding he folded his hands in front of him and tried to keep a calm facade on his face to belie the turmoil he truly felt. Whether the silent men approved of his demeanour in the face of his death, or not, there was no way to know, but they advanced methodically, swords leading the way.

Suddenly, shouts erupted from behind Barall, from where he had just come. The cloaked men on that side all whirled around to face the onslaught of a half dozen, equally armed men. Surprise allowed the new group to quickly overwhelm the cloaked men, killing all with quick thrusts of their swords. Yelling wildly, the newcomers rushed forward, in the forefront, Barall noticed Rillem's burly frame, a relieved expression on his face as he caught sight of Barall. Shock must have shown on Barall's face, for Rillem gave him a crooked grin, then slowed and stopped beside him, allowing the rest of the group to rush passed.

"My lord," he said, only a trifle breathlessly.

"Rillem," Barall replied, slowly overcoming his shock at the sudden attack and even more unexpected rescue. "I am glad to see you."

"My lord we must go."

'Not yet. We must help Destrin."

"There's no time. These men are more prepared and equally numbered. They are also better fighters. This is not a fight that will go down easily. We must get you to safety."

"No, Rillem, I will not leave a man to die. Go and join the fight, I will do what I can for you here."

When Rillem paused, Barall laid a gentle hand on the farmer's arm. Immediately a sense of peaceful confidence enveloped him. The simple touch gave Rillem the feeling that he, alone, could defeat the attackers.

"A priest rarely bears arms, Rillem, because he can do more for a fight without them," said Barall quietly.

With a slight nod, Rillem lifted his sword and moved with purpose toward the ongoing fight. With the battle presumably over his very life just a few steps away, the prayer came to mind. People he knew were fighting for him, to protect him and his endeavors. Lifting his arms high above his head, he began his prayer. Starting with a whisper, he repeated the verse over and over, increasing the volume with each repetition until, at its crescendo, an almost physical wave pulsed out from him in all directions. Though nothing could be seen coming from Barall, its effects were almost instantly noticeable. The men and women with Rillem suddenly felt invigorated and energized; each person feeling stronger and faster and it showed with the enthusiasm with which they attacked.

Their opponents felt the opposite effect as feelings of futility and despair flooded them as their swords became heavier and their limbs sluggish. Even as he watched, Barall could see the tide turning in the fight. Where his saviors had been struggling to maintain their line, they now pushed back. When two of the attackers had fallen, cut down with vicious slashes, the rest turned and fled, throwing down their swords behind them.

As the rescuers cheered their victory, Barall turned to Destrin. He still moved feebly, the dagger in his shoulder embedded deeply.

Kneeling at his side, Barall prepared his mind again, readying the prayer he would send to Endomar, asking for His divine help in healing another of His servants. Reaching out, he pulled the dagger from Destrin's shoulder, causing a new flow of blood to pump slowly from the wound and new groans to escape from Destrin. Without hesitation, he clamped his hands directly on top of the wound, ignoring the blood that immediately covered his hands. Closing his eyes, he focussed his attention on the man before him and the terrible wound in his body. Sending his prayers silently to Endomar, his lips moving with his prayer, warmth spread from his hands into Destrin. In his mind, he envisioned the body mending itself, healing the hurt caused to it, returning health and vitality, flooding the body and mind and soul.

Only when a deep sigh escaped from Destrin did Barall open his eyes and stop his prayer. If it weren't for the blood stained shirt Destrin wore with the three-finger-wide hole in its shoulder, there would be no way to tell he had ever been mortally wounded. Destrin probed at his shoulder, searching with questing fingers for the wound he knew should be there, but was now gone, replaced with fresh, pink flesh. Eventually, he looked up at Barall in wonder and amazement.

"How …" he began.

"Lord Barall has healed you with his prayers," said Rillem kneeling on the other side of Destrin.

Neither priest had heard the man approach, but as Barall looked up, he found Rillem opposite him. Beyond him, surrounding the two priests in a circle, were all of Rillem's companions. All were kneeling, facing inward toward the two priests, with their swords held before them, points down and resting on the ground. With their heads bent, it looked like they were praying. At Barall's inquisitive look, Rillem explained, "We followed you from the camp to make sure you were safe," he started. "We stayed back but when we saw the road blocked by those men, we grew concerned. Then, when they attacked Lord Destrin, we ran like the fox was in the henhouse. As you prayed to save Lord Destrin, we prayed to you."

"You prayed to me?" blurted Barall, shocked at such an idea.

"Not to you, my lord, but for you. To give you the strength and ability to do what you needed to do."

"But you are not a follower of Endomar. You believe in Aronya."

Rillem smiled. "Actually, my lord, we believe in all the gods. And we believe in you."

Barall was stunned. These men and women had risked their lives to follow him, in order to keep him safe, and they did so for a member of the circle that was not the priest of their own chosen god.

"You are true Clerist knights," said Barall at last, rising to thank each one in turn.

# Chapter 15

*"Nearly all men can stand adversity, but if you*
*want to test a man's character, give him power."*
**Abraham Lincoln**

Venick tossed uneasily in his sleep, writhing from side to side as the dream unfolded. He fought to wake, not wanting to see the end of this particular dream, but it was useless. The dream held him solidly in its grip.

In this dream he was afloat on the sea on his own little island among the rolling waves. It was peaceful here, safe and warm, but it wasn't right; something was drawing him to leave this place of quiet solitude. A boat appeared in the mist, bumping gently against the shores of his island. Without a glance back, he boarded the boat, which pushed off from land, the moment his feet touched the bottom. The island quickly faded from sight, but it was soon replaced by six other boats, identical to his. On each of these other boats was, not a person, but a symbol that floated in the air above it. Each symbol represented the other gods in the circle. There was the rock of strength, the heart of love and the tree of health; there was also the death's head of disease and concealment of greed. Last of all was the circle of wisdom. They were all here, all seven members of the pantheon of deities.

But still it wasn't right. Each boat fought for its own place for dominance over the others, struggling for their own survival against the increasing savagery of the sea. Venick, in his boat, with the crossroads symbol of strife, fought like the rest, striving to outdo his friends and fellow priests. Suddenly, a great storm blew over them and the little boats were tossed and thrown about in the high winds and heavy seas like the insignificant things they were against the power of the sea. Looking around, Venick could see each symbol fighting for its life. Some cast spells, praying to their god for the power to control the storm, others for fortification to withstand its might. All would fail, though, of that he was certain, and the circle would shatter, never able to fulfill its mission of equal opportunity for all. Then, as he watched, the heart moved closer to the concealment symbol, tossed there by an errant wave. As the two boats neared, together for only a few heartbeats, they were able to somewhat better withstand the wind and waves. Venick blinked, unsure of what he had just seen, but by he time he could focus again, the two boats had been blown further away again. Could the seven boats, together, survive where individually they were doomed? That was it, he was sure of it, and fought to manoeuvre his boat closer to that of the tree, the closest one to him.

Once nearer, he could see Cura beneath the tree, calling on Aronya for Her protection from the storm. Seeing Venick coming closer, she scowled and moved away. Whether it was fear of him, or of his intentions, Venick didn't know, but he screamed for her to wait, begged her to let him come nearer. Each time, she shook her head, showing his own sign of the crossroads to him. She didn't trust him, he realized, and thought his attempt to help was only a ruse. He tried to call out, to explain how by working together they would fare better, but it was no use, she wouldn't listen or trust his intentions. Giving up, he moved his boat laboriously toward the heart of Sleonde and Dalis.

Surely, Dalis would recognize the benefits of working together, for he would have seen the results from his bumping with concealment of Xelteran. But Dalis, like Cura, was striving to save himself, praying for more power for his little boat. He, too, moved away as Venick neared. In fact every one of the circle members avoided Venick as he tried to get them to work together. His last attempt was the circle of Endomar.

Oddly, Barall was not praying to Endomar, but stood watching Venick sadly.

"We must work together," shouted Venick over the howling wind.

"Yes," agreed Barall.

"Will you help me?"

"Why?" came the reply, with an odd expression on his face.

"We will all die if we can't make the others join with us."

Barall shook his head sadly, eyes downcast at the answer. His expression never changed even as another wave, much larger than any of the previous, smashed over both boats.

⚭

It was a subdued, but angry, group that gathered over breakfast the next morning. News of the attack on Barall and Destrin had spread throughout the camp outside Laufrid. The rest of the circle reported nothing more unusual than some suspicious, dark clad men lingering near the back of the crowd. For the most part, they had all found the people interested, but reserved. Venick noted it quite clearly by saying, "They don't know what to make of us since there's no rebuttal from their current leaders."

It was an odd situation since they had gone out on their own, without Barall, because he tended to draw all the questions rather than the priests themselves.

For now, they sat on the grass at the top of a small hill, sharing a breakfast of grilled sausage, cheese and bread. The aroma of the simple fare caused more than one stomach to growl in appreciation of what was to come. The newly appointed clerist knights stood guard around them, puffed up with pride and purpose, drawing more than one inquisitive look.

"Rillem and his friends came to our rescue," he explained. "They shall form the first company of clerist knights. They shall, at their own request and vow, be the guardians and protectors of the priesthood. Loyal to all, beholden to none, they serve the circle rather than an individual."

There were nods of understanding and acceptance from all around, with the exception of Venick. A frown creased his face so deeply it looked as if it might crack under the pressure.

"What, Venick?" asked Seskia caustically. "Are you angry that you didn't come up with the idea yourself?"

The look on the priest of strife's face vanished immediately, replaced by his usual look of haughty disdain.

"Yes, actually," he admitted to the surprise of everyone there. Venick was always quick to put himself in a favorable light and turn failures onto others. "I approve of the creation of a cadre of guards, and of their service to the circle as a whole. I do, however, have questions. For instance, to whom do these knights report? How do they gain members? And who leads them?"

"I suppose that you think it should be you who leads them," stated Cura, not even bothering to hide the fact that it was a statement more than a question.

A slow smile creased his lips, Venick obviously enjoying acting against their expectations. "Actually, no. I think this group should be independent, other than minor ties to the circle. They will lead themselves, recruit for their ranks on their own, and train, discipline, promote, and schedule on their own. But there must be a leader, a commander if you will, and rules of conduct to be followed."

"Venick," began Barall haltingly. "Your opinions seem quite … extraordinary. I didn't anticipate your feeling this way."

Surprisingly, Venick chuckled, his face and eyes actually mirroring his words. "You are too political, Barall. What you really meant was that you thought I would fight against this idea."

"Well, I wouldn't …"

"But I would. I will also tell you why. We must prepare ourselves for what is coming. The Emissary is growing bolder. He is attacking us directly, in the open, and that smacks of desperation."

He leaned forward, his eyes intent on every member of the circle. "War is coming, my friends, if we are going to bring the truth to the people. We have already seen the split of the people we've talked to. Some will listen and some won't accept what we have to say. But Caven is currently in power and can force soldiers into the field against us. We've seen it twice already and have been lucky both times. We need, we must, prepare for more to come."

Talk broke out as everyone voiced an opinion, either for or against Venick's view, except for Barall who sat with his brow furrowed staring at nothing. The discussion grew rancorous as more than one of Venick's fellow priests accused him of simply forwarding his own god's agenda, and not truly endorsing the knights. Eventually, at a lull in the conversation, Venick held up his hands. "I will not sit here and defend my beliefs. My statements are genuine as is my belief that Barall should formally lead the circle during this time of upheaval."

Stunned silence met his words as the impact of what he was saying hit everyone. Barall's head snapped up from his internal reverie, his mouth agape in confusion at hearing Venick speak as he was, for he had always worked within the circle to put himself or Cerrok forward as the best candidate for leader.

"Isn't he already the leader?" asked Stein.

"Not really, no," replied Cerrok. "Historically there isn't an official leader of the circle, though Endomar usually had the role of neutral arbiter. That role usually led to letting Endomar make decisions, which gave the appearance of leadership."

"Barall is young and inexperienced," Venick continued, "but he is intelligent and, perhaps more importantly, he listens to those around him. And let us not discount the fact that he is a follower of Endomar. The general farmer will put more stock in that fact than in anything else."

General nods of agreement were seen around the circle, and then silence descended again. Slowly, heads turned toward Barall as if expecting his leadership should begin immediately. Barall gave his head a small shake, though whether in amazement at the situation or to remove the lethargy from him, even Barall didn't know. He recognized the irony of his life; barely a season ago he was an Acolyte within the church of Endomar. Now, here he was, roaming the countryside leading priests of six very little known religions, trying to overthrow his own religious leadership.

"Given the events of yesterday, let's assume Venick is right, and the Emissary is gearing for war, what can we do about it? We can't mobilize, or even encourage, the people to follow us to war against the church."

"No," Tella said, "our purpose is to inform and educate the people that they have a choice. There is more than just Endomar available. We do not want blood shed simply to inform people of that choice."

"Perhaps, but can we let the Emissary do what he wants? He's threatening us!" said Cura quietly.

"Yes!"

"No!"

"Wait," broke in Dalis. "How do we really know what the Emissary is planning, either for us, or for his church? Do we really want to just assume that he is out to 'get' us?"

"If I may?" asked Destrin. "I believe you can trust the Emissary will do everything he can to eliminate you."

For the next several minutes, Destrin related everything he knew of Caven's plans for the future of the church and what he had learned from Lassand about Caven's state of mind and the paranoia that was becoming more and more prevalent.

"How did this man ever become the leader of an entire religion?" asked Seskia incredulously.

"It wasn't always like this," said a red-faced Destrin, the defence sounding weak even to his own ears. "He seemed very conservative as a Primate and Wisdom."

"Well," said Barall with a sigh, obviously shaken by what he had heard, "it appears that Cerrok's vision of the future is very possible, which still leaves us with, what do we do now?"

# Chapter 16

*"Wisdom is knowing what to do*
*next; virtue is doing it."*
*David Starr Jordan*

Zithius was striking, regal, as he stood with his back straight and his hands clasped loosely behind him. He was dressed, still, for mourning in a soft doublet of black velvet that was offset by his full head of silver hair and the silver thread that chased itself around the cuffs and throat. Black pants and calf-high boots completed the picture. In all, the king struck an imposing and inspiring figure.

Gazing out the high window of the palace, Zithius turned away in disgust. He used to love the view from his office, given that it overlooked the expanse of Anklesh with the central bay and the cathedral. The cathedral itself used to be his favorite view, with its wonderful, soaring architecture and awesome presence. As a young man, Zithius had found himself at this very window simply gazing at it, drawing inspiration and hope from it.

Looking at it now, isolated, alone and friendless on its island in the middle of the Bay of Faseda, it looked squat and uninviting. The main structure, oddly, was not circular, but more angular. If not for the many towers jutting upward, reaching for the paradise promised in the afterlife, it looked like a castle. Those towers, called steeples when on a church, were each topped with Endomar's circle, and girded around by several minarets that served no purpose that Zithius could see, other than decoration. Up close, the cathedral was built of smooth cut stone, so light in color it was almost white. How the massive blocks were transported or joined, he had no idea, and he marvelled at the thought even now.

By far, however, the greatest feature of the cathedral was a huge window cut into the wall, directly above the pair of huge double doors that allowed entrance to the interior. The window was circular with carved stone through it to connect to a smaller inner circle at the very center. The stonework connecting the inner and outer circles was such that it made the entire thing look somewhat like a flower. The glass itself was apparently etched in some fashion to show some of the historic times of the church but Zithius had never been close enough to the glass to verify that.

The glowing splendor that was the cathedral had darkened with the death of his son. Though Percinal had been dead for some weeks now, the emptiness of his leaving was still keenly felt. Remembering his son brought tightness to his chest, but he quickly quashed the tears that threatened to spill onto his cheeks. It wouldn't do to have the king cry in front of his subjects. He turned to see that he wasn't fooling his guest as Virez stood watching him with sad, compassionate eyes. Perhaps she did understand. While she had not lost a child, she too, was on a precipice of sorts, in danger of losing a way of life, a way to which she had dedicated her very soul.

Zithius laid the blame for both their issues directly at the feet of Emissary Caven. That man had no soul, or if he did, it was one so blackened by self-interest and madness that it wasn't worth saving. Zithius wasn't sure he believed there was an entire pantheon of deities, but he was sure that the Emissary's version of the future was not in the best interests of Cherilla.

Zithius managed a weak smile for Virez and was rewarded with one in return. The Wisdom had come to him shortly after he had received the news of Percinal's death with words of consolation. More importantly, though, she provided information he craved.

The formal courier sent by the Emissary lay the death solely at the feet of Barall, a renegade priest Percinal and his unit had been sent to capture. Zithius knew something of this Barall; enough to realize he was likely not the evil usurper the Emissary claimed. His own man was travelling with Barall and his circle, and sent reports back infrequently.

That information he kept from Virez, at times feeling guilty at keeping it from her, but then reason took over. Without a doubt, she was not telling him everything either. He had noticed her looking at him on several occasions with a look of tension and apprehension that could only be interpreted as her withholding something. It was childish, perhaps, but a king did not reveal all his cards, particularly to those who did not possess what he needed to know.

With a final scowl toward the cathedral, he turned away from the window to again face Virez. "What news today, Wisdom?" he asked tiredly.

"Nothing good, I'm afraid, my lord," she replied.

"So, a normal day, then," he said with a smile.

"Hopefully not, but it does look that way."

The king smiled again. The arrival of Virez was greeted with surprise by everyone in the palace, and with suspicion by more than a few, Zithius included. The relationship between church and state had become increasingly strained over the last generation or two. Zithius' grandfather used to tell stories of cooperation and comradery between them, though, Zithius' father did not have the same relationship, and Zithius himself didn't have even that much.

Where and when this deterioration started, Zithius really didn't know. In his mind, the church grew too big, too powerful, too fast. The priests, and especially the Emissaries, started to consider themselves above those they preached to so no longer was there any collaboration on policies or decisions. Now, the church took more and more liberties without even bothering to inform the king.

Zithius sat tiredly on one of the low couches within the room, gesturing for Virez to sit as well. He rubbed the ridge above his eyes with a low sigh.

"You look tired, my lord," said Virez.

"Really? I can't imagine why, particularly with the news you always seem to bring me."

"Oh, so it's my fault then?" she asked, a smile crooking the sides of her mouth.

"Let's just say you don't help. Now, what today?"

Virez appreciated Zithius' directness and business like manner. It was a refreshing change from life in the cathedral. The Comforts, Primates and Wisdoms tended to gossip and dance around subjects rather than actually discussing anything of merit. The culture within the cathedral was really one of complacency, laced with a large dose of fear centered around repercussions from the Emissary should he feel someone had overstepped their authority or even if they made a decision or comment he didn't like. If Virez looked within herself, she would have to admit this was not to be laid solely at Caven's feet. As the power and influence of Endomar's church grew over the decades, the reigning Emissary took more and more power unto themselves. That much power led to feelings of superiority, which led to actual superiority.

They were now at a crucial breaking point, where forces were starting to work against the Emissary. Her own presence here, in the secular seat of power, was proof of her own feelings toward Caven. Her face reddened as she remembered trying to seduce Caven to advance her own position.

"The Emissary continues his recruitment of young men in the

city," she started. "That much I suspect you knew, however. The men are being conscripted into a holy army to bring Endomar to Ponti and Naer. I don't know why an army is needed to bring religion to people, nor why it is even to be 'given' to them."

The emphasis on 'given' was apparent, even without the sneer that curled Virez's lips.

"And truthfully, I know nothing of either country, despite being neighbors with both. It seems odd, to me, that we have no relations with them."

There was no response from the king, which, in itself, was illuminating. Cocking her head to one side, realization struck Virez at the sight of the expressionless face. She leaned forward intently, her eyes boring into Zithius'.

"You *do* have relations with them." It was a statement, not a question.

A non-committal shrug convinced Virez she was right, but rather than press her point, she waited. It was Zithius who broke first.

"Yes, I frequently talk with both Birdon of Ponti and Caltemsken of Naer," he said. "It would not be wise," he added with a slight nod to her, "for a king to ignore his national neighbors. We have some trade though very little cross-border travel."

"Why?"

The king blinked. "I don't honestly know. From the letters we've exchanged, I find both of them to be extremely introverted peoples, concerned with issues within their borders, not necessarily with the world as a whole."

"Not unlike us," added Virez.

"Well, we do have some internal issues to deal with, don't we?"

Raised eyebrows and a weak smile met his statement.

Continuing, Zithius ticked off points on his fingers as he made them. "So Caven is raising an army. He's using free citizens to do it. He wants to expand the influence of Endomar beyond the borders of Cherilla. I have to conclude that he is expecting to force that influence on Naer and Ponti, otherwise, why the army? Am I correct, so far, in my understanding?"

Virez nodded at the four fingers held before her.

"Fine. Is there anything else?"

She paused at the sudden change in topic, and hesitated before speaking. She had only two other pieces of information. One would be welcomed, while the other could get her beheaded. She didn't know whether the king actually endorsed beheadings or not, but she couldn't help the thought from entering her mind. As she chewed her lower lip, the king waited, but even his patience waned.

"Wisdom?" he asked gently, intruding into her internal debate. "It can't be that bad, can it?"

A forced chuckle soon told him that it could be, at least to Virez. Reaching a decision, she launched into the story of her last night in the cathedral, holding nothing back, as if finally telling the truth opened a flood within her that washed the lies away. She told the story of finding the Emissary, bloody staff in hand, standing over the bleeding body of Kayir; Caven's shock and anger at Destrin's revelation over the guard captain's heritage, and the disbanding of the council of Wisdoms.

"Together, we knew the Emissary had to be stopped, but we couldn't do it alone, and not solely from within the cathedral. So the Wisdoms separated. I came to you to be advisor and aide, Lassand stayed with Caven hoping to glean new information about the Emissary's plans and minimize what decrees he could, and Destrin chose to try to find Barall and his circle of new priests, to guide him as I do you."

Zithius remained silent, staring impassively at the priestess before him. So long did he sit, unmoving and unspeaking, that Virez thought him asleep, except his eyes were open.

"My lord," she started. "I'm sorry for not telling you immediately, but …"

Zithius held up one hand to forestall any further self-recriminations. Leaving Virez where she sat, he moved to the single door in the room and opened it to speak to someone waiting on the other side.

"General, would you come in please?" he asked.

A muffled reply, certainly an acquiescence, and an old, though definitely still robust, soldier preceded the king into the room. General Wilnah was known vaguely to Virez. In the few weeks she had been attending Zithius' court and serving as an advisor, she had seen many of his men, and heard of many others. Wilnah was commander of the army of Cherilla. The army was primarily only for show, in case one of their neighbors decided Cherilla was undefended; still, the general took his duties very seriously. The army was well trained and ready to answer the king's call at any time.

The general stood stiffly at attention, dressed in full military garb. He was tall, well above Virez's head, with only faint traces of his original black hair among the predominant gray. Steely, blue eyes missed nothing as they casually scanned the room, and even under the uniform, she could see the muscled torso and arms.

Refusing the seat offered him by Zithius, Wilnah waited patiently while Zithius resumed his place on the couch opposite Virez. Introductions were made and politely acknowledged, but to Virez, the tension was palpable. Why had Zithius called in the general? He had obviously been waiting outside. Had they known the truth all along? These and a dozen other questions flew through her mind, each one more sinister than the last. She could feel her breath coming faster and her hands shaking, and though she fought, could not control either. So agitated was she that she actually jumped with a small cry when Wilnah addressed her.

"Are you all right, Wisdom?"

Zithius actually chuckled at her reaction, and then outright laughed at the mixture of fear and outrage on her face. "I believe the

Wisdom fears your presence here, my friend," he chuckled. "I think she feels some disaster is about to happen to her."

At Virez and Wilnah's questioning looks, Zithius relented. "Virez, you have told me your story of the reasons for your coming and now fear my reaction."

A whimper escaped Virez's throat and she seemed to shrink in upon herself even as she opened her mouth to reply.

"But," overrode Zithius, "not for what you told me, but when. We already knew what had happened. We knew Percinal had returned and had gone to report to Caven of his mission because my son reported to me first, before going to the cathedral."

Realization slowly dawned on Virez at the impact of Zithius' words: the king, Wilnah, and most probably a good portion of the army and the king's advisors, knew of the murder. Yet they all kept silent. The king, the grieving father forced to endure the loss of his only son without even his body to bury, had done nothing against the man who had murdered Percinal.

"Why?" was all Virez could think of to say.

It was Wilnah who responded. "We are not ready for a war with the church, nor, truly, do we want one. A war over religion is foolish, with no winners, particularly when both sides essentially believe in exactly the same thing, just not in the leadership or methods of governance. Our issues are with the Emissary, not Endomar."

"True," said Zithius, his eyes remaining locked on Virez, "but I believe the question was directed more at me. 'Why' did I not tell you this when you first arrived? 'Why' did I allow you into my home to advise me when I knew the Emissary, your lord, killed my son and plots war with our neighbors? The answer to both questions is trust. I didn't know if I could trust you, Wisdom, or whose side you were truly on. I suspected most of what you just told me, but until you were willing to tell me yourself, you would never have been given access to my inner circle."

Virez sat stunned, looking from Zithius to Wilnah and back. This was not the reaction she had expected. By inference, she was about to be included into the king's group of personal advisors, a position of power.

No! She rebuked herself sharply. Power and influence was not something to be craved or sought after. Travelling down that path led to corruption and the exact situation they faced with the Emissary. Obviously she was going to have to pray and reflect further on her own personal failings. She cared nothing for personal power or wealth and wanted only to work for the salvation of her faith and church and to help improve life for all Cherillans.

"My Lord Zithius," began Virez. "I cannot begin to express my sorrow and anger over what the Emissary has done, and by extension, what we who are in the service of Endomar, have allowed to happen. I have been wrestling with my conscience since that dreadful night, and I couldn't ignore the precepts of my faith and not be honest with you. I promise to help you in every way to remove Caven from his position."

"Excellent!" boomed Zithius with a loud clap of his hands. "Now then, General Wilnah, your thoughts?"

The sudden shift in Zithius' manner surprised Virez. Up until now, the king had been sombre; withdrawn into the grief over the loss of his son, but now he was almost exuberant and full of energy. Though his mood was infectious, Virez caught herself leaning forward in excitement. Things the king had said tickled at the back of her mind. How had he known the truth about *everything* she had revealed? If Percinal had reported to the palace before going to the Emissary and told his father of his mission and its outcome, simple deduction would tell Zithius the true manner of his son's death. But how could he have known about what the Wisdoms had decided to do, and where they had gone?

Realization struck her in an instant, and she looked at Zithius to see him watching her. A slow wink told her he knew she had figured it out and was not at all concerned she was aware the king had spies within the cathedral. The knowledge both amused and upset her. That the king had informants right under the Emissary's nose was strangely gratifying, but that they had been spying on her, too, was not. She would have to investigate upon her return to the cathedral when Caven was ousted. A new thought came to mind then. She was actually involved in a revolution. They were planning the overthrow of a legally elected leader, and the thought chilled her blood.

Obviously the king was an adept reader of faces and people. "You understand, now, don't you Wisdom?" he asked gently. "Now you see the enormity of what we're about. This is not something only discussed or bandied about in theory; this is life, with all the horrors, fears and soul searching that goes along with it. Knowing what that means," he continued, piercing her again with his unwavering gaze. "Are you still willing to help, whatever that might mean?"

To her credit, Virez matched Zithius' stare without blinking. "Yes," she said simply.

"Well then," said Wilnah somewhat awkwardly. "here is what I propose."

❧

The Comfort sat at the desk preparing for the next day's sermon. A cup of steaming tea sat on the desk, still half full, its spicy aroma filling the small office. The period's sermon was about the 'new' pillar of sacrifice. The three lost pillars had filled her thoughts since Barall had come. While she had originally scoffed at the idea that faith had changed over the years, the more she delved into her own records and searched her soul, the more the pillars of humility, sacrifice and patience seemed completely natural. Why had it taken a rogue Acolyte, on the run from the cathedral, and preaching, not the word of Endomar, but of an entire pantheon of gods, for her to see?

A soft knock at her door caused the Comfort to pause in her work, a frown creasing her brow. It was quickly smoothed out with a sigh of self-recrimination. *Patience, patience,* she murmured to herself. Then, "Come in," she called.

A start of surprise rocked her back in her chair as a sergeant of the Emissary's personal guard strode through the door, dressed for travel, his uniform of purple trimmed with white was stained with dust and showing the rumpling of several days.

"Comfort Rischa?" asked the sergeant in a flat tone of voice.

"Yes, sergeant, come in, come in. Sit, please. My you look as if you've been riding for a week. May I get you some tea?"

"No, Comfort. I am here on orders from the Emissary to deal with you."

"Deal with me?" she repeated dumbly.

For the first time, Rischa noticed the sergeant was armed with a sword belted at his waist, one hand resting easily on its hilt. Not one, but two, daggers sat awkwardly on his opposite hip. It was not unusual for the Emissary's guards to be armed; however, they normally gave the priests the courtesy of removing them when not on a protective duty. This man hadn't even given his name to Rischa, or even bowed or signed the Circle to her. Her blood ran cold as the guardsman drew one of the daggers and stood testing its point with one stubby thumb.

"Why?" was all she could manage to say from a throat gone suddenly dry.

The man looked at her as if she had suddenly grown a third eye as he advanced further into the room. Behind him, the Comfort could see several more guards standing watch in the anteroom before her private office, her secretary no where to be seen. As the menacing guard came around her desk, Rischa pulled out her circle, the symbol of Endomar and the focus of her faith. Just holding it seemed to banish her fear and bring understanding to her mind. Retaining her hold on the circle, Rischa stared defiantly into the man's dark eyes.

"Though you may kill me now, the Emissary can't silence the clarion call that is sounding throughout Cherilla. More and more people will learn the truth of the faith of Endomar, and of the different gods and goddesses that exist. Barall brings the truth to all people, and he will bring it to the Emissary as well."

Just as Rischa finished, her last words still sounding in her own ears, the dagger plunged down, entering her chest with such force that she barely had time to register the pain of it, before she died. The guard stood regarding her for a moment, silently appraising his actions and the results of them. The dagger, unremarkable in every way, had perfectly skewered the Comfort's circle, trapping it between the Comfort's body and the blade's hilt.

*Hm*, thought the guard. *Just like the other one.*

# Chapter 17

*"If we work in marble, it will perish; if we work upon brass, time will efface it; if we rear temples, they will crumble into dust; but if we work upon immortal minds and instil into them just principles, we are then engraving upon tablets which no time will efface, but will brighten and brighten to all eternity."*
*Daniel Webster*

"Barall? Barall!"

The shouts reverberated through the camp, rousing everyone who wasn't already awake. Though the sun itself had barely risen from its nightly slumber, someone was awake enough to run around crazily. Barall was still shaking the sleep from his head when the first shouts were heard. They were getting closer, he realized from his small cot within his simple tent, then the unmistakable, more sinister sound, of a sword unsheathing cut through his drowsiness. Fully awake in an instant, Barall flew to the flap of his tent, not even bothering to pull on a shirt.

Outside, he blinked in the early morning light as he took in the scene before him: two clerist knights, Rirodan and Ockun, if he remembered correctly, had stopped the shouter as he had run past

Barall's non-descript and ordinary tent, with the simple expedient of tripping him. Riordan now had one knee pressed firmly to the chest of a young boy, no older than eleven or twelve. Both knights had their swords drawn; Riordan's, for the moment, held back and away from the boy, while Ockun's wavered over the boy's throat and they were shouting questions at the boy who seemed stunned from his fall.

"Who are you? What are you doing here?" demanded Riordan in a menacing voice, made all the worse for the crags and pits that ran rampant over his face.

"What's going on?" asked Barall.

"My lord," stammered Ockun turning swiftly to offer Barall a smart salute. "We caught this boy running through the camp shouting for you."

Barall waited a moment. "And?"

"And, my lord?"

"Yes, Ockun, 'and.' Is it illegal to run or shout? I commend you both in your diligence to my protection, but let's let the poor boy up and hear what he has to say before we run him through."

With a shrug, Riordan lifted himself off the boy, though both guards stubbornly refused to sheathe their swords. Barall, himself, helped the boy to his feet, and then led him into his tent.

⸙

Dalis and Cerrok were just sitting down to a breakfast of warm biscuits and fruit when Cerrok nearly choked on his food, resulting in a bone-breaking pounding from the much larger Dalis, when Barall sped by, running as fast as his legs and formal Comfort's robes allowed.

"Stop pummelling me, buffoon," blustered Cerrok. "What's going on?" he added pointing to Barall, now followed by a knight and an unknown boy.

"Don't know," mumbled Dalis around a mouthful of biscuit.

"Something's going on," stated Cerrok. "Let's go see what it is."

He stood up and strode after Barall, not caring about the untouched breakfast he left behind. Dalis hesitated only long enough to grab up the uneaten biscuits and an apple before hurrying to catch up. The two priests were soon joined by Destrin who, emerging from his own tent had also seen Barall run by. Everyone arrived, together, in a cluster, at the makeshift picket at the outskirts of camp.

While Riordan called for two of the few horses they had been able to scrounge, the others gathered around Barall and the boy.

"What's going on?!?" demanded Cerrok.

Briefly, Barall explained. "This is Fedrinn, a supporter of Endomar who will take on the Initiate's robes when he comes of age. He came to warn me that the Primate is conducting today's sermon at the temple. In that sermon she plans to announce that we attacked cathedral guards and killed them for merely watching your 'demonstrations'."

He was obviously agitated, for Barall couldn't stand still and kept darting impatient glances at Riordan.

"Are you a fool, or just plain dense?" stated Cerrok flatly. "This is obviously a trap."

"That's what I said," mumbled Riordan, clearly unaffected by the looks Barall was shooting him.

"Perhaps, but I don't think so," replied Barall. "It is more likely that they are simply trying to discredit us in the eyes of the people; to show us as brutes having to kill our enemies rather than prove our truth."

"Ridiculous!" sputtered Cerrok.

"Barall," said Dalis in his low rumble, "how do we know this boy? Sorry, Fedrinn, but given what has been happening to us, Cerrok may be right."

The four priests continued to argue, so Riordan motioned

Fedrinn to him. The boy was in the awkward, not-quite-a-man-but-more-than-a-boy phase and was gaping wide-eyed at the priests before him. He was of average height, but rail thin and gangly, appearing to be all legs and arms. A shock of blond hair, just as long and unruly as his arms, topped his thin head, but intelligent blue eyes watched everything and had narrowed at Dalis' implication that Fedrinn was a spy sent to lure Barall into a trap. As Fedrinn approached, Riordan slipped a companionable arm around the boy's shoulders and led him several paces along the picket line to watch the horses being saddled. While their backs were still turned toward the priests, Riordan slipped his knife from his belt with one hand, while his other moved from Fedrinn's shoulder to clap firmly over the boy's mouth. Held securely and with a knife at his throat, Fedrinn didn't dare move. His eyes had opened wide in shock, while his hands had flown to grab onto the older man's encircling arm.

"Now, boy," hissed Riordan into the boy's ear, "I'm no priest, squeamish about doing what must be done, so, why don't you tell me who sent you?"

"Comfort Dowlaw. He told me to find Barall and tell him what Primate Arkadi was going to say."

"Why?"

"The Comfort didn't tell me."

"Why?" The knife pressed closer to Fedrinn's throat, pressing almost gently into the skin.

"He didn't say," came out as a high pitched squeak.

Riordan released him and turned to face the assembled priests, the knife vanishing.

"I believe the boy," he called, loudly enough to cut through their discussion.

"What?!?" roared Cerrok, his face purple in exasperation. "Why?"

For a moment it looked as if the knight wouldn't answer, then, with a sidelong look at Fedrinn, said, "We've had a chat, and my instincts tell me he's telling the truth. And I've learned to trust my instincts."

Oddly, Cerrok seemed to accept that as explanation enough, so with a 'humph,' he turned back to continue his argument with Barall. Only Barall wasn't there. Instead, he had mounted the horse brought to him by one of the handlers when Cerrok's attention had been diverted.

Seeing Cerrok about to renew the discussion, Barall held up his hands. "I'm going, Cerrok," he said calmly. "Trap or no, I am going. The Primate wants to undermine us, but perhaps even worse, she is lying to the people she is meant to guide and lead in faith and honesty. That must be fought.

He continued as Dalis this time, tried to intervene.

"I am taking Riordan with me."

"An excellent idea," said Cerrok. "His skills should prove useful should you run into trouble."

"Skills?" asked Barall.

"Yes. Surely you knew he was once one of your Emissary's guards?"

Barall turned to look at Riordan, who suddenly seemed unable to meet Barall's eyes. Destrin, too, seemed surprised by this revelation.

"This is true?" asked Barall.

Riordan replied with only a shrug and a scowl.

"I've never heard of an Emissary's Guard leaving its ranks," said Destrin curiously. "May I ask why you did?"

For this first time that any of them could remember, Rirodan seemed at a loss of words. He was always ready with a quick retort or sarcastic comment, but not this time. It was strange to see a tall, well muscled, fully grown man, shuffle his feet like a child caught doing something he wasn't supposed to.

"All I'll say," he said finally, "is that there are things the Emissary needs protection from, and others that need protection from the Emissary. I got tired of it being one way over the other."

Barall thought he understood, having heard the rumors about Caven and female Initiates and Acolytes, but he could tell that Cerrok and Dalis didn't know what he was talking about, and clearly wanted to ask. Destrin, however, Barall couldn't read. Whether that was because the Wisdom truly didn't know, or because he did, there was no way to tell.

"Then I'm sure I'm in capable hands," said Barall at last, breaking the awkward and uncomfortable silence. "So can we be on our way?"

"Wait," said Destrin. "If you didn't know of Riordan's history as a guard, why were you taking him in the first place?"

"Because he'd only follow me anyway so I figured this would save time."

"An excellent idea," piped in Dalis.

Dalis, Destrin and Cerrok exchanged looks and grins all around before turning back to Barall.

"Fine," grumbled Barall, "just remember we are not there to start a war, but to stop one."

❧

The temple in Laufrid was old, older by far than the cathedral in Anklesh. Its stone was an aged grayish-yellow color, pocked here and there with missing mortar and weather stains. It was the tallest building in the area, with two towers straddling a triple set of doors. The doors were taller than any two men, and were made of heavy, solid oak, banded with iron. Above the doors were a trio of tall, oblong windows, matched by a pair of windows on each tower.

As with the cathedral, the central feature of the temple was the central, circular window carved into the very apex of the front wall. Easily the height of three men in diameter, the stone carvings of this window were four lines, arranged in parallel pairs that intersected across the center of the circle. The small group gazed up at the window as they drew near the temple. Barall and Destrin expected it, of course, but even then, the size and grandeur of it, still struck them.

The six had made good time in gathering what they needed for the trip and in making their way to the temple, the service just starting as they walked up the few stairs leading to the middle door. After a large vestibule area, another set of doors led to the central worship room.

Inside, the air was still, yet comfortably cool. A cloying odor of the oil used to polish the benches hung thickly, stirred only when the doors were opened. The benches were made of gleaming, polished maple were arranged in four long columns that stretched from the doors at the back to a raised dais at the front. The columns were separated by narrow aisles allowing worshipers access to the benches from either side. A central aisle, wider than the others perfectly separated the two halves.

On the dais, several chairs were arranged, draped in the particular priest's colors: green for a Comfort, blue for a Primate, brown for a Wisdom and the Emissary's purple. One of each color was always placed on the dais for every service to represent the cohesion of the levels and that any of the four colors could lead a service.

Finding seats near the middle of the room, next to the central aisle, the four priests and Riordan sat down to listen, while Fedrinn left to see to his own duties. Cerrok watched him go with barely concealed distrust.

The service followed a standard format for the most part, with the Comfort providing the dictates of the faith and explaining why the faith was important and how adherence to the four pillars would lead to true wisdom. Finally, Primate Arkadi stood to deliver the address. The address was the part of the service where the ranking priest of Endomar provided personal insight and opinion into the faith and current events. It usually took the form of a story with a moral or lesson attached, and most priests were very good at it. They could, through their choice of words, tone and emphasis, draw their listeners into the story. Arkadi was such a speaker.

She was a woman of small stature who would only stalk back and forth atop the dais rather than step down in front of the closest worshippers. She was absolutely stunning with a heart shaped face and large, clear blue eyes. Framing her face was shoulder length blond hair that, when caught in the sunlight, seemed to be made of spun gold.

Her address was well thought out, even if inflammatory and full of outright lies. She masterfully weaved religion and history with threads of fear and secular law. Her words, meant to rouse anger and indignation in the hearts of the listeners against Barall's circle, and Barall specifically, were working. Around them, the circle members could hear mutterings of agreement. One or two even suggested the possibility of hunting the 'traitors' down.

"Enough!" Barall hissed, starting to rise.

A firm hand clamped down over his wrist, keeping him in his seat. "Wait," ordered Destrin from beside him. He was not caught up in Arkadi's address, but was instead intent on listening to her. "Follow your rules of order and wait until the address is over and comments are permitted."

"By then the people will be ready to string me up right here," he shot back.

"No they won't. Not if you phrase it carefully. Arkadi is a brilliant speaker, but only when she has the time to prepare. Force her to think on her feet and she will make mistakes."

Barall thought about what Destrin was telling him. The Wisdom surely knew more about the Primate than Barall. As the assistant to the cathedral archivist, Barall had dealt with practically every member of the church at one time or another, particularly those in the higher ranks as they requested research or specific books, but Arkadi was really just a name to him.

As the address ended, Barall almost expected the crowd to stand up and applaud. He waited, impatiently, as the Comfort resumed the formal aspects of the service. Slowly, time crept along until finally the Comfort and the Primate stood in front of the assemblage and asked if there were any questions they could answer.

After a few people had their questions answered, Barall squeezed past the legs of Dalis to stand in the middle of the aisle. Barall had donned a simple robe of common brown to hide his Comfort's robes thinking to hide his true identity until the best time to announce it. Given the way the address had gone, he was thankful for the disguise.

"Primate, I have a question," he stated as he stepped into the aisle.

"Come forward then, dear, and ask it," she said sweetly.

Rather than advance, Barall stayed where he was. "Which, Primate, do you feel is the most important of the pillars of faith?"

The Primate blinked her wonderful blue eyes at Barall for several seconds, before turning and muttering something to the Comfort, her voice too low to carry to where Barall was standing. With a small frown around her delicate mouth, she turned back to Barall.

"The pillars are not ranked one above another, with one to be followed before another. They are all encompassing and should be used together," she replied at last.

"Thank you, Primate, but that doesn't really answer the question. Which one do *you* think is the most important?"

Again, Arkadi hesitated and Barall understood Destrin's comment about her needing time to prepare. She did not react well, or quickly, to unexpected questions.

"I *personally* believe that the pillar of honor is the most important. Honor requires that a person do what is right, even in the face of possible danger to themselves. It requires that you put the good and well being of the whole before yourself."

The emphasis on 'personally' was clear to everyone in the room. The Primate was not about to bind the church to a hierarchy of the pillars with her own opinion. Obviously, the reputation of the Emissary's temper had reached beyond the borders of Anklesh. Barall sighed inwardly, for that was the answer he needed Arkadi to provide. If he was going to box her into a corner from which she had no escape, he had to keep at her and not give her a chance to think.

"Thank you, Primate, I appreciate your courage to say so and can understand that none of the pillars are any more important than any other. However, in your address you denounced Barall and his attempt to bring knowledge of new religions to Cherilla. As a Comfort of Endomar, himself, would honor not require him to do so?"

Gasps of surprise rippled through the temple as the people were aroused from their lethargy at the prospect of a battle looming. The Primate, herself, was being challenged theologically by this stranger, and she was not someone who took to having her authority challenged.

"Honor requires, my good sir, that one does what is right, not what one wants to do," Arkadi replied icily. "And Barall is not a Comfort, but a mere Acolyte."

"The lowliest Initiate may have the wisdom of an Emissary, if expressed and tempered properly. I would also beg to suggest, that perhaps Barall has knowledge of the topic that pushes him to do what he does."

"But …" started Arkadi, but Barall continued, not letting her interrupt.

"And with that knowledge, wouldn't the pillar of compassion then demand he act?"

"C - Compassion?" stammered Arkadi, clearly struggling to keep up.

"Yes, Primate," said Barall calmly, still standing where he was with hands clasped before him. "Doesn't the pillar of compassion require that one realize that logic may not always be the right answer, and that the heart and soul should serve as the guide?"

"Y-Yes."

"So you see my point, then?"

"No, dear, I'm afraid I don't"

The Primate's answer brought a twittering of laughter from the crowd, but Barall kept any sign of humor from his face. The situation was not laughable to him, but deadly serious for he had to convince not only the Primate of his convictions, but every other person in the room, as well.

"If Barall has knowledge of different gods and goddesses, honor and compassion would demand he present that knowledge to the people. They would require he seek out people with better knowledge of these deities, with experience in worshipping them, to work with him. Would that not be true, Primate?"

Arkadi was visibly sweating now, her eyes darting around the room, as if looking for a salvation that wasn't coming. This man, this stranger, came with ideas and arguments she just wasn't prepared to combat.

"N-No, I don't th-think so. Besides, you are missing the point. He killed in our streets. He killed men the Emissary himself had sent to capture and question him. Question him, sir. Barall was under no threat from anyone, yet still he shed innocent blood. And why? Do you have an answer to that simple question?"

Once Arkadi got going, she was like an untamed horse, unstoppable and wild. She stormed back and forth on the dais, reiterating bits and pieces of her address and raging against Barall and his cause. When she finally ran out of breath and noticed the shocked looks on many of the faces before her. She drew a calming breath and returned to her place beside the now-uncomfortable Comfort at the center of the dais. Everyone was staring at her, while the stranger who asked the interesting questions stood quietly and still in the middle of the aisle.

"My apologies, my friends," she said addressing the people as a whole. "I'm afraid I become very upset when life is taken needlessly. Now, dear, have we answered all of your questions?"

"No, Primate, not quite. I have one more to ask of you."

"What is that, dear?" she asked uncertainly.

"Were you there, Primate?"

"Was I where, dear?"

"Were you there to see Barall kill those men who came only to question him?"

"What? No, of course I wasn't there."

"Then how do you know Barall killed them?"

"Who else could have? Who else would have had any reason to?"

"What reason would Barall have to kill them? Could it be they were not sent to 'merely question' him as you suggest Primate?"

An uneasy and queasy feeling began forming in the pit of Arkadi's stomach. This man was not here to get questions about his faith answered; he was here to question the faith itself. He seemed to know things, or at least to suspect things that even she wasn't quite willing to think.

"Perhaps," she said slowly, thinking her way through the quagmire in which she currently found herself, "he wasn't willing to be questioned and resisted their attempts to arrest him. Perhaps they didn't even get that far, and he simply attacked them."

Barall simply shook his head. "One man against so many? It seems unlikely that a simple priest, an archivist's assistant, would be able to do that," he answered.

"Were you there?" echoed Arkadi, her tone sarcastic.

"Yes, Primate, I was," he replied simply, removing the brown covering robe. His pale green robes matched the Comfort's robes exactly, but still it took several minutes before the Primate and crowd grasped what was happening. Shouts and calls erupted from several throats at once: the Primate calling for guards; the people calling to each other to do something; guards yelling at everyone in general.

Through it all, Barall remained standing calmly in the center of the aisle, staring fixedly at the Primate in her pristine beauty and shimmering blue robes. Around him, the three priests of his circle and Riordan took up positions of protection, doing nothing more than standing around Barall facing away from him, toward the milling crowd.

"You see, Primate," Barall started calmly. Though his voice was calm and he spoke evenly, he could be heard over the cacophony around him. People slowly subsided into silence. "You see how, even now, I am only following the seven basic pillars of the faith of Endomar."

"There are only four …" she broke in.

"Seven!" shouted Barall, losing his calm demeanour for the first time. "I was, as you indicated, a simple Acolyte. But I was an Acolyte assigned to the archives of the cathedral. I have conducted research for you, Primate, as you well remember. I have found evidence of three additional pillars of our faith. Sacrifice, humility and patience all have equal places alongside knowledge, experience, compassion and honor in our worship. I have found evidence of additional six other gods and goddesses, who along with Endomar, reign over us all. What would my honor and knowledge have me do? What would you have me do?"

Arkadi was purpling with rage at this impudent young man preaching to her in her own temple. The guards were being impeded by the mass of milling people and their own distance from Barall but if she could stall long enough they would eventually be able to reach him and end this once and for all.

"You should have taken your findings to the Emissary," she stated matter of factly, sounding more composed than she felt.

"To the Emissary?" he demanded incredulously. "The man who had Comfort Vance, my guide and mentor, killed for his beliefs, the same beliefs that I now share? The man you have just admitted sent guards after me to 'question me'?"

Barall started walking toward the dais and Arkadi, ignoring the curses of Riordan, Cerrok and the others as they moved to stay close to him.

"Are these the same guards, Primate, who attacked me without warning or provocation, seriously injuring one of my companions? The same guards dressed not in the white on purple of the Emissary's men, but in plain and simple brown cloaks?"

"I have done nothing but try to bring knowledge and choice to all people, Primate, and yet the Emissary seeks my death. Twice now, he has sent men to kill me, and twice I have been lucky enough to have faithful friends close enough to me to help. Blood has been shed, I am sorry to admit, but not a single drop has been spilled because we wished it. It is entirely on the hands of the Emissary."

"The Emissary is the Chosen of Endomar, and the one to whom the people look for ultimate wisdom," stated Arkadi weakly. "Surely you are mistaken."

"The people look to Endomar for ultimate wisdom," corrected Barall. "That wisdom is delivered from Him to the Emissary and down through you and your Comforts to the people. None of these people know the Emissary; they know only you and what you tell them."

By now, Barall had reached the edge of the dais and stood looking up at Arkadi. The sun beat down on them both, coming in through the huge circular window high above and behind Barall, so that they stood in the center of a halo of light. The face of the Primate was tightly clenched, the skin drawn across it in fear and uncertainty, as she looked down on the man she had just railed against in her address. This man spoke eloquently and convincingly of his faith, and yet he also spoke about crimes apparently committed by their leader. While it was true that the Emissary's policies lately seemed harsh and radical, he was still the Emissary of Endomar and was to be followed and obeyed.

"Please, Primate. Let us be friends and discuss this before things get too far out of hand," said Barall.

She looked down to see Barall standing beneath her, one hand stretched out to her, reaching up as if in supplication. The sun sparkled off her medallion, sending glints of light in all directions as the circle rose and lowered with her breathing. In contrast, Barall's circle was caught in the shadow created by his own body blocking the light from the window. The signs were too clear to ignore.

In silence, Arkadi turned and walked off the dais, deeper into the temple, leaving Barall standing alone with his hand outstretched to her.

♋

"You tried, son," said Destrin laying a comforting hand on Barall's shoulder. "Truly, there was little hope you could convince her completely."

"I failed completely though," came the despondent reply.

"Not completely, I think," said Dalis softly.

Turning, Barall saw the entire crowd of worshippers was still inside the temple. They had watched him and his small group in silence as Arkadi had left. Now they stood or sat where they were, as if waiting for something more to happen. Already, this had been a most remarkable service, truly the most exciting one in a long, long while. Whispers and mutterings could be heard now and again, as neighbors asked one another if that really was Barall. They were questioning everything they had just heard and were eager to learn more.

Looking to Destrin, Barall raised an eyebrow in a silent question of his own.

"It would be a shame to miss such an opportunity," smiled Destrin.

A grin of his own creased Barall's face as he turned and hopped up onto the now-empty dais. "My good people," he started. "My name is Barall, and you have already heard a lot of rumors about me, so why don't I tell you what I am really about?"

With much scraping and muttering, everyone resumed their seats.

"First, let me introduce Cerrok, Priest of Xelteran, God of Greed."

One hand pointed toward the handsome Cerrok, who somehow managed to look down on everyone in the room from his position at the foot of the dais. The hand then moved to indicate the melancholy-looking Dalis. "And this is Dalis, priest of Sleonde, Goddess of Love and Loyalty."

"We would all like to talk to you today …"

# Chapter 18

*"Human beings, who are almost unique in having the ability to learn from the experience of others, are also remarkable for their apparent disinclination to do so."*
*Douglas Adams*

Several days after the 'great address,' as it was now being called, it was a much-changed camp of the circle that was being dismantled. The citizens of Laufrid had turned out in hoards to hear them talk and all seven priests reported an increased interest and dedication in their respective deities.

It was a bittersweet moment for Barall for he found renewed energy in the discussions of faith and the lost pillars with those who came seeking his counsel but it was tinged with regret at his failing to convince Arkadi. Inwardly he knew he was being ridiculous; that it was impossible to convince everyone, but it still rankled that even when presented with the near-incontrovertible proof, the Primate turned to the cathedral rather than the people around her.

Their success was such that the members had each selected subordinates to remain in Laufrid to continue preaching their respective faiths. The circle was going to move on to another of the larger cities. No one knew which one, the feeling being that the Emissary likely had spies of his own, and there was no point in announcing to him where they were going. If what Destrin and Stein had told them was true, then the Emissary was planning things in the name of the faith of which people should be aware and Barall was finding it hard to remain focused on the goal of returning all of the gods to the people of the world. More and more, he caught himself worrying about how to stop Caven.

*Dear Endomar*, he prayed silently. *Please grant me the wisdom to do what is required and the stamina to see it through to whatever end you have laid out.*

His prayer concluded, Barall returned his attention to the here and now. He was sitting in his tent, the only one not yet taken down, Gibson's diary in his lap. Across from him sat Destrin and Stein, both men dressed for traveling in simple brown shirts tucked into pants that were, in turn, tucked into hard, black boots.

The two men both came to 'advise' the circle. What they were to advise on, or whether either truly had the goal of enlightenment in their hearts, probably only they knew for sure. What Barall did know was that, together, these two men had the political and religious acumen he sorely needed.

"I would like your thoughts on what to do now."

As if the statement un-corked the bottle, both men began talking at once. This was obviously something they had been thinking about for a while and had just been waiting for the chance to talk. It was a sad testament, Barall realized, that they had to be asked before offering an opinion. Destrin was all for traveling directly to Anklesh and confronting the Emissary directly. "It should be done now before the Emissary is able to fully amass and train his army."

The king's envoy agreed but took a different course. "That is true, Wisdom, but a good thing has been started here in Laufrid. The common people are behind Barall and that momentum should be used to gather more support before the Emissary is confronted."

The discussion ranged back and forth with both sides making relevant and telling points. Sitting back, Barall remained silent, content to merely listen. But he was also conscious of the time and the need to get moving, so at a lull in the conversations, he interjected his own thoughts. "Your points are all valid, but you're both suffering from the same double vision I am. The purpose of the circle is not to unseat Caven but to return knowledge and worship of all seven gods to the people."

"Doing the first accomplishes the second," replied Stein immediately, with a wave of his hand as if to brush away Barall's concerns.

Beside Stein, Destrin slowly shook his head, his long black hair swaying with the movement. "No. No it doesn't," he said, speaking to Stein. "He's right. We've both been focusing on what we consider the biggest threat to the well-being of our own interests, not the purpose of the circle as a whole."

Destrin paused as a new thought occurred to him. "Which is the problem all around, isn't it? Caven and the entire church are only looking out for themselves. The church takes in donations at every service that are supposed to be used to help the poor and needy. Instead we build bigger, grander, more expensive temples, and drape our ceremonies in gold and the richest fabrics."

"And buy armies?" suggested Stein quietly.

Destrin cut off the sharp retort before it left his lips, and simply nodded instead.

The sting of Stein's words was lost when he took up Destrin's thought. "And the king is not blameless either. Really, who is? Fantastic parties, the choicest foods, servants, lavish estates. My apologies, Barall, Destrin," he finished, his voice barely above a whisper.

"There is no need for apologies, my friend," said Barall. "None of us can claim to be perfect, can we?"

"No," agreed Stein, "perhaps not. But we can definitely provide better advice than we have so far."

❧

The group set out an hour later, making their way south in the general direction of Lake Xear. What had started with only seven people, each a follower of a different god, had grown to over a hundred as every village, town or city the circle visited gave up some of its citizens who found within themselves the need to leave their homes for a journey with an unknown destination. Men, women and children now streamed away from Laufrid. On their backs, in carts, and in wagons, they carried food and any meager possessions from which they could not part. Sacks of grain, fruit and hard biscuits made up the bulk of the food, but there was also cheese, cured and salted meat, raisins and an assortment of vegetables. There was also a range of livestock accompanying them. Driven by boys with long, supple sticks, or languishing in makeshift pens carried on wagons, were cattle, pigs, chickens and ducks, and one, lone, scruffy-haired dog.

They were a motley assortment that trekked their way south, away from Laufrid's gates, along an overgrown and little-used path until even that ran out. By the time the sun was touching the horizon they were all tired and foot-weary.

The entire camp was ringed with the wagons and carts to provide a kind of balustrade. There was no indication that there was anyone around, let alone anyone with ill intent, but it was better to be safe than sorry. Barall was grateful for the chance to stop and rest for a while. He had ridden a horse, a mild-mannered, dappled gray mare that had been given to the circle by some of the citizens of Laufrid, but eventually gave that up when he became too sore to ride any longer. Now, aching too much to sit or stand, he lounged on one side in front of the fire.

He had used the day to speak with each circle member, Destrin and Stein, as well as Rillem. With each he had spoken at length about their thoughts for the future, both the immediate and long term. The talk with Rillem was particularly enlightening given the man's modest life to date. He held himself in fairly low regard when compared to the others. Rillem was honest enough with himself to know that he was not the man to raise the clerist knights out of its infancy.

"I'm a simple man, my lord," Rillem said to Barall. "I believe the Goddess Aronya called me to follow you that day, to watch over you and what you're trying to do."

There was nothing Barall could say to that. He could not dispute a goddess sending visions or urges to her followers; he had received something similar from Endomar that led to this moment.

"You and the Circle placed me in charge, but I only do it because there is no one else."

Barall smiled. "That describes us all, Rillem."

"Perhaps, but I…"

"I understand, Rillem. I truly do, and if that is how you truly feel, I may even have a replacement for you. But I have a job for you first, if you don't mind."

Rillem's face broke out in a huge grin at the news, quickly replaced by a look of guilty sadness at how Barall would interpret his happiness. "My lord, I'm sorry," stammered Rillem. "I am deeply honored of the trust you have in me, but I know nothing of protection and very little of fighting. Our success in saving you was more, I think, your blessing and the goddess Herself, looking down on us, than any skill on our part."

His words came out in a rush, almost too fast for Barall to catch. Once his hearing had caught up with Rillem's tongue, he recognized the truth of what he'd been told. Every one of the group who had followed him and Destrin, and then defeated the men who attacked them, were common, simple folk. They were no better or worse than any other man or woman, high or low born. It did make them untrained in soldierly ways and perhaps, lacking in the knowledge of what is required to protect themselves, the circle, and the goal itself.

"Perhaps you should talk to your own members? I happen to know you have some former soldiers and guards registered already. I'll ask Tella and Venick if they can help with advice or training until you find someone to replace you."

"Thank you, my lord."

"Now about this special job…"

℘

The circle, their two advisors and Rillem, still in his role of captain of the clerist knights, met to discuss where they were heading next as the moon was rising. The night was warm and clear with the crickets and other night insects sending their serenade into the night and the brightness of the first, early stars dimmed only by the wafts of smoke from their small fire. The scents of dirt and grass were carried to them on the intermittent breeze, bringing with them the omen of rain for tomorrow.

The talk, so far, had been disjointed, with each person arguing for their own opinion, not even listening to each other. There were, however, only three sides. Half of the group, Destrin, Seskia, Venick, and Cura suggested they head toward Wilrien. It was the largest city after Anklesh, and farthest away from the cathedral and the Emissary. "It is a large city with a history of distancing itself from both the king and the Emissary if it benefited their citizens to do so," said Seskia.

"And given its distance, it could be the Emissary's arm hasn't quite reached that far," added Cura, her body language conveying her confusion at being in the odd position of agreeing with Seskia.

A rude sound escaped from Cerrok. At the angry glares, he turned his most charming smile onto the two women. "I find it doubtful, in the extreme, the Emissary would not have control of all his temples," he said with his white teeth gleaming in the firelight.

Even as Seskia returned Cerrok's snort, her green eyes narrowing with menace, Cura's breath caught in her throat. Before Seskia could release what would surely have been a scathing retort, he continued in his beguiling way.

"By taking a route through Erskin on the western shore, which is nearly the size of Wilrien, we can reach a major trading port. Erskin sees merchants not only from all over Cherilla, but the rest of the world as well. From Erskin we can take a ship, south along the coast and avoid having to trek through the Guara to reach Mordrum. And, Mordrum is another large city," he finished smugly.

The Guara desert covered nearly the entire southern third of Cherilla. Its endless waves of shifting sands were abutted to the west and south by the equally endless waves of the Qeter Sea and to the east by the Chiac River Chasm. The chasm was a deep rift, like a crack in the world itself, at the very bottom of which raged a wide, wild river. The three natural features, wonders unto themselves, made Mordrum extremely difficult to reach. With the inhospitable location, there was little doubt as to why the people of Mordrum were hard and secretive people who rarely ventured very far from their desert.

"Mordrum," shuddered Destrin. "A difficult place for a priest."

"Perhaps," said Dalis, "but then Caven may believe we wouldn't think to go there."

Seskia repeated Cerrok's rude comment, not bothering to back it up with an explanation. The discussion degenerated from there.

Barall sat among the circle, lost in his own thoughts while the six members argued around him. Finally, it was the normally soft-speaking Stein who called for quiet. Already, Stein had taken Barall's advice of keeping focused on the true goal to heart. It was a struggle to avoid creeping out of the narrow confines of the circle's purpose for his mind wanted to return to the issue of dealing with Caven and the actual physical threat he posed.

"We must work together, toward the common goal," he said when order was finally restored.

At those words, Venick's head snapped around to watch Stein behind narrowed eyes.

Suddenly, Stein appeared nervous and uncertain. He ran a hand through his normally well-groomed hair, mussing its neat appearance. Catching himself, he smoothed it back into place and settled on running a thumb and forefinger over his moustache and beard.

"You seem nervous, Stein," growled Venick uncharacteristically. Venick's grouchiness was normally reserved for the young, but he appeared to be expanding his rage.

Chuckling awkwardly, Stein replied, "Not nervous so much as out of my element. My role in coming here was to learn about you and your purpose and to advise with the aim of ensuring the realm was protected. I have traveled with you now for several weeks. I have heard talk of new gods and old. I have talked with each of you, and while I am by no means a devout man, I find credence in what you say. Enough that, while I am not going to be switching my allegiances," he said with a slight bow and the sign of the circle to Destrin, the ranking priest of Endomar present, "I will say that I do believe in all seven gods."

"Well thank you for that ringing endorsement," said Tella petulantly, "but why are you nervous?"

"Because," said Cura, "he's now focused more on returning the gods to the people than on the king's business, and it's scaring him to death because he's trying to do both."

"A man of loyalty," murmured Dalis in admiration, to which Stein shrugged.

"Fine then," said Tella, "So you're on our side now. What do you think we should do?"

"Both of your plans have merit," started Stein, "with advantages and disadvantages. So if we agree that no one solution will please everybody, yet both solutions are good ones…"

He paused, leaving his thought unsaid, letting them reach the conclusion on their own. It didn't come as any surprise to him when Barall reached the end first.

"You think we should split up and do both."

# Chapter 19

*"Good people do not need laws to tell
them to act responsibly, while bad people
will find a way around the laws."*
**Plato**

The ink of the letter in Lassand's hands was stained from his tears that had splashed down upon it as he first read it. Even now, nearly a month later, the emotions were just as strong. The difference was that now the sadness had been replaced by a deep, burning, anger.

The Emissary had been true to his word. Troops had marched out of Anklesh, heading toward everything village-sized and larger to root out … what? Caven's ludicrous vision of hereticism and lack of faith?

It was madness to think anyone, let alone the church itself, could force faith onto the people, especially if those people weren't very religion-focused in the first place. Lassand wasn't under any delusions that every person in Cherilla believed in Endomar. Even those that did believe showed it in different ways. Strength of faith was like strength of body; it came in different amounts in different ways. Those who believed the strongest, who felt the faith the deepest, joined the church to become its priests. But there were others, laypeople, who were equally strong of faith. That difference seemed to be something the Emissary couldn't grasp. There were people working within the church that didn't have anywhere near the amount of faith as those to whom they preached. Caven, in particular, fell into that category.

With a rueful shake of his head, Lassand sighed deeply at his own foolish lack of insight. How had he been so blind to not see that man's true nature? Always, Lassand had thought himself to be a good judge of character. When it had come time for the Wisdoms to select a new Emissary, however, he had been completely taken in by what had come out of Caven's mouth, and not listened to what was spoken by the soul.

*We're all paying for that mistake now,* he thought sadly. There was no way to remove a sitting Emissary within the pillars of the faith. They were stuck with Caven unless they could figure something out.

Thinking of the pillars brought Virez's latest missive to mind. Returning the Emissary's edict to his desk drawer, Lassand crossed to his bookcase and withdrew a special book from a shelf. Hidden within its binding was the last letter he'd received from Virez. It was dangerous to have it here, but Lassand deemed it worth the risk. All her other letters had been burned with the issuance of the edict, it being prudent to destroy them. This last, however, arrived only yesterday, so was too new for him to have fully absorbed everything it said. So, he kept it, hidden, until he had time to review it further.

Virez, in her position with King Zithius, was Destrin's contact to provide information. They had all decided that it would be safer to provide any reports through her, rather than trying to get them to Lassand directly. It appeared Destrin was greatly enamored with Barall. The earliest reports had been guarded, yet informative, detailing what Barall was preaching on behalf of Endomar, and on the other priests travelling with him. Now, though, it was obvious that Destrin was a "convert" to Barall's side. Though his letters professed neutrality, the Wisdom lamented the three lost pillars, openly admired Barall's wisdom and clarity of purpose, and hinted at acknowledging the six other gods.

From his relatively safe haven at the cathedral, Lassand really couldn't fault Destrin, or Virez who showed similar feelings for Zithius. Both had been used more like pawns by the Emissary, abused and controlled with an iron hand, than he, Lassand, had been. Not to say that either had to have a dominating person in control of their lives for them to feel useful. It was just that anyone with a new idea, who offered even a modicum of freedom, would be seen favorably.

Of more interest than Barall's religious thinking was the boy's apparent ability to call on Endomar to grant spell-like blessings. He had healed Destrin after the Wisdom had been wounded by the Emissary's men. That would make it the second time Barall had saved someone, if Zithius' report from his son could be believed. The use of priestly spells was something Lassand had a passing interest in. He had found the old stories of fighting priests, leading armies into battle with powerful spells and weapons mesmerizing as a child. In truth, though he would admit it to no one, those stories were part of his draw to the church in the first place.

*Why couldn't it be true?* he thought to himself. Legends and myths got distorted over time, but at their core was a kernel of truth. The real question was what was the truth here? Was it that priests once held such positions of honor and power to actually lead men into battle, or that they could cast spells? With the appearance of Barall, it seemed both might be true, but the Emissary was taking things too far with his edict. Rolling Virez's letter back up, Lassand stuffed it carefully back into the spine of the book and returned it to its place on the shelf. With a last look around to make sure everything was as it should be, he left his rooms, not bothering to lock the door behind him.

The cathedral was built like a fortress with one large building surrounded by seven towers, each large enough to hold four good-sized rooms around a large central room. Lassand made his way down the winding stairs in one tower lost in thought. Around him, the cathedral was alive with activity, Initiates and Acolytes scurrying out of the way as he swept past, robes swirling around him. Like a gracious lord, he acknowledged each one with a nod for those he didn't know and a few words of thanks for those he recognized. Whispers followed him, heads bent together to argue about the Wisdom and his status, and whatever other rumors were currently going around.

Used to this behaviour, he did his best to ignore it, but it was unusually irritating today as thoughts of the Emissary's edict darted around like lightning inside his head. He, Virez and Destrin were definitely in contravention of it, indeed, they were likely the main focus of the hunt, which was why they had to be so careful. Virez and Destrin, to be sure, but also Stein and Zithius, were all in this, with no end in sight.

Suddenly, he could see where Destrin's admiration for Barall came from. If they had a clear goal in mind, and acted to accomplish that goal, the circle of seven was well ahead of the Wisdoms. Truly, what were they trying to accomplish? Was it to oust Caven? If so, why all of the subtleties of spying and intrigue? Even Lassand, a priest for more than thirty years, could think of easier, more direct and permanent ways of doing that. Was it to help Barall and his circle? That didn't seem likely since, Lassand anyway, didn't know Barall other than that he was an Acolyte of Vance's. Vance had been a good man, hard working and dedicated. Hindsight showed that Vance wasn't as crazy as it was first believed, and probably not as dangerous as the Emissary declared. If that were true, then was Vance's suicide to be believed?

Questions and more questions raged within him, each one

leading to more, but always coming back to 'what should I do now.' He sat in a common room off the kitchen in the main building, a plate of cold bread and fish untouched before him. His elbows rested on the table with his head hanging in his hands as he sought the answers he desperately needed.

Someone squeezed into the bench behind him, bumping him slightly.

"Good day, my lord," came the whisper in words couched for his ears alone.

Nokya!

Instantly alert, Lassand looked around the nearly empty room as much as he could without moving his head.

"Good day to you, child," he murmured back. "I was beginning to despair of hearing from you again."

She answered around a mouthful of her own food. "It is hard to get away. The circle of seven consumes his thoughts until there is little else."

"Indeed? I wonder why?"

"Why?"

"The circle is a concern, but not so utterly destructive to us that it should enthral him so."

"Yet it does. He plots their destruction, rails at them and beneath it all, fears them. Why, I don't know."

Lassand stayed silent. Nokya took the opportunity to ask a question of her own.

"You seem troubled. Is all well with you?"

A small snort escaped from Lassand. "I am troubled. There are too many mysteries with too many questions and not enough answers. I find myself at a loss as to what to do."

She wanted to turn around and comfort Lassand. He had found her living on the streets and comforted her when she needed it the most. The help she gave him now, spying on the Emissary, was part returning the favor and part her own sense of honor, instilled in her by the Wisdom and her faith in Endomar.

"When I was a girl, first trying to understand my father and what was happening to me, I ran away. I met an old woman who took me in and got me to tell her what I was feeling; that I didn't know what was happening or what to do."

Lassand listened silently. It was rare that Nokya spoke of her past, and never about her family.

"She told me that when she didn't know what to do about a problem, she would try to find out the truth behind why the problem was happening. Usually that would help her to realize something she didn't know before. Does that help?" she asked.

"It does, my child," came the answer, "it certainly does."

❦

When the church of Endomar was still in its infancy, the cathedral was built on an island in the middle of the Bay of Fasada. It was designed to be intimidating and imposing. The Emissary at the time, a woman named Tarrin, oversaw the last of the construction, which had spanned five decades. She drove the workers hard, pushing them to exceed even their own expectations and abilities and as a result, the cathedral was finished earlier than expected and Tarrin was hailed as a heroine.

That was the official story told. The reality was entirely different. Tarrin was not just intimidating, she was a hard, cruel, even brutal taskmaster. Workers, driven too hard for too long were tired and made mistakes for which they were punished with beatings or imprisonment. Others died as a result of their mistakes, falling or getting hurt too badly to be healed. To hold the prisoners, Tarrin ordered the creation of dungeons in the very bowels of the cathedral. Once they were built, she filled them with all manner of people for all manner of crimes. Rarely were there trials, and even more rarely did any of her guests leave alive.

These thoughts skirted through Lassand's mind as he made his way through the cathedral. The Emissary had ordered the imprisonment and questioning of those his soldiers deemed to be faithless, so following Nokya's advice, he was on his way to visit those dungeons, wanting to see for himself what was happening there. As Nokya had said, problems often required perspective before a solution could be developed.

Being underground, on an island, the dungeons were lower than the level of the water outside, so they were dank and dark, the air smelling of algae. Patches of tar or plaster spotted every wall where water had begun to seep into cracks in the mortar; he had to splash through so many puddles, his robe was wet up to his calves.

The dungeon was not empty. Seven men and two women languished there, appearing, at least to Lassand's inexperienced eye, to be in good health. They didn't talk, but merely stared at him with unflinching eyes. Any questions he asked were answered curtly, using as few words as possible, so he left feeling no further ahead than before. Obviously, the Emissary had followed through on his promise to seize citizens, but it didn't look like they were being mistreated. It didn't help that they wouldn't talk to him, though for that implied a huge mistrust of the church and the clergy, and Lassand didn't blame them at all. At the moment he, himself, had an equal mistrust.

❦

"My lord, may I have a word?" Lassand asked.

The Emissary looked up from his desk in his private rooms, and Lassand took an involuntary step back. Caven's appearance had changed dramatically over the last few months, and more so over the last week. He had been a very handsome, charismatic man, with chiselled features, who took great pains to maintain an immaculate appearance, always with washed and brushed hair, clean nails and neatly tailored and fresh clothing.

Now everything was changed. He had a haggard, hunted look about his unshaven face; his normally bright, brown eyes were sunken with dark smudges under them like he hadn't slept in days and dark hair stood straight up from his head, far longer than Lassand had ever seen it before. The eyes were the worst though. There was fear within them, and uncertainty as they darted around the room, looking anywhere but at Lassand, as though he was afraid to look into the Wisdom's eyes.

Shock and pity filled Lassand and he was unable to voice the issues he came to discuss. The Emissary had withdrawn more and more from the daily activities of the church. He attended the regular services every twenty days, but remained in the background.

With the council of Wisdoms disbanded, the work fell to the Primates and from them to the Comforts and now he could see why. The Emissary looked terrible, and worse, didn't seem to notice or care.

Thankfully, Nokya entered at that moment.

# Chapter 20

*"An elder Cherokee Native American was teaching
his grandchildren about life. He said to them, 'A
fight is going on inside me … it is a terrible fight,
and it is between two wolves. One wolf represents
fear, anger, envy, sorrow, regret, greed, arrogance,
self-pity, guilt, resentment, inferiority, lies, pride
and superiority. The other wolf stands for joy, peace,
love, hope, sharing, serenity, humility, kindness,
benevolence, friendship, empathy, generosity, truth,
compassion, and faith. This same fight is going
on inside of you and every other person too.' They
thought about it for a minute and then one child
asked his grandfather, 'Which wolf will win?' The
old Cherokee simply replied … 'The one I feed.'"*
**Anonymous**

Venick did not sleep well during the entire trip south. His dream
of the circle's destruction came to him each night, tormenting
and torturing him every time he even thought of closing his eyes.
*Coward,* he thought to himself as he lay awake inside his tent. He
berated himself for not speaking up when Barall voiced the plan to

split the circle. They would have believed in Venick's dream. After all, one of his dreams had proven true already, even if they hadn't been able to figure it out before it was too late.

A lantern burned softly beside him, its low light feebly fighting against the shadows within Venick's head. It, like so many other things, was a gift from the people of Laufrid following the revelation the Emissary had attacked the circle. In fact, every place they had visited since had offered the circle something. It seemed that more and more people were willing to listen to them, to hear what they had to say if nothing else, especially since the Emissary's edict was proclaimed. If there had been no unhappiness or discontent with the church of Endomar before, there certainly was now.

The guards must have been sent out weeks before the edict was proclaimed for no sooner had the last echoes died than the purple tabards of the Emissary's guards appeared in every village, town and city throughout Cherilla. There had been a lot of preparation for this declaration, and a lot of spying on the common people as well. That was obvious to all.

Unfortunately, for the Emissary, the common people did not take kindly to being spied upon. As the priest for the god of strife, Venick revelled in the current goings on, and even fancied he could feel himself stronger, more powerful than ever. Malnoch was not a god who espoused spell use, preferring His priests to use their wits and wiles over magic. Seeing the powerful miracles performed by Barall and Cura, Venick sometimes envied them and wondered what he could do with magic as the chaos the Emissary was causing served to increase Malnoch's own power.

The sun crested the horizon just then, and the voices and sounds of a new day came slowly to Venick. Another sleepless night had come and gone. The only thing Venick felt was a sense of exultation at the uncertainty spreading over Cherilla, and his own self-recrimination. With a sigh, he blew out the lantern and made ready for another day of travel. They hoped to cross the Ramer River today, about two days south of the town of Casban, located on the southern shores of Lake Xear. There had been nothing remarkable about Casban so the group hadn't tarried long, preferring to continue on toward Wilrien quickly. Everyone wondered how the other group was faring. By now, they should be nearing their first stop in Erskine.

❦

The sound of the horse, running hard, reached them before the rider came into view. When the horse and rider finally crested the hill, still some distance away, the group visibly relaxed, allowing hands to ease away from weapons. The rider pounded directly to the center of the long caravan where Barall, Cerrok, Dalis and Tella, as well as Zithius' man, Stein, rode together. A young girl, perhaps fifteen, pulled up in front of them. Though young, she had proven to have the sharpest eyes of anyone currently riding with them, and often rode as lead scout. She looked a little shaken from her wild ride, and sat atop the horse sucking in huge lungfulls of air. The horse, too, danced and shook its head, picking up on its rider's nervousness.

Dalis walked over to the horse and lay a huge hand on its neck, immediately quieting it so it stood passively. Without removing his hand, Dalis looked then to the girl. "Peace be to you, Chaudrin," he said gently in his deep rumbling voice. "You have news to share?"

Chaudrin, all long brown hair and eyes, seemed caught in Dalis' own brown eyes. She stared only at him, and spoke as if they sat alone together in a cozy parlor sipping spiced tea. All nervousness and fear seemed to have blown away on the breeze.

"Yes," she said calmly, "there are a number of people waiting ahead."

"How do you know they're waiting, or that they're waiting for us?" demanded Cerrok, his tone and body equally haughty.

Chaudrin, however, ignored him, all her attention focussed on Dalis.

The huge priest smiled over his shoulder at Cerrok, then re-asked the question though in much gentler tones.

"They are dressed and geared for hunting, though they haven't moved in hours. They post guards, but only to the west, while everyone else looks to the east. They are waiting for someone, and likely know we are travelling from Laufrid."

Silence hung in the air at the announcement, everyone absorbing the news with equal measures of unease and resignation. They knew the Emissary's edict would cause them trouble, but it seemed too fast to have happened already since they had travelled from Laufrid on a direct route toward Erskin. The edict had hit Barall particularly hard and he had fallen into a deep lethargy, not talking to anyone and seeming to not care for anyone either. The other circle members each tried in their own way to draw him out, but without success. They all looked to Barall now, out of the corners of their eyes as he sat in his saddle, shoulders slumped and eyes downcast with all the appearance of not having heard anything Chaudrin had said.

Reactions were as mixed as the people. Dalis seemed sad, while Cerrok frowned so fiercely it was a wonder his face didn't crack from the strain. It was stoic, stone-faced Tella who acted, ordering the scouts to continue watching this group, from all sides, while the main body continued slowly on. Ignoring the scowl from Cerrok and the raised eyebrows from Stein, she allowed the horses and wagons to pass her by. Reaching out, she grabbed the reins of Barall's horse as it moved to follow its fellows. Before the shocked eyes of those nearby, she reached across and slapped Barall across the side of his face, the sound ringing through the air.

Shock registered on every face, Barall's most of all as a hand flew to his cheek, the red imprint of Tella's hand already clearly marked.

"Snap out of it!" she demanded fiercely.

Impossibly, even greater shock showed on Barall's face. "Huh?" he said dumbly.

Too fast to stop, Tella reached out and grabbed the front of Barall's robes and pulled him to her until they were practically touching noses.

"You are the leader of this circle. Start acting like it."

Her piece said, Tella released him and wheeled her horse around to join the passing crowd.

For a moment Barall sat in still-stunned silence. Then, as the realization of what had happened truly sunk in, anger suffused the rest of his face red. With a scowl lingering on his still stinging face, he urged his horse to follow after Tella. For perhaps six steps, he pursued her, before his apathy reclaimed him. *What did it matter, anyway?* he thought to himself. *The Emissary has won.*

The horse, sensing its rider's mood change, slowed accordingly, allowing itself to be guided by its fellows. For long minutes, there was tranquility around Barall; no noise could penetrate the shroud of apparent capitulation that surrounded him. To anyone looking, Barall was the picture of defeat, with no hope or point of even continuing on.

In actuality, nothing was further from the truth. The Emissary had surprised them all with his edict against Barall and the circle. None of them had expected the Emissary to turn against his own. Endomar was the God of Wisdom, the searcher for enlightenment and truth, yet what Caven was doing was the destruction of free thinking and honesty. He was doing nothing but hurting innocent people, imprisoning them for thinking, subjecting them to "questioning" and turning people away from Endomar more efficiently and thoroughly than the circle ever could.

The struggle raging through Barall now was not one of giving up, but of how to proceed without more innocents getting hurt. He was deeply troubled by the edict, not only because of the threat to his friends and the people, but also to Endomar. Things were being done in His name that were reprehensible, and should be denounced by every member of the church, down to the newest Initiate.

But they weren't. Troops, unknown even to the Wisdoms, marched on the people, taking delight in the terror they provoked, despite wearing the colors of the Emissary. With all this arrayed against him, Barall could find little hope, and no way out.

As this thought came to Barall, with its accompanying wave of hopelessness, he sensed he was not alone. Against the pressure of lethargy that seemed to weigh him down, Barall looked up to see Stein riding beside him. The advisor watched Barall openly, his face expressionless, unblinking and direct. Barall quickly broke contact, turning his head and lowering his eyes. No one else need be bothered by his shame, by his duty to the people of Endomar and Cherilla.

"You are not in this alone, my lord," said Stein quietly now staring straight ahead.

When Barall didn't even acknowledge he'd heard, Stein plunged ahead. Though possibly breaking his self-imposed covenant to remain detached, Stein felt himself drawn more and more to this boy who was revolutionizing an entire religion: whether the result would be demise or salvation was yet to be seen. The words Barall spoke were heartfelt and honest, with no desire for acclaim or ambition. That, in itself was odd for Stein, a man used to the intrigue and manoeuvring at the king's court, but more than that was Barall's steadfast devotion to Endomar, while never speaking ill of any of the 'new' gods. He was a man, seemingly content with his faith, never questioning or doubting his god, secure in his belief … or was it knowledge? … of his place in the world.

"You always have options, my lord," continued Stein, still content to merely ride beside Barall and apparently enjoy the scenery meandering by.

Not expecting an answer, Barall shocked Stein, and himself, by retorting, "I don't see any."

"No? You have friends and allies, my lord. Not only within your circle, divided though it is at the moment, but there are folk awaiting you ahead, spurning Caven's edict and the threat his guards pose. You have truth on your side, as well as conviction. And perhaps more than anything else, you have the Emissary."

At Barall's confused look, Stein smiled and continued.

"The Emissary, through his own actions to stop you and bring the people to his side, is doing more to push people to you than anything you could have done on your own."

Stein's words worked their way through Barall's clouded mind, their meaning sparking the first embers of hope to flare. His next statement, however, seemed eerily ominous, and oddly prophetic: "All you have to do now is keep preaching … and not get caught."

# Chapter 21

*"Shake off all the fears of servile prejudices, under which weak minds are servilely crouched. Fix reason firmly in her seat, and call on her tribunal for every fact, every opinion. Question with boldness even the existence of a God; because, if there be one, he must more approve of the homage of reason that that of blindfolded fear."*
*Thomas Jefferson*

The origin of the name of the town of Apajue was not something its residents were proud of. Apajue was a large mining town located deep in the Tekil Mountains that ranged across the southeast area of Cherilla. Local history said that when the first miners arrived carrying their baggage and supplies with them, their leader's youngest child spied the ripe apples dripping from the trees and immediately began screaming for apple juice. Of course, young as the child was, still learning his words, the sound came out more like appa-jew, and so the town's name was cast.

While the miners weren't happy with the name, they were fiercely independent and did not take kindly to fools. The circle members who entered Apajue were eyed warily but respectfully. They kept to themselves at first, but as they were constantly looking over their shoulders and jumping at every sound, it was obvious they were running from something. The group was definitely odd to the townspeople: the two women and two men did not appear to be couples, for instance, or the ladies to be high-born or rich enough to warrant body guards. Three carried weapons easily, though not openly enough to be warriors. Even odder, the fourth, unarmed, man was obviously not the leader of the others, for he frequently deferred to them.

It was the second night since the strangers had entered town before anyone bothered to approach them. Their curiosity had been held at bay long enough, so Garzon, the bartender and locally recognized news gatherer approached the table.

"Evening, strangers," he said, tugging a nearby chair over with one foot and settling his bulk into it without waiting for an invitation. Venick and Seskia masked their surprise with looks of open hostility, scowls deeply creasing their faces. Destrin and Cura were not so openly hostile, but even they couldn't keep the surprise off their faces.

Without pause Garzon began speaking, "Now don't be thinkin' you're all surprised. Apajue's not all that big a place that a troupe of strangers don't gather no notice. We may only be miners but we still notice when strangers show up."

"We didn't mean any …" started Destrin lamely.

"No offence taken there, stranger," broke in Garzon, "We's not the most friendliest of folk here, either, but you been here two days now, lookin' o'er yer shoulders and not talkin' to nobody. If yer lookin' fer trouble, you won't find it here. But if yer bringin' trouble, you sure will find it here."

The group looked at Garzon for a moment and the stern, almost demanding look on his face.

Again, it was Destrin who spoke first. "We are not looking for nor bringing trouble. We are simply travelling and talking to people."

"You ain't talked to no one," stated Garzon flatly.

"And you seem to know a lot about us," interjected Cura, her statement softened somewhat by a coy smile.

"True. We may be a bit o' a backwater group, but we watches and listens, and takes care o' our own. And *we* talk."

"And what have you found?" asked Destrin.

Garzon didn't answer for a moment. He looked around the room, pulling his thoughts together before speaking. With a slight nod to himself, he seemed to come to a decision. Rather than answer, however, he raised one beefy arm and snapped his fingers. Immediately, mugs of foamy ale were placed in front of everyone, followed quickly by huge platters of food. Steaming fish and roasted carrots, potatoes and more sat enticingly in front of them. Digging in with vigor, Garzon indicated the others should help themselves as well. Hesitantly, everyone took portions and began to eat. When they had, Garzon began.

"You be members o' this 'circle of seven'," he said directly causing more than one to choke on their food. "This don't bother us none," he continued smoothly, "you's is welcome to talk to whoever'll listen. I should warn you we don't put much stock in gods, preferring what's real."

Despite himself, Venick couldn't hold his tongue any longer. This town was obviously well aware of them and why they were there. While his own faith often used subterfuge, guile and outright lies to further the cause of Strife, honesty and directness could do so equally well.

"And who are you to speak for the town?" he asked, with more than a little edge to his voice. "And how is it you seem to know so much about us?"

Rather than take offence, Garzon seemed amused. "In truth, we don' know nothin' o' you, other than what we seen. You didn't hide out once you was here; you don't seem to want to do us bad, for most of yer people are still outside; most important though, you ain't tryin' to tell us what to do or think. Not like them soldiers who was here."

Stunned silence met Garzon's statements. In answering Venick, he added even more questions. This quiet town, hidden within the Tekil Mountains, was much more than met the eye. The townsfolk obviously worked together and looked out for each other.

There had been no indication of soldiers, or even guards, anywhere in the town, as if the Emissary's edict wasn't even being enforced here. Each of the four looked around nervously, as if expecting to see purple tabards come rushing out at them.

"There are soldiers here?" asked Seskia sharply.

"Not no more, Lady."

"Where are they then?"

"They was asked to leave," Garzon said simply.

Perhaps it was the way in which he said it, or the fact that he wouldn't say anything further, each one of them knew without a doubt, that this town had evicted the Emissary's guards from their walls. The incredulity must have shown on their faces, for Garzon laughed, the cheery sound breaking the tension. "You be surprised there be no soldiers here? Yes, they comes here and tries to force us to answer they's questions."

Garzon's voice turned cold as he spoke of the soldiers, marching into the town as if they owned the place themselves, immediately, starting to separate residents and put them to the question. Because religion was unimportant to the townsfolk and their work in the mines, the guards started seizing buildings and possessions and imprisoning the people within them. Shortly thereafter, the soldiers were overwhelmed by an uprising of the entire town. Weapons were taken from the soldiers as well as the fancy tabards, and the entire lot were taken from the town, down out of the mountains and released.

"They kicked out the soldiers," breathed Destrin incredulously. "They just kicked them out and locked the doors behind them."

To Destrin, a Wisdom and man used to following orders and rules, what the people of Apajue had done was beyond comprehension. How could they have done it, without a thought of the reprisals, of the Emissary's anger and retribution? The statements were a mantra to him, as if repeating the obvious would somehow lead to an answer.

The others, Seskia, Cura and Venick, though thinking exactly the same thing, were growing tired of Destrin's continuous laments. They had removed themselves from the tavern, and retired to the rooms Cura and Seskia shared to discuss what they had just learned. The rooms were small, with two simple beds, and a shared washstand, there was barely room for the four of them to sit without banding their knees together. They had sent word already to the representatives sent by Dalis, Cerrok and Tella who, along with the rest of the camp followers, and the ever-present clerist knights, maintained a vigil in the camp set up outside the walls. Only two knights remained in the town, one each at the top and bottom of the stairs leading to their rooms.

"Enough, Destrin," snapped Seskia. "We know. We were there and heard it too."

"I cannot believe it," said Destrin, "the sheer audacity of it. Do you think they really understand what they've done?" "The real question," said Seskia smoothly, "is, do you? Can you see beyond your own faith, and this town's disobedience of your leader? Can you see the benefit of this to the circle and our purpose as a whole?" Shaking his head again, Destrin waved his hand dismissively at Rettela's priestess, "Of course. The people are not submitting to the Emissary's whims and are standing up for what is right. But, Seskia, can you see that the people throwing off the Emissary's edict may not be all that *you* think?"

"Meaning what?" asked Venick.

"Ousting the guards may simply have been the town standing up for themselves. It may have nothing to do with support of the circle or the movement at all."

⚬⚬

"How can you support a god who wants nothing but conflict and chaos?"

The shouted question was met with a chorus of agreeing shouts. The question was expected, for it was asked every time Venick spoke, just like the others each had questions that cropped up with each new group to whom they spoke.

Venick smiled for he hadn't even finished telling the small crowd of miners about Malnoch when a particularly thin miner, covered in the dust and grit of his trade, voiced the question. The problem was that these miners were openly belligerent and challenging. They had already heard, judged and sentenced the Emissary's guards, so a wrong move or statement here, and the circle would suffer the same fate.

"Malnoch does not demand chaos; chaos without purpose or end serves nothing and leads to destruction. No, my friends. Strife is struggle and competition. Strife is working to overcome that which cannot be defeated. All this leads to progress, for with the struggle to excel comes progress and the desire to excel further."

The crowd murmured at this, for it was a good and plausible explanation for the question, but just as Venick had come prepared for the question, the people of Apajue had prepared as well, and were not so easily swayed.

"Perhaps what you say is true," said a burly, squat man near the middle of the group, he, too, covered in rock dust and grime, and his voice sounding like rocks grinding together. "But to worship your god would mean avoiding a life of peace."

"Not at all," replied Venick, surprised at a new question, but also welcoming the chance to bring Malnoch to these people. "My friends, you are miners. You delve deep into the ground for things I don't understand and in ways I can't imagine. You struggle against the weight of the world to do so, and you struggle against old beliefs and methods to come up with new and better ways to do things. You barter and compete with outsiders who don't know, nor care, of your sacrifices to get this material out of the ground, to trade for things you need to survive. All of that is already strife. All of that is for the glory of Malnoch."

Venick realized he may have pushed it a little far at the end, but he could tell he was winning the crowd over. There were nods as he talked and he could feel the underlying hostility and tension leave the air. It seemed odd to him, that at that moment, instead of relishing the possibility of new worshippers for the god of strife, he wondered at how the others in the circle were faring.

๑

"The goddess of healing is a benevolent and kind Mistress," intoned Cura, her voice taking on a matronly sound. Unfortunately, the crowd of mostly women surrounding her were not taking kindly to what they considered a condescending tone.

"What need have we of any mistress?" came one shout.

Another one came right on its heels, "How can you travel with one who preaches the exact opposite of you?"

More and more shouts erupted from the formerly pleasant women and Cura recognized that she had obviously offended these women somehow. With the revelations of Garzon the night before, it was plain this town protected their own, and an offence to one was made to all. She could not afford to lose this opportunity to gain new followers. With accusations flying at her from all directions, Cura clamped down, hard, on her rising temper. It absolutely would not do to lose control now. Outwardly, she kept her face smooth and calm, her hands clasped lightly in front of her.

It was a trick her mother, a priestess of Aronya herself before her death, had taught to Cura. It was difficult to remain tense and agitated if you had to concentrate on keeping a feather-light touch between your fingers and it worked now for Cura as she waited for the cacophony to die down enough that she could be heard. Eventually, the women recognized Cura's patience and quieted, if not calmed, down. This time Cura did not smile, nor speak pleasantly. She allowed some steel into her voice, to show strength and determination, she hoped, but also her aggravation at the manner of the interruption.

About to continue her prepared talk, Cura changed her mind at the last moment and hesitated. It was always risky to do what she was about to, but under the circumstances, the risk was worth the possible reward.

"Let's skip the sermon," she said at last. "Why don't I just answer your questions since you already have so many? Now, I didn't catch them all, but I'll answer those I did hear, and then you can ask me whatever you'd like. First, you don't *need* any Mistress. That is a choice each person must make for themselves, and no one can force that upon you."

Murmurs of agreement combined with nodding heads to show that at least they were willing to listen.

"Aronya, if you choose to follow Her, is not really a goddess of conscious decision. She is followed and loved because you feel Her in your heart and soul. She is there and, if we listen, She can teach us Her miracles, through which the sick or injured can be made well, rotten food made good or dirty water made clean. That is the path I follow. Not one that my head told me to, but the one my heart required."

"Which I can also say, is probably true of Seskia, the follower of Rettela, goddess of disease. You asked how I could travel with one who believes the opposite of me, whose goddess is in eternal struggle with mine. The answer is simply that I follow my heart. Seskia and I will likely never be friends, never reach a common understanding of the other, but, this quest we share is for the betterment of both our beliefs and, I feel, for the world."

The gathered women continued to question Cura for another hour, by the end of which her throat was parched and desperate for a drink. A proud looking woman, her hair pulled back into a severe looking bun sitting atop her head, handed Cura a mug and then offered a hand to help her down from the small box on which she stood. Cura smiled her thanks at the woman and was bringing the mug to her lips when the women stopped her with another question.

"Why, if you are a priestess of the goddess of healing, do you carry a weapon?"

Cura hesitated. This was something she had not anticipated, but more than that, she sensed there was more to this than a simple question, albeit a relevant and insightful one. This was a test of some sort.

Without knowing what she was being tested for, Cura decided to simply answer the question truthfully and directly. She handed the mug to another of the women who seemed almost as thirsty as she was, then turned back to the one who asked the question.

"The answer to that comes in two parts. The first part is simple, that I travel a lot and need to eat. The bow is the simplest and most efficient method for catching game. The second is not so simple to understand, for it's for protection. As I'm sure you can understand a female travelling alone would be easy prey to unsavory sorts."

"So you have killed," stated the woman who had handed her the mug, in a flat emotionless voice.

"In self defence or for the protection of my friends," returned Cura.

"But … you are a priestess," said one woman.

"You are a priestess of healing," said another.

Cura held up her hands to stem the tide of questions as more murmurs cascaded through the assembled women. At least now she knew what she was being tested about.

"I am a priestess," she called out, "but I'm also a person, just like you. If attacked, will you not fight? If a friend is in trouble, will you not help? But I sense this isn't the truth you're looking for. You question not the why of it, but the how," Cura continued waving toward the unstrung bow she had propped in a corner. "How is a priestess able to use a weapon and still commune with her goddess."

With a look around, Cura could see that she had guessed correctly, so with only a nod, she launched into her explanation.

"It is not so much a matter of 'can't' as it is of 'won't'," she started. "A priest is just like any other man, just like a hardened soldier can be kind. Most priests make the choice not to carry weapons or to carry only non-bladed ones, to bring themselves closer to their god. I take the position that I can bring the work of Aronya to more people alive, than I can dead."

❧

"Quiet!"

Seskia's shout cut through even the strongest throat to bring a sudden silence to the group. Perhaps a dozen men and women stood glaring at her as she stood, hands on hips, glaring back at them.

It was a much smaller group than was around Cura, or even

Venick, for the number of people interested in learning of Rettela, goddess of disease, was never large. The dozen that stood there were just as likely to disparage Rettela as they were to become one of the faithful.

Once she was sure she had been heard, Seskia ran a long-fingered hand through her short hair and took a deep, steadying breath.

"I would tell you of Rettela, but you will listen first. You cannot shout at me of Her 'evil' ways if you have not heard me first."

Already, Seskia could tell which person fell into which group: believers or doubters, just by the expression on their faces at her statement. Just as with Venick, she had come to expect certain things when she spoke to new groups and had come up with ways to deal with them.

"The goddess does not expect or demand sacrifices or murders, nor does She have us brewing and causing sickness throughout the lands. We study all those things and we try to learn what they are and how they work and where they come from."

"Why?" demanded a reed-thin man with oily hair and a pock-marked face. He looked nothing like a miner, or even a business owner, and to Seskia, he had the look of a thief and miscreant. She wondered how he managed to fit in with this crowd.

"Since when is seeking knowledge ever wrong?" she retorted, her expression remaining behind its stony mask.

"When it is used for something that is," came back the man's reply.

"True, but it's not the knowledge that's wrong, but what's done with it. Just like a sword or spear is not evil in and of itself, but turns evil with an evil wielder. Followers of Rettela are not poison-mongers or assassins any more than worshippers of Gefrin, the God of Strength."

As she continued to speak, Seskia methodically marked each person she considered likely to become one of the faithful. Pock-face was the most likely for it seemed evident he had been victim to an illness himself. Her words were meant to educate, but also to control the mob. Nothing she had said had been a lie. They did spend much of their time in study and learning, but they also used what they learned. There were always those in the world who would pay for the knowledge the faithful gathered.

❧

It seemed everyone had had a good day. Venick had just returned from the camp outside the walls of Apajue and reported that the representatives of strength, love and greed were equally pleased with the discussion they'd had. For now, spirits were buoyed by the expectation of new worshippers coming to their respective faiths. Even Destrin was happy, no longer feeling that their every success was also a loss for Endomar.

At last talk turned to what they should do next, and naturally the good spirits degenerated. The discussion ranged from returning to find the others, to staying in Apajue for a while longer, to continuing on with their original plan and travelling to Wilrien. Seskia, Destrin and Cura turned the issue over and over among them, the talk becoming heated at times. No one seemed to notice that Venick sat silently among them, a mug of ale still nearly full in front of him.

"We need to stick with the original plan," said Cura repeating her argument for what seemed like the hundredth time. "We agreed to travel to Wilrien. As one of the largest cities in Cherilla, we can't simply avoid it."

"Of course we can," snapped Seskia belligerently. "We have started something here, in this town. We should stay here and see what more we can accomplish. After that we can decide what to do."

"So because you've had a good day, everyone else is supposed to just stop with their plans and go along with you?" barked Cura.

"Better that than tucking tail and moving on and losing any gains we've made."

Destrin finally held up his hands as if to ward off an attack. "Ladies, please," he said pleasantly, "arguing like this won't get us anywhere. We've found a town that has both surprised us and given us hope for the success of the circle. We really should advise the others that the Emissary's grasp is not as strong as he thinks."

Both women started berating Destrin and each other, their voices getting louder as they tried to talk over the other. Again, Destrin held up his hands to stop the shouting.

"Perhaps we need to split up and go whichever way we think is best," he suggested.

"No!" exclaimed Venick, surprising the others not only with his vehemence, but that he was even still there, so silent had he been.

"We must stay together," he said somewhat calmer.

"What? Why?" demanded Seskia. "I think the idea is a good one."

"Yeah," agreed Cura, "why not?"

Venick hesitated before answering, unsure, now that he had spoken, how to voice his concerns. The others didn't know anything about his dreams, other than the single one he had shared with Barall and the others once Destrin revealed the Emissary had killed Percinal. Now that he was at this point, on the verge of telling them, he wasn't sure they would see the dream the same way he did. In his heart, though, he knew he was right. For too long he had carried the burden of the dream and what it portended. Before he could change his mind, he told them of the dream without leaving anything out. He told them of the boats with their various religious symbols on them; of the violent storm that threatened them all and how, only when they seemed to work together did the storms abate.

When Venick finished, he was somewhat breathless, but also with a feeling of the 'rightness' of what he'd done. It didn't matter what happened now, whether the others believed him or not, he had done the right thing. Perhaps now he could get some sleep.

❦

It was the misty landscape that marked the scene as a dream; the fuzzy edges that blocked the view beyond the area of importance. In this case that area was shown in exquisite, if indecipherable, detail.

The first thing of note was the circle made of solid gold that glittered brilliantly. The circle had no beginning or end, but that was not what was odd about this circle, though, and not what made Venick toss and turn in his sleep. Whirling within the circle was a smaller circle, spinning around and around. As the small circle bounced off the confines of the larger one, Venick noticed something else. Following behind the small circle, trailing after it no matter what direction it went, were six other symbols: fist and concealment, heart and crossroads, and tree and death.

Two by two, each pair followed the small circle as it sought escape from the larger circle …

# Chapter 22

*"Follow your instincts. That's where*
*true wisdom manifests itself."*
**Oprah Winfrey**

The walk down to the cathedral archives seemed to take longer and longer each day. Wisdom Lassand plodded slowly along the now well-known corridors, meeting no one as he walked.

The cathedral was an empty, quiet place these days as more and more priests abandoned the home of Endomar's church. Initiates, normally coming to the cathedral in a steady stream had slowed to something less than a trickle. So it was that Lassand could walk from his rooms in the residence wing, down several levels to the Emissary's office and then further down to the archives seeing no more than a few priests. In fact, there were more guards than priests to be seen these days.

He was now a regular visitor at the archives, the guards barely glancing at him as he passed between them into the dim, musty chamber beyond. Moving directly to the table several aisles over from the main corridor, he found the books and scrolls he had pulled out last night exactly as he had left them. Smiling at his own paranoia over being caught researching other gods, he seated himself, carefully lit the lamp on the table and picked a scroll at random.

Lassand had been coming to the archives every day for the past couple of weeks, for as long as his duties permitted. To the Emissary, he had reported some minor, insignificant successes, which actually wasn't a lie for he had found a few old letters, written from a Comfort to his Primate that made some vague mention of another priest and suggestions of other religions. Dutifully, he turned these over to the Emissary, knowing what was going to happen. Seeing the pages burned in front of him, Lassand nearly fell to his knees and begged Endomar's forgiveness right there. Of course, these pages didn't prove or disprove anything, which was why Lassand had turned them over to Caven.

What was astonishing was that Lassand actually found proof of the existence of other gods – acknowledgement by ancient priests that the circle of seven was right and Caven was wrong. This proof was found in numerous diaries and letters that belonged to well-known and historically significant priests, some of Primate rank. The most fruitful discovery came about a week ago. In the late hours after moonrise, Lassand came across an innocuous-looking book, bound in simple, plain-brown leather and tied with rotting twine. Titled only *Marell*, Lassand plucked it from the shelf expecting it to be another diary for Marell had been a Wisdom.

He knew her name immediately when he saw the book, and since she was alive around the time of Gibson, it was worth a look. Good thing, too, for within its pages, Lassand found more than he was looking for.

⁕

Of all the people who had tried to talk him out of his sullenness, and all the arguments given to him, the one that stuck with Barall came from a girl still in braids, old enough to understand what was going on, yet young enough to not care.

As Barall and his half of the circle were approaching the group camped outside Erskin, three days after the group had first been spotted by the circle's scouts, the girl stayed in the background. The Erskin group was made up of a number of citizens from the city who, concerned about the safety of Barall and his friends, announced a hunting trip to the guards and soldiers who had entered and taken over the city. There were soldiers everywhere, and most everyone the group knew had been questioned and had friends who had gone missing, so there was no love lost on the church. While Barall certainly appreciated the warning, and told them so, he also asked that if the church was no longer in their favor, why would they bother to warn them at all? Dalis and Stein gave him surprised looks out of the corner of their eyes. Both were happy he was at least talking, but his choice of words left something to be desired. Still, the question was valid and they held their breath for the answer.

"We hold no love for the church, but the church is not Endomar," said an older man with more white in his hair than black. "With all due respect to your friends, Lord Barall, we all worship Endomar. And with all due respect to you, what the Emissary is doing is wrong."

They continued to talk for a while, exchanging ideas and thoughts not only of the circle's next move, but also of Sleonde, Xelteran and Gefrin. Then, as each group made ready to go their separate ways, the girl asked the question that stopped Barall short.

"Why do you fight?" she called.

With that one question Barall's own doubts and questions vanished with the wind. He sat straighter atop his horse, shoulders squared as he turned to look at the girl. In a voice returned of its strength, he answered the question as straightforwardly as it was asked.

"Because it's right. Would it have been better to do nothing because the fight was too hard? You have seen what the Emissary is capable of, and all we have done is talk to people. The Emissary is supposed to be the guardian of the faith, of the people, of the balance. The world is currently out of balance, yet the Emissary is doing all in his power to keep it that way. Why do I fight? I fight because, at the moment, there is no one else; because my mentor and friend was killed by the Emissary, simply for proposing a difference of opinion. I fight because it is what's needed to make things right."

❦

"You are mad!" hissed Cerrok. "Despite your fancy words this afternoon, you have learned nothing from Vance."

"Hardly," retorted Barall, "Vance taught me just about everything I know and as I said earlier, we can't stop now just because it's hard."

They were camped barely a stone's throw from where they had met the Erskin delegation to figure out what they should do now that they knew the extent of the Emissary's influence in the city. The arguments started immediately with as many opinions as there were people … until Barall announced he was going into Erskin.

"Are we never going to talk to people again?" asked Barall. "Are we never going to enter a city, town or village again? Because that's what it's come to with the Emissary's edict."

"Yes, but …" started Stein.

"No buts!" broke in Barall. "I am not asking anyone else to come with me. In fact I think I should go alone. That way, should anything happen, no one else need suffer for my decision."

No one spoke for long moments, each looking at Barall to try to find the flaw in his logic, other than the obvious one of wanting to enter a city occupied by soldiers desperately searching for them all.

"Why do you need to do this?" asked Dalis, his deep voice startling everyone in the silence.

"Caven has done all this in search of me," Barall answered immediately. "The God of Wisdom would not condone this. Endomar seeks balance and knowledge, and Caven is suppressing both. What kind of representative of Endomar would I be if I cannot witness for myself, the evils and horrors inflicted on the people? I *must* do this. I have to see what's being done in His name so I can know how to defeat it."

❧

Thanks to their new friends, Barall had a rudimentary knowledge of the city's layout. Behind a high, thick wall, broken only in two places with a wide gate, the city itself was spread out in blocks around a wheel. The hub of the wheel was the residence of the governor, lord of the city who answered only to the king. Surrounding his walled and guarded home were the houses of the rich as well as the high born; those whose birth, brains or ingenuity brought them power. Progressing outward, the areas became progressively poorer. It moved from the marketplaces where goods were sold through the shops and stores to the ware- and storehouses owned by the merchants and traders, until, finally, abutting up against the walls, were the houses of the poor.

Barall entered the gate of Erskin dressed in full priestly garb, complete with the green Comfort's robes and a prominently displayed circle of Endomar. He expected to be stopped by the guards and questioned, and had prepared for it. Following him, a careful step behind and another to the left, was Arion, a clerist knight who had volunteered to attend Barall. The knight was in the guise of a simple guard, following and keeping watch over a Comfort of Endomar. He was dressed simply in loose fitting shirt and pants, with no markings or insignia, with a sword hanging easily on his hip.

With Rillem gone, the management and training of the remaining clerist knights had fallen on Arion's shoulders. True to his word, Barall had kept out of the affairs of the knights. He knew that Tella and Cerrok both offered guidance but for the most part, Rillem was in charge. Arion trained his group in weapons and 'guardianship,' or, as he called it, the ability to protect someone while appearing innocent, or even invisible, to others. Without hesitation, he had nominated himself to watch over Barall on this mission.

"We're only going to look around," Barall had said. "If we can talk to the Primate stationed here, Quince I think his name is, so much the better, but we will try to avoid the guards if we can."

Unfortunately, it was not to be that simple. Within steps of walking through the gate, they were accosted by no fewer than five purple-clad warriors. They quickly surrounded Barall and Arion, positioning themselves to effectively cut each man off from the other.

"May we ask your business here, My lord?" asked one, dressed as a sergeant, his tone just shy of being disrespectful.

"I should think not," sputtered Arion immediately stepping into his role of the pompous, overly protective guard of a Comfort. "The Comfort does not answer to the likes of you."

The sergeant stiffened at Arion's words. His black eyes narrowed, his bushy eyebrows nearly met in the middle, and his hand moved almost casually to rest on his sword hilt.

"Perhaps I need to rephrase the question," he growled. "What is your business in Erskin?"

As Arion sputtered indignantly, the remaining soldiers tightened their circle around them. Barall held up a restraining hand and turned to the sergeant.

"There is no need for violence, sergeant. We are here to see Primate Quince. The matter is of some urgency, though, so if you don't mind …"

He made to move past the soldier when the sergeant reached out and laid a restraining hand against Barall's chest, barring his way. Raising his eyebrows in wonder, Barall looked down at the hand and then up at the sergeant.

"Is there something else, sergeant?" he asked in a voice far calmer than he felt.

"The Primate is not available at the moment," he started. "What was your business with him?"

"Not available? What does that mean?" asked Arion.

"I'm not at liberty to say. Let's just say the Primate is not as faithful as he should be. Now, for the last time, state your business."

"Unfortunately, sir," started Barall, "I, too, am not at liberty to say. I can only tell you that it is official church business, at the order of the Emissary."

Mention of the Emissary seemed to mollify the soldiers somewhat, but the sergeant still barred their way. He stood regarding Barall directly. Slowly, he lowered his arm and with a deferential bow, offered to escort them to the interim Primate.

Neither Barall nor Arion believed the 'offer' could have been refused.

⸎

There were several churches in Erskin, the city being large enough to support more than one, and the sergeant led them to the largest. Here the Primate maintained his office, or had, before he became 'unavailable.' The church was an imposing building, as most of Endomar's churches seemed to be, made of roughly dressed gray stone and standing at the end of a wide street, dominating the view along the entire way. Two wide double doors, intricately carved with a design that was indecipherable from where they stood, bisected the front wall. High above them, above even the second stories of the nearby buildings, was a window.

The window was a massive circle carved out of a single block of stone. Rather than a simple, plain window, the architects had used more stone to include a design. Two pieces, mirror images of each other, started together at the very bottom of the circle and flared upward at an angle, becoming further apart as they ascended. When those arcs hit the upper part of the circle, both sides curled gently toward each other to join again in the middle, below the height the ascending lines had reached.

One of the soldiers, seeing Barall eyeing the window, thought to question him. "Odd that the god of wisdom would mar his own symbol that way," he said. "What do you suppose it means, Comfort?"

Taking on the look and tone of a patient teacher, Barall simply gave the answer he knew the man expected, even though Barall was beginning to suspect it meant something else entirely. "The circle is there, good sir, around the perimeter, encompassing all. The design on the inside, believed to be that of a shield, is meant to signal us to be on guard against foolishness and pride."

"Hm," said the guard. "It is hard to be on guard against such things though, is it not, my lord?"

"Most difficult."

"Which is the hardest?"

"That would depend on the person."

"For yourself, then, my lord."

"It would depend on the situation."

The sergeant smiled and gestured to his companions. "This situation, my lord."

Barall turned to see the five soldiers now joined by an equal number of more soldiers, closing ranks on he and Arion again. "Is there a problem, my son?"

"How long did you think it would take?" sneered the sergeant, coming so close that Barall could smell his rotten breath. "Did you think to simply walk into this city without us spotting you? Is that pride or foolishness, Lord Barall?"

❦

Barall woke up dazed and confused, unsure of where he was or what had happened. There was a mind-numbing pounding in his head that was making it hard to think, and a searing pain running across his left thigh he couldn't identify. He moved a hand to his head first and felt a large bump there, extremely tender to even the lightest touch. Moving next to his leg, he found a long, straight cut, blood soaking his robe and still oozing slightly. Clamping his hand over the cut, a wave of nausea swept over him.

Slowly, as he regained his senses, he was able to take in more of his surroundings. The ground on which he lay was cobbled, not dirt, and there were sounds coming from all around him. What did it mean? The sounds were chaotic, rising and falling at odd intervals. There were voices: angry, in pain, triumphant, cursing.

*Too much, move on,* Barall told himself. What did the cobbles mean? He was outside, but somewhere inside. A town, no, a city.

Erskin.

And with that tiny piece of knowledge, it all came flooding back.

❦

Almost as one, the ten soldiers surrounding Barall and Arion drew their swords.

"W-what is this?!?" squealed Arion, fumbling pathetically to draw his own weapon. Finally getting it out of its scabbard he spun around trying to figure out which way to face since there were swords all around them.

Snickering came from more than one soldier until abruptly cut off by the sergeant. "You will come with us," he said, making it an order.

"No, actually he won't," stated Arion firmly, no longer the useless hireling he had been pretending to be. The act had accomplished its desired effect. The guards had underestimated him and not only allowed him to draw his weapon, but to look around and mark the number and location of each of the enemy. Now with the situation getting dire, it was time to protect his charge. The sword was held confidently and unwaveringly, despite the odds arrayed against them. Barall could only hold his breath in fearful hope that what was about to happen, actually would not. Too much blood had already been spilled. Arion's whisper to him shattered that hope. "Have faith, my lord. We only need to survive until help arrives."

"Help? What?" blurted Barall.

The soldiers, mistakenly thinking he had been calling out for help, laughed roughly. "There is no help for the likes of you, zealot!" sneered one.

As if that were the cue they were waiting for, half of the soldiers moved forward, swords leading the way. Arion sprang into action, becoming a whirlwind of arms, legs and sword. Somehow, miraculously, he was able to fend off the advancing soldiers, striking down two in flashes of steel and blood with as many strokes. The others were held back by his spinning blade and their surprise at his skill and speed.

A roar from the sergeant sent every soldier into the battle, but they all approached more cautiously this time. Arion was in constant motion, gathering a second sword from one of the fallen soldiers. At eight against two, even Barall could see the futility of continuing the fight. Two more men lay dead, their lives lost because of him. This was what the Emissary's edict had wrought, where his leadership had brought the church, but it was not what Endomar stood for.

Pulling himself straight, Barall grabbed the circle that hung around his neck. Closing his mind to the raging battle around him, he began to pray for Endomar's blessing, hoping he wouldn't be too late to help Arion. The prayer was on his lips when the soldier slipped past Arion and slashed Barall across the left thigh. The pain of the sword tearing his flesh as easily as the meagre robe covering him forced a scream of agony from Barall's throat and he collapsed to his knees. With a malicious grin, the soldier slammed the hilt of his sword against Barall's head, sending the priest to oblivion.

෨෬

Now that he was awake again, Barall tried to figure out what was going on. He rolled carefully to his knees and took in a scene more horrifying than any he could have imagined. Men were fighting everywhere, their cries and curses echoing madly off the enclosing walls abutting the street. There were more than a dozen of the Emissary's soldiers now, more than before he had been knocked out. Fighting them was an assortment of men and women. Some were dressed plainly in simple pants and shirt while others looked like they had come from the city. One man was dressed as what looked like a butcher, He even held a meat cleaver in each hand.

As he watched the melee in front of him, Barall heard Arion's voice shouting orders toward someone. Only now did Barall notice his guardian knight.

How Arion had managed to survive, he couldn't understand. The knight had obviously fought hard for he bled from several cuts and he was breathing heavily. He stood over Barall, still, guarding his charge from any of the soldiers who might come after him. If Arion was here and sending orders ... Barall boosted himself to a sitting position and looked out over the fight. Yes, there were Bryce and Camon, and over there was Elsar, knights, all of them.

They must have followed him into the city, disobeying his orders to follow what they perceived to be the higher purpose of protecting the circle.

An overwhelming sense of pride and purpose filled Barall, along with guilt for he had placed these men and women in this danger. They fought for their lives now, because he had insisted on entering the city. Everything that was happening was his fault – and Caven's. Between them, the people were not being instructed or educated or guided in Endomar's ways but were being forced to take sides that would only continue to clash.

It was all so clear now, so easy to foresee: war was coming. Not one to overthrow a tyrannical overlord or a king debasing his people, this war would be based solely on religion; a battle of faith. Freedom of faith, in Barall's mind, but to those who followed of the Emissary's vision of the truth, it would be exactly the same. To them, they were the ones fighting for freedom of religion while those who followed the circle of seven were the ones threatening the faith's freedom. This issue had to be decided some other way, without the entire country being torn apart by it. If only he could sit down with the Emissary and discuss things; show him the proof of the six other gods and prove there was room, in fact a necessity, for all of them. Surely, they could come to an agreement.

That was it.

He would travel to Anklesh to meet with Caven. It was time for this meeting to happen, before any more lives were lost.

The battle had continued while Barall had been thinking, and bodies from both sides now lay, unmoving, on the cobbled street. From the blood pooling around them, it was obvious they were dead. *More lives to atone for,* thought Barall sadly.

"I need to help," he said aloud, moving to stand, though his leg screamed at him.

The prayer to bring Endomar's blessing to the knights and their allies came easily to Barall's mind again. It had worked in Laufrid and he was confident it would work here too. He shut out the pain in his head and leg; ignored the screaming of the wounded and the sight of the dead, but then, as he began speaking the words, they turned to ash in his mouth, the words dying on his lips before they could leave his mouth.

Running down the street toward them, swords already drawn were another two dozen guards.

Arion saw them too and, like a true knight, though he blanched at the sight, he stood his ground between Barall and the soldiers, gripping his swords tightly. Barall took in the sight of Arion and, in a moment of precognition, knew what he had to do. Moving to Arion, he grabbed hold of the man and spun him around to face him. Looking at him intently, his fingers digging into Arion's arms, Barall told him to run.

"There is nothing more you can do here," Barall said quickly. "Run. Get into the church and hide or duck out the back."

"No, my lord! No!" Arion argued emphatically.

"You will!" demanded Barall. "Only you can prepare the knights. I *must* go to Anklesh to see the Emissary. That is the only way this can ever end."

"They will kill you."

"No. They can't. The edict named me specifically so they will have to take me to the cathedral and the Emissary. You must take the news to the others. Let them know what has happened."

"Tell them that I failed and you have been captured, more likely killed, and that I ran without even trying to protect you?"

"Yes. No. I am ordering you away. NOW!" You must leave before they get here. This must happen for the end to come."

# Chapter 23

*"It requires wisdom to understand wisdom: the
music is nothing if the audience is deaf."*
**Walter Lippmann**

The small camp was torn down and deserted less than an hour after Arion stumbled into Cerrok's tent dishevelled, distraught and thoroughly disgusted with himself for, as he saw it, abandoning Barall.

After being ordered away, he'd shouted the retreat to his men, praying they heard and obeyed, as he sneaked into the church, the huge doors decorated with the odd symbols Barall had pointed out. The Comfort had grown excited at seeing the carvings within the large window over the doors. Arion didn't see why. To him it looked like a deformed circle caved in to a point at the top and pushed out to another point at the bottom.

Quickly exiting the dim church through another door, Arion stole a change of clothes, discarded his sword and, as nonchalantly as he could, made his way through the city and out the gates on the side farthest from the camp. A long trek around the city during which he nearly faltered in the overwhelming guilt of leaving Barall and his men, brought him to Cerrok's tent. The priest's face registered a range of emotions: shock, horror and anger chief among them. In the end, Arion had to give Cerrok credit, for despite whatever he might personally think of Barall and his decision to enter Erskin, upon hearing what had happened, those opinions were put aside.

Cerrok ordered the camp to be struck. He then sent runners for the other circle members, for food and water for Arion, and lastly for a map of Cherilla. The camp sprang to life as the orders spread and Tella, Dalis and Stein converged on Cerrok's tent at a dead run, terror filling their hearts at what could have happened.

For the second time, Arion told his story, seeing almost the same reactions he had from Cerrok, only this time he added his own opinions on what to do next. "I have already begun planning the rescue," he stated simply, his expression almost daring them to disapprove.

"No!" exclaimed Cerrok ignoring Arion's look, focussing on Tella and Dalis. "Surely, the soldiers will be expecting it, as well as looking for us. They won't be so foolish as to think Barall was alone and they'll know the rest of the circle will be nearby."

"Agreed," Tella said. "I see the camp already breaking. That's good. They should be told to scatter, go in all directions and spread the word what's happened here."

A deep frown spread across Cerrok's face as Tella spoke. "Yes, yes. I was just getting to that," he said irritably.

"I'm sure you were," replied Tella smoothly. "Now, when the rest of the camp heads out, the four of us will …"

"… make our way east and north …" interjected Cerrok.

"… toward Anklesh," finished Tella.

The two priests stood glaring at each other, the tension in the tent palpable. Into this awkward anger, Dalis waded, "It seems the two of you are in agreement, but to journey all the way back to the hornet's nest, as it were, seems unwise."

Whether it was Dalis' slow method of talking, his large size, or the simple fact of asking the question, as soon as he started speaking, both Cerrok and Tella turned away from each other and focussed on him. He'd also carefully included the point that the two were actually agreeing on the plan.

They eyed each other suspiciously for a moment until Tella finally spoke. "The soldiers will expect us to come after Barall now, before they have a chance to move him. But, instead of doing that, we will move ahead of them to their most likely destination."

"Anklesh?" asked Stein doubtfully.

"Yes," nodded Tella. "It's a guess, but a good one. Barall is a Comfort of Endomar, the leader of the circle and the one most prominently named in the Emissary's edict. Out of all of us, Barall will be taken to the cathedral to stand before the Emissary."

Stein looked thoughtful for a moment, then began to pace. "Interesting," he said at last. "Very clever in fact. If we could get there fast enough, it's possible I may be able to offer additional help, too."

"Excellent!" exclaimed Cerrok, clapping his hands together for emphasis. "Arion, continue your rescue planning, but for somewhere in or around Anklesh and discuss your ideas with Stein. We'll try to get you information about how they're travelling if we can. Dalis, perhaps you can talk to the camp and explain what they're to do: pack, scatter, spread out and spread the word. Make no mention of what we'll be doing though. There's no telling what would happen if anyone got caught and the Emissary found out what we're planning."

"Tella," he continued, an oily smile creasing his handsome features. He tossed his head, his long blond hair falling down his back in sharp contrast to Tella's shaven pate. "Thank you for your explanation of the plan. We'll depend on you to arrange the supplies we'll need."

Tella's face grew hard, her blue eyes like flint. She crossed her arms over her chest, but Dalis noticed that both hands were fingering the daggers she always wore on her belt.

"And you?" Tella asked, her voice emotionless, cool, "what will you be doing?"

"Well, my dear," said Cerrok condescendingly, "I'll determine our best route to take and find volunteers to go into the city to gather information about Barall and any plans they have to move him."

Tella was unimpressed with Cerrok's taking on the role of leader and doling out tasks to everyone. He was only trying to better his own status, at least in his mind and those of his followers. As her anger mounted, Tella grew calmer and more focussed. The lines of tension around her eyes softened, and the muscles across her shoulders relaxed. To most, these would be good signs to see, but not so with Tella. Seeing them, Stein placed a restraining hand on her arm, hoping to bring calm back to her and stay her hand. With his eyes, he begged her to stay calm, but then he turned to Cerrok. "We shall do as you have suggested," he started. "After all," he continued, turning to Dalis and Tella, "we all need to work together if we're to rescue Barall and allow the circle to continue its work."

With slight prodding, Tella led Stein and Dalis out of Cerrok's tent, sending a scathing glare his way. The trio walked in silence down the path from the tent, not noticing the surreptitious figure enter the tent behind them. When far enough away Tella whirled on the two men, fire in her eyes.

"I will not take orders from that ... that ..." she sputtered.

"Pompous jackanapes?" suggested Dalis.

"Insensitive clod?" offered Stein.

Tella blinked in surprise, brought up short by the unsmiling comments of the two men. "What?" she finally managed to say.

The tension spent, everyone smiled, and Tella even laughed a little at herself. "Fine. All right. I suppose I'm overreacting a little, but that man boils my blood."

"His plan does make sense, though," said Stein. "It is unexpected and, therefore, has a good chance of working since the Emissary won't be able to plan against it."

"As long as the guards cooperate and don't simply kill Barall first," added Dalis grimly.

ⅭⅦ

The small, non-descript man entered Cerrok's tent as soon as the others left and had their backs turned. He was dressed the same as many of the camp's members, in ordinary browns and grays, and there was very little about him that would distinguish him, physically. He entered the tent and stood silently, waiting to be acknowledged by the priest.

Cerrok was bent over the map of Cherilla, studying it with all the intensity of a general planning his next campaign. When he finally stood, he moved away from the man at the entrance and poured himself a glass of wine. It didn't matter the hour of morning to him. What mattered was that things were finally starting to fall into place. That bitch Tella notwithstanding, Barall could not have timed things any better than if Cerrok had planned it himself.

Finally, still without turning around, he addressed the man. "Keep an eye on her."

With a bow, the man left as silently as he had come, leaving barely a ripple in the tent to show he had been there.

Cerrok drained his glass, and with a smile on his face, pointed down at the map, his fingertip coming to rest on Anklesh. "Soon," he whispered. "It will end."

ⅭⅦ

The lathered and exhausted horse caught up with them on the city-side of the Chiac Chasm. The gorge plunged down, deep and ragged, like the world itself had cracked and split open leaving a tear in the very earth. Far below, winding along the base of the chasm, right up to the steep sides on both edges, was the Chiac River. The waters of the river were fed from the Lake of Rain located high in the Tekil Mountains. As such, the waters rushed on in a frothing, churning maelstrom, fuelled by the drop from the mountains and the constricting confines of the chasm walls. Where the river itself was at least twice as wide as strong man could throw a small stone, the chasm walls flared outward as they soared upward. By the time the top yawned open onto the landscape, it had doubled its width again.

Across the span, a massive bridge had been erected. How or when it had been built, no one knew, but the bridge was the only way across the chasm without avoiding it entirely. The caravan had taken their time crossing, not wanting to put too much strain on the bridge, or themselves. At the sound of the horse, several clerist knights moved to positions at the rear of the column and drew their swords. A man came clattering into view and drew up short at the sight of the bared weapons. The horse stopped immediately and stood with its head bowed nearly to the ground, its sides heaving as it drew in great gulps of air.

"Peace, good sirs," said the stranger spreading his arms to show he was unarmed, "I mean no harm."

One of the knights sheathed his sword with a look to his companions and stepped forward several paces. "What has you riding so hard that your horse is dying beneath you?"

Before the stranger could answer, Destin and Venick rode into sight, coming to see what was happening. Catching sight of them, trailed by what were obviously two more knights, the stranger's eyes widened in shock. He then clapped his hands and started giggling maniacally.

A barked order from the knight following Destrin and the man closest to the stranger redrew his sword. He advanced on the man and levelled the blade at his chest.

"State your business, sir," demanded the knight of the stranger, only a slight licking of his lips truly betraying his nervousness.

The sword quelled the stranger's amusement and again his arms where held out, but instead of talking to the knight holding the sword, he addressed Destrin and Venick.

"You are members of Barall's circle?" he asked, offering a slight bow from the saddle. "I have been searching for you to deliver news of great urgency."

The knights murmured quietly with the priests for a moment keeping themselves between them and the stranger. Reaching a decision, one knight nodded and spurred his horse forward.

"I am Riordan," he said. "What is your news?"

"You are the circle?" pressed the man suspiciously.

Riordan narrowed his eyes as if judging the man before him. "Aye," he said at last.

"Thank the seven gods."

Murmurs and whispers erupted at the man's oath. Knights exchanged looks, and even Destrin seemed shocked, though he quickly smoothed his face to hide it.

"What did you just say?" demanded Seskia from behind Destrin, causing the older priest to jump in surprise.

"Your pardon, mistress," bowed the stranger, "but I thanked the gods for delivering me to you."

"Seskia, please," hissed Venick, "let Riordan do his job."

The priestess glared at Venick, but held her tongue as Riordan turned back to the stranger, a single eyebrow raised in invitation for the man to continue.

"I was told to find the second half of the circle and tell you that Lord Barall has been captured by the Emissary's soldiers in Erskin."

"What!?!" came exclamations from around the chasm, the shouts echoing weirdly off the steep walls.

"My lords, ladies, please," begged Riordan, never taking his eyes off the man. "Let us hear the whole story first."

Still atop his horse, the man explained Barall's insistence on entering the city, accompanied by a single knight, the battle and Barall's capture. "Lord Dalis bade me find you and recommend you make haste to Anklesh."

"Fah!" spat Seskia. "He is dead already. If not now then long before we could ever hope to reach the city."

"No," exclaimed Destrin and Riordan together.

"The Emissary will want him alive to question him himself," said Destrin.

"And the guards will parade their prize slowly through every hamlet between Erskin and Anklesh," added Riordan with a nod to Destrin. "We can reach Anklesh in time, but we must travel fast and light."

"Impossible," said Seskia. "It took us weeks to get here, and that from Laufrid."

Riordan didn't bother to answer, but turned away and began barking orders to the men and women of his knights. Like Arion, he had been recruiting and training the people that came to them. Now, as he got his people moving, the circle approached him. Before turning to them, however, Riordan released the stranger, telling him where he could find food and water. Finally, with that done and the man out of sight, the knight turned to the priests.

"We *can* reach Anklesh. The soldiers will dawdle and plod along for they'll have to pull a prison wagon; they won't risk putting him on a horse. They can't and won't kill him; they'll have to take him to the Emissary as Destrin said. But they can only move as fast as the wagon, and will put their trophy on display at every chance. We can take a boat along the Rainer River, just east of here, up into the lake of Rain. The Rainer is calmer than the Chiac, though the going will be hard and the lake juts to the north to the very outskirts of the mountains. What took us weeks to cross on foot, we can do in two days by boat. From there, it's hard riding all the way to the cathedral."

❧

The mood in the Cathedral was markedly different from that in the two parts of the circle. With just one, hastily written report, the Emissary turned from a dour, despondent man, who would as easily ignore someone as lash out in a verbal tirade, to a man who could almost be called giddy. He strode through the halls of the cathedral with a near constant smile on his lips, even warmly greeting those priests, guards and visitors, he knew.

Barely a week ago, the cavernous hall was mockingly near empty from its normally overflowing mass of worshippers and devotees of Endomar who clamored for seats at the Emissary's sermon. It wasn't that there were fewer believers, or that people's faith had diminished, or even that the Emissary had loosed soldiers into the city to question the people: it was the Emissary himself.

His sermons ranted about blasphemy and raged against Barall and his circle and the 'righteous vengeance' that Endomar would wreak upon those who did not follow the Emissary. Conspiracies were everywhere and behind every passing remark was deception and condemnation. His fear that the people did not love or trust him was being made truth by his own actions.

But now, with word coming of Barall's capture, everything changed. Reading the report of the arrest, Caven had grabbed Lassand by the arms and began dancing him around the room. When the Wisdom heard the news of Barall's capture, he was deeply shocked. Though he had never met Barall, he had come to think of the man as highly intelligent and careful so the news he had walked into Erskin, seemed foolish beyond anything he would have expected.

The books and documents Lassand had found several weeks ago had spurred him into deeper research. Everything he had found, while not great in terms of volume, was vastly significant in terms of its value. Barall and his circle were right and the Emissary was wrong. Such a revelation was difficult for Lassand to accept, for his entire life he had been taught that Endomar was the only god. Even now, despite what he had found, he questioned the truth of it. What was the need of any other god, after all? Wasn't Endomar enough?

Endomar taught about balance in all things: among the pillars of faith, between men and women, and so on. It was logical that a single god was not balanced, even neutral Endomar. There had to be evil if there was good, night if there was day. Similarly, if there was wisdom, there had to be its opposite.

The Emissary started outlining his newest plan. "We need to find the rest of this circle," he was saying. "The heretic was one of our own so the one we wanted the most, but the others are just as dangerous. I want the soldiers to increase their questioning of the people, particularly in the central region. That's where he was found, so that's likely where the others are. They've been going to every town they can south of here, so the people know damn well where they are."

"But, my lord …" started Lassand.

"I want a message to go to every Comfort and Primate to announce the heretic's capture. Those between Erskin and here are to denounce him in their sermons and start public displays condemning him when he is paraded through their regions."

"And he is to be paraded, Lassand," he continued. "Chain him up within the wagon so the people can see him. I want him on display to show what happens to any who defy me."

The Emissary was breathing heavily and his eyes were wide and staring. He was so excited and keyed up he couldn't stand still. His hands, too, seemed to be in constant motion, either waving in the air or wringing together.

To Lassand it was like the Emissary was a new man, with vast resources of energy that he was burning off. He spoke quickly, almost too fast for Lassand to understand, as if he had to get the ideas and thoughts out in order to make room for others. He talked about increasing the soldiers' duties, giving them more power, and of using Barall like a scapegoat for the church's problems. While Barall was certainly the spark, he only ignited the inferno that had been smoldering for a long time. The true problem with the church was its over-reaching presence throughout Cherilla; the power of the church had grown beyond ministering to the souls of the people into areas they should never have gone – like politics. Its leader, the man standing before Lassand now, was not only becoming mentally unhinged, but believed the people should worship and unquestioningly obey him, not Endomar.

Caven was still the Emissary, however, the man legally placed into power by the council of Wisdoms. There was no way to remove him, and no one to replace him. As Lassand saw it, his role was still that of an advisor, helping the Emissary to see different options that likely weren't being considered. If that advice could save the people, it would be best for him to maintain his role.

"Some suggestions, Emissary?" offered Lassand.

"Yes?" returned Caven, his eyes wide in eager anticipation of some new way to humiliate Barall.

"Perhaps instead of chaining the prisoner up within his wagon," he started, careful not to use Barall's name, "he could be moved to a central location for a day or two. Chaining him up could be seen by the people as being too cruel."

He could see the thought of being too cruel to Barall did

not concern the Emissary at all but at the same time the people's perception, as well as their own priest's perception, of the church, was of great importance. This was especially true if there were six new gods to compete with for the people's love and attention.

To appease the Emissary, Lassand offered him a carrot that would be too good to pass up. "By leaving him in the open, guarded of course, the Comforts will be able to speak to the people right there, while the people can see the prisoner in front of them."

The idea took hold of the Emissary as he could see the benefits of a static display area. "Good. Yes," he said nodding vigorously.

"Then, my lord," Lassand continued pushing his good fortune, "I think we need to consider recalling the soldiers from the field."

"What? No!" exploded Caven. But then, "Why?"

Taking courage from the fact the Emissary was at least willing to listen; Lassand explained that, really, Barall was the only one of importance. "The priests of these other gods have been around, presumably, for a long while and no one has listened to them or given them any notice until Barall joined them. It stands to reason that the people know and listen to Endomar. If His priest is removed, the other priests will either fade away, or, more likely, will follow Barall here."

A thin smile spread across the Emissary's face.

⚬⁄⊅

She ran down the hallway, any thought of dignity was ignored as her legs pumped as quickly as she dared. Her brown robes, normally kept pristine and neat, flapped wildly while the tan sash swung around her waist. Rounding a corner she could see two armed guards part way down the corridor. The guards saw her, too, and immediately drew their weapons. While this did not surprise her, she did stop several paces from them. Through gasps and panting breaths she gave her name and why she was there. While his companion knocked politely on the door and stepped through, the guard immediately in front of her stayed in position, his sword still drawn and held across his chest exactly parallel to the floor, like a barrier to prevent her proceeding any farther.

The woman took this time to improve her appearance by smoothing her robe and straightening her hair. The guard, moving from proper protocol gave her a nod of approval and a smile. She returned the smile and then waited impatiently, rocking from one foot to the other.

Finally the door opened again and the guard motioned for her to enter. Nodding her thanks and with a final smoothing of her robe, she strode purposefully through the door. Once inside, she paused on the blue plush carpet and allowed herself a moment to adjust to the room. The furniture was opulent and included a large desk of solid maple, and several comfortable chairs. Another door was slightly ajar off to her left through which she could just make out a huge, rumpled bed. It was a tidy and business-like room, despite the position of its sole occupant.

"Well, Virez," said Zithius pleasantly from one of the chairs where he sat reading from a sheaf of papers and sipping tea, "what has you running through the halls of the castle at such an early hour?"

Virez bowed politely to the king and stepped forward. "Something has happened," she said directly.

"So I assumed," he replied smiling. "Sit down and tell me what's going on."

Taking a seat next to Zithius, Virez waved away his offer of tea and looked him directly in the eye. "The Emissary's soldiers have captured Barall in Erskin," she said. "They plan on carting him back to Anklesh to be placed at the Emissary's feet."

Zithius became immediately alert. Though he didn't move from his chair, his body became tense and he focussed directly on Virez, the papers in his hand forgotten.

"When?" was all he asked.

"It is unclear," she replied. "The orders are for the soldiers to parade him through every village between here and Erskin, and the Comforts are to use him in their sermons. Likely several weeks at that pace."

"Good. We have time to think of what to do. Now, Virez, I need to know your loyalties."

"My lord."

"No, Virez, for once and all, you need to choose. Are you with Caven or Barall?"

He talked with a calm voice, but with earnestness she had rarely heard before. He also, she noticed, offered her a choice between two of Endomar's servants, neatly excluding himself from the equation.

"My loyalties are in question?" she asked, no small amount of indignation and bitterness creeping into her voice.

"Everyone's loyalties are in question," Zithius snapped. "The entire country is rising up, ready to boil over like water left on the fire. The people are divided between the circle of seven and the Emissary. With the edict and the soldiers he sent, the people are moving away from Caven, but he still holds control over the soldiers. So again, Virez, I ask you, where are your loyalties?"

"It seems your sources are as sharp as ever, my lord. The Emissary has grown increasingly cruel and self-centerd. His sermons are more about how we should obey him, instead of leading us in the ways of Endomar. But more than anything, his treatment and opinion of the common people, that they're no better than ignorant fools to be led around by the nose like cattle, tells me who to support. My loyalty is with the circle."

The tension in the room deflated noticeably and Zithius relaxed and let out the breath he had been holding. His eyes closed for a moment as he took several more breaths. He truly hadn't known how Virez would respond to his challenge since she had grown up in the church to become a Wisdom. Normally, reaching the upper echelons meant a deep devotion, not only to Endomar, but to the Emissary, as well. The Wisdoms chose their leader when a current Emissary died. Caven had been selected and elected by the council, not that long ago, less than a decade, yet in that time, he had disbanded the council, been rumored to have ordered the removal of dozens of his own people and was now going after the common people.

"Perhaps we can arrange something to either hurt Caven's plans, or help Barall. With the soldiers out of the city, something might be able to be arranged," he said.

"On that issue, though," Virez added, "the soldiers are all being recalled."

"What?"

"Caven has ordered the soldiers, all of them, to return to Anklesh."

"My god," breathed Zithius. "They're all coming here?"

"Yes."

"But they're spread all over the country right now?"

"Yes."

"Hmmm."

"You are thinking something."

"Indeed. There is potential for us to help. Let us get some breakfast and discuss it, shall we?"

# Chapter 24

*"We learn wisdom from failure much more than from success. We often discover what will do, by finding out what will not do; and probably he who never made a mistake never made a discovery."*
**Samuel Smiles**

The figure that huddled in the corner of the wagon was a miserable looking wretch of a man. He lay curled into a ball among the dirty straw covering the floor, his once clean robe now a mess of grime, blood and vomit. As bad as he looked, though, the smell was even worse. The wagon pitched and bounced over the uneven road, yet the figure never moved, seeming more dead than alive until only the keenest of observers would be able to notice the green eyes still alert and aware.

The wagon had been Barall's home for the past several weeks. He had been taken, immediately upon his capture, and held in the city jail while the soldiers tried to decide what to do with him. He languished there for most of the day before being taken out and dumped into the prison wagon. It had a wooden base with thick metal bars imbedded deeply into the base and across the top. Large wheels extended part way up the side of the cage, turning slowly as two oxen struggled to move the weight behind them.

He didn't travel far that first day, only to the main entrance of the church where he stood in the cage, robe covered in blood and tears from the battle, and surveyed the scene before him. Though night had fallen, torches had been set up for bringing the wagon and he could see blood and debris still littering the street. The bodies had been removed so he had no idea how many had been killed or wounded on either side. Soldiers in the purple and white of the Emissary milled about, slowly working at cleaning the street, but generally just gawking at him.

For the next three days, soldiers came and berated him, shouting insults and slurs while talking to every person within earshot of the results of heresy against the Emissary. Each evening, when darkness fell and the streets emptied, different men came to him. These men did not shout and they made sure there were no other people around. The torture did not start right away. They simply talked to Barall about his life, where he was born and how he was raised. While Barall suspected what was happening, he couldn't understand where it was headed. What was the point, after all? What did it matter that he was the youngest of five children, with three sisters and a brother who lived in a farming village outside Tyron in the far northwest corner of Cherilla? All he knew, at this point, was that not answering was not an option.

As a priest, Barall was fairly isolated from the world. He hadn't travelled throughout Cherilla or even Anklesh much for that matter. He did, however, read voraciously, and talk to every visitor to the archives he could. This gave him some insight into different types of people; how some people could, at a glance, discern another's true nature and whether they could be trusted or if they were a good person or not. Barall did not have this skill, but even he could tell that the men who came to him that first night were not men he would want to cross. By the fifth night, the pleasant nature of these men changed completely when they took him out of the cage and forcibly walked him into the church moving quickly through the audience chamber where the Primate would conduct their sermon. While Erskin was large enough to warrant a Primate to be permanently assigned to it, along with four Comforts, this night there were no priests around, yet the questioners seemed to know exactly where they were going.

The three men who led Barall moved through the church without a light, moving unerringly in the inky blackness past rows of benches, around the altar and through a door that Barall could perceive only as another space of blackness. Through the door was a set of steep narrow stairs leading down. Barall nearly stumbled several times and only a hard grab onto the back of his robes by the guard trailing him kept him from tumbling the rest of the way down to wherever the bottom was. Barall expressed his thanks to the guard who had grabbed him when suddenly one of the others, walking just in front of him, whirled and struck Barall across the face.

"Silence!" hissed the man, anger burning in his eyes.

Shock merged with pain as Barall tasted blood from his split lip. A growl from behind followed by a slap across the side of his head, and Barall started moving again with an understanding that these were the Emissary's interrogators and the nice chats of the last few nights were over. Horror stole over him that this was happening to the people in every village and city in the country and all at the order of the Emissary. An almost physical transformation came over him as this realization hit. His back straightened and his shoulders pulled back and on his face, a look of determination replaced the shock. He was still afraid at the prospect of being tortured, but the knowledge of what the Emissary was perpetrating on the people gave him strength and the determination to endure whatever they did to him. Too, there was solace in the fact that, by now, Arion would have made it back to the camp and the circle would be gone, the camp disbanded and everyone scattered. He had no knowledge of where any of the circle members were or their plans for the future. What the circle was about, their ultimate purpose, was no secret, and he would gladly share that information with everyone.

❧

Orders from the cathedral came far quicker than anyone thought possible, but the directions were clear: Barall was to be carted up and returned to Anklesh with any village on route to have the opportunity to see the prisoner, and the Comforts to openly condemn him.

For the most part, during the first days of the trip, the guards ignored Barall, apparently worrying more about looking for an ambush than about him, but as they progressed without incident they looked for sport to relieve their boredom. For that, they turned to their prisoner. The remains of their meals were thrown to Barall for him to eat. Patrols would bang on the bars or shake the cage while he slept, just to annoy him and keep him from sleep. Anything they could think of to irritate him was fair as long as he wasn't killed.

The questioners were hindered in their job somewhat by the fact that they felt they couldn't permanently harm their prisoner. He was being taken to see the Emissary and would have to be able to talk when they reached the cathedral. So far, Barall had refused to cooperate, which meant he told them everything. The leader of the questioners, a rather unassuming man named Vahchen, was completely at a loss as to what else to try.

Vahchen had earned his position, and his reputation, by never failing to get to the truth. He did this, oddly for a man of his profession, by learning as much about his prisoner as possible and verifying what he was told. While this often meant some delays it resulted in better results and fewer apologies or uncomfortable explanations. Barall continually stonewalled him by telling the truth each and every time. It wasn't believed, of course, but since that first night, in the basement of the church, Vahchen hadn't been able to find a lie anywhere. The priest had been beaten, starved, ridiculed, humiliated and debased in every way the questioners could imagine. In a way, it was almost inspiring the way Barall took the continual punishment and yet did nothing to make it easier on himself. Vahchen had seen stronger men lie of their own guilt or involvement, admitting to things they hadn't done or seen, just to save themselves pain. But this priest … this boy … seemed to go out of his way to bring even more punishment onto himself.

The guards had sent word of Barall's capture to Anklesh, within an hour of his capture and while they waited for instructions, the standard twenty-day observance time came up. The fool of a woman, Prestia, who now served as Primate in Erskin, thought herself superior to Vahchen, and in charge of the 'religious' aspects within the town. Likely in an attempt to curry favor with the Emissary, she decided to use the prisoner in her sermon. She had him removed from his wagon; put a fresh robe on him to hide most of the bruises inflicted by Vahchen's men and placed him, shackled, on a dais at the head of the church, behind the altar where she stood. What this did, in effect, was place Barall in a position of superiority, behind and above the Primate even though he stood complacently and followed the protocol of the service. But then, the Primate made the biggest mistake of her career, erasing forever any hope she might have of advancing. She gave Barall the opportunity to speak.

It was probably unintentional, but Prestia got too caught up in her own sermon; too excited at the reaction of the crowd to her condemnation of the circle and the heresies of Barall. She was too stupid to realize the people were not reacting to her and her words, but to the presence of the questioner and the Emissary's guards. The people had quickly learned to put on great shows of support for the Emissary and disdain for Barall and the circle. The Primate went on at length, railing against those who did not take the Emissary into their heart, and against Barall and his quest. She explained that the 'true' reason for the circle's existence was to destroy the Emissary and bring Endomar's name to ridicule. Then she turned to the calmly listening Barall and asked: "Isn't that true, Acolyte?"

She probably thought she was being clever, assuming Barall would be too cowed by his capture and being put on display to even think of a response but he quickly proved her wrong. Being placed at the forefront of the church, behind the altar, Barall was alone and untouchable for no guard would violate the altar during a service. Being asked a direct question during the service, he was now allowed to answer it, however he saw fit. Where Prestia raged and played on the fears of the people, Barall simply spoke to them of how he became involved in his quest, how he learned of the other gods and that all he was trying to do was to educate and inform the people that they had a choice. Even the sight of his guards slowly making their way up the sides of the church, suggestively fingering their weapons, did nothing to stop the young priest from talking. He surely knew the punishment Vahchen would impose, but obviously didn't care. He had an audience of hundreds willing to listen to him, and there was nothing the Emissary, the questioner or the guards could do to stop him.

⁊

Vahchen's opinion of Barall went up a notch after that and there were very few people who Vahchen deemed worthy of even a modicum of respect. Barall had earned it by answering every question with the truth and holding tightly to his faith. Faith held little place in Vahchen's world since it didn't keep his belly full or a roof over his head. History was littered with people gifted with brilliant insight and intelligence who wasted it on pursuing quests of faith for god and if it was one thing Vahchen detested, it was wasting one's gifts.

From everything he had learned and everything he knew of the man, Barall was not wasting anything. This was a man who had faith in his god and complete certainty and devotion to his cause. Whether this made him more or less dangerous was not for the questioner to decide. He only had to deliver Barall to the Emissary, and his task would be complete.

One day more.

ぐ.ク

The towers of the palace of King Zithius were visible to Barall through the bars of his cage. They were still a day out of the city, but the sight of the towers glinting brightly in the sun brought the end of the journey into sharp focus. He had told the questioners everything he knew; it was the only course he could take, knowing that to lie to the hard faced and cold-eyed questioner would only do himself harm. He knew the circle would have scattered, thrown themselves and all the followers to the four corners of Cherilla. Likely they had thought of rescuing him, but had wisely chosen the mission over foolish sentimentality over a single man. He didn't want to die, and if honest with himself, was hurt they hadn't even tried a rescue. Logically, he understood and approved of that decision, but emotionally he was scared.

It had taken weeks to travel from Erskin to Anklesh, nearly three times longer than it should have. They had plodded along, stopping at any cluster of huts that called itself a village, as well as in the larger towns of Laufrid and Guilder. In each place Barall was put on display in whatever passed for the town's square. From there the local Comfort would harangue the people about the evils of defying the will of the Emissary and the blasphemous ways of Barall and his circle. After the first sermon in Erskin, they hadn't made the mistake of asking Barall any more questions. However, since he was something of an oddity to most people, someone who openly defied the cathedral, the townspeople came to gawk and see for themselves who all the fuss was about and, thus, gave him the chance to talk, until the guards found out. They would take turns beating him while another sought out the questioners. After that the questioners had taken to paying townspeople to shout obscenities at him and to pelt him with rotting food, which they doled out in great quantities. Through it all, Barall maintained his resolve and determination.

That determination nearly faltered in Guilder, however, when the Comfort strode out of the church to view the prisoner first hand. It was not Rischa who faced him through the bars of his crude prison, but a fat, haughty man, easily twice Barall's age and three times his size. The Comfort more waddled than walked, his huge girth, barely covered by his formal robes, the fabric straining to stay together as he rocked from side to side and his tree-trunk-thick legs struggled to move him forward. He sweated profusely, though the day was cool, and mopped at his brow and jowls continuously with a dirty cloth. Approaching, he gave Barall a disdainful look before sniffing rudely and turning to Vahchen. "This is him, then?" he squeaked in a high-pitched, pig-like voice.

"Yes, my lord," replied Vahchen. "You have received word from Anklesh on what is to be done?"

"Yes, yes, of course," wheezed the Comfort with a wave of his cloth, sending the reek of damp sweat through the air. "All is ready."

"Where is Comfort Rischa?" interrupted Barall, having heard a similar dialogue at every village they came to.

"Harrumph!" snorted the Comfort, "You'll find no friends here, boy. My predecessor was not worthy to speak the Emissary's name, let alone be in his service. She has been punished as a heretic and sent to confess her sins to Endomar. Do not worry, though, for you'll be with her soon."

Barall rocked back in his cage, stumbling and falling onto his back in shock as thoughts of the gentle, brown-haired woman flitted through his mind. Words of angry retort burned his tongue, desperate to be unleashed in support of Rischa, killed because of her support of him.

 ∾

It was obvious, now that he was only a day away from the Emissary, that he wasn't going to be killed by these men. He was being taken to Anklesh and the Emissary, so there was nothing to fear. The circle and their followers had dispersed and he was being taken to confront the Emissary – the perpetrator behind much of the wrongs being done in the name of Endomar. He tried to plan that meeting, but it was difficult since he didn't know much about the way the Emissary thought and had no insight into how the man might react. He also didn't know if the Emissary would choose to confront him in private or with an audience, so in the end he simply focussed on what he thought most likely.

The Emissary would be gloating and cocky, overconfident in the capture of the circle's leader and would likely confront Barall publicly, in front of whomever he thought he needed to impress or defeat. In capturing, and therefore conquering, Barall in full witness of all those people, the Emissary would gain their support and obedience. But it would be the Emissary's mistake to presume Barall would not fight back. Almost from the beginning it was inevitable there would be a confrontation between the circle and the church and Barall was prepared to debate the Emissary, to spell out the facts and truths he had come to learn. In the end, while he hoped to be able to convince the Emissary of the circle's benevolence, he was under no illusions as to his chances of success. The Emissary was smart and would not allow an upstart priest to diminish him, especially in front of those likely to be there. The public audience would be ended, and then, Barall knew the questioners would be called and an excuse for the prisoner's death concocted. His only hope was that he be able to put enough doubt and questions into the heads of the Emissary's adversaries to allow the circle's momentum to continue.

☙

"The prison train is but one day away, my Lord Emissary," stated Lassand.

"Excellent," gushed Caven, rubbing his hands together gleefully. "It's about time."

"Well, Emissary, they were told to stop at every town and village between Erskin and Anklesh to show the people the result of going against the will of Endomar."

"Yes, yes, but it has still taken far too long. It is time he was here. Time he answered for his crimes."

"One more day, Emissary."

"One long day," grumbled Caven petulantly. He brightened visibly, and then seated himself in one of the comfortably padded chairs. "What has your research found?" he asked as he motioned for the heretofore silent Nokya to serve them.

The others in the room had stayed silent as Lassand and the Emissary talked, but at the mention of Lassand's research, they all perked up. The two men and one woman served as a type of advisory committee to the Emissary when he had recognized the need for additional information and insight into what was happening inside his own church. Chestun and Fael, the two men, and Shawney, the woman, represented the levels of Initiate/Acolyte, Comfort and Primate respectively. Thinking of how it would look to create a committee after he had only recently disbanded the council of Wisdoms, this new group was created quietly and called together only at the whim of the Emissary. Really, it was a waste of everyone's time for the Emissary rarely let them speak. Tonight was no different. They had been summoned and sat in silence as first the Emissary ate and then recounted his plans for Barall and the church. These were all things they had heard before and the Emissary cared very little for the issues their respective groups had asked them to relay.

Nokya served hot tea to everyone and then removed herself to the back of the room, silent and forgotten until needed. Once the tea was sampled, Lassand explained that his investigation had revealed nothing conclusive, but much circumstantial evidence that could be harmful to the Emissary's position. As the Wisdom continued, he scanned the glances shared by his fellow priests, and the deepening scowl forming on the Emissary's face, trying to determine who might be a possible ally and who to avoid. Since word had come of Barall's capture and the Emissary's orders for his handling, Lassand had doubled his efforts within the archives. He had found references to 'all' priests and odd occurrences of 'seven' too often to be ignored, yet always in infuriatingly obscure terms. It was like the authors wanted to convey the truth or a message, but couldn't just come out and say it which made it frustrating beyond words, for everything else was explained fully.

"Ahem," coughed Chestun, to the shock of his friends, "if I may, my lords?"

The Emissary looked over at him slowly as if unsure the man had, indeed, spoken. The Initiate/Acolyte leader remained steady under the Emissary's stare, his clean-shaven head dry and his bright, green eyes, calm.

"Yes?" asked the Emissary coldly.

"Please forgive me, my lord," started Chestun, "but it sounds to me that what Lord Lassand is talking about is the silence decree."

Caven shared a glance with Lassand then turned back to Chestun. "Silence decree?" he asked.

"Yes, Excellency. Although it doesn't really have a name, that is just what I call it. I am somewhat of an historian, and frequently visited the archives when Comfort Vance was alive. He was doing research into something or other when I offered my assistance. I believe he was looking for information on someone named Gibson, but even he couldn't find any references to him. Together we searched the archives, growing more and more frustrated, until I came across a passage in a book describing Emissary's laws. It had no name or date, and no reason for its being given, but it essentially called for a complete end to any mention of 'the subject' or 'the others,' upon penalty of death."

There were gasps from Fael and Shawney, and raised eyebrows from Lassand. Only the Emissary seemed unimpressed and unaffected. No one spoke for a time, and it was like no one dared breathe for fear of disturbing the Emissary's thoughts.

"And then?" asked the Emissary almost in a whisper.

"Emissary?" asked Chestun.

"What did you do then?" came Caven's clipped reply.

"Why … nothing, Emissary," said Chestun, starting to lose his composure in the face of the Emissary's anger.

"Nothing?"

"N-no, Emissary," stammered Chestun.

Lassand, seeing this turning badly for the young priest, interrupted with what he hoped was a conciliatory tone. "Perhaps, Chestun, you can help me, then. We will look for the reasons for this 'silence decree' as well as continue to look for Gibson. He seems to be the turning point for everything."

Before Chestun could respond, the Emissary added his own thoughts. "I believe it would be best for you to work with Lassand. Perhaps you will find something more useful than more questions."

❦

Everyone had finally left an exhausted Caven an hour later, and Nokya was drawing him a hot bath. The stresses and strains of his position wore on him and Nokya knew the heat of the bath would help to ease the knots from his muscles. She had listened to Lassand and the other priests discuss Barall with the Emissary, and knew of the plans being made for tomorrow when he was due to arrive. There was nothing she could do to help Barall, and truly she wasn't sure she would even if she could. She had known little about Endomar when Lassand found her and brought her to the cathedral to live but she had found safety and love and a place to belong among people who loved her. Endomar was the first and only love she had ever known, and Barall was working to weaken His church.

But Lassand was adamant that it was Caven, not Barall who was destroying the church. Barall, he said, was restoring the balance and returning truth to the people and the church. Only time would tell who was savior and who the destroyer, she supposed, but there was one thing she knew for sure, and that was that Caven was not a good person. She had been the Emissary's personal attendant for several months, and while she was no wilting flower when it came to the bedroom, Caven was truly a monster. Acolytes, like her, were often used as attendants by the higher ranking priests, and so were often privy to all sorts of gossip and internal strategies. It seemed most of the upper echelons within the cathedral knew, or suspected, the Emissary guilty of rape, abuse and likely the murder of dozens of young Initiates and Acolytes. Nokya hadn't been able to confirm this conclusively. She had seen the Emissary with any number of young women, but she couldn't be sure if she'd ever seen any of them again, having never gotten a good look in the first place. All this meant she had to be extremely careful in her dealings with the Emissary. His moods changed lightning quick; he was extremely smart and, despite his recent paranoia and erratic decisions, was still respected by most of the church and Cherilla.

With the bath drawn, she added several handfuls of herbs and some fragrances to the water and ensured a glass of sweet wine was ready. She then moved to advise the Emissary that all was prepared. Exiting the bathing room on silent feet she called quietly to the Emissary. He didn't bother to answer her, but came to the steaming room as Nokya busied herself preparing his bed, laying some warming stones on the mattress and pulling up his blankets. So preoccupied was she with her own thoughts of Barall and the Emissary, the right or wrong of them, that Nokya didn't even hear him return.

"You seem out of sorts tonight, Nokya," he said, somewhat sleepily. "Is something the matter?"

"No, my lord," she bowed embarrassed. "Just silly thoughts, not worthy to bother your Excellency."

A little flattery tended to go a long way with Caven.

"Isn't their worth something for me to decide?" he chided with a smile, using his good looks and charm to his advantage. "What are you thinking of this late night?"

"Only of this Barall," she replied quietly, unsure of how he would react.

"What of him?"

"My lord, I'm just confused. Would it truly be so bad if there were other gods? I mean, mighty Endomar calls for balance in all things, and isn't that all Barall is proposing? If people were to leave Endomar because of this, then they were never truly His to begin with, they were mere pretenders all along and your church would be left with the truly devoted and those worthy of attending."

He was on her in a flash, almost before she stopped speaking, strong fingers grasping at her neck, his face contorted in rage with blotches of red spotting his cheeks. He pushed her down onto the bed and climbed on top of her, straddling her until all of his weight pressed into her throat, squeezing tighter and tighter. Beneath him, Nokya clawed and scratched at him, trying to reach his face, his arms, his chest, anything to loosen his grip. It was futile, and in seconds her strength waned and her struggles ended. Still Caven squeezed, not willing to let go, seeing only red as his rage remained in control.

"The only balance is what I proclaim there to be."

# Chapter 25

*"It is characteristic of wisdom not
to do desperate things."*
**Henry David Thoreau**

The late morning sun gleamed brightly over the bustling city of Anklesh, shining down on people up and about their daily routines who knew that today was going to be anything but routine. The importance of the day and of the person entering the city caused a subdued hush throughout the normally frantic market. The port seemed to have a fraction of the regular traffic. People already lined the streets from the cathedral to the west gate, the most likely entrance through which the prisoner would emerge. They also crammed the warehouse district and along the southern shores of the Bay of Frasada since the only access to Cathedral Island was by the boat launch located there. The Emissary's guards, recalled from their assigned locations when Barall had been caught were now performing guard duty throughout the city, a feat that had not escaped the notice of several people.

The first was King Zithius, whose responsibility it was to guard and protect his people, including the Emissary and the entire church. A long-standing agreement allowed the church their own contingent of armed guards but the Emissary had greatly exceeded the limit the force was to include, and was now in command of an army roughly equal to Zithius' own standing force. The king could call up many times the number permanently on duty, but had not seen the need to as of yet. Once the Emissary's soldiers started entering the city, most of Zithius' advisors recommended he close the gates to any more and refuse them entrance. Only Wilnah seemed to be thinking ahead and pointed out that doing so would leave the city essentially under siege with half the opposing army already inside the walls, and the other half outside wanting to gain entry.

The others who noticed the rapid increase in the number of the Emissary's soldiers were the clerist knights. Created by Barall, and thus far without any uniform or insignia, they were unknown to both the Emissary's and king's soldiers and could blend in with the rest of the people. They used their anonymity to scour the city, searching for information of what the Emissary had planned. It was sheer luck the separate parts of the circle found each other. Both groups had made their way inside the walls under cover of darkness and quickly found hiding holes for the priests before venturing out for information and food.

Cerrok immediately ordered his group to move to join the other and each group took turns telling of their experiences since they separated. From then, Cerrok again started issuing orders, keeping everyone busy while keeping his loyal followers close. More and more Cerrok was withdrawing from the group, keeping his own counsel and rarely speaking to the others, other than ordering that plans be finalized for Barall's rescue and for the escape from the city afterwards. He hadn't really been seen since the two groups arrived in Anklesh.

Since planning for Barall's rescue had begun as soon as he had been captured, they were essentially finalized with only some fine tuning needed now that they were in the city and had more first-hand knowledge of what was going on. Stein had broken off from the group immediately upon entering Anklesh to go and report to King Zithius. His knowledge of the city and the guards had proven invaluable, just as Destrin's insight into the cathedral had been. But Stein had yet to return, and the circle was growing worried. He didn't know both halves had joined together and found a single safe house, but the knights were constantly on vigil and were looking throughout the city. They hoped it was the overabundance of Emissary's guards that kept him away, but the circle couldn't walk up to the palace and ask for him either, so they were forced to wait and hope he was well.

The two groups of knights, led ostensibly by Arion and Riordan, combined forces and spread themselves out to gather information, protect the circle members and continue their training of the new volunteers. Due to his greater experience in administration, Riordan assumed overall command and parceled out assignments, duty rotations and reported to the circle. This made Arion more than happy as it gave him the chance to focus on training and the rescue plan though he still struggled with his conscience over leaving Barall in Erskin to be captured and tortured and trekked across the country to face his enemy.

The two knights sat inside Riordan's makeshift office discussing the day's activities.

"A couple of the new ones show promise," Arion was saying. "Baxter, Besoin and the woman Gazere, are all ready to advance."

They sat together, at ease in each other's company as only two soldiers could be. The room was sparsely furnished, but functional, with only a desk and two wooden chairs. Arion sat in one of the chairs in front of the desk, his feet propped on the other, watching Riordan who leaned casually against the desk.

"We really should come up with some kind of ranking system for all these …"

"Initiates?" suggested Riordan, his face stoic and unsmiling.

Already, the two were familiar enough to recognize the other's sense of humor.

"Yeah, Emissary," retorted Arion with a smirk.

"Hm, maybe you're right."

"But so are you. What about something like Recruit, Accepted and Knight? That pretty much explains the levels and keeps the religions out of it."

"An interesting turn of phrase, considering we're clerist knights," remarked Riordan thoughtfully. "But we can debate philosophy another time. How is the rescue plan going?"

The younger knight hesitated before answering, a sign of his insecurity or … mistrust. Riordan did not take offence at this possible insult, because if their places were reversed, he was sure he would be wary of trusting anyone as well. Very few people knew how or when Barall was to be rescued, and the safest thing to do was keep that number to a minimum. The fewer who knew about it, the safer it was for them all. All this went through Arion's mind as he sat across from Riordan, debating whether to reveal anything. The older knight had become mentor, friend, and teacher and had been chosen, of them all, to lead the knights. He would form them into a group, honor bound to obey, protect and defend, not only the priests of the circle, but all priests and each other as well. They were forming a true brotherhood, protectors of all faiths, and trust had to be a part of that.

"The expectation is that the Emissary will question Barall himself, but not right away. It's likely Barall won't be, shall we say, 'fit' to see the exalted Emissary. After weeks of being paraded through every village between Erskin and here, beaten, starved, housed in a wagon, he'll have to be cleaned up. Of course, they won't house him in the guest suites …"

"The dungeon," stated Riordan.

A nod from Arion confirmed the guess. "With Destrin's knowledge of the cathedral, our own study of the guards and some disguises, we have a good chance of springing him from right under the Emissary's nose."

They talked for a while longer, discussing the next round of training for the recruits. Before leaving, Arion recommended a change to the schedule of the knights assigned to guarding the circle members. "With Cerrok barely moving and staying so silent, some of the men are complaining. Normally I wouldn't change a rotation for that," said Arion with a shake of his head, "but with so many knights ready for duty, it wouldn't hurt to give a few of the others a chance."

❧

In the last seconds before Arion's form emerged through the door, spilling light into the hallway, a dark clad figure scrambled away, silently merging with the deeper shadows. The knights had secreted the circle away in a run-down-looking neighborhood, not the seediest or roughest part of the city, but certainly not the best. Within this neighborhood sat a dilapidated house, made of weathered boards bleached gray by years of sun and rain. Large gaps were apparent between many of the boards and several windows had been broken, their shutters torn off and used to board up the gaping holes.

Most of the fugitives stayed holed up in the interior rooms just in case some over-eager guard took it upon himself to check on some movement seen in an apparently abandoned house. Riordan, however, kept his office in a windowless room on the outside wall at the back of the house, saying the gaps in the wall allowed some light and air into the room. Whatever the reason, the skulking figure retreated quickly upon hearing Arion get up from his chair. In the dim hallway even the meager sunlight spilling in through the cracked and warping boards would have shown his position clearly. Wrapping his black cloak around him and tucking his head into its folds he became virtually invisible.

Arion, with a final wave, shut the door and made his way along the hallway, passing within steps of the hidden man. As he passed, the man maintained his breathing, quiet and regular, but some sound must have escaped for Arion stopped suddenly, his head cocked to one side as if listening. Turning slowly, his hand dropping to the knife at his waist, Arion peered into the darkness; straining all his senses to catch whatever it was that had triggered them. As Arion turned away, moving his head first one way, then the other, the cloaked man relaxed slightly until a loud thunk sounded through the hallway. Barely moving, the man moved only his eyes to see the knife, swaying slightly, imbedded two full fingers into the paneling just a hair's breadth from his ear.

"That was not an accident," said Arion grimly slowly drawing his sword. "Come into the light," he ordered, his sword leveled at the man's chest.

Before the man could decide whether Arion was bluffing or not, Riordan burst through the door, his own sword in hand.

"What …?" he started first seeing Arion, and then noticing the mass at the end of Arion's sword. "What's this?" he asked, more curious than alarmed.

"Don't know," replied Arion. "Saw him moving away from the door as I was leaving."

"A spy? Here? Who knew we were here?"

"All good questions. Perhaps we should ask our friend?"

❧

The large black cloak lay crumpled in a corner of Riordan's office, tossed there after a thorough search of both the cloak and the man revealed nothing more than a slim knife belted at his waist. The man himself sat silently in a chair in the middle of the room. There was nothing extraordinary about him. He was of average height with a slight build, sporting neatly trimmed brown hair and eyes, nearly the same brown as his hair and seeming more suited to a courtier than a spy. So far, he hadn't said a word, or answered any question put to him.

As if they interrogated strange men caught listening in on their private conversations on a regular basis, Arion and Riordan slipped easily into a casual banter over the man's head.

"Do you think he's deaf?" asked Riordan leaning in close and peering into the man's ears.

"He wouldn't be much good as a spy then, would he?" countered Arion. "Maybe he's just dumb?"

"Doesn't that mean he can't speak? That's even worse."

"Good point. What do you think our friend here was doing outside your door?"

"Listening."

"Spying."

"Spying by listening."

"Why, friend?" asked Arion of the seated man, a strong hand on his shoulder.

The man just stared straight ahead, his lips compressed into a thin line.

"A quiet one," commented Riordan, laying a hand on the other shoulder.

"Thoughtful."

"Introspective."

"Stubborn," murmured Arion, noticing for the first time something on the man's back.

As he had given the man a shake to punctuate the banter, the back of his shirt had shifted enough for Arion to catch a glimpse of a tattoo drawn on the man's back, a piece of it reaching up onto the back of his neck. Faster than the blink of an eye, Arion shoved the man forward with one hand, holding him there strongly as he struggled. Confused, Riordan nevertheless maintained his part and acted as if this were all part of some plan and drew his dagger to hold it to the side of the man's neck while raising his eyebrows in silent question to Arion.

With a dagger held firmly against his skin, the man ceased his struggling. Over the back of the man's head, Arion motioned with a nod of his head for Riordan to look at what he had seen. With his other hand, Arion pulled down the back of the man's shirt. The tattoo, seen in it's entirety without the covering, caused both men to stare, wondering what it could mean, both for themselves and the entire circle. The tattoo showed two hands, each clasping the other with fingers together and thumbs intertwining.

It was the symbol of Xelteran, god of greed.

※

The six circle members, plus Destrin and their ever present knight guards, had assembled at Riordan's request in what was a huge dining room. They used the room for large gatherings, since the table was still intact and functional, being able to seat twice the number currently there. Once the last person had been seated, Riordan wasted no time in getting to the point. "We have captured a man this morning listening outside my office."

"What?!"

"Outrageous!"

"My god."

"Who is he?"

This last was spoken into the silence that eventually descended as Riordan said nothing more. The commander turned to the speaker,

"We don't know, my Lord Cerrok," he said. "We thought perhaps you might."

"Me?" barked Cerrok indignantly. "What makes you think …"

"No, no, my lord," interrupted Riordan smoothly, "not you specifically, but 'you' as a whole," he said spreading his arms to include the whole room. "Does anyone have any reason to wonder why we should be spied upon? Keep in mind that it was not a member of the circle who was being listened in on, but me, and lastly, we have reason to believe this man was not working for the Emissary."

Stunned silence met Riordan's latest announcement, as everyone struggled to understand what the possible meaning could be. That they were being searched for was obvious, and that the Emissary would send spies after them, while unlikely when he had a near army of soldiers looking for them, was not impossible either, but if what Riordan had said was true, then who else was after them?

"How do you know this?" asked Seskia quietly, her mind already moving on to how to further protect themselves.

"I would rather not say, and I would ask that you trust me, as one who has sworn to protect you and the mission from *all threats*, that what I have said is true."

If anyone noticed the emphasis placed on the 'all threats' or that Riordan's eyes flicked briefly toward Cerrok, then no one said anything. Instead there were nodding heads of trust and appreciation from the priests and stoic pride and determination from the assembled knights. Discussion circled around the room, the talk going nowhere of use until even the repeated theories and questions ended and quiet suffused the room again. Slowly, realization dawned on everyone that they truly had no idea why anyone would want to spy on the knights, not with any certainty.

With a glance at Arion, who had selectively positioned himself directly across from Cerrok, Riordan brought up the second purpose for calling the meeting. "We must also decide what to do with the prisoner."

"Kill him," said Cerrok simply and immediately, his tone indicating that he was issuing an order rather than offering an opinion.

"What?" exclaimed Seskia. Though she had no doubts Cerrok would look out only for himself, she was surprised at the cold-bloodedness of the statement. She narrowed her eyes in frustration as she tried to figure out his purpose.

"Of course," Cerrok replied calmly. "If he was caught spying, and we don't know who he was working for, then he's too dangerous to keep around."

"So now we just kill people who don't agree with us?" asked Cura sarcastically.

"They would do no less to us."

"So that means we should be more like them? That's an intelligent argument."

"I suppose you have a better idea?" huffed Cerrok indignantly.

"Interrogate him," Cura shot back. "Find out who hired him, and why. Find out what he's learned already and what he's told his employers. Then we can decide what to do."

The argument between the two priests was almost comical to Arion. Cura was short and plump with fiery red hair and a temper to match. Opposite her was Cerrok, nearly twice her age, extremely handsome and charismatic, and with an equally hot temper. The look of stubborn force on Cura's face was enough to give any man pause but into this fierce storm, Cerrok waded as if uncaring, or unaware, of the impact he was having. He argued vehemently for the killing of the captured spy, a point that Arion noticed with narrowed eyes. With Barall only a day away, to the knight's commander there was no doubt what the spy was really after, and why he was listening to the knights and not the circle.

❦

"Sit down, Stein," spat Wilnah more forcefully than he had intended. "You need to calm down."

"My dear general," said Stein from where he was pacing worriedly in front of the windows high in the palace, "I'm afraid this is about as calm as I'm likely to get."

He spoke good naturedly, his friendship with the army general too strong to take offense, especially when they were risking far less than the third man in the room. Of them all, Zithius actually seemed the calmest as he sat on a plush couch, covered in soft, butter colored leather. Ostensibly, he was reading one of the seemingly endless reports that required his attention but the image was spoiled by the small smile that turned up the corners of his mouth as he listened to his two advisers bicker. Though Stein had been gone for most of the past year, first searching for, and then traveling with, Barall and the circle of seven, he and Wilnah returned immediately to their former relationship.

Not willing to look at Zithius, knowing the strain he was under, Stein turned back to the window, and looked out over the expanse of Anklesh. Despite the sprawling vista of the palace grounds, just starting to lose the splendor of autumn colors; the graceful architecture of the noble houses and the sparkling bounty of the Bay of Fasada; even to the unsightly poverty and neglect apparent in the poorest sections, none of this could attract his eye today. Only the massive crowds were to be seen today. From his perch high in the palace, it looked to Stein as if every man, woman and child in the city had turned out to watch Barall's entrance. The movement of the crowd reminded him of the tides of the ocean, such was the ebb and flow. It was sickening and fascinating at the same time how people would flock to see the horrors inflicted upon another being.

A touch on Stein's shoulder made him flinch, so absorbed in

his thoughts that he hadn't even heard Wilnah approach. "It is too late for misgivings, my friend. The plan has been made and is now in motion."

"I know that."

"Then why are you acting so strangely?"

"I am thinking of the oddity of people."

"Rubbish."

"Actually, I was. I find it uniquely odd that nothing brings out more people than the prospect of spilled blood."

"And is that what you expect to happen today, Stein?" asked Zithius.

"If not today, Sire, then soon. The Emissary will not and cannot, allow Barall, or the circle to continue to thwart him. The people across the country are divided and taking sides. We heard rumors as we traveled of fights breaking out among townspeople over who to believe, and it's only going to get worse until the whole country is involved. We are on the brink of a civil war, and I can't see any way to stop it."

The king and general had listened quietly as Stein spoke, both having learned that Stein's unique insights were often correct.

"I agree with much of what you've said," started Zithius, "particularly about human motivations. I can even see why you believe blood will be shed, though perhaps not on the scale you suggest."

"I hope you are right, my lord."

"But you don't think I am."

"No."

"Why?"

Stein ticked off the points on his hands as he made them. "The circle traveled across almost the entire country bringing word of the other gods. Everywhere they went, they met with the people, convinced many to convert, and gave a lot more a reason to start thinking. The Emissary was becoming erratic and paranoid before Barall or the circle was ever heard of. Unbeknownst to anyone, the Emissary gathered an army of soldiers, trained them and unleashed them simultaneously across the country to quell what he called 'an uprising.' In my opinion, my lord," he continued looking directly at the king, "we should have acted then. The army should have marched to protect the people. I can understand why that didn't happen, for that would definitely have resulted in blood running through the streets. But," Stein's thumb joined the four fingers already raised, "that is merely a matter of timing given what we are about to do. The Emissary may, quite literally, lose his mind."

As if on cue, a roar could be heard rolling up from the throng below. For it to be heard from where the three men stood every throat in the city must have been shouting itself hoarse.

"Our men are in place?" asked Zithius gravely.

"Yes, Sire," answered Wilnah, "with orders to invoke the law and deliver Barall, under heavy guard, directly to the palace."

"Good," nodded Zithius, rising from his couch. "Then you should be away, general. Be safe, my friend."

The two clasped hands, regarding each other in friendship, perhaps both sensing the momentous times they were invoking. Finally, with a simple nod, Wilnah broke away and, with a sweep of his cape over one arm, strode purposefully from the room.

"A good man, Wilnah," said Stein.

"Hm," agreed Zithius. "As are you, Stein. I appreciate your candor and honesty, may they yet prove to be wrong."

"I pray to all the gods they are, your Majesty."

# Chapter 26

*"Six essential qualities that are the key
to success: Sincerity, personal integrity,
humility, courtesy, wisdom, charity."*
**William Menninger**

A scream of pure primal rage tore through the Emissary as the runner delivered her message. The poor girl, one of the few new Initiates received by the Church lately, cowered on her knees before the Emissary, probably still wondering what it was she had done to so anger him. The Emissary sat upon the gaudy throne he had had commissioned and placed in the grand reception hall. In one sense, it was an incredible creation, the craftsman having carved an intricate network of interwoven circles to form the sides, seat and back. A hollow circle was placed in the center of the back, exactly placed so that when the Emissary sat down, his head was perfectly centered within it. Containing graceful curves and gently tapering legs, the throne was to be 'unveiled' publicly, when Barall was brought to the cathedral to be questioned, but the Emissary had been using it privately ever since its completion.

Now, the Emissary's plans, as well as his grandiose vision for the overall destruction of Barall and his circle, were being thrown into disarray by King Zithius of all people. Inwardly, Lassand marvelled that it had taken the king this long to act, but was glad that he finally had. To be honest, he wasn't aware of this law the king was invoking, but it was a masterful play for it had completely thrown the Emissary sideways, placing everything in turmoil.

Lassand needed more time for his own research so the reprieve was welcome. With Chestun now helping him, the search of the archives was proceeding rapidly. Chestun knew the archives, their layout and basic filing and sorting system, better than Lassand so they had been able to refine the search somewhat. The Wisdom was guardedly optimistic about Chestun's loyalty, believing it was more toward the circle of seven than to the Emissary. General comments he made led Lassand to believe the Emissary's policies were not well received.

With Chestun capably conducting the search in the archives, Lassand was spending his time in what would be considered treason since he was investigating the Emissary. Rumors had abounded for months, if not years, about the Emissary and the young Initiates and Acolytes assigned to serve him. None lasted long. In fact Nokya was the longest serving Acolyte by several months. It was odd, actually, that Nokya was not here. Ever since the Emissary had captured Barall, he had been using the throne, barely budging from it, and if he ever wanted anything, he would rap his knuckles on the arm or ring a small bell he kept on his person, and Nokya would appear to attend him.

Lassand pushed thoughts of the girl from his mind as the Emissary rose from his throne with a guttural growl. He had taken two steps toward the kneeling Initiate, his circle-topped staff gripped tightly in both hands, before Lassand could jump to his feet from where he sat behind and to the left of the throne.

"My lord," he said quickly, unsure what the Emissary intended.

The Emissary took another step before stopping suddenly, Lassand's presence finally registering within his rage-filled mind.

Still gripping his staff, he scanned the room to see if anyone else had seen his momentary loss of control. Seeing no one else but his personal guards, he took the time to lean on his staff and take a few steadying breaths. Even from behind Lassand could clearly see the change. Between one step and the next, the Emissary transformed himself from a murderous rage to what looked like nothing more than a belaboured leader with the burdens of responsibility and duty weighing heavily upon his shoulders.

With a weary hand, the Emissary reached out one hand and laid it gently on the Initiate's head, "Bless and thank you child," he said bestowing a beatific smile upon her.

The girl looked up at the Emissary, her face alight with faith and trust. "I am so sorry, my lord," she said breathlessly, "to have had to bring such news to trouble you."

As soon as the Emissary dismissed the young Initiate his demeanor changed again, returning to its former state. He turned toward Lassand, a feral sneer curling his lips, his fingers curled inward, looking like grasping claws.

"I want Zithius arrested," he growled. "Now. Today."

"Emissary …" started Lassand placatingly.

"Now!" shouted the Emissary. "He tests me. He steals from me what is mine. What is more, he thwarts the will of the church. My will. Who does he think he is?"

"My lord, he is the king …"

"King, pah!" spat the Emissary. "King of men. I am the Emissary of Endomar. The Emissary of god, the only god. I am above the laws of the common man."

Lassand could only stare for several heartbeats, hoping the Emissary was only joking; hoping that this man, whom he had helped to place in the highest position possible within the church, did not think himself better than everyone. The position of Emissary was not one of rule, but of guidance, teaching and learning. Caven was leading them, the church and all its followers, down paths they had no right to go. As he saw the look of hatred on the Emissary's face, Lassand realized something else. The entire battle with Barall, the Emissary's obsession with the circle, raising his own army, preparing plans to bring Endomar to neighboring Naer and Ponti, all of it was smoke-screening. It had nothing at all to do with Endomar or His church, and everything to do with Caven's own quest for power. What Lassand had perceived, at first, as a legitimate defence of the church against the loss of its faithful, was truly just the Emissary's excuse for grabbing more power. What end the Emissary was actually after, was anyone's guess, but Lassand felt it was all just to increase Caven's own feelings of self-importance by providing a 'legacy' of sorts to leave behind. For Caven, this was an expansion of the church's influence and membership through any and all means possible.

"Of course you are the Emissary, my lord. But there are still laws to be obeyed and rules to follow. You cannot simply arrest the king because he disagrees with you."

Lassand knew he was treading on risky ground here, especially with the Emissary's current state of mind, but something had to be said or the Emissary would order a full scale attack upon the palace. The Wisdoms were doing everything in their power to prevent a war from happening.

"Why don't we summon Nokya to fetch some wine, and we can talk about what to …"

The Emissary whirled on Lassand, his voice a shriek of anger. "Do not mention that name again," he howled.

"What? Who?" stuttered Lassand dumbly.

"That blasphemous servant you brought to me," replied Caven through clenched teeth.

"N-Nokya?"

"Yes."

"W-what has ha-happened?"

"She questioned why it was wrong for there to be other gods. Clearly that is blasphemy, and I have punished her accordingly."

❦

Lassand stumbled along the corridors blindly, not knowing or caring where he was going.

Nokya was dead.

He was as certain of this as he was that the Emissary had killed her. Lassand didn't doubt that Nokya had asked the Emissary about the other gods. She was inquisitive and curious, and who better to ask than the Emissary? He was supposed to be the most wise and learned of them all, and, therefore, the one best able to answer the difficult questions. Instead of welcoming the questions and using them to start a discussion into the unlikelihood of alternate gods, or why Endomar was the best choice to worship, the Emissary killed her. He killed a poor, sweet girl. And yet, the Emissary was not the only one at fault. Lassand, himself, had placed Nokya in danger by asking for her help. He had convinced her of his desperate need for information, and of her ability to gather it for him, never truly considering the price she would have to pay if the Emissary found out. True there had been rumors, but that was all he had considered them, until, of course, he had started looking deeper. By then, it was too late to pull her out without the Emissary getting suspicious. Her blood was on his hands, as much or more than on the Emissary's.

As that thought coursed into his head, he paused in his mad wanderings and looked at his hands. Turning them over and back, he searched for the tell-tale blood, but found only pale skin and wrinkles. The fingers curled into fists as anger washed through him, filling all his senses, and his breath came in staggered gasps as the fierceness of the emotion hit him. Looking wildly around, Lassand saw, for the first time, where his ramblings had taken him.

He was deep in the cathedral, near the archives, and still within the residences. In fact, he was very near to Comfort Vance's room.

With barely a pause to consider what he was doing, Lassand strode off toward where he thought Vance's room might have been. What he intended to do he wasn't entirely sure, but the prospect of seeing the room of the man who started the debate of the other gods was something he hadn't considered before now. Even in his grief and anger, logic and the need for more information presided.

After several wrong turns, and a few wrong doors, he came upon a door marked with the broken circle. Barely glancing at the symbol of lost faith, he pushed through the door, wondering if, soon, his own door would bear the same mark. Inside, the room was in disarray and unkempt with books and clothes piled in every available space. What little furniture could be seen was buried beneath the remains of Vance's life; his personal effects and curiosities, his work and study. Momentarily reverent about being there, Lassand could only stand on the threshold and gaze about. In his current state of mind, it seemed right to be there - to return to the spot where it all began, to see if it also led to its ending. Almost immediately Lassand's eyes were drawn to the chair, located in front of the dark and cold fireplace, covered in ugly, dark brown splotches where Vance's blood had soaked into it. It looked like only the body had been moved, for everything else seemed to be in place. There was no way for Lassand to know that for sure, but it didn't look to him like the room had been entered since the Emissary's men had killed Vance. It was likely the room had been searched, and then left alone, with no one willing to go to the bother of emptying it, and no one wanting to move into the room of a traitor.

To start, he just let his eyes roam, seeing if anything jumped out at him. Not really expecting anything, he was surprised at what he found peeking out from underneath the chair where Vance had been killed. From his vantage point standing near the door, Lassand could just make out the distinctive shape of a dagger. Bending on creaking knees, and stretching one hand under the chair, he was finally able to get a finger on the hilt of the weapon and edge it closer. Grasping it, he nearly dropped it again when he saw the dried blood caked onto the blade. Realizing that he was holding the dagger that killed Vance, Lassand's mind whirled with plans of vengeance. The Emissary had brought murder into the halls of the cathedral. Whether it started with Vance and his, admittedly unwise, decision to publicly proclaim the existence of other gods, or with the disappearance of the girls assigned to attend him, didn't matter. Rumors were rampant around both issues, but one of them said that Vance himself suspected the Emissary of direct involvement, and confronted his lord about it.

Using a scrap of cloth torn from one of Vance's robes, Lassand wrapped the dagger carefully and placed it on the chair where he wouldn't forget it. Then, he turned back to the room and began his search.

ᔕᔓ

Barall was taken through the crowded streets of Anklesh under a large contingent of soldiers loyal to King Zithius, who were drawn up in close order to surround the wagon and oxen that pulled it. The journey to get here had obviously taken its toll on him for he was weak and dishevelled; looking more like a wild man than a priest. Still, the change in guards and the near battle that had erupted when the king's men announced the change in custody was impossible not to notice. As the spilling of blood seemed imminent, Barall tried to call out to them to stop, but he was interrupted by the arrival of an older man possessing an air of competent command that seemed to garner the respect of both sides. After a few quiet words to the leader of the Emissary's guards, there was a nod to the king's men, and Barall was led off.

Now, hours later, Barall had had time to reflect on the end of his journey. His entrance into Anklesh had been enlightening in many ways as people lined the streets, obviously there to gawk at the Emissary's prisoner as he was taken to meet his fate. The gray haired soldier who had staved off the battle appeared beside his cage and introduced himself as Wilnah, general in charge of the king's army. It was Wilnah who pointed out things Barall hadn't noticed.

The people looked at Barall, but only in glances, their eyes locked on the people around them and speaking in whispers to their neighbors. Every person wore some kind of identifying color, purple for the Emissary, or white for the circle of seven. Each person had chosen a side and was openly declaring their allegiance. The other thing was the cathedral itself. With all he had learned, all that had happened, Barall's faith was strong and the sight of the cathedral still filled him with awe as he looked upon its numerous towers and graceful arches. Since seeing churches in several other cities, a theory had begun forming and when the great church came into view, he strained to see it to verify his burgeoning theory. Like the other churches, it was centered by a massive pair of double doors and topped by an even bigger circular window. In this case, the window was carved with spokes radiating inward toward a smaller, centered circle. But this was not what caused his breath to catch in his throat. A new revelation was shown to him by Wilnah and now fairly shouted out to him: there were seven towers located around the perimeter of the cathedral.

*Seven towers for seven gods,* he thought excitedly.

Upon reaching the palace, the gates were unceremoniously slammed shut on the rest of the city, allowing the soldiers to relax and Barall to be released from the cage for the first time in weeks. Escorted by two pairs of guards, he was allowed a bath and a change of clothes before finding himself led to an empty sitting room with a table heavily laden with trays of food and several pitchers. The conflicting aromas soon threatened to prove too much for him since he had only been given scraps to eat since he was captured, but he dug into the food with an energy he didn't realize he possessed.

Just as he was finishing, the door opened and Wilnah entered with several others. Barall smiled to see Stein again and rushed to embrace his friend.

"It's good to see you again," said Stein smiling.

"And you, my friend. Do I have you to thank for my timely rescue?"

"Not exactly, no."

Whatever else might have been said was lost when Virez entered the room. Seeing her, Barall first stiffened in shock and what might be interpreted as fear but then his eyes narrowed suspiciously and he looked from her to Stein to Wilnah, before returning to Virez.

"Wisdom," he said cautiously, making the sign of the circle.

"Comfort Barall," she said calmly. "It is my honor to meet you. I'm relieved to find the plan worked."

"Plan, Wisdom?"

"The plan that got you here, at least for now," came a deep, but not unkind voice from the doorway.

Virez stepped to Barall's side, whispering, "bow," to him as she turned to face the newcomer.

"My Lord King," she said as she bowed.

"King?" blurted Barall, noticing the rich cut of Zithius' doublet, the soft leather of his boots, and the jewelled handle of a dagger belted at his waist. Too late, Barall realized he, alone, hadn't acknowledged the king. Rather than simply bow, he dropped to one knee and bent his head.

"Oh, I see why you like him, Stein," said Zithius, amusement in his voice. Then, "Rise, Barall, all of you. Let's not pander to formalities today."

As he said this, Zithius bent and helped Barall to his feet, exhaustion and embarrassment plain on the younger man's face.

"You have been through quite a year, young man," said Zithius while supporting Barall's slight frame easily. With a nod of his head, the king indicated a comfortable looking chair near a merrily crackling fire and led Barall to it while everyone else found seats for themselves.

As he sat, Barall looked around with a mixed expression of fear at what may be coming and shock at being in the presence of a Wisdom, a general and the King of Cherilla. In his heart and mind, Barall still considered himself just the boy who worked in the archives. Never had he expected to be keeping such company as this.

Knowing him best, Stein suspected what his friend was going through, so explained what was going on. "We likely don't have much time before the Emissary comes to try and collect you, so while I have told the king what I know of you and the circle it might help if you could explain it to everyone."

"W-where do I start?" stammered Barall.

"Why not start with what you know about what Comfort Vance was looking for before his death, and go from there," suggested Virez.

&

Barall talked for most of an hour, telling them everything he knew. For the most part, his audience stayed silent, letting him tell the story in his own way and in his own time. He tried to keep his personal feelings out of it and relate only the facts, but it was impossible, and his rancor at the Emissary's lack of consideration for his people, his own priests and the church, came through. When he fell silent, and Stein offered him a glass of chilled juice, he sank back into the chair, with an expectant look on his face, waiting for them to respond to what he had said. He did not have to wait for long as everyone had questions, mainly to clarify what he had already said, but also to gather Barall's impression or opinion of events. When finally the questions ended the group split in two with Virez coming to see Barall, and Wilnah and Stein joining the king.

Bless you, Barall," said Virez, earnestly making the sign of the circle over him.

"For what, Wisdom?" asked Barall. "I didn't do anything that anyone else wouldn't have done. I just happened to be the one in whose lap it fell."

"I'm not sure I believe that."

"It's true. It started because I thought whoever killed Comfort Vance, would come after me next. There was nothing noble or virtuous about it."

"Rubbish," stated Zithius flatly.

Surprised, Barall looked up to see the three men had already finished talking.

"Your leaving the cathedral may, indeed, have been done out of a feeling your life was in danger, but that does not account for the time since then."

"Do you know what courage is, my boy?" asked Wilnah.

When Barall shook his head, "Courage is not the absence of fear. Fear disables us and makes it so we can't think or move, unless it is to just run away. Courage is acting despite the fear."

"But …"

"Forget your reasons for leaving," Zithius started, "was it fear that led you to join six unknown priests and priestesses of unknown gods?"

"Or to stand up in every town and city across the country to proclaim your support of all seven gods?" added Stein.

"Or to continue your work despite the Emissary's edict and the mobilization of an army?" chimed in Virez.

"Or to allow yourself to be captured, questioned and brought all the way back to Anklesh?" said Wilnah. "These are not acts done out of fear. These are acts of courage and faith."

"Your faith," concluded Virez, coming up to Barall, "is the strongest and deepest I've ever seen. It was strong enough to join a group dedicated to bringing lost gods to Cherilla and strong enough to stand up and promote their existence. Only one whose faith is strong could do that, for only they would believe that the people will still be there for Endomar, and our lord for them. In the end, Endomar is stronger as those who don't truly believe will find solace with another god."

The description Virez provided was the simplest Barall had heard, and truly went to the heart of the matter. Just as Barall was about to respond, a knock came at the door.

A guard stepped into the room and announced, "A delegation from the cathedral has arrived."

"Who speaks for them?" asked Virez.

"Emissary Caven, himself, my Lady."

# Chapter 27

*"We are made wise not by the recollection of our past, but by the responsibility for our future."*
**George Bernard Shaw**

"I want that boy, Zithius, and I want him now," demanded the Emissary. "You have no right to him."

The Emissary pointed a long slender finger at Barall, who sat off to one side, his arms free and his hands clasped loosely in front of him. Dressed in a clean, fresh robe, he felt almost normal again. But what felt best was the weight of the solid silver circle and chain Virez had given him. The Wisdom had removed the circle from around her own neck and placed it around Barall's with a smile and a nod, before she left, not willing to yet reveal her presence at the palace to the Emissary.

Barall remained silent and still, listening to the exchange, wondering how Zithius, a politician, would deal with the irrationalities of the Emissary.

"I have every right, Emissary, as you well know. The law is clear. Any religious prisoner is to be held by the state until the commission of a crime is verified. I'm surprised you tried to avoid the law, Emissary," replied the king, mildly rebuking the Emissary.

"I tried to avoid nothing, Zithius. It's a never-used law."

"You have that many crimes committed in the cathedral that would cause it to be invoked … Caven? I presume I can call you Caven, since you have taken the liberty of calling me by name?"

The Emissary bristled at the king's cavalier attitude. His brows narrowed in anger and his hands clenched at his sides. He looked from side to side, searching for his guards, his anger only mounting when he remembered they were forced to remain in the courtyard below, except for his captain who stood outside the door. They were under the watchful eyes of the king's soldiers. It was humiliating for one of his rank, Emissary of the church of Endomar, probably with more power and influence than this pathetic, weak fool before him, to be forced to walk alone, without suitable guards or attendants.

"I don't recognize that name any longer," stated the Emissary dismissively. "Just as I don't recognize your hold over my subject."

"Your subject?" said the king slowly, as if unsure he had heard correctly.

"Yes."

Zithius looked over at Barall, a look of profound sadness on his face. Knowing what was coming when the king's face hardened as he looked back at the Emissary, Barall silently begged the king to patience and prayed that both men would remember the seven pillars of wisdom. Nothing good would come of hot tempers and grandstanding.

"You would do well to remember, Caven," sneered Zithius, purposely breaking the Emissary's name into two slow, distinct words, "this man is, first and foremost *my* subject. As such, I am duty bound to protect him. Especially since all he has done is work to educate the people and strengthen the faith of the worshippers of Endomar."

Shock registered on the faces of both Barall and the Emissary, neither predicting the king would so openly support Barall. Thus far, Zithius had been extremely careful to straddle the fence, neither supporting nor denouncing either side, in a delicate balancing act he had been performing since the circle of seven had appeared. Now, with the Emissary standing before him, Zithius had declared his allegiance to Barall and the circle. The Emissary recovered with a seething tantrum, ranting and raging against Zithius, Barall and Vance and anything else that permeated his thoughts. Spittle flew from his lips and his arms waved and punched the air as he screamed his fury at the world.

In his mind, the Emissary reeled. Never had Zithius been considered an ally, but neither was he an enemy. But now, everything was turned on end. As much as he believed in his heart that the king was a useless figurehead, kept in a position of power at the whim of the people and the church, he also knew the king was well-loved and respected. With his support thrown behind Barall, people may be swayed to follow the circle of blasphemers.

Finally gaining some control over himself, the Emissary took several deep breaths. When he looked again at Barall, the cause of all his turmoil and anguish, the Emissary moved toward him, eyes locked on the prisoner, like a predator stalking its prey. Barall watched him come, unmoving and seemingly unafraid. Still he was grateful when the two men charged with guarding the prisoner were not willing to believe in the Emissary's good intentions and moved forward to stand beside Barall as the young priest rose from his chair.

"You have brought this church to the brink of ruin," hissed the Emissary. "Because of you people are turning away from the light of Endomar and if it's the last thing I do, I will be triumphant. You will never be Emissary."

The venom in the Emissary's voice startled the guards but did nothing to Barall. The younger man listened without reaction, remaining still and composed. Only when the Emissary mentioned

Barall's supposed goals, did he show any reaction. A look of confusion and dismay came across his face.

"Oh, Emissary, how I have prayed for you. I do not covet your position. I want nothing more than to return to the archives and work for the education of all people and a return of the church to its former glory."

"Bah! You have done nothing but sow dissention and promote false gods."

"No, Emissary, I have not. I have tried to return the world to balance, as you should have done."

"Do not think to tell me my role, boy. I am the Emissary."

"But a poor one," retorted Barall, a chink appearing in his cool composure. "You have sought to increase your own power and influence, not Endomar's. You have sent soldiers among your own people, not protected them. You have denounced learning and made discussion and debate illegal, not welcomed it with open arms."

"You dare," started the Emissary, pulling his staff back as if to strike out with it. What his intentions were, however, were interrupted when the door to the room burst open to admit general Wilnah and the captain of the Emissary's guard.

"My lords," said Wilnah, politely ignoring the tensions in the room, "the city is rioting."

෴

What actually started the riot was something that would never be determined but likely it was some comment made by one side and overheard by the other. The comment, whether innocent or intentional, was irrelevant for it was taken as an insult. Surely words were exchanged, quickly growing heated and angry which led to blows and weapons being drawn. From there the escalation was inevitable. Friends of the initial pair would be the first to join in, each side blaming the other for the first insult, the first punch, the first weapon, the first to spill blood. As it spread, the truth of the reason behind the fight would become less and less important as all that would matter was that the person you were fighting wore a different color, or worshipped a different god. It was the most anti-Endomarian thing to do, for only through enlightened disagreement and heart-felt discussion could true wisdom be attained.

Word spread rapidly throughout the city, and while most people shut themselves in their homes and clutched tightly to loved ones in fear of what was happening, others ventured out onto the streets. The soldiers who were dispatched to quell the bloodshed made matters worse. Both the Emissary and Zithius, informed simultaneously, since they were locked in a battle of their own, issued orders to their respective forces. Each ignored the other, and neither cared about what the other was doing, even though all they were doing was adding more men to the fray.

Only Barall, now all but forgotten, and Wilnah, saw the danger.

"My lord, perhaps we should let the Emissary's forces put down this uprising," suggested Wilnah quietly.

"What?" exclaimed Zithius in surprise.

"My lord … our forces are not friendly to each other, and are professionally trained. By sending our men, and the Emissary sending his, they will either be targeted by the mobs, or will decide to join them."

But Zithius would not be swayed and his men rode just ahead of the Emissary's guards. Turning from Wilnah, Zithius could see Barall striding calmly away from his guards, looking for all the world like he was leaving. The Emissary left with his own men so the king had thought he had a reprieve where the young priest was concerned.

"What's this?" demanded the king.

"I'm going to do what I can to help calm the people," replied Barall matter-of-factly over his shoulder. "The general is right, my lord, the soldiers will make things worse, not better."

"And you will make it better," said Zithius incredulously, "the leader of this so-called rebellion and the cause of the riot? You think walking alone and unarmed into a city gone mad, with half wanting to raise you to Emissary, and the other half damning you as a blasphemer, will help?"

"I have the strength of truth and the shield of faith …"

"You have nothing, not even the wisdom your god granted you, not if you can't see the danger, the risk, the inherent bad sense this decision makes."

"I'm not a prisoner of yours, so you can't hold me. I can only say that I must do this, as much as the Emissary must do what he must, until the end. For as much as I had to leave the cathedral then, I must leave the palace now."

The king stared at Barall for a long moment, weighing his options, while Barall waited impatiently. Finally, uncharacteristically chewing his lower lip in worry, he grunted, "Fine. But you go with a contingent of guards and will listen to them when it comes to your own protection."

⚭

The city was eerily quiet, broken occasionally by pockets of roving bands aligned to one side of the fight or the other. Smoke curled in lazy circles from fires set inside the walls as looters could not pass up such a good opportunity.

The Emissary and his personal guard of twenty men were resting in an alley while scouts ranged ahead, checking the route toward the cathedral. Since leaving the palace, they had run across only a smattering of other people, and those had turned and fled at the sight of the armed and mounted group. The Emissary was impatient to keep moving, and grew more anxious the longer he was forced to wait. His horse, sensing his rider's mood, danced and whinnied, but the Emissary did nothing to try to calm it.

Suddenly the clip-clop sound of several horses from a street nearby was heard. Silently, the guards closed ranks around the Emissary and drew their swords. As the sound drew nearer, the Emissary called softly to the captain of his men, "I am too important to the church and this country. I cannot be taken. You will attack on my command … and you will fight to kill."

The captain gave the Emissary a sidelong look, but nodded his head after only a moment. The captain, the same who had spoken to Wilnah upon Barall's entrance into the city, was beginning to seriously wonder about the Emissary's state of mind when a squadron of soldiers walked past the mouth of the alley. In their midst, Barall sat his horse easily. The soldiers walked by the alley barely glancing in, their focus intent on the road ahead. The captain relaxed, knowing there was nothing to fear because these men were loyal to the king and were likely tasked with quelling the riot. They were professional soldiers and maintained their temperament in difficult situations. If they passed by, they were on a mission not involving the Emissary and no danger to him.

But then, the Emissary shocked him again by ordering them to attack.

"But, for what purpose, Emissary? Surely getting you to safety and putting down the riot are of more importance. We can return to Barall once you are safe."

"Do as I say, captain. Barall is not to return to the palace, but to be taken to the cathedral. If he happens to be killed in retrieving him, so be it."

"Emissary …" started the captain, seeing his own men shuffling and looking at one another uneasily.

"Now, captain," the Emissary said, for the first time looking directly at the man. "I am the Emissary and am to be obeyed in all things. My will is law and to disobey me is to disobey Endomar. Do it now!"

With no option open to him, save facing the Emissary's wrath and possibly being denounced, himself, as faithless, the captain gave the command to attack. The battle was over before it could really start. Outnumbered by over three to one, the soldiers guarding Barall were cut down with brutal efficiency. There was no one else about to witness the cowardly attack on the king's men, and even the guards who conducted the slaughter seemed to have no heart in it. A stunned Barall could only gape in astonishment as the Emissary rounded the corner of an alley and manoeuvred his horse alongside Barall's. For a long moment he did nothing but stare at Barall, a self-satisfied, smug expression on his face. Then, when Barall opened his mouth to speak, the Emissary slapped him, hard, across the face.

"Do not dare to speak to me," roared the Emissary. "You are beneath me, not worthy to converse with the likes of me. Be silent and obey and perhaps you will live a while longer."

"Captain," he turned to his guard commander, "continue to the cathedral and kill anyone who gets in your way."

❦

The Emissary's words were easily said, but none of the guards with him wanted to fight their way through the entire city since the only real access to Cathedral Island was by boat, and the launch that brought them from the island lay on the far side of the Bay of Fasada. From the palace it was a long way around, over the Bridge of Micarad, and they hadn't even come within sight of the bridge yet. Surely the Emissary wasn't serious about killing more people. It was bad enough they had killed the king's soldiers in cold blood, but the Emissary was ordering them to kill even their own side. Most of the men were praying they didn't meet anyone. Of course, that wasn't about to happen, so swords were kept bared. For a while, they were lucky, scouts ranged several blocks ahead and were able to steer the group away from any others. As they walked, the Emissary stared at Barall, sitting his horse, a pace or two ahead.

"Your rebellion will soon be over. You are beaten," sneered the Emissary.

"It is not 'my rebellion,' as you call it, Emissary," said Barall sadly. "The people that you have stepped on, beaten down and oppressed with your draconian measures and tactics will not stay that way forever. Nor will the king continue to allow you to harm his subjects. You are alone, my lord. In this great, wide world, you have no one whom you can really count on or trust."

As if Barall's words were somehow anti-prophetic, the group rounded a corner, and saw the Bridge of Micarad, covered end to end in people. The bridge spanned the Bay of Fasada over the narrowest point in the channel that connected the bay to the sea. The bridge was a spectacular sight. Made of white stone in a graceful arch over the glittering water, it soared upward to an impossible height, so that, at its highest, even the tall-masted trading ships could glide easily underneath.

The people lining the bridge weren't fighting; in fact they weren't doing anything but staring out over the bay as if watching the cathedral, the palace and the rest of the city. The road the Emissary's group rode along was blind to the bay until just as it broke upon it. There was no warning for the Emissary as the scouts held back, not wishing to reveal their position. So intent and incensed at Barall's statement, the Emissary blurted out his true feelings without realizing where he was or who could hear.

"I am loved by the people and adored, Acolyte. My name is known throughout the land, while you wouldn't be recognized in the cathedral."

As he spoke the people began to file off the bridge, and even more people started to enter the small square that fronted the entrance to the bridge. Numerous soldiers in the king's livery, weapons drawn at the sight of the naked blades of the Emissary's guards, stood in a semi-circle around none other than the king himself, with Virez at his side. Further along the way, Stein appeared, looking dishevelled and out of breath, while the six priests of the circle members and what looked like every clerist knight followed. But the one man who truly caught Barall's attention was the one who separated from the group descending from the bridge and came walking toward them. Leading them all was the bulky form of the very first knight, Rillem.

# Chapter 28

*"We thought, because we had power, we had wisdom."*
**Stephen Vincent Benet**

"For too long, the people have been allowed to be complacent in their devotion to Endomar," continued the Emissary, oblivious to the crowd growing around them. "The church has allowed this to happen. And then you come along, and your equally pompous Comfort Vance, and think to challenge me? Vance was dealt with … but you? You pick up right where he left off announcing to the world about seven gods, declaring the world out of balance, spreading your lies and fear to everyone. No more! It ends here and now. Captain," he called out to his guard. "Kill this blasphemous wretch immediately."

There was no response at first, then, "My apologies, Emissary, but I don't think that would be a good idea."

"What!?!" screeched the Emissary, whipping around to find the man. "How dare …"

Only then did the Emissary see the crowd gathered, his guards keeping everyone back with a close circle surrounding he and Barall. Most of the faces were hard, very few showing any sympathy or support. Looking around and thinking quickly, he saw King Zithius with Virez, and knew now where the Wisdom had vanished; there were also a lot of well armed men he didn't know, not wearing any kind of uniform.

"Captain," he called out again, somewhat more conciliatorily, "you will kill this blasphemous wretch immediately, if he doesn't answer my questions to my satisfaction."

"Well met, Emissary," hailed Zithius. "Is all well here?"

"Zithius," replied the Emissary coolly, "I'm surprised to see you out of your palace."

"You would be surprised at what we do, my son and I."

If Zithius thought the mention of his dead son would shock the Emissary, he was mistaken, for there was no reaction; no indication the Emissary even knew the king had a son. For now, Zithius kept his thoughts to himself, too.

"I'm sure I would," said the Emissary sounding bored. "If you will excuse us, we will be on our way back to the cathedral."

"Actually, you won't, Emissary. You have seized my guest, knowing the law requires you to prove your claim against him before any sentence is carried out."

The king paused as if letting his statement sink in. "However," he added, "since you mentioned questioning Lord Barall, let's do just that."

"What?"

"We will, all of us here, stand witness to your questioning."

Much to the Emissary's chagrin, the whole odd group stayed, and he was forced to conduct his questioning of Barall himself, in public when he had planned to do it in the privacy of his throne room, with Lassand and Vahchen at his side to assist him. All the clever questions he had prepared to prove Barall was conducting a ruse, that he was a blasphemer against the church, seemed to fly out of his mouth. He peppered Barall, who was forced to stand alone in the center of the square, with every speck of knowledge and rumor ever heard of the quest and the circle of seven. Barall acknowledged just about everything he was accused of. At the beginning, he answered each question with a simple, "Yes, Emissary" or "No, my lord" and to the crowd watching, it was like the Emissary was walking all over him. The two men, however, knew the opposite was true.

By not responding in the expected manner, Barall was completely undermining the Emissary's attacks and the questions became wilder and further away from the Emissary's plan. As the Emissary started to lose control, Barall expanded his answers to add questions and comments of his own.

"Endomar is the greatest god there is," started the Emissary.

"Then by your own logic He is also the worst," interrupted Barall calmly. "For there to be balance, where there is a greatest there must be a least great. Don't you agree?"

"That is blasphemy," said the Emissary. "I am the inquisitor in this investigation, you are to answer questions, not ask them."

"I do only as you bid, my lord."

Barall was taught to argue by Vance which was a common event in the archives as they worked together, hour after hour and day after day. Vance was an excellent debater and often caught Barall in this method of asking questions rather than answering those put to him, infuriating Barall to the point where he would say something he would regret for it would often point to the position that Vance was arguing. Turning the tables on the Emissary, while entertaining, was also doing something else: it was enraging the Emissary to the point where he was making mistakes, and uttering statements that were only furthering Barall's position, rather than his own.

"So you admit, freely and willingly, to making up three ridiculous and unheard of pillars of faith?" questioned the Emissary.

"No, my lord, I do not. I learned of the forgotten pillars in the diary of Gibson, a Wisdom of Endomar. A Wisdom, my lord, and therefore one who would have taught untold numbers before me."

"Gibson is unknown …"

"And why is that, my lord?" interrupted Barall, shocking the Emissary to silence. "Why is it that a Wisdom in your own church has been forgotten? How have three pillars upon which our faith is based been eliminated, and why?"

"That is preposterous."

"And why do these three pillars so frighten you, my lord? Humility, patience and sacrifice complete the circle that is our lives. Is it, perhaps, because you, the Emissary and highest of our order, do not exhibit these traits in even the smallest degree?"

The Emissary was nearly apoplectic with rage and several people from the crowd gasped in shock and outrage that the Emissary was spoken to in this manner. Caven's grand plan for Barall's interrogation had rapidly descended into his being questioned instead. This fool of a boy obviously didn't know who he was dealing with, or what he was capable of. Many in the crowd shared that lack of knowledge, obviously, for many of them laughed as well. It was all going so badly, and the people were starting to turn against him. Barall had already admitted to proclaiming and promoting these other gods and goddesses and to defying the Emissary's edict. This last was a mistake of the Emissary's, in bringing it up at all. The question had actually made Barall laugh to hear it. His laughter caused the crowd to laugh as well. The Emissary's face burned in embarrassment at the remembrance of the laughter. It brought something else too, though. A new tack came to mind, one he had not considered before, but one that could galvanize the people to support him over Barall. The people would flock to his banner, out of fear, yes, but their reasons were irrelevant.

"What do you know of magic?" asked the Emissary, ignoring Barall's question.

"Magic, Emissary? Nothing at all," was Barall's confused reply.

"Really, boy, come now, we've all heard of your magical abilities; how you destroyed the doors to the great church in Guilder and healed a man you, yourself, wounded."

For a moment Barall was silent as he contemplated his response, looking around at the faces in the crowd. Unknown to the Emissary, the bulk of the spectators were Barall's friends: the circle was here, as was the king, Stein, Riordan and his knights, as well as Wisdoms Virez and Destrin. Where Wisdom Lassand was, Barall didn't know. Looking closer, Barall finally caught sight of Rillem, the man looking like he hadn't changed a bit in the months since he and his wife, Valleria, had left to perform a special task.

Barall tried to read Rillem's face, to gather some kind of clue as to whether things were ready. The knights had travelled to Anklesh at Barall's request several months ago to prepare for what Barall called, "an eventuality hopefully never to come to pass." Since being captured, Barall had prayed diligently that Rillem had heeded his request and been able to get everything in place, then, as he neared Anklesh, he could only hope the knight even knew Barall was coming. Seeing Rillem walking from the Bridge of Micarad, Barall's knees had nearly buckled in relief. His friend had smiled to see Barall, but then his face creased in concern and worry and not a little anger. Not able to talk, they used generic facial expressions and slight movements to try to get their messages across. Rillem took Barall's direct look and barely noticeable shake of the head to mean he was to do nothing yet and so stayed back, eyes glued to the unfolding scene.

The curt nod the knight saw now though, changed everything. Returning the nod, to show he had seen and understood, Rillem eased his way through the crowd, tapping several men and women as he passed. The interrogation was irrelevant - they all knew how it was going to end, anyway, and the time to change that end was approaching.

Still ignoring the Emissary, Barall found the priests and priestesses of the circle standing together not too far from where Rillem was positioning himself. The circle watched with varying looks on their faces. Most were as expected: Cura with concern and worry creasing her understated beauty, Cerrok with boredom and Tella with fierce determination and loyalty. Surprisingly Dalis stood with his massive arms crossed over his barrel chest, a look of deep anger on his face. Both Destrin and Arion had a hand on one of Dalis' arms and seemed to be speaking softly to him. It was then that Barall noticed Dalis' hands. In each one he carried a massive stone hammer, gripped tightly and apparently ready to be put to lethal use. Barall had never seen the priest of love and loyalty show anger, and to see him now, so obviously full of fury and barely contained violence, made him realize how little he really knew them. Doubt crept into Barall. Was Vance right about the other gods? Were the men and women that formed his circle really the high priests and priestesses of all but forgotten religions? Was he doing the right thing? That last, more than any other question plagued his thoughts and dreams.

By now, the Emissary, reading Barall's silence as indecision and guilt, crowed in glee. "I see you hesitate and look around for an answer. The truth is not found out there, boy, but in here." The Emissary tapped his chest over his heart. "The heart knows the truth, even as the mind concocts lies. Tell us, finally, the truth you know swells within your heart."

Barall cocked his head, listening to the Emissary. Although wrong about Barall, the Emissary's words were true nevertheless. All of the Emissary's questions and opinions had mirrored all of Barall's inner questions that he had struggled with since he had met Cura and Dalis that long-ago spring day outside Anklesh. But those questions came from his mind, refusing to believe something simply because it contradicted what he had been taught up until then. Faith is not a thing of the mind, but of the heart and soul. A man does not believe in Endomar because he is told to or because he has physical proof. True faith believes despite being told not to, and without proof. That was what Tella, Venick, Seskia and the others exemplified every day.

Like morning dew touched by the summer sun, doubt evaporated from Barall's mind. The truth always lay within his heart, but he just now recognized it for what it was: his faith. It had upheld him throughout all the ordeals of the past year and led him to take up with Cura and Dalis. Even now, he had faith that what he was doing was right. The Emissary was not a man who was pure of faith or who worked for the benefit of Endomar; in just about everything the Emissary had ever said to him, he proved this. Straightening his back and turning to face the Emissary again, he prepared himself for what was likely to come.

"Emissary, once again you are wrong. Everything I've said has been truthful and honest and, as you suggested, from the heart. What you call 'magic' is the beneficence of our great God Endomar answering a heartfelt prayer. You, Emissary, are supposed to be the model for the people to follow, to educate and instruct us in our spiritual lives, and to maintain the balance in the faith. In all these areas, and more, you have failed. It is time for you to ..."

A scream tore through the still air. A woman clapped her hand over her mouth and pointed with the other. Looking where she pointed, the crowd gasped in unison as thick, black smoke could be seen rising over the tops of the buildings.

೫

The king marched several paces into the square to get a better view before turning to the soldiers behind him. "Halden," he called, "take the men and as many volunteers as you can muster. Check all areas for fire and report back as soon as possible on the fire and the riots."

The man, Halden, saluted and rode off immediately, several others following behind. Zithius, the picture of regal authority, now turned to Barall and the Emissary.

"This is over, Caven. You've proven nothing against this man. No crime has been committed, and it seems to be an internal church matter."

"Zithius, you too have been taken in by the lies of this man. I will not let you, nor anyone else, stand in my way."

"It seems as if everything Lord Barall has said, then, is true," called a new voice from the crowd.

Everyone searched for the speaker, and then, from the direction of the bridge, Wisdom Lassand strode into view.

"King Zithius is right, my lord. Barall has done nothing but work for this church without any regard for himself."

The Emissary was flabbergasted. Lassand had been his right hand, guiding and advising him. It was Lassand who recommended a search of the archives to find and destroy any proof of other gods, bringing numerous books and letters and diaries to be burned. Yet here he was, advocating for Barall? It didn't make any sense.

"L-Lassand?" stammered the Emissary.

"Yes, Emissary?" replied Lassand evenly.

"W-what are you doing h-here?"

"I heard of the riot, my lord, and of this interrogation, though I admit I expected to find you in the palace, not in the middle of the street. I came to bring you the latest finding from our search for proof."

The Emissary's eyes lit up in renewed triumph. Lassand's searches had found references to other gods, those usually casual mentions to a non-Endomarian cleric. Those books or papers had been burned, their existence removed from the archives and forgotten. For Lassand to have ventured out to find them, he must have found something truly damning to Barall - something that would end this pointless debacle once and for all. Motioning Lassand forward into the area of clear space surrounding he and Barall, the Emissary made a great show of welcoming Lassand and bestowing upon him the blessing of Endomar.

"Wisdom Lassand," intoned the Emissary, "you are welcome to this proceeding. Tell us, what great news you have to share?"

Lassand clutched a book to his chest, its leather bindings blending in to the brown of his Wisdom's robes. That he again was in the brown of a Wisdom instead of the blue of a Primate was lost on the Emissary as Lassand looked around at the faces familiar to him: Virez, the Emissary, and Destrin. Finally, coming to rest on Barall, the Wisdom shifted uncomfortably and held the book tighter.

"My lord, I believe we should discuss this in private," he said.

"Nonsense, Lassand, my one true loyal Wisdom," replied the Emissary with pointed looks at Virez, standing next to King Zithius, and Destrin among those who could only be the remaining members of the circle of seven. "I know you have come here to help end this long year of constant strife. Know that I recognize your worth and want everyone here, too, to know of your dedication to the church and to me."

The words meant little to Lassand, for any respect he had for the Emissary, had died with Nokya. The paternal-type feelings he had for her, a waif of a girl who had propositioned him on the street one day years ago, were coursing through his veins, breeding feelings of anger and revenge. He truly believed that as much as he saved her that day from a life of pain and abuse, she had saved him too, for until then, he had felt his life had lost its purpose and he had lost his focus. Nokya gave him direction and a reason to get up each morning. It was as close to love as he had ever really gotten.

The feelings of guilt he felt over her death were still very much present and he knew he would feel the burden of her death and the responsibility for putting her in that situation in the first place for the rest of his days. He would work tirelessly to prove to her, and to himself, that neither of their lives were in vain.

"Lord Emissary," started Lassand, "I have, just today found this book that may resolve the debate on the existence of other gods."

As he spoke he moved away from the Emissary and spoke more to the crowd. He acknowledged Virez with a smile and a slight nod of his head, and then bowed low to the king, which would surely irritate the Emissary, but Lassand was beyond caring. These people had done more to promote and protect the church and the people than the Emissary ever had. Destrin, whom he had not seen since the night of Percinal's murder, seemed thinner, more haggard than Lassand remembered. Was it, perhaps, that travel disagreed with him, or life as an outlaw? Regardless, Lassand came right up to his friend and clasped him, warmly around the shoulders.

"It is good to see you," said Destrin returning the embrace awkwardly, for the two men had never really been close, and more often than not, were adversaries.

"And you, too," replied Lassand honestly. Then, quietly, so only Destrin could hear, "You've done well, the best of us all in fact. Your travels with the circle seem nothing short of a miracle. Now let's see if I can match your accomplishments, but be ready, he won't be happy."

With those words, Lassand moved away from his puzzled and worried friend. Destrin followed Lassand's movements with a wary eye never hearing such praise from Lassand before, or such criticism of himself. Obviously, the task of remaining at the cathedral and working with the Emissary had taken a great toll on the normally staid and composed Lassand. Something big was coming, Destrin decided, so he'd better warn the others, but turned to find the knights already preparing. A knight moved to stand in front of their priestly charge, with another taking position behind. The priests themselves readied their own weapons, not willing to let others fight their battles for them. Dalis, so ready to charge to Barall's rescue earlier, had somewhat calmed down, apparently prepared to let Lassand's plan play out.

No longer able to delay the Emissary any longer, Lassand turned again to face his lord. "Emissary, this book is an older version of a book we, ourselves, keep, a chronological listing of every law, edict, directive and order issued by the office of the Emissary."

Lassand paused as if to let his words sink in, and continued to walk around. The crowd, obviously, didn't know that such a book existed, but the Emissary merely looked bored.

"And?" asked the Emissary. "What did you find?"

Lassand smiled. "I don't know."

❧

With the Emissary distracted, Halden moved closer to the king and gave his report in a hushed voice.

"Neither side has any advantage, Sire," he said, keeping one eye on the exchange between the Emissary and Lassand. "Our soldiers and the Emissary's are staying out of it, but the people are getting more daring because of that. Someone decided that the owner of one of the warehouses near the shipping docks was on the other side, and set fire to his goods. The fire is contained within the building, but obviously tempers are starting to flare and people are getting bolder. I recommend we call out our full force to stop this before it gets any bigger."

"Sire," interrupted Stein from behind Halden, "there may be another way."

"Speak," ordered Zithius.

"The people are fighting because they don't know what the truth is. So, we spread the word that the leaders of the two sides are in discussion to resolve the issue. Ask the people to stand down to let Barall and the Emissary conclude their … business. That request will be backed up by your soldiers for any of those who don't obey."

"Good," said the king decisively, "only have it said the Emissary and Barall are locked in battle - it will be more credible."

❧

"What!?!" the Emissary fairly screeched.

"Approximately four or five generations ago, an internal decree was issued and a law proclaimed. All we know is that it was called the *Forgetting Law* and where all other entries provide a brief explanation of the law, this one has been obscured."

"Then it's useless," stated the Emissary with a dismissive wave of his hand and a scornful look at Lassand.

"No, Emissary, it's not," said Barall quietly, while a look of relief spread over Lassand's face.

"No question was put to you, boy," shouted the Emissary.

"And yet I must answer anyway, you foolish, foolish man," Barall yelled back, finally losing his temper. "I have been nothing but truthful with you, Emissary, but my truth frightens you, not because of what it says but because of what it contradicts. The existence of the six other gods and goddesses is not what you rail against, but what their existence and acceptance would do to your precious plans for your own legacy."

"Wisdom Lassand," Barall called out, "despite what the Emissary believes, and orders others to believe, prayer can work miracles. I should be able to reveal the truth behind the *Forgetting Law.*"

Barall stared at the Emissary as Wisdom Lassand walked over to him. When Lassand reached him, Barall finally broke his staring to see a look of such profound fear on the Wisdom's face that Barall immediately reached out to him.

"Wisdom, are you all right?" he asked worriedly, his hands grasping hold of the Wisdom's own.

"Well met, my lord," breathed Lassand. "You are, indeed, the true savior of our church - probably of us all."

"I don't …" started Barall.

"I know you don't think so, but of everyone, the Emissary, the Wisdoms and Primates, only Comfort Vance and yourself saw the real danger to the imbalance. Only you saw through the veils the Emissary lay across everything he did. Only you had the courage to act and the tenacity to see it through. My fear is not for me at all, I am nothing, but you, my son, are in grave danger."

Despite what Lassand predicted, Barall actually relaxed and smiled. Still holding on to the Wisdom's hands, he looked first to the Emissary and then to the circle of seven and King Zithius.

"Look at them, Wisdom," he said. "Of everyone here, who is the most afraid? I tell you, for certain, it is the Emissary, for in his heart, he knows he is already undone."

Before speaking again he manoeuvred the book in Lassand's hands so the Wisdom was holding it open, the pages facing Barall. The title of the laws and proclamations could be read easily, flowing down the page in neat orderly rows, until, near the bottom where the name of the law and a brief explanation would normally be printed, only a blank and the word *Law* could be seen. In the empty space before the word, and for several lines beneath it, there was only a cloudy mass, looking like milky tea. After a slight nod of satisfaction, Barall looked into Lassand's eyes. "You must promise me something, my lord," he said quietly.

Lassand looked at him quizzically, but nodded.

"Be safe. You know that whatever my prayer shows, the Emissary will claim victory. My time is nearly done, but yours is just beginning.

I believe with all that I am, you must be safe, for in you lies the balance."

Not giving Lassand any time to respond, Barall closed his eyes and began to pray. As curious as Lassand was about the prayer, or spell, or whatever it was, he found it impossible to concentrate. He had long suspected priestly magic was possible, but the feeling that Barall was expecting his own death was too unsettling to allow him to follow what Barall was doing. There were no arcane gestures or strange words and from what Lassand could make out, all Barall was doing was praying. Suddenly, it was over and Barall looked up and smiled. Together they looked down at the book together to see that, where the words had been unreadable, they were now clear and legible. Lassand could not hold back the gasp as he read:

> *Forgetting Law:*
> *There are to be no Gods, other than Endomar. By proclamation*
> *of the Emissary, every priest of this church shall forget, on*
> *penalty of death, the existence of the circle of Gods.*

# Chapter 29

*"More than any other time in history, mankind faces a crossroads. One path leads to despair and utter hopelessness. The other, to total extinction. Let us pray we have the wisdom to choose correctly."*
**Woody Allen**

Lassand and Barall looked at the book, then at each other before reading it a second time and turning to look at the Emissary who hadn't moved since Lassand arrived. He stood in exactly the same place and had watched as the Wisdom moved around and ended up at Barall, listening as they discussed magic and the reading of the purpose of the *Forgetting Law*. Once again, Barall had disrupted all of the Emissary's plans. The interrogation was supposed to be his pre-eminent moment when he would rid himself of Barall and the circle of seven and any talk of his not being the foremost Emissary of all time would be put to rest. Now, he was nothing but a laughingstock, someone you looked at, before looking quickly away. From now on he would be pitied, not respected or feared.

He used to see fear in almost everyone's eyes when he walked into a room. It was intoxicating. People feared his opinion going against them. Now, it seemed, the only ones who feared him were his own men. His priests avoided him, the people found reasons to skip his sermons every twenty days, and his soldiers debated his orders. It was a move away from the church's traditional role of ruling by the threat of damnation if donations, servitude and piety were not given in large amounts. Even the people who, right now, were rioting on his side, were doing so only out of fear of what he would do if he found out they supported his enemy.

Things were to change under his rule. The people and priests alike were to return to their proper places in the world. Priests were above reproach, except from within the church, and were to be obeyed in all things. They were consulted for their learned and wise opinion on all matters of importance: social, business and political. Why couldn't the people see the changes he was implementing were for the betterment of all?

The Emissary looked around and realized that not one of the people standing around gawking had bent their knees to him. Who did they think they were? Better than him? They were nothing. Peons and cretins, all of them, but none more so then this stripling boy. He was an Acolyte who dared to grow hair on his head, as if he were mature enough to do so, a whelp, who dared to cross him and disrupt all of his plans.

Looking at the people now, the Emissary could see them staring back at him but it would end here. It didn't matter that Zithius was here, too, for the king was useless, like a toothless dog barking to make himself heard, but with nothing of substance to back it up. The Emissary's guards had grown to such a proportion that they could easily handle the number of permanent soldiers maintained by the king. His Wisdoms too, were irrelevant. He had worked and succeeded without their so-called 'guidance' for so long, the entire rank had been collapsed, leaving only Barall, for he controlled the hearts of all the lost ones out there. All those people who foolishly followed the circle of seven would learn, with Barall's death that his lies and deceits were only the mad dreams of a boy bent on glory and power for himself. The Emissary would be magnanimous, he decided, and allow all of those people to return to the fold without punishment or retribution. Of course, their names would be recorded and they, and their families, would be watched for any signs they lacked true devotion.

"What have you found?" asked the Emissary, the disdain he really felt, kept from his voice.

As Lassand read the words revealed by Barall's prayer, the Emissary's hand tightened forcefully on his staff, the pain of his grip filling him, centering his mind into sharp focus as he stared at Barall from across the square.

"And we are to believe this?" he spat contemptuously. "That you have cast a spell, when true priests are unable to work magic? We are to believe that this spell was cast honestly, to reveal the hidden truth, and it just so happens to provide vindication for your preposterous claims? Since you are the only priest of Endomar claiming to be able to perform such a feat, I find your 'results' suspicious."

"Of course you do, Emissary," replied Barall softly, but only Lassand heard as the Emissary continued.

"I hereby declare this use of 'magic' blasphemy as it has been outlawed by the church for countless generations. Your performing it here, in front of all these witnesses, makes it known beyond any doubt."

This last was said in a shout to the assembled masses, but to Zithius in particular. Then, to his guards, the Emissary added, "Arrest him, and take him to the cathedral for his punishment to be decided and carried out."

Shouts erupted everywhere as people voiced their approval or displeasure at this pronouncement, and watched as several guards made their way to Barall, drawing swords as they came. Lassand tried to step between the guards and Barall, but the priest pulled him gently aside.

"Remember your promise," Barall said, then raised his hands in front of him.

Just then a dagger materialized in the middle of the lead guard's chest, a perfect circle of blood forming on his tunic as he reached blindly for the hilt jutting from his body. There was enough life left in him to look up into Barall's equally shocked eyes before toppling dead at the feet of his companions. Chaos ensued as everyone moved at once. The king's soldiers enveloped Zithius in a ring of steel, deadly swords pointed outward in all directions, shields raised. Slowly and steadily, they moved backward, like a giant porcupine, removing the king to safety. Riordan's knights leapt to ensure the well-being of their charges, trying and failing to get the circle away from the murder site. The priests remained where they were, not willing to abandon Barall without some idea of what had just happened. Weapons were raised, however, and eyes watched for the source of the attack. The remaining men guarding the Emissary split; half moving to protect the Emissary, with the other half continuing toward Barall, sure he had just killed their comrade. The guard closest to Barall raised his sword to strike, when suddenly Rillem appeared, knocking Barall's slight frame aside easily.

Barall fell heavily to the ground, jarring his shoulder and banging his head on the stone of the street. Behind him, Rillem blocked the sword thrust meant for Barall, then stepped back and stood protectively over the priest. Around them, several plainly dressed men and women surged out of the crowd, drawing swords as they came. Seeing them, the supporting Emissary's guards came forward as well, perceiving these new people as a threat to their friends and the Emissary. With no confirmation or time to ask, the two groups met in a resounding clash of metal on metal.

Cries of "for the Emissary," fought with "protect the circle," as the battle raged. The band of knights recruited by Rillem and Valleria charged into the fray without hesitation though most of them had never even met Barall or any of the circle members. The knights, though, were untrained and the guards were professional and disciplined, so while inferior in numbers the guards were taking a heavy toll on the knights.

Barall watched in horror as the knights ran to his aid, and his horror mounted as the fight ensued and then turned badly. He rose to his feet, hoping to somehow stop the fight before any more lives were lost. As he stepped forward he was stopped by a hand on his shoulder. Turning, he gasped in pain as a dagger was thrust powerfully into his stomach. His hands clutched at the wound, the dagger slicing into his palms as it was cruelly removed, then plunged in again, this time into his chest. The second wound made Barall gasp again, but he managed to look up to see his attacker. Recognition filled his eyes, but his voice was gone, stolen by the excruciating pain. The attacker shoved against Barall, removing his dagger and forcing Barall to stumble back several steps, but not to fall. Without another glance, the attacker tossed his dagger to the ground, to be lost amid the blood and bodies around them, and blended into the battle.

The Emissary's Guards saw Barall stumble back, clutching his stomach. They moved in to arrest him, but the Emissary took matters into his own hands. Throwing off his protectors, he rushed forward and with all his strength spun his staff in a wide arc and brought its heavy, weighted top down on Barall's neck. A primal scream of rage tore through the Emissary's throat as he felt the power of his blow break skin and bone. Barall crumpled before him to lie in a growing pool of blood.

The Emissary's ecstasy was short lived, however, for immediately he felt white-hot pain lancing outward from his chest. Like Barall only moments before, he stared dumbly down at his chest and the sight of a dagger quivering there, blood spilling onto his robe.

# Chapter 30

*"Just as a fire is covered by smoke and a mirror is obscured by dust, just as the embryo rests deep within the womb, wisdom is hidden by selfish desire."*
*Bhagavad Gita*

The new Emissary strode along the corridors of the cathedral going over his upcoming sermon, the first since the riot and death of Barall. It had only been two weeks since those events and in that time, he had barely had time to breathe much less prepare a sermon, but it was his duty and it was expected to be a packed house. The purple robes of his office felt particularly heavy today, moreso than the weight of the wool would account for. Still, he walked purposefully with his head erect. He would show the people he was proud to hold the position, and was dedicated to preserving the church with all its traditions.

Reaching the entrance to the worship hall, he paused a moment, nervousness finally showing itself as he smoothed his robe and adjusted the circle around his neck. Noticing the smiling face of his Initiate attendant, he offered a sheepish grin of his own in return.

"Just gathering my thoughts?" he suggested weakly.

Not hesitating a second, the Initiate replied with a completely serious face, "Of course, Emissary," she said.

The Emissary laughed, a jovial sound in a place that hadn't heard much laughter in a long while. "Off with you, scamp," he said good-naturedly. The girl smiled, showing beautiful white teeth and ran off, leaving the Emissary to enter alone, as was custom.

He opened the door just as the great gong sounded, announcing his arrival. A Primate, selected for his booming voice, called out, "Rise for Lassand, Emissary of Endomar."

☙

The formalities of the service concluded and Emissary Lassand rose from his plain chair and approached the podium. He surprised everyone by passing it by and coming to stand in the very front, just ahead of the first row of benches. He stood for a moment in front of the entire hall, looking out upon the sea of people staring back at him, and smiled. The sermon he had delivered had included references to all seven pillars of faith, an acknowledgement to Barall and the sacrifices he had made for his god. Normally this part of the service was for the people to ask questions, but that would not happen today. The Emissary was going to use this time to deliver his own message for the direction of the church.

"My friends," he started. "I know this is normally your time to ask questions, but I beg your indulgence to let me talk a while longer to tell you some things. These things will be of the past, the present and the future. I will speak of the past to dispel some of the rumors you have, no doubt, been hearing, as to what caused the rift in the church and what really happened at the bridge of Micarad. The present will be to let you all know what I have done to begin to heal, not only this church, but the balance as well. I will tell you of the circle of seven and introduce you to the high priests and priestesses who form the circle. As for the future ... well, that remains to be written, doesn't it? Will Caven be considered visionary or misunderstood? Martyr or hero? Will I? All remains to be seen, but I will tell you of the plans to return balance to the spirit and to our realm."

He spoke first of the *Forgetting Law* and admitted the church had, indeed, ordered the forgetting or elimination of the six other gods. He didn't know why, but a team of scholars were scouring the cathedral, royal and private libraries to find the answer and the people would be informed as soon as the answer was found. Next, he spoke of Barall and all he knew of him, right up until the time of his death. He spoke honestly and deliberately of what happened by the bridge; of how an unknown attacker had killed an Emissary's guardsman moving to arrest Barall; how the Emissary himself had killed Barall in the ensuing confusion and how a farmer named Rillem, dubbed a clerist knight by Barall, was killed defending the dead body of his lord.

"Clerist knights," continued Lassand, "are new to the church, to every church. They represent an independent group of men and women, loyal to no particular priest or god, whose purpose is to protect and serve the priests of the circle of seven. They have already proven themselves worthy and necessary over their short existence."

Moving on, the Emissary spoke more of the circle of seven, and how the church of Endomar would no longer call itself the only religion. There were other gods for people to worship and it was the job of every priest to let the people know why they should choose which religion to follow, and why Endomar was a good choice. "For beyond the *Forgetting Law*, there is much circumstantial evidence to point, at least in my mind, to the existence of alternate gods and goddesses."

This declaration, from the sitting Emissary was met with shock. True, while Lassand had already shown himself to be almost the direct opposite of Caven, no one suspected an outright reversal of position. Not even Lassand himself would have been willing to go quite that far – not until he had read two books.

The first had been Gibson's diary, provided to him by Destrin, with the approval of the circle and the second was Barall's own journal, apparently started after he had met up with the other priests and read Gibson's diary himself. The first page of Barall's journal was an indication of the type of man he was:

*It amazes me at the amount of knowledge that has been lost to the world – the existence of other gods and the ability to use magic being probably the most important. The reason for this is unknown, being one of the things that have been lost. While I cannot condone the actions of others for I feel it was done purposefully, I also cannot imagine what kind of reason there would be that would lead them to believe their only recourse was to destroy knowledge.*

*The church of Endomar, and I can only believe the churches of those other gods and goddesses, is not to hide knowledge from the world. They would want to educate, at least their own followers in their methods and methodologies. Lack of knowledge could only hurt the world."*

Within the journal, Barall wrote about his theory of the churches in Cherilla, including his last entry about his thoughts around the cathedral. Lassand checked into Barall's theory and found even more information to support them than he would have thought possible. Within Cherilla there were seven major cities: Anklesh, Wilrien, Laufrid, Tyron, Vanerry, Erskin and Mordrum, each containing a large church. The churches were built roughly the same of large blocks of stone with huge, intricately carved, double doors and a central circular window situated atop the doors.

"When Barall cast his revealing spell on the book of laws, it did much more than show us the purpose of the *Forgetting Law*. It was as if a veil was placed over so much more than just the law. Books we had been searching for were found easily, doors were discovered, leading to rooms not known to have existed, items, carvings and symbols, throughout the cathedral, were suddenly noticed, in plain sight, though never seen before. For example," the Emissary continued with a flourish, gesturing behind him with an outstretched hand, toward where Dalis and the other high priests sat, "we found these."

The priests of the circle sat in a loose semi-circle at the back of the dais upon which Lassand stood. Above them, at the Emissary's words, Initiates dropped six tapestries to unfurl directly over a circle member to reveal the respective symbol of the priest's deity. To the Emissary's left, the signs of death for Rettela, concealment for Xelteran and the crossroads for Malnock were depicted in red thread on black cloth. To the right, in black thread on red cloth, were the tree, the heart and the rock of Aronya, Sleonde and Geffrin. Gasps of astonishment and wonder escaped from more than one mouth but to the Emissary's disappointment, several people angrily rose from their seats and stomped from the hall. It was too much to ask, he knew, that everyone would be open-minded and welcoming of the 'new' religions. With a look toward Chestun, Lassand made sure that the people who left were noted in order to receive a personal visit in the near future to discuss their concerns.

"I have surprised some of you, shocked others," said Lassand with a smile, "and they're not over yet. We found these tapestries throughout the cathedral, each one in a different tower. You will note the similarities, of course, seven cities in Cherilla, with seven churches and each church has a window symbolizing of a different god. There are seven towers within this cathedral. Within six of these towers, we found those same symbols carved into the seventh stair, and then found a room never seen before. In the seventh tower, with a circle carved into the seventh stair, we found this."

Behind him, the final tapestry was lowered, centered between the other six. On its pristine white fabric, displayed in inky black and blood red were the six godly symbols surrounding a golden circle. Lassand stood for a moment and simply gazed out at the people in the hall. He hadn't expected, or really wanted, to be Emissary, but standing here today, having conducted his first sermon as head of the church and announcing to the world that Endomar was not only acknowledging six other gods, but welcoming them with open arms, he felt something else. He felt at peace. The feeling surprised him. Nokya was dead, as were Barall and Percinal. Dozens of citizens had been killed in the riot, and the church itself was divided. Still, the feeling remained.

Perhaps Barall was right; maybe it wasn't peace he felt. Maybe it was balance.

இ

Destrin rose from his position at the center of the circle members, after being appointed the Endomarian representative to the Circle of Seven by the Emissary and accepting it graciously. The group met to discuss simple procedural issues today, such as how often they would meet, where and why, but the discussion quickly turned bitter. Though many years his senior, Destrin tried to emulate Barall, but was finding it hard to deal with the arrogance and superior attitude of Cerrok. The Wisdom wanted everyone to be able to express their honest feelings and opinions, but the priest of Xelteran persisted in disrupting the meeting by complaining about everything from the food to the location and meeting topics. It was just a continuation of Cerrok's attempts to gain control of the circle, but Destrin was at a loss for how to get the priest of greed under control. The Emissary could offer no help to his friend for he didn't know Cerrok, or Xelteran, and preferred to leave the inner workings of the circle to Destrin. It was better that way, Destrin knew, for the circle needed to find their own way and resolve these kinds of differences themselves. Up until now, Destrin, with the support of most of the Circle, had tried to bring Cerrok in line by dealing with his issues quickly and directly, not giving him time or need to object. Everyone suspected that at least one of the daggers that started the melee at the bridge that killed Barall and Caven were, if not thrown by Cerrok, then ordered by him. The problem was that there was no proof of this, which Cerrok also knew. They didn't want to push against Cerrok too hard, until they had that proof – which was left to the knights to find.

For the time being, that issue had to be put aside. The circle had ended its meeting with the members deciding to travel to the respective cities where their churches were located. Each had been given a letter of introduction and orders of cooperation from the Emissary to the individual Primates in each church. They would not be welcomed with fanfares or open arms, and each would travel with a large contingent of knights. They had debated whether to support the knights with Emissary's guards, but feelings against the purple clad soldiers were still too raw for either side to be comfortable. One of Lassand's first tasks as Emissary had been to offer unconditional release to any guardsman who wished to leave. It turned out that Caven's methods for recruitment included intimidation, threats and duress, so many guardsmen accepted the offer.

As the meeting broke up, Destrin held back with Tella, talking of nothing in particular while watching the others file out of the room. Once they were alone, Destrin turned to face Tella directly.

"What do you think?" he asked her.

"I think there's a lot of work to do," she answered bluntly. "We need to determine our purpose and find some way to solve our differences."

"That may be easier said than done. We have quite opposite theologies, not to mention, personalities," he said.

Tella considered that for a moment. It was no secret she and Cerrok shared no love between them, and she also didn't care much for Seskia either, but personality differences were a part of every interaction, every relationship. It was their differences that gave the world creativity and imagination and the ability to solve problems. While the circle had travelled together for most of a year, they had a purpose of informing people of their existence. Now that people knew of them and their gods, they needed to re-establish their purpose and redefine their goals.

As if reading her thoughts, Destrin said suddenly, "I think I'll suggest our purpose be to maintain and protect the balance."

"Hm," said Tella non-committedly.

"Obviously, given what the church has done, the balance is in need of protection," he said plaintively.

"Your church."

"Yes, my church."

"So you would, potentially, work against your own church?"

"Yes."

Tella's eyebrows raised in an unspoken question.

"The balance protects everything," said Destrin. "Too much good, too much evil and the world will … tilt, for lack of a better term. For whatever reason the church, my church, nearly destroyed us all. That cannot be permitted to happen again. By dedicating the circle, with representatives from all seven religions to the protection and maintenance of the balance, we essentially monitor each other. Despite being neutral, Endomar became too strong, too all-encompassing, and the world was nearly thrown into chaos. No matter what Barall, and perhaps even our new Emissary, believe, I suspect the riot and bloodshed that happened was more due to the upset of the balance than a battle over the recognition of new gods."

Tella was impressed for it seemed Destrin was a much-changed man than the one who appeared before their fire that night so long ago. He was going to be an excellent addition to the circle.

"Now all we need to do is beat its acceptance into Cerrok," said Tella with a straight face.

❧

Cerrok walked by himself away from the meeting, proud and confidently sure of himself and his plans. Things were going almost exactly as he'd planned. Destrin, while a surprise appointee to the circle, Cerrok had expected the new Emissary to assume that role, was a weak fool. It will be child's play to wrestle control of the Circle from him.

As Cerrok rounded a corner, he nearly collided with Riordan. The leader of the clerist knights stood blocking the corridor, with one hand on the hilt of his sword and the other leaning against the wall. He looked quite formidable in the uniform recently adopted by the knights: a black leather jerkin with seven red slashes across the breast from left shoulder to right hip, black pants and boots.

"My lord," said Riordan, "a word if I may?"

"Riordan, I'm a busy man."

"Spying and murder do tend to take up one's time."

"You dare accuse me of …"

"I do. We caught your man spying on me, which was why you argued so hard for him to be put to death. We also know that it was your men who started the riot and who killed the guard trying to arrest Barall. Whether you were involved in the murder of Barall remains to be seen."

"You know nothing, fool," spat Cerrok. Then with a toss of his long hair he tried to step around Riordan.

The knight reached out, almost casually, and threw the priest up against the wall, pinning him there easily with one arm pressed against his throat. Riordan moved his face in close to Cerrok's.

"We know, Cerrok, and the knights will always be watching."

Released at last, Cerrok sniffed disdainfully and, without a word or look back, continued down the hall. Riordan knew he had made an enemy, and a powerful one, but it was necessary. The knights would protect the Circle from all enemies – even one of their own.